HEART
OF A
ROYAL

HEART
OF A
ROYAL

HANNAH CURRIE

WhiteSpark

HEART OF A ROYAL

WhiteSpark Publishing, a division of WhiteFire Publishing
13607 Bedford Rd NE
Cumberland, MD 21502

ISBNs:
978-1-946531-53-7 (paperback)
978-1-946531-55-1 (hardcover)
978-1-946531-54-5 (digital)

For Isabel and Katie

When I wrote about Kenna, I was thinking of you.

You both make me so proud.

The world was crashing around me
I couldn't find my way
My life had skittered somewhere out of reach
All I knew was fading
Leaving me behind
All alone, too scared to even stand

But then,
there You were
Still and steady, sure and good
Holding out Your hand for me to take
Asking me to trust You
Telling me I could
Showing me the way
That I might know
Your strength and light and hope
Your care and love and peace

You're the reason I can breathe
In the middle of this whirlwind

ONE

If mortification could kill, I'd be six feet under. And Nurse Kristiann over in the corner would probably still be trying to hide her laughter at the funeral. Some help she was. A word, a jerk of the head, even a cough would have been enough to warn me the three of us were no longer alone.

"Well? What happened next? Did Prince Thoraben find another pair of pants or did he have to stay sitting there until the princess left? What did the king say? Was he mad?"

I did my best to ignore Kristiann's muffled laughter and the bemused prince standing in the doorway and focused instead on the wide gray eyes of the little girl in the hospital bed. The one intent on getting me into trouble. Even if she had no idea she was doing it. Not that I could really blame her. I had been the one to tell the story.

"He, uh..."

Seventeen years and nine months of living in the palace should have taught me better than to share personal information about the royal family. I'd never betrayed their confidence before, steering well clear of anything which would put the family I all but called my own in a bad light, but Roni had looked so worried this morning, staring out the window, the bright shirts she favored swapped for a colorless gown as she counted down the hours till her heart surgery. Even her curls were drooping. I would have done anything to make her smile, so when she asked if Thoraben, who she idolized along with the rest of Peverell, was as perfect as he seemed, I'd told her the first story that came to mind.

"Well?"

"Uh..." My gaze drifted beyond Roni to Ben, still standing in the doorway, all six foot of him. He'd crossed his arms now, a half smile quirking the side of his mouth as he leaned against the door, no doubt waiting to see what I'd do next. As if I had any idea. What had I been thinking? And how had I not noticed him standing there? King Everson aside, Prince Thoraben was the most powerful man in Peverell, drawing the public eye wherever he went. Once upon a time, him catching me sharing one of his most embarrassing moments would have only made me embellish it more, teasing out each moment until we laughed so hard we couldn't talk.

Once upon a time, we'd been children. "He...um..."

A hand rubbed its way across his smile, doing nothing to wipe it away. I don't know what manner of pleading or apology he saw in my expression, nor how much he'd make me pay for it, but with a shake of his head and a few strides forward, he finally spoke.

"He made up a story about needing to leave, borrowed his little sister's pink jacket under the very gallant guise of carrying it for her, tied it around his waist—desperately hoping it was long enough to cover the split in the back of his pants that lengthened as he stood—and walked back to the car. Where he proceeded to sit for the next forty minutes, waiting for his father to finish his meeting, not sure whether he regretted more the fact that he'd tried to impress Princess Taryn with a cartwheel or that his little sister and her best friend, Lady Kenna, had witnessed it and were still giggling. Thankfully, his father, the king, never found out."

"Prince Thoraben!" Roni straightened in her bed, a thin, almost translucent hand fiddling with the gown she wore, tucking it tighter round her shoulders. "You're in my room!"

He grinned as he pulled a chair over to her bed and sat. "I heard you were having an operation this afternoon and thought I'd come and see if you were okay."

I hadn't thought her eyes could have widened any more, nor my respect for this man grow any higher than it already was. Somehow, they did. "You heard about me?"

"Sure. Lady Mackenna here talks about you a lot." He winked. She blushed. "And me, it seems." Heat rushed across my cheeks again as he turned to me, eyebrow raised. I should have been thankful he found the situation so amusing. Perhaps I might have if I hadn't been so busy berating myself over the fact that, once again, I'd let my heart get in the way of my better sense.

A princess always considers her words carefully before speaking.

A princess must be respectful at all times.

I wasn't a princess. Not in blood nor in title, but while I lived at the palace and acted in their name, the same rules applied.

"She thinks you're handsome," Roni piped up, drawing his attention back to her.

"She does, does she?"

And there went the tips of my ears. Burnt to a crisp. Any second now my hair would start smoking and set off every alarm in the place. Roni's heart might not have worked properly, but her matchmaking mind certainly did. Last time I visited, she'd tried to set me up with Blake, one of her nurses. The time before it had been her uncle. Apparently, she'd now decided to skip those options and go for the most eligible man in Peverell. As if he even had the option of marrying me.

I sent a desperate glare in Kristiann's direction, begging for intervention. Surely, she could come up with something. Nurses always had something they could do. Take a temperature, check a dressing, chart the level of pain...

"Yep. And the nicest man she's ever known. I said she should marry you because she's a princess and you're a prince but she said she's not really a princess so she couldn't but my mom said she might as well be because she acts like one but when I told Lady Kenna that, she said—"

"You know, maybe *you* should marry him," I interrupted, not sure where she was going with this conversation but certain Ben didn't need to hear it. Amused as he currently seemed.

Roni sighed. "I can't. I'm too young. Mom said so. But you're not, Lady Kenna. You're exactly the right age, and you did say he was—"

"Okay, Roni," I interrupted, again. Yep, definitely going to get me in trouble. "I think we've told Prince Thoraben enough of our secrets for today. Look, Nurse Kristiann is going to check your blood pressure now—" whether she needed to or not—"And then as soon as your mom arrives, you'll be ready to go."

The loss of her beautiful smile was instant and like a hammer to my chest. If mortification wouldn't kill me, perhaps regret would finish the job. Why couldn't I keep my mouth shut?

"Oh, sweetie, I'm sorry..." I reached out to take her hand, tucking it between mine. "I know this is scary, but you've done it before and Nurse Kristiann and her friends will look after you and Doctor James is so good at what he does that you won't even know—"

"What if the Rebels come while I'm asleep?"

I started at the change of subject, coldness blanching the heat from my face like an avalanche. Even Kristiann seemed taken back, pausing halfway between her cart and the bed, cuff dangling forgotten in her hand.

"Is that what you're worried about?" I asked, careful to keep the trembling from my voice. Not the seriousness of the operation, not the pain or the recovery, but terrorists attacking while she was under? What had brought this on? I looked at Kristiann, questions in my eyes. All she had to offer was a shrug.

"Did someone say something to you about the Rebels?" I asked Roni. She nodded, the action tipping tears from her eyes.

"The nurses were talking yesterday when they thought I was asleep. They said a Rebel group was suspected of being near the hospital."

"Oh, honey, that hasn't been proven. It's just people talking. You don't need to worry about that."

"But if they attack while I'm in surgery, I won't be able to hide."

This time, the hammer to my chest took my breath away. I wanted to wrap my arms around the precious little girl and assure her I'd always be there to protect her—but I couldn't. Even within the walls of the palace, we lived in fear. *Especially* at the palace, because we were the ones the Rebel group were after.

A glance at the man beside me showed Ben's smile, also, had given way to stoic sadness. Was he thinking about the last time the Rebels had attacked? The day he'd lost his mother and the kingdom of Peverell their beloved queen? There had been minor skirmishes and attempts since, but nothing to rival that one. That day had changed us all.

I squeezed Roni's hand, refusing to let my fear grow hers. The poor girl had enough to worry about, and surely even the worst of criminals had enough decency not to attack a hospital full of chronically ill children. I hoped. My smile was genuine, if a little shaky.

"You'll be safe here. I promise."

"How do you know?"

How? I didn't. Not at all. But I couldn't tell her that. My mind sped through a thousand answers, trying to find one that would satisfy Roni, never quite landing until Ben's hand reached out to cover both of ours. Whether he did it to comfort Roni or simply to offer strength, I didn't know. But in that moment, the words came.

"Because Prince Thoraben will protect us." I leaned in closer, gesturing with my free hand for her to do the same, a thrill of success jolting through me when she did. I would fix this. She might still have a hundred things playing on her mind today, but Rebels wouldn't be one of them—even if the thought of them attacking had me jumping at shadows for the rest of the day. My voice dropped to just above a whisper. "I don't know if you've seen, but he looks pretty impressive dressed in his uniform. He even has a sword! The Rebels would take one look at him standing there in all that majesty and run for cover as quickly as their weak little legs could carry them."

Her giggle was worth every bit of embarrassment saying such a thing in front of Ben cost me. I hoped he would believe it to be a silly bit of prattle meant to calm the nerves of an anxious child and not the truth...but the ears once again singeing my hair had me doubting it. I tilted my head forward just enough to let my long hair cover them, ignoring Ben's knowing smile as I did. The man saw far too much.

Roni's mother's arrival was just the distraction I needed.

"Oh look, your mom is here. We'll go now, but I'll be back to see you tomorrow. You be the brave girl I know you are, okay?" I gave her thin hand another squeeze before standing to greet the woman who'd entered. I couldn't hear what Ben whispered as he bent down to Roni's ear, but whatever it was, it brought a smile to her face bigger than any I'd seen today. It was all that stopped me crying as I blew her a kiss and walked out, Ben closing the door behind us. Seeing these kids in pain was always difficult. Seeing them scared wrenched my heart. But seeing them smile?

"Thanks."

I didn't qualify what it was I was thanking Ben for as we walked down the hospital hall together, but the word alone seemed enough.

"Kenna?"

"Hm?" *Stop thinking about the Rebels, Kenna. You're safe. Truly. They won't come here. They wouldn't. Roni is fine.* The breath I filled my lungs with smelled of disinfectant laced with some type of flowery air-freshener, but it was enough to ground me. I glanced at my watch. Who next? Martin in bed eleven would be getting back from his appointment soon. I'd missed him last week. And I'd promised Jordana a visit, although with grandparents, two aunts, and several cousins currently in with her, that could probably wait till later. There was only so much room in there. Perhaps Millie? Chatting with that precocious two-year-old always brought a smile to my face. She'd have woken up from her morning nap by now.

"About the Rebels..."

"Don't worry, I'm not really counting on you to protect us. I just said that to keep her happy. I know, I should have kept my mouth shut." Regarding more than just the Rebels. King Everson would be furious if word ever got back to him about the story I told. But I couldn't change that now, so there was no point in ruing it. Bed five for Millie. I turned to head back to the other end of the ward.

"No, wait, that's not what I—" Ben stopped, frowned, that action in itself enough to give me pause. I hugged my purse against my chest and waited, hoping whatever he had to say wouldn't take too long. "They're not—" He pursed his lips. Another sentence broken off. Another frown.

He looked down the hall, smiled at a passing doctor, looked back at me, considering for a long moment before he quirked his head. Grinned. "You think I'm handsome?" I stopped just short of whacking his arm. One did not hit a prince. Even if the prince was practically one's brother and well-deserving of it. Especially since, as Mother reminded me almost daily, he *wasn't* my brother.

"What are you doing here anyway?"

"Looking for a wife. Though apparently, neither you nor Roni are takers."

"Very funny. What are you really doing here?"

"King Dorien and Prince Marcos are on their way from Hodenia. They'll be at the palace in—" He checked his watch. "—approximately forty-seven minutes."

My purse dropped several inches before I caught it. "And you're only just now telling me? It takes twenty minutes to get to the palace! And I'm not dressed or—"

"You look great."

I was wearing jeans and tennis shoes. Designer, of course, stylish, perfect for an afternoon tromping around the hospital, sitting cross-legged on beds while chatting with kids. Not so much for greeting visiting royalty. And if I was this nervous...

"Alina's going to be a wreck."

Alina wasn't a wreck. Livid, but not a wreck. It was almost dizzying watching her stalk her way from one end of the suite to the other, her irate chatter stopping only long enough to take the required breath every minute or so.

"He sent me away. How could Father send me away from his office? Prince Marcos is in there."

"They're having a meeting."

"Yes, regarding me."

"You don't know that."

"Don't be dense, Kenna. Why else would King Dorien and Prince Marcos come all this way—*in person*—to meet with Father if it wasn't to discuss my engagement?"

There was little point in attempting to reason with her. I'd already tried, pointing out numerous explanations for the unexpected visit which had nothing to do with her. Alina waved them all aside with a swish of her manicured hand, certain of her conviction. I gave up trying after the fifth attempt and made myself comfortable in her sitting area, content to sit and wait.

It wasn't as if this was the first time Alina had swooned over a man. Every couple of months it was someone different, although she always came back to Prince Marcos. Personally, I didn't know what she saw in him. He was handsome, certainly, but in a swarthy way. Like a sea captain of old. Tall, dark wind-swept hair, deeply tanned skin, clothing pressed and pristine. Too perfect almost. Although, perhaps that was part of what attracted Alina. She'd always hated mess or anything out of place.

Alina walked to the mirror again, checking her appearance even though all she'd done since the last time she'd checked it was a lap of the room. Admittedly, the suite was large, but she hadn't been walking fast. Berating her father's high-handedness with the occasional gush over Prince Marcos and the fact that he was the only man in the whole world she could ever marry, yes. But not exactly breaking a sweat.

"Alina, you look beautiful. Truly. Come and sit. There's nothing you can do but wait."

"I will not sit and wait, Mackenna Sparrow. This is my future. The rest of my life."

Mine too, though apparently she'd forgotten that. "Alina—"

"We'll break in. One of the maids will have keys. They have to clean his office. I'll tell them it's an emergency. Who do you think would be most likely to believe me? Perry? Emilia? Risine?"

I was saved from having to come up with a reply to that ridiculous train of thought by a knock at the door. Alina ran to open it so fast she almost tripped over her feet. Almost. Princess Alina of Peverell was far too particular to ever *actually* fall. Even in the three-inch heels she favored.

"Yes?" she asked of the maid standing there.

"The king requests your—"

Alina was gone before the girl could finish, her white, summery dress flying out like a cape behind her as she ran down the marble staircase. Though I followed, my steps were much slower. Partly to give Alina time but, though I hated to admit it even to myself, as much to prolong the inevitable. Whether it happened today or in a few months' time, Alina would get engaged. And then?

You can't hold on to what should never have been.

No, I argued with the voice in my head, but maybe, just for today...

Alina's squeal of delight brought a smile to my face and an ache to my heart. I walked around the last corner and into view of King Everson's office in time to see her turn from her father to throw both arms around Prince Marcos's shoulders. The indulgent smiles of both kings behind them was proof enough that she'd been right. Alina, princess of Peverell, my closest friend and the sister of my heart, was engaged to Prince Marcos.

As the four of them walked back inside the room, Alina's hand clinging to Marcos's arm like she had no plans of ever letting go,

I turned and walked away. King Everson would call for me soon enough but, for now, this was Alina's moment. And for the first time in seventeen years and nine months, I wasn't a part of it.

TWO

The weather-smoothed stones making up the tower's half wall were warm as I rubbed my hands across them, relishing their familiar feel, committing each curve to memory. The palace might have been an imposing structure to the rest of Peverell but for me, it was home and this tower, my hideaway. Something I desperately needed today. Open to the elements, closed to criticism and the continual need to please. High above life's challenges, with only the weather to contend with, I could almost let myself believe I was at peace.

There were no clouds in the sky above me today, no wind whipping my hair across my face in stinging streaks of auburn. I wished there had been. It would have given me something to think about other than the fact that the only life I'd known was about to be torn out from underneath me. The life of a princess. Elaborate gowns, priceless jewels, the best education Peverell had to offer—everything Princess Alina herself had, everything a girl could ever dream of.

But, like any dream, waking up was inevitable. Even knowing change was coming hadn't lessened the shock. In a single moment, Alina's engagement had brought it all crashing down— the uneasiness, the feeling of not knowing where I belonged, the wondering what my future held. If I even had one.

"I knew I'd find you here."

I swallowed back a shriek loud enough to startle every bird in the tree below me before breaking into a sheepish smile.

Ben. Of course, it was. For the second time today, he'd snuck up on me. This time, however, I didn't mind that he had.

"Prince Thoraben. Welcome to the East Tower."

"Come on, Kenna. Must you call me that? I've told you—it's just Ben."

His tone was wry, his reprimand expected. It was an old argument. One we pulled out and rehashed every few months, despite the futility of it.

I used to call him Ben. Growing up, side by side, it made sense. I'd called him Ben since the day I'd learnt to speak, Thoraben being far too much of a mouthful for a toddler. I'd called him that right up until his eighteenth birthday when Mother had pulled me aside and reminded me that though they treated me like part of the family, I wasn't truly one of them. Like I needed reminding. The man standing beside me would always be Ben in my mind but to speak it aloud?

"It's not appropriate, you know that."

"Not in front of dignitaries or the public, certainly, but there's no one here but us." He shrugged one shoulder, his wistful half-smile tugging at my heart. "I miss being Ben."

And I missed him simply being Ben, but we were royalty, with a long list of rules, regulations, and social expectations alongside the privileges. At least, *he* was royalty. Once Alina married, I didn't know what I would be.

I turned back to the view, leaning my elbows on the warm bricks. It took only a few seconds for Ben to follow suit, his stance mirroring mine as we let the wall bear the weight of duty we'd grown so accustomed to carrying. I could have continued our old argument but what was the point? Neither of us would ever concede.

"What are you doing up here, anyway?" I asked instead. "Shouldn't you be entertaining Prince Marcos or something?"

"I wanted to check you were okay. Are you?"

"Of course."

"Really? Because you missed afternoon tea."

"What?" I looked at my watch. Groaned. Over two hours I'd

been up here, staring at the city below, lost in a maze of contemplation. The sun would be setting soon, and I hadn't even realized. "Your father's going to kill me."

"I told him you weren't feeling well."

"And he believed it?"

"He has other things on his mind. Much like you, apparently. Is it Roni?"

I sighed. It should have been. The poor girl was having her heart operated on, yet all I could think about was myself. "No. It's just—I can't believe Alina's getting married."

"It's really such a shock?"

"Yes. No. Maybe." I shook my head, trying to make sense of my thoughts. "She seems so young."

"No younger than our parents were."

Not in years, perhaps, but certainly in maturity. Alina was much like the dresses she favored—beautiful, striking, timeless, but little prepared for the harsher side of life. She was excited about the match. After all, she'd admired Prince Marcos for years, droning on and on about his good looks. But good looks weren't everything. And marriage was so...final. What if he hurt her?

"He's a good man, Kenna."

Tears sprang to my eyes at Ben's gentle commendation. I blinked the wetness away before they could fall. I couldn't let Ben see me cry. I would never live it down.

"She has to marry. You had to have known it was only a matter of when."

"No, I know." Neither was it a surprise to hear it was Prince Marcos who she would marry. When one government then another the world over had fallen to the demands of equality, the nation of Hodenia had been the first to reinstate its long-forgotten monarchy as a single voice of reason. Earning, surprisingly, the respect not only of its people but of much of the western world. Peverell had followed suit not long after, though with far greater resistance. Even sixty years later, there were still Rebel groups who opposed the decision and made it their goal to wipe out the royal family. Though I hated Roni's fear regarding the Rebels, it wasn't unfounded. A marriage to Hodenia would strengthen Peverell's monarchy like little else could, offering not only the endorsement of their name but their protection.

Even if it did mean Alina would move to another country.

"To be honest, I'm surprised you've gotten this old without being married yourself," I told Ben. "Spending too much time in the stables and not enough on the dance floor?"

I shouldn't have teased him, especially since I knew avoiding his abundance of female suitors was exactly the reason he went there, but it was too easy.

"You won't call me Ben but you'll call me old."

"I wasn't—" But he was grinning again. Stopping short of elbowing him in the ribs, I looked down on the city below us.

It calmed me, the view from this tower. The marketplace stretched out before me, a river of people winding its way through the center of town. Cobblestone streets and tall wood houses, little changed since they'd been built four hundred years ago. A landscape frozen in time.

The houses weren't uniform, though that added to their charm rather than taking away from it. They looked almost like a pebbled pathway from this height—their roofs varying shades of brown, the shapes they made melding together despite their odd angles. And in the distance, surrounding the town, the hills. Green, undulating, capturing the sun as it set each night only to release it to the far horizon the next morning.

"Actually, I've already chosen my bride."

My gaze flew to Ben's, my breath caught somewhere between my lungs and the air around me. I forced myself to look away before he read too much into the shock on my face. *Breathe, Mackenna. Breathe.*

He'd chosen his bride. Of course he had. It was wise. Good. Kingly. He would be king one day. He would need a queen to rule alongside him. Someone beautiful, someone he could confide in, who would stand with him and be his strength as he ruled and love the people as much as he did. It was the shock of his declaration that stole my breath, not envy for his unknown bride.

Definitely not envy.

"Does your father know?"

"He knows."

Something in Ben's tone made me wonder how happy King Everson was with his son's decision. Perhaps that was why the marriage hadn't yet gone ahead—the king didn't approve of Ben's choice.

If that were the case, there was still hope for me. I inwardly sighed, ruing the emotions railing inside. I was not in love with the Crown Prince of Peverell. I couldn't be. And even if I was— which I wasn't—I wasn't allowed to be. He was my friend, that was all. My best friend and the brother I'd never had.

I'd counted Ben my friend since the day he didn't give away my hiding place when Alina and I were playing hide-and-seek as six-year-olds. He could have easily, especially since Alina asked him outright if he'd seen me. He'd told her it wasn't his game to give away. Even as a nine-year-old he'd been diplomatic.

It was the fact that a wife would come between the two of us which bothered me, not the woman herself. The day he married, our close friendship this past decade would become, by necessity, a treasured but distant memory. Something to be savored on lonely days.

"Someone I know?"

"Yes." He didn't even consider my question before answering. Though, I supposed, that was not so strange given we'd moved in almost the same circles our whole lives. While I looked at the view, Ben was looking at me. I could feel his stare even without turning. His laughter, too. "You won't ask me who she is."

And put myself through that pain? Not likely. While I didn't know, I could still fool myself into thinking our friendship would never change. "I don't believe it's any of my business."

"But you want to know."

Of course I wanted to know. "Absolutely not."

"You do. I can see it. You hate surprises, and the very fact that I've chosen someone at all has you surprised as it is. You can't bear not to know her name."

He was right, of course. There were times I wished Ben didn't know me quite so well. This was one of them. And just for that, I wasn't going to ask. Not even for a hint. I would not give him the satisfaction of proving him right. Even if the curiosity killed me, which it very well might.

"When will you make the announcement? At the Midsummer's Ball?" No doubt that was when they'd announce Alina's engagement. If there was one thing King Everson liked, it was the attention of a crowd, and the ball tomorrow night would provide him ample. He'd want to proclaim the news himself before anyone else beat him to it.

"You're really not going to ask."

I ground my teeth together in an effort to keep my mouth shut. Much more goading from him and I knew I'd give in. I was already listing in my mind all the women I could think of who he'd shown even the slightest bit of interest in over the past six months. If I had to guess, I'd choose Princess Celeste as his mystery bride. They'd become fast friends the week she came to visit, and he'd admitted to me himself that he thought she was beautiful.

"Stubborn as always, that's my Kenna."

I barely kept the grin off my face at my achievement. It would ruin the illusion of control entirely if I did. My jaw might ache for days from the pressure I'd put on it in the last thirty seconds, but I'd not given in.

"Very well then, no. There will be no announcement made regarding my engagement tomorrow or anytime soon, as the woman I've chosen is not yet of age."

I raised my eyebrows, chancing another look in his direction. Was that a blush creeping up the back of his neck, pushing its way past his ears?

"I'm not that old, Kenna."

I tamped down a smile. No, twenty-one wasn't as old as it had once seemed but using the excuse that she was not yet of age made the girl he'd chosen seem very young. Of course, that ruled out Celeste. She'd celebrated her twenty-second birthday last year.

"Does she know?" I asked.

"Know what?"

"That you—That she—"

"That she is the one I've chosen to be my bride and the future queen of Peverell?"

Something like that. "Yes."

"No."

"What?" What was wrong with him? "You haven't told her? Not even hinted?"

"I'm waiting for the right time. There are a number of negotiations still to be made before such a thing could be announced, even if she were old enough to marry, which, like I said, she isn't. Don't worry. I'll tell her. There's plenty of time. Father has promised I may choose my own bride and isn't rushing me to marry."

No, he wouldn't be. Not if he didn't approve of the match. Until announcements were made, there was still a chance that Ben might change his mind to a more appropriate choice.

Prince or not, the man beside me deserved a whack to the head. At the very least a bucket of ice water dumped over him. Anything to wake him up to his foolishness. I settled for what I had on hand and threw a leaf at him. It fell short, not even catching his notice, which was probably for the best anyway.

I didn't know who the girl was Ben had set his eye on, but I already felt sorry for her. He had no idea how difficult it would be for a girl to become his wife. Even if his bride was a princess already, the adjustment to life as the future queen of Peverell would be immense. It wasn't something that happened overnight.

"Well, my congratulations to you both. Or, at the very least, to you, as clearly she has no idea of your affections."

"My affections?"

Oh. He hadn't said he loved her. I'd assumed. Wrongly, it appeared. Or not. I wasn't going to ask. I'd made enough of a fool of myself already.

"How did you know I was up here, anyway?"

That earned me a laugh. "Changing the subject, Lady Mackenna?"

Absolutely. "You can't grow up in the palace and not know a thing or two about diplomacy." Or avoiding awkward topics. *Smile,* the tutor had told Alina and me over and over again. A well-aimed smile will diffuse many a fire. And while disarming the opponent with one's smile, change the topic to a safer one.

Ben turned to face me, crossing his arms as he leaned a hip against the wall. "Smile and all that?"

"You were taught that too? Here I thought it was only in 'How to be a Princess.'"

"No, first lesson of diplomacy in 'How to be a King' as well. Of course, the second was to pull out one's sword and lop off the offender's ear, but I'm assuming that wasn't part of your lessons."

A smile spread across my face as I fiddled with a dried leaf sitting on the tower's ledge. "You'd have to actually hit their ear first."

"You bested me once in a duel. That doesn't mean I can't aim."

I looked his way, raising my eyebrows as I did my best to seem innocent. "And yet you never did give me a rematch."

"Didn't want you crying when I won. Father might have found out and then we all would have been in strife."

I turned to face him. "You assume I would have been the one crying..."

Ben narrowed his eyes in warning, something that would have been far more effective had they not been sparkling with mischief. "I'll have you know, Lady Mackenna Sparrow, that I am quite the swordsman. You might joke that enemies will run at the sight of me, but that sword I carry is very real. And I think my uniform quite suits me."

I swallowed, forcing the image of him dressed in full regalia from my head before I blushed or did something equally stupid. Thick brown hair so dark it was almost black, the tiniest bit of curl showing through despite regular cuts to keep it tamed, eyes that had girls the country over debating whether the color was chocolate, mahogany, or rich coffee brown, a grin which came as easily and frequently as his laugh... Add the sleek black pants, bold red coat and gold sash, belt and medallions of his military uniform and—He had no idea.

"But, all teasing aside, you always come up here when you're stressed. With the hospital this morning and the news of Alina's engagement this afternoon, it wasn't too difficult to figure out where you'd gone. You know, I'm almost jealous of you having this place. If ever I needed a good reminder of why I do all this, looking out over the city and my people would be it."

The scoff was out of my mouth before I could pull it back. "Please. It's your castle. You have every right to have this particular tower for yourself."

"No, it's your place. I know it's important to you to have a place of your own." He jiggled his eyebrows. "Though how you've kept it a secret from Alina baffles me."

How he knew about it baffled me. He spoke as if he always had, though I'd never told him, nor seen him up here. How long had he known? And what other secrets of mine did he know?

"I love your sister and her endless chatter of gowns and tiaras, but sometimes I need to get away from it all and remind myself that I'm not a princess. That I'm only here because your mother..." I stopped, but I might as well have kept talking. Ben knew as well as I what I'd been about to say. "Forgive me."

"Because my mother died the day Alina was born and your mother stepped in to help? Kenna, it's okay to say it. You're here because Mother isn't, and while I miss her still, almost two decades on, I could never rue the pleasure of knowing you and your parents because of it. Neither would she want me to."

Prince Thoraben was going to make a wonderful king someday. I'd always known it, but that moment proved it once again. He had the right amount of compassion to make his subjects feel like they mattered, while still being in control. Yes, he would make a good king. Even if I'd be watching from afar.

"I hereby decree it to be your tower once I'm gone, then." Crouching down, I wrote his name in the dust near our feet as I'd once defiantly written my own. *Prince Thoraben's Tower.* My throat thickened, tears once again threatening as I stared at the words. My scribbled name was long gone, and his would be soon, but the reality would remain. I was leaving the palace. King Everson's summons would come any day now, and my life here would be over. I would never again feel the wind whip away my worries here in this tower nor feel the peace that came from knowing I was part of something so much bigger than myself.

"You don't have to go, you know."

I stood slowly, brushing the dirt off my finger as I considered his quiet words. He was kind, even if he was wrong. "Alina won't need me once she is married, and without her here, there will be no reason for me to stay."

"We could find a reason."

An ant crawled through the dust in which I'd written Ben's name, scuttling its way over two pebbles and half a brittle leaf before hurrying on. I envied its single-minded purpose. It knew where it belonged, where it was going. Short as it was, its life had meaning. Mine?

Forget it, Kenna. Just because your life is falling apart doesn't mean it's over. Or that you have no purpose.

I shook my head, attempting a smile. "Your father has been more than generous already. The agreement he made with my parents was only to last until arrangements could be made for Alina's marriage. For almost eighteen years, I've lived the life of a princess. It's time I stopped pretending to be someone I'm not."

I couldn't be sure, but he almost seemed sad at the prospect.

"Still, there's no rush to leave."

Not from his perspective, perhaps, but he wasn't the one living someone else's life. An upcoming wedding would mean Alina's schedule would be filled with fittings, engagements, media appearances, lessons, and more decisions than anyone should ever have to make. Once she was married and settled in Hodenia, the kingdom's focus would be solely on Prince Thoraben's own nuptials—whether he liked it or not. I would simply be in the way.

I took one last look at the view, capturing it in my heart before forcing myself to turn away. No, it was time to leave. Time to go home.

Wherever that might be.

THREE

"L ady Mackenna, as of yesterday afternoon, Princess Alina is engaged to Prince Marcos of the Kingdom of Hodenia."

King Everson didn't waste any time getting to the point, and for that I was thankful. It was intimidating enough to stand before his throne as he meted out my fate without having him drag out the details. When I'd imagined this meeting, it had been in his office, perhaps with Alina present, not here in his room of judgement, alone except for a smattering of guards and two of his advisors. Both of whom wore frowns as deep as the king's as he stared me down.

I tucked shaking hands behind my back, lifted my chin, and reminded myself that I was almost eighteen. Too old to be wishing Mother stood beside me.

"They will be married the morning of her eighteenth birthday, at which time your services as her companion will no longer be required, nor will you be welcome here. You have until then to remove yourself from the palace."

My hands slipped from their hold. I'd be leaving, I knew that, but—

"Lodgings have been procured for you and your parents in one of the cottages. My advisors urged me to do so, reminding me that to dispel you from the kingdom altogether would not endear me to my people—and I'm sure you understand how important public relations are."

He stopped to take a breath. He might as well have taken

mine. No longer required, unwelcome—the words echoed in my mind, battering against my heart with a physical pain. I could have forgiven his choice of words, had it not been for the sneer of hate behind them.

Important to the people—but not to him. Not to the king who'd given me everything I had. The man who'd made me who I was today. He might as well have proclaimed me a Rebel. Were it not for his advisors and the opinion of the people, I would have been exiled like one of them.

King Everson had never been overly warm toward me, not like he was with Alina, but I'd always thought he cared at least a little. How wrong I'd been. He didn't care. To him, I was simply a means to an end, and he'd reached the end.

Alina's betrothal had only just been made official and already, barely twenty-four hours later, the king was ending the agreement he'd made with my parents. I could stay for three more months he'd said, but if this was the hostility I was going to receive from him, I did not want to.

"I shall leave tomorrow, Your Majesty."

"I will send staff to help you pack."

I stared at the wine-colored velvet behind his throne and tried not to let the satisfaction on his face hurt me. He'd won. Without even asking it of me, he'd gotten exactly what he'd wanted all along. He wanted me gone. Today, if possible. But I wouldn't do it, not even for the king. One more night I would claim. One more ball.

"Thank you, Your Majesty." I touched my skirts, preparing to curtsy and leave when he spoke again. His malevolent words stilled my movements, chilling my heart.

"One more thing, Lady Mackenna. Once you leave, you are to have no more contact with my son. I want you nowhere near Prince Thoraben. Ever again. He is the Crown Prince of Peverell, and it's time he stopped gallivanting about with commoners and started acting like it. I have put up with the friendship between you and him this long because of the debt I owed your mother, but no longer. My debt is paid. I owe your family nothing more. Thoraben has far more important things to do than play the fool with you—first and foremost finding himself a suitable bride.

"There will be no more meetings—not here or in town—and certainly no lovers' trysts in the tower. If I hear of any contact between the two of you, I will exile you and your family from Peverell immediately. Do I make myself clear?"

Lovers' trysts? Was that what he thought yesterday had been? How dare he insinuate such a thing. I was so offended by his assumptions of my character that I almost missed his ultimatum and what it meant.

I would never see Prince Thoraben again.

A bride would never come between us...for the king already had.

"It wasn't a—"

"Do I make myself clear?"

I stared at the floor, wishing I had the courage to stare into the king's eyes. He'd hurt me, but if that wasn't painful enough as it was, he knew it. He'd planned it. It wasn't enough that his benevolence was at an end, he was determined to take away the one thing I would always cherish—the friendship I had with his children. My voice was barely a whisper as I agreed, knowing I had no choice but to do so. "Yes, Your Majesty."

"Good. You are dismissed."

I ran out of the room, barely remembering to curtsy in my haste to leave. He hated me. The king hated me. All these years, I'd never known, yet now it was clear. Marble floors, the priceless paintings gracing the walls, tall gold vases of flowers—they were all a blur as I ran. Mother, I needed Mother. She would know what to do. She always did.

Bursting through the door to Mother's suite, I flung myself into her arms. The maids she'd been talking with left quickly as she wrapped her arms around me.

"Mackenna. What is it? What's wrong?"

The words I tried to speak came out in sobs as I clung to her comforting frame. All I could think was that if I stayed here long enough, everything would be fine. Mother could fix it. Every pain I'd ever had, she'd fixed. Whether it was a kiss to my scraped knee, a word of wisdom, or merely a listening ear, I would come to her feeling as if the world were about to end and leave knowing it still faithfully continued.

"He hates me," I finally got out. "The king hates me. He's sending us away. We're leaving tomorrow. And he won't let me see Ben again. Ever."

I thought she would react. Commiserate, offer sympathy, maybe even be angry on my behalf. She did none of them, continuing to silently hold me until I pulled back. Perhaps she hadn't heard me. "Mother?"

She looked at me then, her expression showing none of the righteous anger I'd expected, selfishly even hoped for. Though her green eyes, so much like mine, were sad, the rest of her face was stoic. Resigned even, as if she'd seen this day coming. If that were the case, she might have warned me. Not that I would have believed her, being so blinded by the king's generosity that I hadn't noticed his black heart.

"Come, sit with me a moment."

She took my hand as if I were a young child again and, like that child, I followed her, tucking myself in against her side as we sat on the edge of the four-poster bed.

"Mackenna, did you ever wonder why the people love you so much?"

I frowned. What did the people have to do with this? We were talking about the king throwing me out, not the people. Still, I found the best answer I could. "Because, like them, I'm common?"

"I suppose that is part of it but, Kenna, it's far more than that. They love you because you're like their queen."

"Queen? You mean, Queen Ciera?" Mother nodded. "But I am nothing like her. I have dark hair, she was blonde. I'm tall. She was short. I've seen enough photos and portraits around the palace to know she was beautiful. I'm—"

"Also beautiful, but it wasn't physical features I meant. It's her character. You have the same heart. The same love and compassion for our people. The king sees that. Everyone who knew Queen Ciera and now knows you does. But while the people love you for it, I think it probably causes King Everson pain. You remind him of the wife he's mourned all these years.

"If you were his daughter, he would likely cherish that in you, but you're not. And although Alina looks like her mother, she is nothing like her as a person. The people want you to be their next queen. The friendship they know exists between you and Thoraben only encourages that hope."

"But—" I glared at the ornate rug near my feet. If frustration had been fire, the rug would have been ablaze. No. This time, Mother was wrong. Very, very wrong. "You know as well as I that I can't be queen. I am no more eligible to be Prince Thoraben's bride than you are." And even if I were, I had nothing to offer him. My family had no connections nor wealth to strengthen his rule. Perhaps if we had, the king might have overlooked our common status, but we had nothing except what he'd already bestowed upon us. When we left the palace tomorrow, we'd have even less. We were faithful friends and loyal subjects, but that was all. And that would never be enough.

"Still, eligibility aside, I agree with them. I can't think of anyone more suited to being Peverell's next queen. Twenty years ago, the king likely would have thought the same."

I laughed at the absurdity of such a statement before realizing Mother was serious. "King Everson. The same king who moments ago threw me out of the palace." There was no part of the man I knew that I could reconcile with that statement. Especially today.

"He wasn't always so bitter. He was different back then. Queen Ciera's death changed him."

"Different? How?"

Mother stroked my arm, the motion more irritating than

soothing in my current state. I said nothing, though, too curious for her answer to interrupt her train of thought.

"He smiled more, for one. He walked through the city and took the time to speak with his people—much as Thoraben does now. In fact, Thoraben is a lot like his father was at the same age. It wasn't a difficult decision at all for your father and me to move to the palace the day you were born given how well we felt we already knew the royal family. We were heartbroken to hear of Queen Ciera's death but thrilled for the chance to help our beloved, grieving king in any way we could."

I smoothed my hand across a crease in the bedspread, wishing I could smooth away my doubts as easily. Her words wouldn't settle in my mind, refusing to sit nicely alongside my assumptions. All this time, I'd thought my parents had had no say in the matter. When the king orders you to do something, you do it, even if it means giving up your home and everything you know to move to the palace only hours after giving birth to your first child. I'd thought it an order. Had it truly been a request? And one they'd happily agreed to?

"And you should have seen how proud the king was when Queen Ciera gave him a son. He called a week-long holiday. There was partying wherever you looked. King Everson announced the birth himself, crying as he did so."

"King Everson cried? In public?"

"No doubt hard for you to believe." Mother smiled. I didn't bother agreeing with her. She already knew it was. "But not so much for his people. It was further proof of the kindhearted man he was. Every time we saw the royal family, which was frequently, he'd be the one carrying Thoraben. First in his arms then proudly on his shoulders.

"People still respect him now, but it was a different respect back then. A respect born of love and devotion rather than fear. Queen Ciera's death changed everyone."

"And rid them of their common sense, it would seem. They have to know I could never be queen." It was crazy. Ludicrous. And downright impossible. I expected Mother to laugh along with me at the mere thought, but she was strangely silent as she considered me. Too silent. There was far more to what she was thinking than she was saying aloud. "Mother?"

"Would you want to? Be queen, that is."

"What? No." Why was she even asking that? To be queen, I would have to marry Prince Thoraben and that would be... strange. Very strange. The few times such a crazy thought had crossed my mind, I'd banished it immediately. Where was the point in wondering? He belonged to someone else. Sure, I loved dancing with him—who wouldn't?—and yes, he was my best friend, but embracing? Sharing a suite with Ben? Secrets? And... more? Heat crept up my neck, racing across my cheeks as I determined, once again, to banish the thought. I scrunched my face, shaking my head. Hoping Mother didn't identify my blush as anything but what it was—pure mortification.

Not that it mattered what Mother thought since it wasn't as if either of us could change anything.

I looked at her and regretted it immediately. She was considering me again, taking in my words but trying to figure out whether I really meant them or not. I did. "I am not marrying Prince Thoraben." Mother's only reply was to purse her lips, still hunting for something beyond my words. Enough was enough. "Mother."

"I'm only saying that, while I think it wrong the king would forbid you from seeing Thoraben, the very fact that he has proves he considers you a threat. He's scared the people will love you more than they did Queen Ciera—perhaps he even fears what will become of the kingdom if Thoraben rewrites the law and marries you—so he's done the only thing he can and taken you out of the picture."

I pulled back from Mother's embrace, shocked by her words. I hadn't thought anything could have surprised me more than King Everson's hate. I'd been wrong. Had it been anyone else, I might have thought Mother was joking, but I knew she wasn't. Conviction hung from every word she spoke. She truly believed

I would be queen. And claiming King Everson was scared of me? I was glad the maids had left.

"The king could have you tried for treason for saying such a thing."

"Then he would have to send to trial most of his people, for they are all saying it. However it comes about, they want you to be their queen. Surely you have seen the respect they hold for you?"

I had, it was impossible not to. They called me Lady Mackenna, curtsying to me and giving me the same respect they afforded the royal family. Mr. Slaughter, who had to be in his nineties despite having the mischievous grin of a ten-year-old, was the one exception. He addressed me as Princess Mackenna, no matter how many times I corrected him.

Then there was Mrs. Olive, who always had a bunch of flowers for me whenever I came into town, the school children who stood to attention when I passed, and little Ella Smoak, who was so awestruck the first time she saw me in the marketplace that all that had come out of her mouth was a tiny squeak. Two years on, she'd more than found her voice, chattering what felt like a few hundred words to the minute whenever we had the chance to talk. Every time we parted, she'd tell me she wanted to be just like me when she grew up.

Their love and respect was humbling, to say the least, but I'd always thought it came out of reverence for their king. While I lived in the palace and ate at his table, I was his representative among the people. Could it truly be that their deference was for me myself rather than who I represented? It was almost too much to consider.

"They love you, Mackenna."

They shouldn't. I was neither royal nor noble, and they knew it. We all did. "Their reverence is misplaced."

"I don't think so."

I crossed my arms. "I am a commoner, like them."

"You've never been common."

"How can you say that? You know as well as I that, had Queen

Ciera not died, we would never have come to the palace. I would have grown up, attended school, and gone to work in town as you and Father did. Not royal, not noble. Simply a commoner."

"And yet, she did die, and we did come. You may not have royal blood in you, but you, Mackenna Sparrow, will never be a commoner."

"Then what am I, Mother? Answer me that."

A breath, a heartbeat of silence, and then—

"Perhaps you are our future queen."

A knock at the door had me scrambling from my mother's side, as if the king himself stood there and heard our conversation rather than the maid who entered. I wondered if the guilt was written across my face as clearly as it was my heart. Mother smiled at me but didn't say any more. Our conversation was at an end for now, but I couldn't regret the fact. She'd given me far more to think about than I'd anticipated. For the first time ever, I left her presence feeling more weighed down than when I'd come.

FOUR

True to his word, the king had sent staff to assist me in packing. They were in my suite when I returned, much to my maid's confusion. I sent them away. Avrel too. I'd already determined to take very little when I left. A few outfits, certainly none of the ballgowns or dresses they had been wrapping. Apart from the fact that there would be no room for them in our new, much smaller house, they all felt so fake now. As if the king had never wanted me to have them in the first place.

I needed to think. Sitting atop my bed, I pulled out my journal and leaned back against the mountain of pillows. My pen was poised, but the page remained blank. So many emotions assailed me that I had no idea where to begin.

Did the people truly think I would be a good queen? They wouldn't if they could see me now, cowering in my room as afraid to leave the palace as I was to stay. The truth was, I didn't know where I belonged anymore. As contrived as it now felt, the palace and its lavishness was the only life I'd ever known. I might have been common by blood, but I'd never lived like it.

And Queen Ciera? Was I truly like her?

She'd died the night I was born, a Rebel attack on the palace sending her into early labor with more complications than could be resolved. She'd left behind not only a grief-stricken king and baffled toddler looking for his mother but a mewling infant in desperate need of care. When bottles of various milks and formulas hadn't been able to settle the tiny princess, palace employees had been sent throughout the city to find help. My mother had been brought to the palace, me bundled in her arms. Father followed the next day with what little possessions we owned. We never left.

I often wondered how different my life would have been had the king had a little more patience with his newborn daughter. Alina likely would have taken a bottle given more time, but King Everson liked to be in control. I imagine hearing his tiny daughter screaming, even for a few minutes, while dealing with the loss of his wife and the Rebel situation was too much to bear. He would have tried anything to get her to settle, even the care of a stranger. Once Mother was there and little Alina quiet, the relief would have been too great to send Mother away. Not that I could hold any of that against him. He had just lost his beloved wife.

Out of the generosity of her heart, Mother cared for Princess Alina and me as if she'd given birth to twins, rather than me alone. Three-year-old Thoraben also found comfort in her capable arms. In a moment of immense gratitude, the king decreed that I was to be allowed the same privileges his daughter had—the best of everything, the life of a princess—until the day Alina married.

Some days, I wondered why my parents had agreed. Even now, almost two decades after that life-changing night, they wore palace life uncomfortably. They could have sat with the royal family at meals as I did but usually chose to eat in their suite or with other staff. They could have reveled in a life of luxury, being draped in fine gowns and jewels equal their status as the king's guests but instead chose to dress simply and continue working—Father in the stables training the king's horses and Mother cleaning alongside the maids.

We were an ill-fitting group—King Everson the head of his family and my parents the heads of mine, with Thoraben, Alina, and me floating somewhere in the middle. Part of both families, I supposed. Not quite siblings, but closer than friends. Mother had never taken the place of Queen Ciera in anyone's minds, yet she'd mothered the queen's children, being available to all three of us any hour of the day or night. And I was her payment, it appeared. At the very least, that seemed to be the way the king saw it.

When my pen finally began to write, lists, rather than musings or recounts, wound their way down the page.

Alina was getting married.

Ben had chosen a bride.

The king was throwing me out.

The people wanted me to be queen.

It was the last point that still had me reeling. The first three points, I'd expected in some form or another. Even the king sending me away wasn't all that much of a surprise, though the way he'd done it and his threats still infuriated me. But the people? Me, their queen? Why? What did they see in me?

And what was I to do about it? Could I do anything about it? Because they were wrong. No matter what Mother said, they were wrong. And if they continued to speak of it, like Mother said they were, sooner or later, the king was going to hear about it. I couldn't bear to think of someone being punished because of me, nor what the king might do to me if he heard. Exile would be the least of my worries.

A knock came at my door, so tentative I knew it had to be one of my maids. Any other employee would have knocked loudly, Mother tended to crack the door open and call my name through the opening, and Alina barged right in. The men of the castle, king and prince included, knew better than to come at all.

"Lady Mackenna?"

I was right. It was Elayna. I smiled to myself at that small achievement. I was so unsure of myself right now that I'd take any victory. "Come in."

Elayna was the first through the door, but Meri and Avrel were close behind her.

I watched as they took in the half-packed room and my eyes. I didn't look away, though even without looking in the mirror, I knew my eyes would still be red from my earlier tears. I'd never been one of those girls whose faces showed blotchy evidence of a crying fit. I could wipe the tears off my face and no one would know the difference—if not for my eyes. I couldn't wipe the red away from the whites of my eyes.

"It's true then, what Avrel said? You're leaving?" Elayna asked.

I nodded, afraid if I opened my mouth, my tears would begin again. Even that was too much for the one tear that dripped its way down my cheek. I quickly wiped it away. The maids were silent for a stunned moment before all speaking at once.

"Oh, my lady..."

"They're sending you away?"

"When will you go? Are we to go with you?"

Their predictable reactions brought a smile to my face, albeit a waterlogged one.

Petite Meri trembled with the effort it took to hold her composure together. The hand which had first gone to her mouth when I nodded now sat alongside its mate in Meri's apron pocket. The light cotton wasn't enough to hide the way she wrung them together.

Where Meri trembled, Avrel stood tall like a guard at attention. There was a fierceness in her face she rarely let show but I'd always known was there. I'd seen it once before when she'd spoken of her younger sister being mistreated. She'd confront the king himself if I told her he'd been the one to hurt me, and no doubt lose her employment in the process. I'd have to keep her too busy to have the chance.

Then there was Elayna. Though her expression hadn't changed since my confirming nod, there was no doubt in my mind that she was sorting through what such an announcement would mean. She'd probably already written several lists in her head and begun prioritizing them.

My kind-heart, my warrior, and my manager. The three of them had been my personal maids since my tenth birthday, when I'd moved from my parents' suite to my own. I appreciated their advice more than they gave themselves credit for, their friendship too. They weren't old enough to be my mother but could certainly pass as older sisters. And beloved ones at that.

They wouldn't be coming with me—I'd settled with that already—but I did hope they kept their positions within the palace. They were far too adept at serving as personal maids to be wasted in the laundry room.

Tears blurred my vision, but not so much that I missed the look Elayna sent Meri's way. Buck up, it said. Pull yourself together. I felt like telling Elayna not to bother. It felt nice to have someone upset that I was leaving. I reached out to tell Meri that it was okay to cry, but she'd already walked away.

It took her twenty-three steps to reach the window. I know. I counted every one of them. Laying her shaking hands on the sill, she simply stared. I don't know what she saw out there—perhaps it was more what her mind saw than her eyes—but when she turned around, she was calm. She walked back slower, each step more certain than the last.

"Forgive me, Lady Mackenna."

I sighed as I closed my journal, placing it on the nightstand, the pen balanced on top. If anyone should be apologizing, it was me. The three of them had been nothing but wonderful. Having a heart that cared was nothing to apologize for, even if one was a maid. At least, that was what I thought. I supposed the king might think otherwise, wishing his employees to be devoid of emotion and opinions entirely, but I could not be like that. We held different roles in the palace, certainly, but these women before me were no less human than I and therefore had every right to express their emotions.

"No, Meri, I'm sorry. I'm leaving tomorrow and until this moment, I didn't even think what that would mean for you—"

"Tomorrow?" Elayna interrupted. For an instant, her confidence faltered and I could see I'd surprised her, but then she blinked and found balance again. "So soon?"

"I chose the time," I quickly said, before Avrel had the chance to lay the blame on anyone else. I needed her. Here.

"Of course," Elayna said, as if she hadn't suspected anything else. "That doesn't leave us much time. What would you have us do first?"

They were being so strong, all three of them, even Meri. Her hands had begun to tremble again but, determined not to let it show, she'd crossed her arms across her middle. I could still see the shaking but appreciated the effort. I had to be strong too. I could spend my last twenty-four hours in the palace moping and mourning or I could go out in style, making the ball tonight a night to remember. I chose the latter. The king already thought me a threat, though I'd never given him any reason to do so. Perhaps, tonight, I would.

I swung my legs around, sliding off the edge of the bed, and swiped at the last of the tears. Tears were for the weak, and if ever I needed to be strong, it was now.

"I have a plan..."

I didn't go to lunch in the dining hall, choosing instead to have food delivered to my room. It was easier that way, and I didn't think the king or whoever else happened to be eating in the hall would appreciate the picture I currently presented anyway. They likely would have had the guards shoot me on the spot, certain some monster from the deep had wandered inside. I touched a tentative finger to my face. Still wet. Still smelling like the mud puddle where I imagined the slop plastered across it had been found.

It was a delicate operation, timed to perfection, this beauty regime. It had begun two hours ago with a half hour long soak in a rose petal-laden warm bath. How Avrel had talked the gardener into providing her with so many rose petals, I wasn't entirely sure, but it was so luxurious that I certainly hadn't complained.

They'd washed my hair next before rolling it around large curlers which made me feel as if half the kingdom balanced on my head. Then the mud mask, polish on my nails, and numerous sprays of something heavenly-smelling on my wrists and neck.

Of course, anything would smell good when compared with the mud. I truly hoped Meri declared it done soon. Much longer and I doubted they'd ever get rid of the stench. No matter how beautifully regal they made me look, one whiff of the mud and every ball-goer tonight would be sent running.

The curlers they'd rolled my hair in weren't all that comfortable either, balanced as they were across my head. Still, if they gave my normally straight hair any fullness at all, they would be worth it. At the very least, they kept my hair away from the mud.

"Now, Meri?"

I knew I was trying her patience asking so often but, soothing as it had been when she first slathered it on, the mud was starting to prickle and itch. If she didn't take it off in the next few minutes, I was going to order her to, and if there was one thing I'd learned growing up alongside Princess Alina, it was how to give an order, albeit with a charming smile.

"Very well. Into the bathroom with you. Careful you don't wet your hair though."

I was out of my chair so quickly it crashed behind me, clattering on the marbled floor. I was fortunate it didn't hit anyone on its way down, though, from their muffled giggles, I didn't think they would have minded.

The water felt wonderful on my face. Smooth and luxurious, sluicing effortlessly across my heated skin, soothing the places which had only moments ago been smarting.

"Don't get your hair wet," I heard again. I grinned, pleased to be able to do so. Though I did my best to keep it dry, my exuberant washing had sent a few rogue droplets the wrong way. I cupped water in my hands again, splashing it against my face. If the purpose of a mud mask was to make me delight in washing my face after removing it, I would call it an absolute success.

A tap at the bathroom door had Meri peering in. She looked in my direction, but I knew she was examining my face rather than looking at me. I don't know what she was hoping to see but she must have found it.

"Good. Now, dry your face and back to the chair."

I smiled into the towel she threw me. I'd never before seen Meri so bossy. Elayna, certainly, even Avrel on occasion, but never Meri. She was more the follow-directions type. Then again, I suppose I had asked for it when I'd told my three maids to do whatever it took to make me into a princess.

I did my best to stay still while they flitted around me, somehow managing not to get in each other's way despite working in such close confines. Though I sat in front of a mirror, there was little point in trying to see my reflection with at least one of them—usually Meri—constantly blocking my view. Avrel and Elayna worked on freeing and styling my hair while Meri continued to slather dubious concoctions on my face. At least these smelled good.

The next half hour was a daze of doing what I was told.

"Purse your lips."

"Close your eyes."

"Open them again. Now close. Open."

"Look up. Look down. Turn this way."

A few pointed stares, tweaks, far too many pins, and a rush of hairspray later, they deemed me ready. All that was left was the gown. I did my best to stand still as the maids lifted it over my head, the delicate fabric brushing against my shoulders in a cool whisper of silk as it danced its way to the floor. I'd long ago given up any illusion of modesty or personal space when it came to my maids, something I was reminded of again as the three of them pushed and pulled at my ribs and sides, caring far more for the fabric of the gown and its painfully slow-rising zip than my comfort. It was no small relief when they stepped back.

"There. All done. What do you think?"

Turning to the full-length mirror behind me, I got my first glimpse of my outfit in its entirety. I gasped, then grinned as my maids laughed. They were proud of their work, and rightly so.

My normally dead-straight hair had been pulled back into a loose chignon, low to one side of my neck, gentle twists down each side of my head giving the hair a fullness I hadn't thought possible. A few tendrils of curls framed my face—just enough to soften its patrician lines and draw attention to my moss green eyes. I didn't know what Meri had done with her sponges and brushes nor where she'd learned such magic, but I loved it. Almost as much as I did my gown.

I spun twice, watching as the skirt flared, danced and settled. A shimmering, sapphire blue, the one-shouldered gown was fitted to the waist before cascading to the floor in rivulets of silk. Strands of silver thread running through the bodice from shoulder to waist made it look almost as if I'd walked through a moonlit waterfall and captured the moment in time. It was perfect for the Midsummer's Ball.

I was still trying to find the right words to thank the women when Meri ran into my wardrobe, returning seconds later with a decorative wooden box. I should have guessed they would pull it out tonight. The box itself, though pretty, wasn't all that remarkable. But what it contained... I sighed, my heart catching as she opened it, holding it out to me.

My silver tiara. The one I'd cherished since my sixteenth birthday when King Everson had given it to me. To Alina, he'd given a gold crown so laden with gems it was a wonder it didn't give her a migraine every time she wore it. Me, he'd given the silver tiara. A cheaper yet still more than adequate gift for a princess's companion, I'm sure he thought. He had no idea how right he'd been.

I picked up the tiara, running my finger along the loosely tangled silver vines which made up the band. Tiny sapphire forget-me-nots rose delicately at intervals around it. Had I had to choose between the ostentatious gold of Alina's crown and the quiet simplicity of the forget-me-nots, I would have chosen the forget-me-nots without even a thought.

But I couldn't wear it.

I placed it back in its box, heart aching as if I'd trodden on my maids' dreams in the process. "Not tonight."

"But why not?" Meri asked. "Haven't you always wanted to?"

Of course I had. It was beautiful. Stunning in its simplicity. I'd tried it on more times than I could count as my maids and I played the charade within the privacy of my suite, but I could never wear it—especially not tonight. Tonight was Alina's night. Dressing up was one thing but I wouldn't take the attention from her by wearing that tiara...though it was probably the height of vanity to even think I *could*.

I'd always stood in her shadow. Always would. She was the princess, I merely her companion. No number of frills or jewels would change that. Not even a simple, silver and sapphire tiara. Still... I turned away from Meri's disappointment before it could mar my common sense. "Sorry. I can't."

Meri's reply was cut off as my door burst open, Alina barreling through in a flurry of pink satin. The skirt of her gown reached so wide, I wondered how she'd even fit through the door. Then again, this was Alina. She'd probably told the doorposts to move and they'd been only too thrilled to jump aside.

"Alina. What are you doing here?" Not that I didn't want to see her. I just hadn't expected to see her until tonight at the ball. I'd been counting on it, in fact, wanting to keep my appearance and gown a surprise until the moment I walked into the ballroom.

Too late.

"I had to show you—Wait, wow. Look at you. You're gorgeous. I want your gown. Let's swap."

I stared at her gown. Me, wear that pink monstrosity? I hoped she was joking. Tonight was supposed to be my final hurrah. Dressing as an oversized marshmallow wouldn't really help that, nor my shaky confidence any. Not to mention how terribly the pink would clash with the deep auburn color of my hair.

"I, uh—"

"Kenna. I'm kidding. It wouldn't fit me and anyway, it's the wrong color. You know I only wear pink to balls. But I do love it. Well done, maids." She swished a hand of approval in their direction. I tried not to show my relief too obviously.

"What did you want to show me?"

I should have complimented her gown, it would have been the proper thing to do, but I had yet to find something I appreciated about it. It was overly big, overly pink, and overly frilly. Alina was the only one in the entire kingdom—dare I say, the world?—who would choose to wear something so...pink.

"My ring. Oh, Mackenna. You have to see it. Prince Marcos gave it to me. See? See?"

I tried my best to see it, but she was waving it so close to my eyes that all I could see was a glimmer of gold as it flashed by. I swerved backward to avoid being hit with it. Meri would not have been impressed to have spent two hours glamorizing my face only to have it redecorated by Alina's ring.

Grabbing her hand, I finally stopped it moving enough to look, though Alina continued to bounce with excitement. She suffered none of the misgivings I had about her arranged marriage. I wasn't sure whether that comforted me or worried me further. Did she not know how much her life was about to change?

The ring rivaled her dress for size. Or, at the very least, sparkle. It would have caused my face some serious damage had it actually hit me. I could see why Alina was so excited about it though. The central jewel cluster was enormous, with a pink gem bigger than my thumbnail surrounded by smaller sapphires and white diamonds. As if that weren't enough on its own, the gold band encased even more diamonds as it wound its way around Alina's finger.

"He had it made for me. Can you believe it?"

Strangely, I could.

"Marcos—he gave me leave to call him that—came and showed it to me now, asking if I approved. I have to give it back, of course, since Father won't announce our engagement until tonight so I shouldn't really be wearing it in case someone sees, but I begged Marcos to let me show you first and he said I could. It's a pink diamond in the middle there. They're rare, you know, pink diamonds—or that's what Marcos told me. He had to send halfway across the world for it, but he did it anyway because he knew pink was my favorite color. Wasn't that kind of him?"

Kinder than I'd given him credit for, even after all Ben had told me about him. I worried for my friend. She was...Alina.

Flighty, naïve, and, for the most part, sheltered. It was fortunate Ben had been the firstborn—and therefore heir—for though Alina was stunningly beautiful and the kingdom's darling of a princess, she would have struggled to run a country. She didn't have the temperament for it. Or perhaps it was *because* she was second born that she was like that, for while the king spent hours pouring knowledge and teaching into his son, he poured only money and indulgence out on his daughter.

"Do you mind?" I asked her. "That your marriage is arranged, that is."

Alina giggled. "Have you seen Prince Marcos? He's gorgeous."

Not what I asked, though I supposed in her mind it probably answered the question. The rulers of two kingdoms had agreed upon this matching of their children and, no matter what King Everson thought of me, he adored his daughter. He wouldn't do wrong by her. And Ben had approved Marcos. Even if I couldn't trust the king, I could trust his son.

"Oh, I forgot you had this. You have to wear it."

What? I spun around, wondering what it was that had captured the flighty princess's attention now. Oh, my tiara. It still sat there on the dresser.

"I don't think—"

"Then don't. Just wear it. Here." Before I could stop her, she'd plonked it on my head. It was a little askew, but clearly good enough. Alina's eyes widened. "Yes. Definitely. It's perfect. You'll wear it."

Command given, she swished out of the room as fast as she'd come. I was a little mollified to see her stop outside my door to recapture a piece of skirt which had had the audacity to get stuck under the door. Not everything went her way.

But, it appeared, something was. Though my maids tried their best to hide their satisfied smiles, the triumph peeked through. Princess Alina herself had decreed I wear the tiara, so wear it I would.

It didn't take long for them to secure the tiara, my hairstyle fitting around the piece as if it had been created to do just that. Perhaps it had. Silver, strappy heels were next and then—

"There, you're ready."

There was a hitch in Elayna's voice as she spoke, almost as if she were holding back tears. Or perhaps excitement. I wasn't sure exactly. In turning to see, I caught sight of myself in the mirror.

I'd never known it to before, but I am certain in that moment time stood still.

A tiara and some shoes. That was all that had changed since the last time I'd looked in the mirror, and yet I barely recognized the woman staring back at me. Tall, elegant, stately, beautiful—it was everything I'd hoped for, and more.

Forget "princess"—they'd turned me into a queen.

FIVE

I almost took the tiara off four times on the way to the ballroom. For something so light I could barely feel it, it weighed heavily on my mind.

Take it off. Leave it on. Take it off. Don't you dare.

The words warred in time with my footsteps as I walked, their refrain a battle cry for a fight I didn't want to have.

If it had only been me it affected, I would have removed it. But somehow, this night had become bigger than me, and the tiara more than a pretty piece of sapphire-studded silver. It wasn't even that Alina had ordered me to wear it—as I had no doubt her crown would far outshine mine—or the way I felt wearing it, that strange mixture of shyness and confidence.

Alina had a say, my emotions tried, but neither of them were what kept the tiara firmly on my head. That honor rested solely on the proud shoulders of my three maids.

I'd finally given them permission to make me the royal they'd been begging for since the day I'd met them. And they'd done it, all the while knowing that this first chance to do so would also be their last. I might have been besieged with uncertainty, but they suffered no such doubts.

I'd seen them crying as they pushed me from the room. Even Elayna. They'd humbled me with their reactions, all teasing and laughter gone from their faces as one by one they'd curtsied deeply before me.

I'd been curtsied to many times before, but this felt different.

It had to have been the moment making me feel so emotional. After all, in the course of today I'd been threatened by the king, shocked by my mother, coated in mud, prodded and poked, ordered about by the princess, and dressed like a queen in the most beautiful gown I'd ever seen. I was certain it had been my ears mishearing a whispered "Queen Mackenna" as the three maids dipped their heads toward the ground.

My steps slowed, the grand wooden doors to the ballroom looming before me. They were closed, as I suspected they would be, arriving half an hour after the ball had begun. King Everson was a great believer in punctuality and expected his guests to follow suit. I could still enter through them though. Alina had done it enough times, choosing to wait until all the guests were present and every eye watching before making her grand entrance into the room. It was what I'd planned to do tonight.

Only now I was here... My heart thudded in my chest, a hand going to my tiara again before—again—dropping to my side empty. I couldn't take it off. Whether I walked through those doors or found a side entrance, this was my maids' moment as much as it was mine. There were few achievements a maid could aspire to or profess but tonight, I was theirs. Their masterpiece.

I looked beautiful, but more than that, I felt beautiful. For the first time in almost eighteen years, I wouldn't be just the shadow behind the princess. My appearance instilled in me a confidence that I was frightened to claim. Equally loud voices screamed from within me, yelling over each other in an effort to be heard. *See me! Notice me! Look at me! I'm beautiful...* But then, every bit as strong, *Don't look at me. It's not real. It's a part. There's the princess. Over there...*

Four steps forward, one single knock on the door. That was all it would take. *Come on, Kenna. You'll never get this chance again.*

Still, I hesitated.

It terrified me how eagerly I anticipated the spotlight and the attention I knew I'd gain. I could so easily go with the emotion and be the person my maids believed me to be, floating on the waves of giddy delight...but I wasn't that person. I couldn't be.

Though I looked like a princess, everyone here knew I wasn't one. Bold confidence pushed me forward, timidity pulled me back. Together, they had me stumbling.

"Here, miss, let me help you."

A hand steadied me, and I looked up to see Prince Thoraben, looking every part the fairy-tale prince in his black dinner suit, dark hair combed into perfect submission. His eyes widened, his hand pulling back immediately as he realized who I was.

"Kenna." He blinked twice before letting his gaze skitter down my gown and back up again. He looked surprised. I doubted I looked much different. Startling appearance aside, I had assumed the royal family was inside the ballroom already. He must have been running even later than I was, which wouldn't gain him any approval from his father. For either of us. "Forgive me. I didn't recognize you. You look...uh...that is..."

My face flooded with heat far worse than the mud Meri had caked it in. Had Thoraben been alone, I might have teased him, but he wasn't. Standing behind him were two of his very male companions, both of whom were staring at me as if I were a prize they couldn't wait to start bidding on.

I knew them both, having seen them around the palace over the years. Lord Ashe was kind enough, if a little proud of his good looks—which, I had to admit, he had a right to be. Ben might have been named Peverell's Most Eligible Bachelor every year since he was ten, but Ashe had taken the title of Most Handsome the last three years running.

Lord Waitrose, on the other hand, was not a man I would ever want to be caught alone with. He'd ruined more girls' reputations than any man I knew, though nothing had ever been proven. Fortunately for him.

Unfortunately for the rest of us. Had there been a single witness willing to testify against him, Peverell's old morality law would have forced him into marriage by now. Not that anyone really believed the king would force a marriage because of a simple kiss, but it was still the law, and therefore enough to keep most people in line.

Waitrose excluded. Or perhaps his parents were just rich enough to pay off any witnesses. I was surprised to find him a friend of Ben's…though, I supposed, if he was friends with the prince, he'd be unlikely to go for the princess. Keep your enemies close and all that.

I tried a smile, all the while wishing I still wore Meri's mud. It might not have stopped my face exploding with heat, but its hard casing might have held it in. Perhaps the muted light out in the hall would make me appear charmingly rosy rather than a beet-root in a ballgown. I should have gone directly into the ballroom instead of loitering outside trying to decide whether to make a grand entrance or sneak in through a side door.

"What's this?" Ben flicked a finger at my tiara. "Trying to out-shine Alina?"

Though his voice was teasing, his words were more than my shaky composure could take. I reached up to pluck the tiara out of my hair but his hand on mine stopped me. "Kenna, I'm kidding. It suits you, and Alina would never wear something so understated." His hand dropped back down. "Coming in?"

Was that a compliment he'd given me? Or a reproach? I was still trying to work it out when I realized he'd already changed the subject and was waiting for an answer. Coming in? With the three of them? Not likely.

"Not yet."

He raised his eyebrows. "Ever?"

Caught. "I will…" In a few hours, when everyone was too high on festivities to notice another person arriving. I couldn't do this, not even for my maids. It wasn't me. And I hadn't even seen the king yet. I knew any shard of confidence I clung to would shatter the moment I saw him.

"Come on. We'll walk you in. Right, fellows?"

The two men bowed deeply as Ben grinned. "It would be our honor."

I glared at Ben. He knew exactly what I was doing, standing outside the ballroom, and had taken away any chance I had of sneaking in. Which I had suddenly decided was definitely the right thing to do.

Ashe and Waitrose both offered their arms, eager to escort me. I accepted them, it being impolite to do anything else. Ben's protest was immediate.

"Oh no, you don't. I'm the prince and therefore should have at least half of the honor of escorting such a beautiful woman, should I not?"

To my eternal gratitude, he took Lord Waitrose's place at my side. Waitrose looked disgruntled but then, as Ben had said, Ben was the prince. Waitrose was relegated almost to the role of servant as he went to knock on the grand wooden door, a role he played none too comfortably. I lost track of him as the doors opened, the music stopped and every eye, it seemed, turned to me.

No, Prince Thoraben. They were looking at Prince Thoraben, bowing to him as we passed. Surely, they were. He was the prince. But I heard the murmurs as the three of us walked down the center of the suddenly open ballroom toward the raised dais where King Everson sat and—while stately, princely, handsome, and regal—neither of my escorts would be described as beautiful.

"Look up, Kenna. They won't bite."

I hadn't even realized I'd dropped my attention to the floor. I raised my eyes to the level of people's knees. Ben would laugh, but he had no idea how much courage even that had taken. The sooner I got away from the prince and found my way back to the shadows, the better it would be for all of us. But the shadows were not where we were headed. No. Ben, traitor that he was, had led me right to the one person I'd hoped to avoid.

Hot lights burned against my back along with the eyes of hundreds of people as I walked up the few steps to the dais and curtsied before the king. "King Everson."

I hated the tremble in my voice as I said his name, but it was nothing compared to the shaking within me. I felt Ben look at me but didn't acknowledge him. After a moment, he placed his free hand over mine where it still clutched at his elbow. I bit back a sob at the kindness of the gesture. I would not cry in front of the king.

My foolish pride chose that moment to overpower my good sense, and I looked into the king's eyes. It didn't take a mind reader to see that he'd noticed me and, unlike the rest of his people, was far from impressed. No doubt he thought I'd somehow schemed to make a grand arrival on Ben's arm. There was fury in his eyes as he looked between the two of us, but he couldn't say anything. Not in front of so many people. It didn't matter. He'd already said everything he needed to this morning.

"Thoraben, you're late."

"Couldn't be helped."

Ben's cheerful answer did nothing to assuage his father's displeasure. "I suggest next time you try harder. There are people waiting to see you. One woman in particular I think you'll enjoy seeing again. Lord Ashe, I'll thank you to see Lady Mackenna back to her place."

I doubted he meant anywhere within the ballroom, though it was a small enough nuance that only I would feel the jibe. It was rude of him, callous even. King Everson hadn't even acknowledged me with a single word, but I was too relieved to be dismissed from his presence to care. If either of us had any say in it, I would never have to talk to the king again.

"Kenna," Ben said under his breath as I pulled my arm from his. "You okay?"

To speak would have been to let loose the tears clogging my throat, but I did offer a small smile and nod. Whether he believed me or not didn't matter. He had his responsibilities and I had mine. Tonight, neither of those overlapped. I was the first to look away, turning aside to smile at Ashe as he walked me down the stairs. My breathing still felt labored, but at least my legs had stopped shaking.

The music began again, our magnificent—and magnificently awkward—entry forgotten as the dancers waltzed their way across the floor.

"What was that about?"

"What?" The shadows. How fast could I find my way to the shadows? The ball was already wearing on my nerves, and I'd been here less than five minutes. Perhaps I'd go out into the gardens. Or to my tower. There, I could enjoy my gown and the way it made me feel without having to appropriately react to every person's opinions on it. No one would notice. The spotlight I'd craved earlier was uncomfortably warm.

Except then I'd miss Alina's announcement, and I had to be here for that.

"You. The king," Ashe said. "I can't be sure, but I think the king snubbed you."

I sighed, glancing at the dais where King Everson had risen from his throne to stand beside his son. Though their expressions were amiable, the furious whispers rebounding back and forth between them belied the true tone of their conversation. I could only hope I wasn't their topic. The sooner I left this place, the better. Even if it did mean never speaking with Ben again. I might not have my friend, but I'd have my dignity.

"He's the king," I said by way of an answer. "He can do whatever he likes."

Perhaps I shouldn't have been so flippant, but there was no way I was admitting to this man who I knew little better than an acquaintance how much the king had hurt me. I pulled my arm out of Ashe's. "Thank you for your escort."

The pink gown of a passing woman reminded me I should probably find Alina. Check she wasn't too dizzy after floating about on her cloud all day.

"Wait, don't you want to dance?"

I stopped. There was a lot of noise in the room tonight, I'd probably heard him wrong. I turned back anyway, to check. Tall and handsome enough to turn every head in the room, Ashe was still waiting. For me, it seemed. "Dance? With you?"

"Well, I was hoping you might, but if you find me so abhorrent..."

"No, no, that wasn't what I meant. I was surprised, that's all. You've never asked me to dance before."

He let out a short laugh, his gaze not leaving mine even as he shook his head. "Have you looked in a mirror tonight? You, Lady Mackenna Sparrow, are the most beautiful woman at the ball. Why wouldn't I want to dance with you?"

Oh. A smile bloomed across my face before I could hide it. Mother would tell me that the beauty I held inside was far more important than what people saw outside, but it stoked my battered ego no end to hear him say such a thing. Alina could wait. This ball had suddenly become far more appealing.

"Don't let Princess Alina hear you say that."

Ashe grinned and looked around the room, checking, I assumed, for Alina. "She's not exactly lacking in admirers," he said. I followed the direction of his nod. Though I couldn't see Alina, being almost a head shorter than Lord Ashe, I saw enough pink frills peeking amidst the pant-clad legs of her entourage to know he was right. Even with a single glance, I'd been able to count at least eight men clambering for her attention.

"So, now you've seen that the princess is taken care of, will you dance with me?"

His eyebrows quirked as he looked at me, hope in those eyes surrounded by lashes a woman would kill for. It wasn't fair. My maids had spent hours making me this beautiful, and he'd probably pulled on some clothes and come. Not that I was really complaining. How could I, when I blushed just looking at him? Only a fool would refuse such a man.

"It would be my honor."

SIX

My worries over the king and the life I was about to lose dissipated under the entrancing spell of the dance. I'd always loved dancing, and Ashe easily claimed the distinction of being one of the best partners I'd had the pleasure of dancing with. His hand was strong against my back, not so much that I felt threatened but enough that I knew he wouldn't let me fall.

The music of a full orchestra swirled around us as we waltzed, amplified yet not splintered by the fresco-painted ceilings dripping with chandeliers. The Midsummer's Ball had always been my favorite, though the Celebration Ball came a close second. There were four major balls held at the palace each year, each with their own charm.

The Black and White ball was the first, where tradition stated that every person attending wore black and white and the decorations followed suit. Of course, Alina never did, always standing out like a flamingo among ravens in her brightly colored gowns. No one complained. She was the princess, after all.

The Midsummer's Ball came next, though I always felt it should have been the pinnacle of the year rather than haphazardly thrown in the middle. It was always beautiful. Warm enough to wear evening gowns of silk without all the furs and coats of the rest of the year. And the women did, parading about in every bold color of the rainbow with not a bit of black, white, or pastel to be seen.

I'd wondered as a child what it would look like from above, if

I could have climbed one of the chandeliers and tucked myself in amongst it. The dresses swirling out like bells as the women spun and danced, colors mixing together as they whirled about. Unlike the marble floors in much of the rest of the palace, the ballroom floor was wood polished to such a gloss that it reflected everything above it. As if the dancers spun on the mirrored surface of a perfectly still lake.

Tall vases of brightly colored flowers stood at attention around the walls of the room, their blooms arching toward the floor as if they, too, ached to join the dance. The clash of so many colors could have looked garish, but somehow it never had, instead beckoning me to join the rainbow and the promise of things to come.

In direct contrast to the Midsummer's Ball, the King's Ball, next on the calendar, was far more subdued. Rather than a full orchestra, a simple quartet played, and while flowers once again decorated the walls, even they knew not to droop or sway out of line. It was a ball for visiting dignitaries and royals, a chance to show off the elegance of Peverell and ensure the tiny kingdom wasn't forgotten. People danced but, ever so careful not to portray their own nations badly or offend anyone else's, their movements lacked any joy.

And then, finally, the Celebration Ball, where every inch of the ballroom was festooned with golden lights. They dangled from the ceiling, twisted amongst the boughs of greenery draped along the walls and spun around every pillar. Even the king's throne wasn't exempt. There was no specification for the color of the women's gowns but, in the spirit of the season, most of them were some manner of red, green, or gold. It was a ball for the people, with every class from the lowest of public servants to the royal family joining in the merriment. The colors and wonder beckoned me at the Midsummer's Ball, but it was the people that made the Celebration Ball shine.

I wondered if I'd still be invited to the balls once I left the palace. Somehow, I doubted it. With Alina married and living in

Hodenia, King Everson wouldn't even have to justify my lack of an invitation.

"So, who do you think she is?"

Ashe's question brought me back to the present. It said a lot for my state of mind that I was dancing with one of the most eligible men in the kingdom and not paying him any attention. Had the waltz not been one I'd performed a hundred times, I probably would have tripped over my own feet by now.

"Who?"

The song finished, moving seamlessly on to another. Ashe didn't let go of me, so I kept dancing, telling myself not to read anything into the reasoning of such an action.

"The woman the king wants Thoraben to notice."

"Oh. I don't know. It could be anyone." Or, just as easily, no one. I wouldn't have put it past the king to invent someone to get Thoraben away from me. He'd made no secret this morning of how much he detested the friendship I shared with his son. He'd ordered me never to see Thoraben again, and mere hours later, I'd walked into the ballroom, dressed like a queen, on none other than Thoraben's arm. It wouldn't have mattered to King Everson that Ashe was there too. He wanted Ben away from me.

"Anyone except you."

My gaze flew to Ashe's, trying to ascertain what he meant by such a comment. Had he guessed, even from so short an encounter, how much the king disapproved of me? As far as the kingdom was concerned—as far as I had known until this morning—the king thought of and treated me as a daughter.

Ashe grinned, taking the opportunity to lean close and speak directly into my ear. With the amount of shivers racing down my spine, I almost missed his words. "Don't worry, the king doesn't like me either."

I smiled with unexpected pleasure as I turned under Ashe's raised arm. If he was trying to charm me, he was succeeding. "No? What did you do to earn his ire?"

"Showed an interest in Princess Alina. He doesn't think me worthy and left me in no doubt of it. Not that it came as any surprise. My family isn't the most affluent despite our title. It would seem I had no chance anyway." The glance he sent Prince Marcos's way was brief but telling. Though the official announcement had yet to be made, Prince Marcos's presence here tonight was enough to cause conjecture.

"Are you disappointed?"

Ashe shook his head. "No. Now I have the chance to court you."

What? Court me? This time I was certain I'd heard him wrong. No one wanted to court me. Certainly not someone of Lord Ashe's standing, even if the king didn't approve of him. "Me? But I'm—"

"Oh. Forgive me. I thought I understood from Thoraben that you were unattached."

"I am."

"Then it's only me you disapprove of?"

"No, not at all. I—"

"Then I might have a chance?"

I quelled the urge to shake my head. He might have had a chance if he stopped interrupting me. But I couldn't truly say yes, could I? I was leaving tomorrow, and the only reason he'd danced with me tonight was, by his own admission, because I looked beautiful. The moment the ball ended, the façade would be gone, and I'd be simply me again. A me I'd never known. He couldn't like that girl. I didn't even know that girl. Much as I might regret it, I had to tell him.

"I—that is…I'm leaving."

"Peverell?"

"The palace."

Ashe smiled. He actually smiled. Here I thought he'd stop dancing with me on the spot and move on to someone with far less complications and he was smiling. "No problem. Actually, that makes it easier. Less guards to deal with. When are you moving? I could help. Though, I suppose, you already have plenty of that already."

"Yes, I do. But—"

My feet moved on the floor as my mind raced with how to finish that sentence. Did I even want the undivided attentions of Lord Ashe? I'd barely gotten my mind around the fact that I was dancing with him, and now he was asking to court me? Did he truly think of me like that? Or was I part of a game he was playing? Alina made it look so easy, conversing with men. I felt like a baby bird being pushed out of the nest, the ground very quickly approaching and no idea where my wings were.

"But...?"

I should say no. I barely even knew where I'd live tomorrow, let alone what my life would look like. Complicated didn't even come close. And the idea of bringing a man into that uncertainty? Ludicrous.

"Lady Mackenna?"

It was his eyes which swayed me. Blue, piercing, looking all the way to my heart—and approving of what they saw. One glance and I was captured. I found myself agreeing against my better judgement. "Yes, I'd like that."

"Excellent."

I spent the rest of the dance vacillating between excited anticipation and sickening dread. It was becoming all too familiar a feeling. This time, when the song finished, Ashe stepped back and bowed before taking my arm and escorting me to Alina's side. Or, at least, as close as I could have gotten. Her crowd of men had doubled in the time I'd been dancing. I was surprised none of them had noticed Prince Marcos's presence and come to the same conclusion Ashe had. Perhaps they had and simply hoped for one last chance to change her mind—as if she'd had any say in the matter at all.

"Until we meet again, my lady," Ashe said with a wink and a bow before disappearing into the throng.

There were so many things I could have done at that moment. Left the ball, sought out refreshments, hidden in the bathroom, made eye contact in the hope of finding another dance partner. Instead, I stood and watched, a smile tugging at my mouth as I thought about what had happened. Lord Ashe had singled me out—and wanted to do so again.

"Punch, Mackenna?"

There was laughter in Alina's voice, and it only took one glance in her direction to see why. Five of her admirers had brought her drinks. She'd spend the entire night in the bathroom if she accepted them all. I took one with a word of thanks, walking to her side as the crowd of men parted. With a toss of her blonde hair, she sent them all away. Within seconds, we were alone. I shook my head, impressed once again by the power of this diminutive woman.

"Don't think I didn't notice your entrance, or the fact that you were late."

I lowered my glass, surprised by the sudden change of Alina's tone. The laughter that had been there only moments ago was gone, disapproval taking its place. Was she angry at me? True, she changed moods as often as she changed gowns, but this was the Midsummer's Ball. Her betrothal ball. I wouldn't have thought anything could pop her bubble of bliss, least of all me. Whatever it was I'd done.

"I took longer than usual to get ready."

"Truly, Kenna? You think I'm going to believe that? You were almost ready when I saw you. I'm not blind, you know. You came with Thoraben."

"What? No. How could you think that? You of all people should know that would never be."

"No?" Fuchsia nails tapped against the side of her glass as Alina drilled me with a glare. "Then why the grand entrance? Why were you clutching at his arm like that? Why do your outfits match? If you wanted to hide it, you might have tried a little harder."

"Our outfits don't—" My eyes found Ben in an instant, as if I'd been tracking him around the dance floor without even realizing. Alina was right. In my nervousness earlier I hadn't noticed, but his waistcoat and tie were the same color as my gown.

Exactly.

His tie even had flecks of silver in it.

"It wasn't planned." I sighed, hating how defensive I sounded—and that I had to defend myself at all to this woman who was practically my sister. "I was simply running late. My maids had to change my hairstyle to accommodate this tiara you insisted I wear." Not that that had taken long. It was the number of detours I'd taken between my suite and the ballroom while searching for my courage which had made me late. "I was about to walk in when Thoraben, Ashe, and Waitrose arrived. They, being the gentlemen they are, insisted they escort me.

"Surely you noticed Lord Ashe by my side along with Thoraben. And that it was him I left the podium with, not Thoraben. And Ashe I danced the first two dances with."

"Then you hold no secret designs on my brother?"

Was she serious? "Of course not. I can't believe you even thought that. You know what he is to me. What he's always been. Come on, Alina. It's Thoraben, for goodness' sake."

"Good. Because you know Father would never approve." I held back a scoff at her words. Didn't I know. My heart was still aching from his scorn so purposefully delivered. "So, you and Lord Ashe then? Or are you going to tell me that was merely a coincidence too?"

"Actually, he asked to court me."

The squeal she bestowed upon my left ear was deafening. "You said yes, didn't you? Please, tell me you said yes. He's so tall and handsome and please, please, please tell me you said yes."

The instant change in her was remarkable. Gone was the anger, back were the giddy smiles. I couldn't help one of my own as I answered. "I did."

"Good. Are you going to tell Thoraben?"

"I don't know. Probably not. He's busy meeting people."

"One person in particular, I'll bet."

So, there was a woman. I found myself again searching the ballroom for Ben. I almost lurched forward when I saw him captured in the arms of a woman I didn't know. Of course, they'd probably call it dancing but, arms wrapped tightly around Ben's neck, her expression filled with more hope than a hound on a hunt, the woman clearly wanted far more than a dance.

"That woman? The one dancing with Thoraben now?" I pointed with my chin. Alina found him and nodded. "Who is she?"

I wasn't sure whether the expression on Alina's face was pity or veiled laughter at my expense. Either way, I regretted asking.

"You don't know?"

I hid a scowl behind indifference. Clearly, I didn't know or I wouldn't be asking. I could walk away, ask someone else even, but that would make me seem far more interested than I was. I was interested, but more because it was becoming almost embarrassing watching the woman's possessive hold on Ben and ridiculously loud flirting than anything else. I could hear her trilled laughter from halfway across the room.

"Should I?"

"She was your friend once too."

I frowned, still drawing a blank as I ran through the list of girls Alina might consider my friends. I hadn't had many over the years, not many close ones anyway, though Alina wouldn't realize that, counting every person who ever smiled at her a friend. It wasn't that I was unwilling to make friends, simply that my position in the palace made it difficult.

"Outspoken? Had a crush on my brother since, well, forever?"

My mouth dropped open in shock as I stared at the woman. "Wenderley? That's Wenderley?" I tried my best but still couldn't reconcile any part of the pleasant, but plain, girl I'd once known with the gorgeous, flirty woman dancing with Ben now. "You're teasing me."

Alina laughed. "No, not at all. That's Wenderley, all right. I talked to her earlier. She and her family have moved back to Peverell where, it seems, she's finally caught her man. Though I daresay Thoraben's not minding her attention quite as much as he used to."

Ben laughed at something Wenderley said before spinning her out and back into his embrace. I looked away, the ache building in my heart too painful to continue watching. Ben had said he'd chosen a bride. I don't think I'd truly believed him until this moment.

Lady Wenderley Davis. How had I not thought of her? Titled, wealthy, and from a family with connections stretching halfway across the world—if not further—it was a wonder she hadn't been first on my list of suspects. The fact that she was beautiful only added to her perfection. And she'd moved back to Peverell? Convenient...

"How old is she?"

The question was out of my mouth before I'd thought through the wisdom of it. I kept my face neutral, hoping Alina wouldn't read anything into it while telling myself I was being paranoid. It was highly unlikely Ben had shared with his little sister that he'd chosen a bride who wasn't yet of age. My question would mean nothing to her.

I hoped.

"Seventeen, I think. Wasn't her birthday usually around the date of the King's Ball?"

"That's right." I remembered now. It was the week before. Come the King's Ball this year, Wenderley would be of age. Would the negotiations Ben hid behind be completed by then? Would that be when he announced Wenderley as his bride? He could hardly choose a better time, the ballroom being filled with visiting dignitaries.

"Oh look. Father is calling me over. It must be time. Can you believe how exciting this is? I'm going to be married. To Prince Marcos."

I laughed at Alina's exuberance as she bounced up and down, her skirt not sure whether to float or sink as she did so. Different as we were, Alina was still one of the closest friends I had, and I'd miss her greatly when she moved away. I was excited for her. How could I not be? But I did wish I could freeze time and hold this night in my heart forever. The people we were right now, this very minute.

Because, whether any of us admitted it or not, the moment the king made his announcement, everything would change.

SEVEN

Ileaned against a pillar as the king droned on. It wasn't particularly comfortable, being both cold and starkly upright, but then, neither was standing still for so long. You'd think the king was giving an economic report with all the excitement he was showing. One year at a time. For the past hundred years. The history of Peverell and Hodenia in a moon-sized nutshell.

Certainly, the engagement was as political as it was practical, but it was still the announcement of the upcoming marriage of his only daughter. Even Alina's smile was starting to sag where she stood at his side. I would have made a face or done something to cheer her, but with her in the spotlight and me in the shadows, she'd never see it. I doubted she could see many of us at all, bright as those lights were on her.

"...Peverell has long looked to its closest neighbor, Hodenia, as an ally in times of peace and war and valued the strength of its trade..."

I wondered what the time was. It felt like I'd been standing in this position for hours, but it had likely only been half an hour. Half an hour too long. A simple, "It is my honor and delight to announce the engagement of Prince Marcos of Hodenia and my daughter, Princess Alina of Peverell," would have sufficed. The king could have gone back to effusing about Peverell's history to those who wanted to hear, and Alina could have been making her way around the crowd, smile about to break her face open with delight as she accepted everyone's good wishes. Instead, we were all still waiting, standing at attention as King Everson preached.

"...and so, it is my great pleasure to announce that—" Finally. I pushed away from the pillar, standing tall again as I freed my hands to applaud. "—King Dorien and Queen Galielle of Hodenia will be joining us for the King's Ball. They will be spending some time in Peverell so it is hoped you will offer them the greatest courtesy..."

The pillar once again claimed me. I was starting to wonder if King Everson had forgotten why he'd begun speaking. He might as well start announcing Thoraben's engagement also. By the time he got to the point, Wenderley would be old enough to marry.

I let my gaze rove over to where she still stood beside Ben. They weren't holding hands, as far as I could tell, but neither was there much room between them. I still couldn't believe she was back. Her family had moved to Hodenia a few days after her twelfth birthday. I'd seen her two years later when they came to the Celebration Ball but not since. For people as well connected with the palace as the Davises, it had been strange to see them so little.

But now they were back, and I couldn't help but think there was only one reason.

They looked good together, Wenderley and Ben. The perfect king and queen. Tall, regal, neither gaunt nor obese. It was all too easy to imagine a crown sitting comfortably atop Wenderley's rich caramel hair and a sash draped over her shoulder. They were silly thoughts, really, for who could stereotype a royal couple? Yet still, they suited each other.

Murmurs around me brought my eyes back to the front. Prince Marcos had walked forward and lain a hand on the king's arm. His face was turned away from the crowd as he spoke quietly in the king's ear so there was no chance I could even guess at what he was saying, but it was interesting nonetheless. Alina had brightened as well, perhaps due to the same hope I held that the speech was almost over. Had King Everson made the announcement then? It didn't look like it, but I couldn't be sure.

King Everson frowned slightly then nodded, stepping backward as Prince Marcos took his place in the spotlight. For a moment, I thought the prince was going to address the crowd as the king had done, but instead he turned and faced Alina, holding one hand out to call her forward. I regretted letting my mind wander. Unlike everyone else who'd been dutifully paying their king attention as he lectured, I had no idea what was happening.

Marcos's voice was quiet as he took one of Alina's hands. Her face glowed with excitement, and none of the confusion I felt. There wasn't a sound in the room as, to a person, we all strained forward to hear.

"Princess Alina of Peverell, I have long admired you from afar, watching as you grew into the beauty you are today. You are the queen I hope to have by my side as I rule one day in my father's stead." Wait, was he proposing? In front of all these people? My hand went to my mouth, charmed by the prospect.

"Your father and mine have made their own agreements but I should like to ask you all the same. Princess Alina, will you marry me?"

A collective gasp of delight rose up from the dance floor where we stood as Marcos pulled from his pocket the sparkling diamond ring and held it out to Alina. I am certain in that moment the whole of Peverell fell in love with Prince Marcos. I didn't know what choice either he or Alina would have had had either of them refused the match, but it was kind of him to ask. Ben was right, Marcos was a good man. He would do right by Alina.

"Yes. Oh, yes."

Cheers rose from every corner of the room as Alina launched herself into Marcos's arms. For an instant, he seemed nonplussed at the action, but he recovered quickly, embracing her before sliding the ring onto her finger. I didn't know how many carats were in that ring—thousands, it seemed—but Alina's smile outshone them all as she stood proudly beside her husband-to-be.

The orchestra began playing again, but instead of dancing, the floor cleared, making room for the newly engaged couple.

Arm in arm, Alina and Marcos walked down the few stairs to the middle of the room and began dancing. I could have been mistaken for Alina's mother with the immense pride overflowing me in that moment. I knew my own mother would be crying happily somewhere, likely tucked up against my father's side as they watched from a corner. Had I even remembered to tell Mother about Alina's engagement when I spoke with her earlier? I couldn't remember. Perhaps not, though I doubted she'd hold it against me.

"Mackenna? Is it really you?"

I blinked my tremulous emotions into submission before turning to the owner of the voice I hadn't heard in almost three years.

"Lady Wenderley, welcome home."

Up close, it was easier to see the girl I'd once known. She might have been dressed in a ballgown showing off every enviable curve she had rather than the shorts she'd always favored as a child, but behind the makeup and long lashes, her eyes were the same.

"Home? Yes, I suppose it is, though it feels like forever since I've called it that."

"You're back to stay?"

"I am."

Her gaze roved toward Ben as she answered, but she didn't offer any more information. Neither did I feel the need to ask. Some things were better not said. If I was right, and she'd come at Ben's request, we'd all know soon enough.

"Isn't this ball divine? The colors are gorgeous, and would you listen to that music? Though, I suppose, you're so accustomed to the grandeur that you barely notice it anymore..."

Not notice this? "Hardly." Even a blind person would notice the grandeur of this room. Between the flowers, the perfumes, and the silky warm scent of the candles, you could smell the opulence. And, of course, after the dancing, there would be dinner.

All eight courses of it. Already the first course would be being plated and served, its aromas frolicking through the halls. Stand in the right archway and one could be driven mad with longing for the dancing to be over and dinner to begin.

Wenderley laughed. "Forgive me, Mackenna, but you look so different. I didn't even recognize you when Thoraben pointed you out earlier. When did you get so tall? And that hair. Are those curls real? Tell me they aren't or I might pull all mine out in protest."

I grinned. "They had help."

"Oh, thank goodness. It simply wouldn't be fair if you looked this perfect all the time."

"Me, Wenderley? Look at you. You're wearing a gown. Dare I believe you've finally realized they're not as constricting as you once thought?"

"Ugh. This heavy thing? Over pants? Heavens no. But how else am I to keep Thoraben's attention?" Tilting her head, she shrugged before leaning in closer to me. "It turns out men like a woman in a gown." While I was still shaking my head over such a ridiculous comment, she pulled away with a grin and a wink. "And it must be working, for Thoraben already told me how charming he thought I looked this evening."

"Nothing's changed then. You still love him."

"Oh, everything has changed. I know now that—uh—" Breaking off, Wenderley glanced around the room, her gaze once again catching on Ben before returning to me. It was like he centered her, for when she looked back, she was calm. "That is, I know that the world is far bigger than Peverell."

Somehow, I doubted that was what she'd been going to say when she first opened her mouth.

"But yes, I still love him. More and more with each day. It's like an ache inside me. I keep waiting for the day he'll turn around and see me, you know? Not as his little sister's friend but as a woman. A wife."

If only she knew he already had.

"I mean, wow, have you looked at Thoraben lately? Really

HEART OF A ROYAL

looked? He was always handsome but he's a man now, and every inch a king. Can you imagine being held in those arms of his? All muscles and strength and security. And I don't mean to dance." She raised her eyebrows, hinting at something far more intimate. She was in love, that was for certain. "One day, Kenna. One day that will be me. I'll soothe away his worries and stand proudly beside him as his queen. I know it."

I smiled, not knowing what else to say. It was a relief when, at that moment, the newly engaged couple's dance came to an end. I clapped along with the rest of the room as Marcos bowed to Alina, kissing the back of her hand. Her other hand fluttered around her chest, the lights catching the glisten in her eyes. She was so happy. If only for this moment, I was glad I'd stayed. Love was such a beautiful thing.

"Thoraben invited me on a ride tomorrow morning."

And a painful thing.

"Alina will be busy with Prince Marcos and all their wedding arrangements, but I don't suppose you'd like to come?" Wenderley asked. "We'd have to have a chaperone anyway, and who better than a friend of us both? Thoraben wouldn't mind, and I'd love the chance to catch up—at least when Thoraben and I aren't speaking or doing...other things..."

I continued to smile, though my delight at our renewed friendship dimmed at the reminder of why she'd returned. Kind as she was to invite me, I had no desire to watch them fawn over each other for a few hours. Ben might not mind if I came, but I doubted he wanted me there either.

"Thanks, but I have plans tomorrow."

"Oh. Well, maybe next time."

Again, I smiled in lieu of an answer. There wouldn't be a next time. She was moving in as I was moving out. Still, if I had to lose Ben's friendship to someone, it could have been worse than Wenderley. Perhaps she would be kind enough to allow Ben and me to be friends again once they were married. It wouldn't be the same as it was now, but the friendship might still be there. An echo of what once was. Or perhaps I'd let the echo die out. Yes, perhaps that would be best.

"Wenderley, Kenna. I see you've found each other."

It was as if Thoraben had been summoned by our thoughts of him. Suddenly there he was, standing in front of us, full glass in his hand, smile on his face. He handed the drink to Wenderley.

"Dance with me?"

I looked away, not wanting to intrude on their moment. Perhaps I'd go freshen up in the bathroom or procure my own drink since the besotted prince had neglected to bring two glasses or—

Wenderley poked me in the ribs, glancing toward Ben with her eyes when I looked at her to see why. What? Oh. Ben wasn't asking Wenderley. He was asking me. That must have been why he'd only brought one glass—and given it to Wenderley.

"Kenna? Will you dance with me?"

EIGHT

While I'd been staring at the ground, trying to make myself invisible, Ben had been holding out his hand, inviting me to dance. Me, not Wenderley, as I'd thought. And now I looked rude.

"Sorry. Um, are you sure?"

Twin sets of confused eyes stared at me as heat spread across my face. It was Mother's fault, this sudden attack of nerves I felt in Ben's presence. Or the king's. Maybe Alina's, for having the audacity to be willing to consent to an arranged marriage. My maids' even, for doing exactly what they were ordered and dressing me up like this. I danced with Ben at least once every time there was a ball, usually twice. No wonder my hesitance to accept baffled him.

"Why wouldn't I be?"

Because Mother had put in my head that the people thought I should be the next queen. Because the woman Ben had chosen to be his bride was standing right beside me. Because, even without turning to check, I knew the king would be plotting my demise for merely being within speaking distance of his son. Because it felt like the whole room was staring at us. Because suddenly I wasn't sure I wanted to...

"No reason."

I told myself to have courage as I took Ben's hand and walked to the center of the ballroom. Wenderley's laughter following us didn't help. She had no problem with me dancing with the man she loved. I was being ridiculous. I shook my head as if somehow that might banish the doubts. It didn't.

"You don't have to, you know. Dance with me, that is. I mean, I want to dance with you but, well, if you didn't want to dance with me..."

We stood in the middle of the dance floor, facing each other, the music and other couples already having begun to swirl around us. But instead of dancing or even touching me at all, Ben was giving me the option to leave. He must have seen me shake my head and thought it was aimed at him.

"I do want to," I hastened to assure him. "I thought you were asking Wenderley."

"I've already danced with her."

He had. Twice. Not that I was watching.

Ben's right hand settled on my waist, his left holding mine securely as we began to dance. I stared at his shoulder, not quite trusting what he might see in my expression if I looked directly at him. I didn't want him trying to decipher what I was thinking while I was still trying to figure it out for myself.

"What's wrong?" he asked.

"Nothing."

"You know, I'd be more inclined to believe you if you didn't look terrified of me."

I missed a step, quickly doubling the next one to catch up, all the while trying to ignore his quiet laugh. And the way my palms were sweating. It was too much to hope that he'd be a gentleman and not mention how slippery my hand was in his.

"Scared of you?" I tried a laugh, annoyed at how hollow it sounded. "Hardly."

He wasn't deterred. "Yep. As scared as you were the first time you went on a ski lift. You hide it pretty well. Your fear doesn't show, but your determination to conquer it does."

I twisted twice under his arm before coming back face to face. "I'm not scared." Not of him anyway.

"Then tell me what's wrong."

"Nothing."

"You know I know you better than that. Is it Alina's engagement?"

He wasn't going to let this go and, unlike in the tower, I doubted I could get away with completely changing the subject. Or smiling my way out of it. "No. She's happy and you were right. Prince Marcos seems to care for her. It's just something Mother said earlier."

Step left, step back, one step forward, half turn. Smile at the couples swirling past us.

"What did she say?"

"Nothing I'm telling you."

"Because it's about me?"

"What? No." I ducked my head, suddenly captivated by the way the blue of my skirt shimmered under the lights. It really was a stunning gown. And I really wasn't blushing. At all.

"I hope it was something good," he whispered far too close to my ear.

I jerked my head back. Infuriating man. "You're arrogant."

"You're blushing."

"Oh, grow up."

He grinned as he spun me out, around, and under his raised arm. "Most people would say I have. Wenderley certainly seemed to think so. I lost count of the number of times she told me how strong my arms were."

No doubt.

"Surprised to see her here?" I asked Ben instead.

"No. Father told me she was coming. I believe he invited her himself this morning."

Before or after he'd thrown me out of the palace? I ground my teeth together in an effort to dispel the bitterness rising within me. I didn't want to hate Wenderley. She'd been my good friend once and could be again. But, like everything else of late, all that had changed. All because of the king. Whether he'd disapproved of Wenderley in the past like I'd assumed or not, he was her most ardent supporter tonight.

He wanted Wenderley for his son. He didn't want me interfering. It was as simple as that.

"You really do look beautiful tonight," Ben said softly, the words brushing past my ear and soothing my nerves before dissolving into the music. "I meant that when I said it before. I wasn't only saying it because of Ashe and Waitrose, or because it was polite."

I chanced a look at Ben's face and found sincerity etched there, without a single trace of laughter. It was sweet of him to say such a thing, especially given his confusion when he'd first come across me outside the ballroom.

"Thank you. You don't wash up too badly yourself."

Which was the understatement of the year. He looked more than okay, but he had plenty of women to tell him that. And likely they had been all night. He didn't need me adding to the number.

I settled easily into the rhythm of Ben's hold as we danced. Unlike Lord Ashe's, Ben's hold was familiar. I'd been his dance partner for as many rehearsals and lessons as Alina had, likely more given how fortuitous our dancing instructor thought it was to have someone dance with Ben who wasn't his sister. "Different dynamics," I could still hear the instructor saying in that irritatingly smooth voice of his. I think that was simply a tactful way of saying I didn't complain as much as Alina.

People watched us as I twirled my way around the room on Ben's arm. I tried to ignore them. Their whispers too. Though I knew they were talking about the two of us, there was no way I could hear their words over the music, and it would do me no good to make assumptions. They could just as easily have been commenting on the color of my dress as my dance partner.

"Broken any toes yet?" I asked Ben. It was an old joke, but one that still brought a smile to his face. He'd broken my little toe once during a dance lesson when he'd trod on it, and though it could be argued that it was as much my fault as his—given my foot was supposed to have stepped back and not forward as I had—he was the one who'd stepped on it.

"Very funny."

"They're probably too polite to tell you."

"Unlike you, you mean?"

"I'm not trying to impress you."

He laughed at that, gaining us even more attention. I tried my best to keep a straight face and pretend I wasn't the cause of it.

"No, you lost that chance when you threw up in my lap as a five-year-old."

"Are you going to hold that against me forever?"

"Yes," he answered smugly.

I shook my head, though I was smiling as much as him. "I was five. And, if I remember correctly, you were the one who convinced me to go on that swing before spinning me around so many times I got sick. I still claim it was your own fault."

"You ruined my favorite pants."

"You ruined my love of swings. I haven't been able to go on one since without feeling nauseous."

"Really? I didn't know that."

"And there we have it. Proof you don't know me as well as you think."

I spouted the words off in triumph, but Ben wasn't smiling anymore. He didn't seem angry or annoyed or anything like that, rather...thoughtful, perhaps? I wasn't sure. He stayed silent for a whole promenade of the ballroom. A score of questions poked at my mind, begging to be asked, but neither they nor the mundane comments I usually filled silence with made it out of my mouth. He was silent, so I was too.

Finally, I could take it no more. I said the first thing that came into my head. "I'm leaving tomorrow."

"What?" Ben's step faltered, coming to a complete stop so suddenly I almost tripped over him. I pulled at him to keep moving. We were already gaining enough attention as it was. I breathed a sigh of relief when he continued dancing, though he did it with all the finesse of a pile of bricks. "Why?"

I shrugged. "It's time. Alina's engaged, and you soon will be too. I have to find my own life." It was the easiest answer, and the one I thought him most likely to accept. I was wrong.

"What did Father say to you?"

"Your father?"

"I know you spoke with him earlier."

Ben's choice of words brought a wry smile to my mouth. Me, speak with the king? Far from it. He'd spoken to me. I'd been given very little option but to listen and obey whether I liked it or not.

"He was..." Cruel, condescending, threatening. "...more generous than I had expected. He has procured one of the cottages for my parents and me, and though he offered us time, I decided the departure date. Alina might have needed us once, but she doesn't anymore. I see no reason to stay."

Ben was silent when I wished he would speak. I wanted him to beg me to stay, to tell me that no matter who or when he married, I would always have a place in his life, but he said nothing. It was foolish to hope for such a thing anyway, when I already knew there was no chance of it being true. I was thankful for the music, for not only did it hide the thunder of my heart, it gave me the courage to hold back tears. Had I blurted out my news in a more private setting, I was certain I would have been weeping by now, but my pride would not let me in front of so many people. How had I not realized this would be goodbye?

"I'll come visit, then. The cottages aren't far."

"No!" He couldn't. The king had made that more than clear. I couldn't risk it, not even for our friendship.

"Kenna?"

"Don't come. It would only—Just don't. Please, Prince Thoraben."

I don't know how he finished the sentence I'd left blank, nor what he thought of me right now, but I'd suddenly realized the truth. He couldn't come, not because of the king's edict or for the sake of the bride he'd already chosen, but because I didn't want him to. Until Ben's engagement was announced, I had to stay away from him. It was the only way to quash any hopes the people might have for the two of us. I couldn't have them thinking we were any more than friends, something that would be inevitable were he to visit me away from the palace. Whether people loved me or hated me, they had an opinion. They always would. But I didn't have to feed it.

"Tomorrow?" he asked.

I nodded.

He quirked an eyebrow. "No wonder you dressed up tonight."

I laughed. I couldn't help it. Of all the things I'd been preparing myself for him to say, all the defenses I'd been running through in my head, that had not even come close to featuring.

When the song finished, he took my arm and delivered me to the edge of the ballroom as he'd done in our lessons a thousand times. It felt bittersweet, to think this was the last time we'd do this. To anyone else, it would have looked like the end of any dance, and yet we both knew it wasn't. I wanted to hug him or hit him or something. Anything to release some of the tension inside me at the thought that this was truly goodbye.

Instead, I simply stood there as he brought my hand to his lips and kissed it, his eyes never leaving mine.

"Thank you for the dance, Lady Mackenna."

I should have stayed, should have taken my turn in the line to congratulate Alina and her prince and farewell the people I'd come to love during my life at the palace. As far as appearances went, I was still part of the royal family tonight. But I knew it wasn't true, and soon the people would too. The excitement of Alina's engagement would cover my absence at dinner, and if not, King Everson would come up with a socially-acceptable excuse. I couldn't have eaten anyway. Blinking back tears, I surveyed the grandeur of the ballroom and its people one more time before walking out a side door and leaving it all behind.

NINE

My maids jumped to attention as I threw open the door.
"You're early."

"What was it like?"

"What's the matter?"

I stood dazed in the doorway, willing my foggy brain to work.
I heard their eager questions, but it was as if the words hit an
invisible barrier in front of me and dropped benignly to the floor
without even an echo of them reaching my thoughts. A wave of
fatigue had me clutching at the doorknob for balance.

"I'm tired."

As far as answers went, it was pathetic, but those two words
spurred the women into action as if the king himself had uttered
them. Elayna took my hand and led me to my dressing table,
holding the long skirt of my gown aside so I could sit. Meri came
over with a basket full of sponges and creams ready to remove
my makeup, Avrel close behind her with a warm towel. All I had
to do was sit, and they would prepare me for bed.

I couldn't even do that.

"You may go." Their hands stilled. "Please." My voice shook
with weariness. One more minute and I'd be a sobbing mess.

"Let me at least help with your gown," Elayna said.

I shook my head once. "I can do it."

I don't think they wanted to leave, especially with me in such
a state, but to my immense gratitude, they did. I wondered if I'd
ever appreciated them more.

I wrapped my arms around my middle as a few errant tears began to drip down my face. It had been balmy, bordering on stifling, in the ballroom but now, alone, I felt cold. It was a chill that went beyond temperature, as if my body was so tired it couldn't even regulate itself anymore. I needed sleep, but I knew I wouldn't be able to. Though my body was exhausted, my mind was far from restful. Warmth. I needed warmth.

I pushed myself to my feet, tripping as the heel of one of my shoes tangled with my gown. I kicked the shoes off, not even bothering to pick them up. I'd do it in the morning before my maids found them and did it for me. The walk of a few yards to my expansive closet had never seemed longer. I didn't even bother to turn the light on. I knew what I wanted. My red hoodie. Oversized and old, it was comfortable as a hug. Within seconds, I was warm.

Tucking my hands in the sweatshirt's deep pockets, I let myself sink to the floor and simply stared, not even having the strength left to cry. Memories from tonight skittered through my mind in no particular order. The froth of Alina's pink marshmallow gown. Prince Marcos's face as he'd asked Alina to marry him. The feeling of Lord Ashe's hand on my back as we danced.

Lord Ashe. He'd certainly been a surprise. Was he truly as charmed by me as he'd appeared, or had it simply been the romance in the air tonight? Flattered as I was by his attentions, it was difficult not to be suspicious of them. He'd admitted an interest in Alina. Was I simply the next best option when she wasn't available? Did I even care?

He was coming to visit me after I left the palace. Or, at least, that was what he'd said. He hadn't said when and didn't know where I'd be living, but I supposed it wouldn't be too difficult to find me given I'd be living in one of the king's cottages. Built almost as long ago as the palace itself, the row of three-room, wooden bungalows sat in an all but forgotten corner of the palace grounds and were used primarily for senior staff and guards required to be on call night or day. I couldn't remember when they'd been dubbed the King's Cottages, but the name fit them well, dated as they were. Barely visible from the palace itself, they were the perfect place to send someone you never wanted to see again.

What would my parents think when Ashe came to visit me there? Father would probably be happy. He liked Lord Ashe. I wasn't sure what Mother would think after all she'd said today.

I sighed into the empty room. How had my life changed so much in one day? Even my room looked different tonight, though I couldn't say why. I was taking so little with me that nothing had actually changed. I'd never been one to hang things on walls, though I had chosen the pale blue paint on the walls and the decal of tiny flowers dancing around the center of them. It had been my first big decision as a ten-year-old moving away from my parents.

I could still remember how life-changing a decision it had seemed at the time. It took me a full three days to finally settle on white flowers rather than purple and pink butterflies. I could have changed it as many times as I wanted over the past seven years—Alina changed her suite's decor once a year at least—but I never had. It had seemed too much of a waste of the palace's funds to redecorate on a mere whim, and I'd always liked those flowers anyway.

I suppose the room felt different tonight because I knew this was the last night it would be mine. Part of me was thrilled at the thought of a new adventure out of the public eye, but a bigger part was terrified of the unknown. I'd learned to hide it, a necessity growing up in the royal family, but I'd never been confident in new situations. I longed for the days when my greatest responsibility was choosing flowers over butterflies for my walls.

A tentative knock sounded at my door. I knew it had been too much to hope my maids would truly leave me, distraught as I was.

"I'm okay," I called out, hoping it would be enough to placate them. I mightn't have looked it, gown puddled around me as I sat here on the floor, but I really was okay. Or would be.

"Kenna?"

In an instant, my musings fled, leaving shock and no small amount of wariness in their wake. That was not the voice of one of my maids.

"Uh..." Scrambling to my feet, I stood frozen against the wall. What was Ben doing at my door? He'd never come here before. Something must be wrong. Or right. Or...I don't know. What did he want? Why was he here? He was supposed to be at dinner.

"Can I come in? Only for a moment. I brought you something."

"Uh..." Yes? No? I shouldn't. He shouldn't. He knew that. We both did. But I couldn't deny I wanted him to, if only to find out what he was doing here.

My gaze flew down my clothing. The red hoodie clashed terribly with my sapphire gown, but I stopped short of tugging it off. It was warm, and it was just Ben. He'd seen me in far worse.

"Please, Kenna."

I walked over to the door, pausing with my hand on the knob. This was a bad idea. I'd already said goodbye. I was only putting myself through more pain to do it again.

I opened the door.

Ben had ditched his jacket somewhere but was still dressed as impeccably as he'd been at the ball. Unlike me, he'd even kept his shoes on. I tucked my bare toes a little further under my gown, though it wasn't like it was a secret given my heels added two inches to my height. And really? I wore a red hoodie over a blue silk ballgown likely crushed beyond repair. A lack of shoes was the least of my fashion faux pas.

"I, uh, brought you this."

He shoved a wrapped gift toward me. I caught it without thinking, still confused by the fact that he was here at all. He seemed to find it as strange as I did, barely looking at me as his gaze flitted back and forth down the hall. I suddenly realized why. If anyone was to see us...

"Care for a walk?" I asked.

"Now?"

I held up the present. "I want to open this and I'm assuming since you came to deliver it personally you want to see my reaction, and you and I both know you shouldn't be in my room so..." I shrugged, figuring that covered all the main points. It was a relief when he nodded. He could have come in, I trusted him and with the door shut we wouldn't be seen, but a walk seemed a wiser idea.

"Want to get some shoes first?"

I looked down at where my feet would have been could I have seen them and smiled before heading to my closet and slipping my feet into the first pair of flats I came across. They were yellow. With bows. Of course they were. I thought about changing them for another pair, but Ben was waiting and I was getting more curious by the second as to what was in the rectangular gift I still held. Or, more precisely, what picture or photo, since I was fairly certain it was a frame. It was a shimmer catching my eye as I walked past the mirror which reminded me I also still wore my silver tiara. It was a good thing I wasn't trying to impress the prince for, dressed like this, I would have failed magnificently.

I didn't suggest where to go, neither did Ben ask, but somehow, we found ourselves up at my tower. I'd never been up here this late at night. The sunrise I'd seen, the sunset and twinkling of hundreds of house lights in the early evening, but never a darkness like this. Even the moon hid its face. And yet, the stars... Thousands upon millions of them. The longer I looked, the more peeked out until I couldn't find a single inch of the sky without one. Pinpricks of hope amidst the darkness.

Beautiful.

I stared at them, captivated, until my neck ached and a scuffing of feet behind me reminded me I wasn't alone. Distracted by the view, I'd forgotten why I'd even come up here. I moved back to the patch of light spilling from the open doorway and pulled at the first piece of tape.

"Wait."

I looked at Ben. His face was a study of uncertainty as he stood there, his eyes on my hands.

"It's nothing big. Kind of silly, really. I was going to give it to you for your birthday, but then you said you were leaving tomorrow and I didn't know whether I'd see you and I wanted you to have it, even more now I know you're leaving and...well...now I've probably talked it up too much when I was trying to talk it down and..." He rubbed a hand across his forehead. It didn't wipe away the frustrated frown lines. I smiled, more intrigued by the second. "Oh, just open it."

Ignoring the tape this time, I tore off the paper and put him out of his misery—but not mine. I gasped, too many emotions railing within me to do anything else. I'd guessed it was a frame, but there was no way I could have guessed at the photo it held.

"How did you get this?"

Ben shrugged, but even in the muted light I could tell he was pleased. "Not all paparazzi are bad. This one's actually pretty good."

I wasn't sure whether he was complimenting the photographer's stealth or technique but either was true. I tipped the photo closer to the light, laughter and tears still wildly warring within me. He should have known better than to give me such a sweet gift when I was already tired and overwrought.

It was a photo of the three of us—Ben, Alina, and I—but as far from our usual formal portraits as one could get. I remembered well that day, if not the photo itself.

It was two years ago now, in the middle of a week of absolute bliss. The three of us had traveled with King Everson to the icy northern country of Tycassia for trade talks with their ruling family. Only, when we arrived, it was to discover it was the king alone they wanted to entertain. I thought we'd get right back on the plane and go home, but King Everson merely asked our hosts for the name of the closest snowfields and told us to go enjoy ourselves. We'd fled before he could change his mind, laughing in disbelief at our good fortune.

For one whole week, the three of us swapped our crowns and the weight of a country for skis and the freedom of being like everyone else, tumbling and laughing in the snow. Snuggled head to toe in puffy, bright colored snow jackets and pants, childlike plaits peeking out beneath beanies and goggles, we were as unrecognizable as the next person. No one watching, no reporters or cameras—or so I'd thought—we were simply a trio of friends having the time of our lives.

The photo I held captured in time one of our many snowball fights, or, at least, the beginning of one. I was amazed at the detail the photographer had caught. The half grin on my face as I assured Alina there was no snow marring the perfect pinkness of her beanie, while trying not to give away Ben standing directly behind her, hands full of snow raised above her head, pure mischief on his face. An instant later, she'd been covered, and it'd been all out war. The photo summed up the delight of that week and brought back a thousand memories—all of them treasured.

"But how did the photographer know it was us?" I doubted even Mother would have been able to pick us out of the crowd of people on the mountain that day.

"Actually, he didn't. He was just another guy enjoying the snow with friends. He'd been taking photos of the scenery while he waited for them to come back from getting lunch when he saw me grab the snow. Anticipating what I was about to do, he started taking photos, partly for the fun of it and partly because he actually was studying photography and thought it'd be good practice. They turned out so well that he found me later and asked if I wanted them, still having no idea who we were. I think he was a little shocked when I told him. I have another twenty or so, detailing the next few minutes after that moment, but I've always liked this one the best."

I could see why. This photo would take pride of place in my new room at the cottage. Even if it hadn't been us, it would have been an exceptional piece of photography. The fact that it was us, and instantly buffeted me with memories, only added to its charm.

"But he never sold them to any magazines? He could have been paid thousands."

Ben shrugged. "I offered him a better deal."

"It must have been quite some deal."

"I told him he could photograph my wedding if he kept these a secret."

He said it like he hadn't changed some amateur photographer's life with such a promise. No wonder the photos had never surfaced. That was quite an honor.

"You like it then?"

"Ben, are you serious? It's—" Too late. I saw the delight in his eyes at my slip, as if I'd been the one to give him the gift, simply by saying his name. Perfect gift aside, I had to keep my distance from him, even regarding something as meaningless as his name. I was leaving tomorrow. He was all but engaged and I was leaving. "I love it."

"Alina will lecture me if she hears, telling me how an eighteenth birthday is a huge milestone and should be celebrated with jewels and expensive gifts. I got her a gold watch with a different gem for each hour of the day but—"

"It's perfect. Really, Thoraben. I can't think of anything I would have liked more. Thank you." I smiled up at him, surprised to see him so serious.

"Don't go tomorrow."

What? How did we get back to that so fast? "I have to."

"Why?"

"I just...do." As far as explanations went, it was terrible. Barely an explanation at all, but how could I tell him the truth? That his father wanted me gone, that the people wanted us to marry, that staying where I wasn't wanted was pure torture. "I have to."

"But tomorrow? It's three months until Alina weds, and even after that you could still stay. You know you'd be welcome. You're part of our family."

I wished it were that simple. It might have been, had Alina been an only child. But she wasn't, and whether Ben knew it or not, he was the reason I had to leave.

"What difference does a day make? Tomorrow? In a week? A month? It's all the same." And the king wanted me gone. I had to remember that. I wasn't welcome here anymore.

I walked over to the wall and stared up at the stars, reminding myself of all the reasons I shouldn't cry. I was thankful for the darkness as a pair of renegade tears escaped anyway. It was late and I was exhausted, that's all it was. I hoped Ben would let it go and stop trying to convince me to stay. My emotions were so tiredly muddled right now that I didn't know how much longer I could resist.

And I had to resist.

The weight of the entire kingdom felt as if it rested on me and the pitiful bit of strength I had left. I wasn't the woman any of them thought I was. Not the king, not my mother, not the people, not my maids, not Ben.

I closed my eyes against the pain as he came up behind me.

"Kenna..."

His voice was soft, the hand he placed on my shoulder as gentle as the man himself. Any other night, I might have accepted his unspoken invitation and stayed. Talked. Let him convince me I could find the peace I sought here. But I knew better. There would be no peace for me here. Not as long as King Everson had an unmarried son.

I stepped aside, swiping the tears from my face as I did so. "I should go."

Ben stared at me for a few seconds before turning and offering me his arm, gallant as always. "I'll walk you back. Can't have you tripping on that gown and falling down the stairs. Nice outfit, by the way. I think the yellow shoes really bring out the color of your eyes. And that red? Hmm..." He was grinning again. Teasing. I slugged him in the arm, like old times. This Ben I could deal with.

We made it to my room without mishap. I opened the door and walked inside, surprised when I turned around to see him still waiting there, staring at me. I'd thought he'd return to dinner.

"Prince Thoraben?"

He walked forward, stopping just inside my room. Reaching out, he ran a finger along the edge of my tiara. "I like that you wore this tonight. It suits you."

"Thank you." Suddenly it hit me. This was goodbye, and I wasn't ready. I didn't know if I ever would be. "Prince Thoraben—"

"Can I give you a hug?"

What? *No. Yes?* I hadn't hugged Ben for, well, I couldn't actually remember the last time I'd hugged him, or if I ever had. We'd never had that sort of relationship. Dancing together, yes. Teasing, yes. Ganging up on Alina when she needed to be reminded that she wasn't the queen yet, yes. Throwing snowballs and taunts back and forth and looking out for each other, certainly. But hugging? It would be awkward at best.

And yet, the expression on his face was so sad as he stood there that I couldn't find it in me to say no. He wasn't his father. He was my friend, and maybe me leaving was as painful for him as it was for me. He'd given me a gift I knew I'd always treasure. Surely, I could do this for him in return.

"Yeah, I'd like that."

I heard his sigh as he reached for me, wrapping his arms around my back as he crushed me against his chest. I held myself stiff for a moment, unsure of what to do before giving in to the weariness I felt and melting into him. He was warm, his arms so certain, and right now, I really needed a friend.

"Kenna? Are you crying?"

Was I? Probably. I looked up at him, trying to find a smile to reassure him I really would be fine when suddenly his lips were on mine. My mind went blank for a moment before an emotion both warm and utterly terrifying shot from my head to my toes, stumbling me backwards out of his arms. The pain of regret I saw in his eyes hurt me, but I couldn't look away. We stood there, silently staring at each other for what felt like an eternity.

"Forgive me," he finally said. "I shouldn't have..."

No, but that didn't stop me wondering why he had. The hands which had only moments ago held me to him dropped to his sides.

"What about your bride?" What about Wenderley? I watched as he opened his mouth and closed it again, thinking better of the words. I didn't have the heart to let him lie. "Go. Please. You shouldn't be here. Go back to dinner. I'm sure you've been missed."

He opened his mouth again to speak, but I was done listening. It was bad enough that he was in my chamber so late at night. If anyone ever found out he'd kissed me, we'd both be ruined—and that was likely the best-case scenario. "Please, Prince Thoraben. Leave."

He waited there, out of reach but not out of sight for an eternal few more seconds before letting out a sigh. "Goodbye, Lady Mackenna. I'm sorry I hurt you."

By some strength I didn't know I possessed, I held the tears back until he left. The instant I heard the door click into place, I turned my back to it and let them go, the wood my backrest as I sank to the floor. Waterfalls of silk spliced with silver became both my cushion and blanket as I cradled my knees to my chest and wept.

TEN

Morning couldn't have come soon enough, nor the night passed any more slowly than it did. I don't know what time it had been when I'd finally pulled myself from the floor and stumbled into bed, but I needn't have bothered. I hadn't slept. Instead, I'd spent the midnight hours wrestling with the memory of that moment I couldn't seem to forget. Why, Ben? Why?

Had it been an accident? Had I made him kiss me? I'd played through every moment we'd spent together last night and couldn't think of anything I'd done, yet who could know the mind of a man? He'd told me I was beautiful. Perhaps he'd simply forgotten who it was he held in that moment. Or had it simply been goodbye? Was I reading too much into the gesture? And his regret.

I'd felt protected in his arms, but now, I didn't know what I felt. Back and forth I'd gone, vacillating between anger, confusion, and hurt as the dark hours sluggishly crept by.

When the sun finally poked its tentative fingers of light through my curtains, I'd come to only one conclusion—no one must know about the kiss. Ever. I would carry the secret with me to my grave. It was the only way.

I avoided looking in the mirror on my way to the bathroom. I hadn't undressed at all before falling into bed, and the only makeup I'd removed had been through tears. I didn't need actual proof of how terrible I already knew I looked.

But that was all behind me, or would be as soon as my oversized bath filled with water and I could sink myself into it. It was a new day. I would wash away the memories with the mess.

I checked the water again. Almost done. Some of the pins had fallen from my hair as I tossed during the night. I pulled the rest out, cringing as they stuck to clumps of hairspray. I'd have to find my tiara later. I didn't see where it had landed when I'd flung it at the floor.

Turning off the water, I undressed, letting my gown and hoodie fall to the floor in a haphazard pile. Yet another thing on my list to be seen to before my maids arrived. They wouldn't mind cleaning up after me, but doing so would raise too many questions, even if they weren't uttered. They were likely already worried enough about my mental state after the way I sent them from the room last night.

I sucked in a quick breath as the hot water touched my skin but lowered myself in anyway. Second by second, I felt my cramped muscles relaxing, and my mind along with them. I was glad I'd made the water so hot. Had it been any cooler, I might have been lulled to sleep by its comfort.

I allowed myself to simply sit for a few minutes before getting to work. It had taken almost seven hours yesterday to prepare me for the ball. I hoped to wash away all that in seven minutes. Ducking my head underwater, I soaked my hair. I'd start there.

Ten minutes of scrubbing and a thorough washing of my hair had me feeling almost normal again. I could have stayed in the bath for longer but forced myself out, my mind racing with all the things I had to do.

By the time Meri peeked her head through my door to check if I was awake, I'd dressed, tidied the room, steamed most of the crinkles out of my gown, made my bed, and chosen the twelve outfits of clothing I wished to take with me. My red hoodie was on the top of the pile. It carried memories I wasn't sure I wanted, but I couldn't leave it behind.

"Lady Mackenna?" Meri said, blinking with surprise as she walked further into the room.

"Morning, Meri. Sleep well?"

"Not as well as you, it appears. You're looking rested, my lady."

I smiled. Appearances could be deceiving. Look good and no one will ask how you feel.

"Shall I call for your breakfast?"

"Yes, please. And for Elayna and Avrel also, if you don't mind. I'd like to leave before lunch, if possible."

The tears in her eyes were almost my undoing. I sucked in a deep breath and made myself stand taller. "Will that be a problem?" My words were too harsh. In trying to be strong, I'd become cruel. I opened my mouth to apologize but Meri was already ducking her head in a curtsy.

"No, my lady. I'll see to it right away." She scrambled out the door before I could try again.

I felt myself start to crumble but refused to shake. I could do this. I could hold myself together for as long as I needed to. My turbulent emotions might have stolen my sleep, but I would not let them control my day. I walked over to my window seat and picked up the cushion sitting there, hugging it to my chest as I stared out the glass to the field beyond. The grass was dotted with purple wildflowers almost too small to see. I might have missed seeing them at all had they not been swaying.

Mother liked wildflowers, always telling me how they reminded her she had worth. I'd never understood how a simple weed could bring about such profound thoughts, but they were beautiful. Stunning in their simplicity. The cottages were beyond the tree line on the other side of that field. Perhaps I'd pick some of the flowers on my way through. For Mother. It might dispel some of the guilt I felt at rearranging her life without asking.

The clatter of a trolley bringing breakfast reminded me I wasn't alone. Someone needed to oil its wheels. One of them at least had a definite squeak.

"Your breakfast, my lady."

I turned around, opening my mouth to thank Avrel, only no words came. The scene before me stole them. That wasn't breakfast. That was a feast. And my maids, all three of them, stood proudly to attention behind the heavy-laden table dressed in their formal uniforms, the ones they only wore when serving in the presence of the king. Even Meri, who I'd treated so rudely. Their honor brought tears to my eyes. I didn't deserve their allegiance.

"We couldn't just let you leave. And when Chef heard this was to be your last meal, he sent up all your favorites."

I nodded, still mute. Sooner or later, the words would come, but even if they did, I doubted I'd be able to speak past the emotion clogging my throat.

"Come, sit. Eat."

I did as I was told, sitting down at the chair they'd provided before my legs gave out on me. I'd never be able to eat all of this alone, but I doubt anyone expected me to.

Spinach and feta muffins, still steaming, sat beside a tray boasting a rainbow of fruit. Berries, peaches, melon, plums. Was that even—I moved aside a strawberry—it was. Roasted coconut chunks. My not-so-secret pleasure.

And if that weren't enough, another tray held plates full of chocolate pastries and yeasty cinnamon scrolls—straight from the oven—drips of sticky icing meandering their way down the sides and melting between the layers. I doubted even the king ate this well every morning.

"Join me?" I asked my maids.

"Oh no. We couldn't."

I expected their immediate refusals but was having none of it. Not today. If they were going to treat me like a queen, I was going to act like it—and they were going to obey.

"Sit down, all of you. There's enough food here to feed all four of us to exploding with leftovers, and I wish to share my last meal here with the three kindest women I could ever hope to meet. I'll let you do all the packing and cleaning and serving you wish as soon as we finish, but please? It would mean so much to me."

It went against the rules. It wasn't part of their job description. There weren't even enough chairs, I belatedly realized. But, to my immense satisfaction, they did, Meri pulling over a tightly packed case to perch on.

"To my friends," I said, raising my glass high in the air. "Thank you more than I could ever say for everything you've done for me. I can't imagine ever finding better or more honorable friends."

They ducked their heads, shy smiles on their faces before raising their odd assortment of glasses. Like the chairs, they were making do with the cutlery and crockery that had been sent with the food. Meri used a thick mug and Avrel a teacup but neither of them seemed to mind. Any one of us could have called for more place settings, but I liked it this way. It was the impromptu gathering sweet memories were made of.

They still served me first, waiting until my plate was full before taking any for themselves, but I didn't mind. They were sitting, sharing a meal with me. I couldn't ask for much more than that.

"So...how was the ball?" Meri asked, a tiny grin on her face as she peered at me. "Did you turn any heads?"

She jumped suddenly, looking in Elayna's direction. Elayna must have elbowed her, chastising Meri for her impertinence no doubt. She needn't have. My three maids were about as far from impertinent as a person could be. And I had every intention of answering Meri's question since, elbow or not, I knew all three of them were longing to hear my answer. After all, they had been the ones to spend the entire morning and much of the afternoon getting me ready.

"Actually, I did." I paused, biting into a cinnamon bun as I let that piece of information satiate their imaginations. "I believe Lord Ashe Marsh was particularly swayed. He asked to court me."

"He didn't." Elayna dropped her fork with a loud clatter, quickly ducking down to collect it. Or possibly to claim a few extra seconds to compose herself. Meri and Avrel had no such compunctions, letting loose squeals which weren't overly loud but were so high pitched that I covered my ears with a short laugh anyway.

"He did." It felt good to laugh.

"Oh, but you're leaving." The delight fell from Avrel's face.

"I know, and I told him such. The news didn't seem to bother him at all. I think he was actually relieved to hear it. Something about fewer guards to have to deal with." I took another bite of the cinnamon bun, enjoying every messy mouthful of it.

"He's right, you know," Elayna said, carefully placing her fork beside her plate. Even in eating, she was particular. "You won't have as much protection away from the palace. No maids, nor guards—at least, according to the gossip in the kitchens this morning. It seems strange that the king would send no one with you after you've been so close to the princess all these years."

Though I tried to keep my expression from changing at Elayna's comment, my feelings toward the king were still so raw that I was certain something would show on my face. Elayna might not have believed it of the king, but I certainly could.

"You'll be careful, won't you? It isn't the same out there as it is here. Men can be...different...when they're alone with a lady. Not every man is a gentleman."

The memory of Ben's kiss washed unbidden through my mind. I pushed it aside and took a sip of my juice. Prince Thoraben was a gentleman. A true gentleman. One moment's mistake didn't change that. We'd been in the tower alone twice in the past week, and he'd done nothing even close to untoward. And after the kiss, he'd walked away when I'd sent him. I had nothing to fear from Ben. So why was my heart racing triple time at the mere thought of seeing him again?

And why was I even thinking about Ben? It was Lord Ashe we were discussing.

"I'll be careful," I promised. "Thank you for all you did for me yesterday. For all you've done for me. I won't forget it."

I wanted to ask them what they would do when I left, where they would go, whether they even knew, but I couldn't. Anyone seeing us would think we were four friends, smiling and laughing together as we shared a meal, but I knew better. We all did. There were cracks in the charade if one looked close enough.

Meri's smile was watery with tears. Avrel had almost picked her muffin to pieces, and had yet to eat any of it. And Elayna... Tears of my own threatened as I looked down at my plate. It was Elayna's pain which tugged most at my heart for she always seemed so strong. No matter what Meri or Avrel were doing or feeling, I could always count on Elayna to be my rock.

My rock was crumbling.

Elayna rearranged the cutlery again before straightening the corners of the napkins so they aligned. If she couldn't bring order to my life anymore, she could at the very least order the napkins. I had to bring this meal to an end before we all fell into too many pieces for even Elayna to pull back together. The breakfast feast which had had my stomach begging to be fed only moments before now made me feel ill. There was no way I'd be able to force anything past the teary lump in my throat anyway. The kitchen staff might as well enjoy the leftovers while they were still hot.

I pushed back my chair and stood, not surprised when the three of them followed suit. "This has been wonderful, but I really should keep packing."

"But you barely ate anything."

I didn't see the need to point out that neither did they. "Perhaps you could wrap a muffin for me to eat later? I'd like that."

Elayna nodded. "Of course." I watched as she began tidying up the mess we'd made of breakfast, happy to have something to occupy her hands. I had no doubt the muffin I'd requested would turn into a basketful. And likely come with berries, some roasted coconut, cinnamon scrolls, and probably even a chilled bottle of the apple and mango juice I loved. Even in my leaving, they'd be looking after me.

My resolve almost faltered as I thought about telling these three women goodbye. Alongside Alina and Ben, they would be the ones I'd miss the most. I would have stayed for them. If the choice had been mine, I would have moved to the employee quarters and lived out my days serving alongside these three women I counted as friends.

But that choice had never been mine. It, along with a thousand others, had been taken out of my hands when I was born the same day as the princess.

I had to keep moving forward. It was too late for regrets.

The strength of that conclusion carried me through a morning of goodbyes. Goodbye to my maids, my guards, and Alina who assured me she'd come visit. Goodbye to the suite I'd called mine and its luxurious sunken bath. Goodbye to the only life I'd known. The tears had been there, waiting at the corners of my eyes, but I'd held them back with the constant reminder that this had been my choice.

"Ready?"

I looked to Mother and Father, waiting at my side. Our belongings had already been taken over to the cottage. All that was left was for us to follow them. I wished I hadn't eaten any breakfast at all. The cinnamon bun I'd so enjoyed at the time was now making me feel nauseous. Or perhaps that was simply the regrets swirling through every cell in my body despite my resolve to ignore them.

What had I done? I'd thought myself so bold telling the king I would leave. Now it felt foolish. A moment of foolishness I would regret for the rest of my life. Like hugging Ben last night.

I shook my head, furious at myself for being so weak. For letting my fear and pride get the better of me. For caring at all. For better or worse, the decision had been made. There was nothing I could do to change it.

"Let's go."

"You're certain?" Father asked. "You look tired. We don't have to leave today, you know. You had a busy night—" My heart thudded, dropping to somewhere around my toes. How had he found out about...? "—with Alina's announcement and all that dancing." My heart slowly crept back up where it belonged. The ball. He was talking about the ball. "We could wait another week, or another month. I know Alina would appreciate having you close during this time. We could move out when she does, after the wedding."

I smiled sadly. He sounded like Ben. Same argument, same gentle tone. And for exactly the same reasons, I couldn't give in. Much as I wanted to right now.

"The staff have already moved all our things. They'd have to move everything back again if we stayed."

"They wouldn't mind."

They might not, but I knew someone who would. Though neither of my parents had made comment of it, there was someone very important missing from this moment.

The king.

He should have been here to bid us farewell. Instead he'd called his son and all his advisors into a meeting about the King's Ball. One that hadn't been scheduled yesterday. One I was almost certain could have waited until tomorrow. He was avoiding us. I had no desire to see him myself, but I was furious with him on my parents' behalf. He wasn't only disrespecting me, he was disrespecting them.

"Let's go."

Out of the corner of my eye, I saw my parents look at each other, silently conferring as to whether to take my word for it or not. I knew they were worried about me, though neither of them had said it directly. They didn't need to. Mother walked close by my side, one arm ready to steady me should I need it, and Father had already taken the two bags I carried filled with things I couldn't bear to let a stranger handle. Like the gift Ben had given me last night and the now-pressed flowers Alina and I collected one day years past as we planned our imaginary weddings. Each item precious, priceless—and as fragile as I currently felt. My parents expected me to break any moment. They were closer to the truth than they knew.

Mother looked at me again with that expression only a mother could give. That one that looked beyond my face to the very heart of me, summing up my physical and emotional health in an instant. I raised my chin a little higher in the air and walked to the front door before they could ask me again.

"This is it, then, Lady Mackenna?"

Despite my melancholy, I easily found a smile for Mr. Stanley, the doorman. I loved this gruff old man with his lifetime of stories. He'd been guarding the palace's grand front door, overseeing every person who came and went through it, for almost forty years. He might have been barely seen or heard by that cast of thousands, but he'd noticed every one of them.

"Yes, sir."

Leaning heavily on the long stick he carried, he bent his arthritic back half an inch, bowing to me before straightening again and nodding. "I wish you well, my lady."

His respect was my undoing. I blinked fast, trying to hold back the tears but they fell anyway. Not even bothering with the list of reasons why I shouldn't, I leaned in and hugged Mr. Stanley. I'd held it together all morning, and a barely even visible bow had pulled me apart. An unsteady hand patted my back. "All will be well, child. All will be well."

He adjusted his waistcoat when I stepped away, tugging it back into place. I'd probably embarrassed him. But then, he was smiling. It was tiny, barely even a change to his normal stern face, but it was there. The crinkles at the corners of his eyes were like a puppeteer's strings as they pulled up—the tiniest bit—the edges of his mouth.

"Goodbye, Mr. Stanley."

"Goodbye, my lady."

It felt surreal walking out of the palace. I'd done it thousands of times over the years, but I'd always known I was coming back. This time, I wasn't. Yet there was no fanfare, nor any people lining the paths to bid us farewell or cheer as we passed. I'd given so much to the kingdom over the years, my parents had given even more, and now we were leaving, almost in disgrace.

Mother and Father would still work at the palace—they'd be back there this afternoon, as if nothing had changed—but we all knew everything had. The mixed family we'd been part of for the past seventeen years had been raggedly torn in two. I wondered if I'd ever stop feeling the pain of it.

My parents talked to Mr. Stanley behind me, their words little more than a quiet mumbling in my ears. I didn't wait for them. Tears blurring my vision, I walked through the garden and across the field, purple wildflowers brushing at my ankles as I passed, almost as if to comfort me. It would have taken more strength than I had left to bend down and pluck some.

The cottages loomed in front of me. I counted along to the one I knew was ours before pushing open the door and walking inside.

It was small, smelled of disinfectant and air freshener, whistled as if one of the windows wasn't quite closed—and had a bed made up ready for me. I pulled off my shoes and sank into it, not even caring that the pillow was too flat or the sheets starchy as if they'd been pulled from plastic only minutes ago.

It was a bed. That's all that mattered.

Rolling onto my side, I curled into myself, hands tucked beneath my chin, and finally fell asleep.

ELEVEN

I woke to a pounding in my head and the echo of far more emotions than anyone should have to deal with while their hand was asleep. Had I moved even once while I'd slept? The numbness of my hand proved otherwise. I stretched it out in front of me, opening and closing it to get the blood flowing again, wincing when it did.

A note on the bedside table caught my eye. It took a few blinks for the words to slide into focus.

> *Mackenna,*
>   *Your lunch is on a plate in the kitchen. We considered waking you but decided you needed the sleep more. We'll be back in time for dinner. See you then.*
>   *Mother*

I blinked again, this time in an attempt to clear the confusion from my mind. I'd missed lunch? As if on cue, my stomach growled. Loudly. How long had I slept? A glance out my window showed trees casting shadows three times their length, the sky long since having surrendered its brilliance to a softer light. No wonder my hand had gone numb. I'd been lying on it all day. I couldn't remember the last time I'd slept so long. Although neither could I remember a night when I'd slept so poorly. If at all.

But no, I'd left that all at the palace. That had been my resolution this morning, and I was determined to keep it. Even if—

"Lady Mackenna?"

I started at the sound of my name, muffled though it was through the door. A series of knocks accompanied the voice my mind was still too fuzzy to recognize. It took me a few seconds more to realize I'd have to answer the door myself, given I no longer had maids to do it for me. *Commoner, remember?*

The man was just turning away when I opened the door, but I easily recognized his wide shoulders and the way his thick, blonde hair brushed against his collar. Not wild, but not quite tamed. I'd stared at it enough while we danced last night, wondering whether he liked it that way or it simply refused to sit flat.

"Lord Ashe?"

He might have left his tuxedo at home, but the effect of him in jeans and a polo shirt was just as staggering, if not more so. Dressed in their finest, their flawed edges softened by music and mood lighting, everyone looked good at a ball. It was in the unforgiving light of the sun the day after a ball that true faces were shown. Ashe proved even more handsome. Did he think the same of me? Or was he already regretting having asked to court the princess of the Midsummer's Ball only to find a plain servant answering his knock? His smile when he turned claimed the former, but time would tell.

"Lady Mackenna. You are here. I've not come at a bad time, I hope?"

"It's just Mackenna now. And no, not at all." My schedule had been left at the palace alongside my title and responsibilities. There was no such thing as a "bad time" anymore.

"Splendid. Forgive me for waking you. I realize it's late but wondered if you might like to take a walk with me."

"Wake me? Why would you think that?"

He grinned. "The handprint on your face."

My eyes widened as I raised a hand to cover the place he'd gestured to. Why hadn't I taken the time to look in the mirror before opening the door? Was my hair as much a mess as my face? At least my clothes were presentable, not having changed before crashing into bed. Although, that had been at least six hours ago, as my still pounding head reminded me with drum-like regularity...

Ashe caught my hand, gently pulling it down. "Please, Mackenna. Don't let it worry you. It's almost faded. Believe me when I say there are princesses and women all over the world who wish they looked as charming as you upon waking."

His easy compliment embarrassed me almost as much as the thought of a bright red handprint blazing across my face. I pulled my hand from his, fighting the urge to close the door on him and run straight back to bed.

And stay there.

Maybe forever.

When I'd agreed to Ashe's request to call on me, I hadn't expected him to come the very next day. My head still boggled with the fact that I was gone from the palace at all, and my heart...

Well, I didn't know what my heart was feeling, but there was definitely an imprint of Ben there that hadn't been before he'd—

I took a deep breath, pushing back the memory I knew I could never forget. Perhaps in time...

"Mackenna? Are you well?"

I had to stop this. Ben wasn't here. Ashe was. And there was the difference.

"Yes. Forgive me. Still gathering my bearings."

"Of course. And forgive me again for waking you but, now you're up, would you like to go for a walk with me?"

"A walk? Now?" It was almost evening. My parents would be home soon. And I really needed to eat something. But it was a final realization which had me faltering. "With me?"

"Unless you didn't want to?"

"Um, no. I, uh..." I could feel the blush creeping across my face. Actually, stampeding was more like it. At least it would blend in with the handprint there. Taking a walk together, just the two of us, no maids or guards, felt so...so...intimate. As if we truly were a couple. Would he try to hold my hand? Did I want him to?

I shook my head, irritated by my own foolishness. I had to get into my head that I wasn't a princess anymore. Already, not even twenty-four hours away from the palace, the differences were obvious. Not only the house I now lived in, its entire floorplan smaller than my palace suite, but little things. Like the fact that I'd had to answer the door myself. It made me seem so arrogant to assume someone else would do it, but I'd never actually answered a door myself, always having had visitors screened and announced.

But I wasn't that princess anymore. I didn't live at the palace. I had no need of maids or guards to chaperone me here. I was a normal girl with a handsome man standing at her door asking for her company on a simple walk. Nothing to be afraid of.

If only I could convince my thumping heart of that fact.

I tried a smile, hoping it would convince us both. "Let me get my shoes." And as many bites of a sandwich as I could in the process. I'd embarrassed myself in front of Ashe enough in the past couple of minutes. He certainly didn't need to hear my stomach growl.

Though Ashe offered me his arm as we left the house, I didn't take it, choosing instead to hold my long skirt out of the dust. I could have done both. I was no novice to the challenge of bringing to submission a billowing gown while being escorted by a gentleman—years of etiquette lessons had seen to that—but I wanted that distance between us. Ashe's attentions were all still so new. After all, I had only agreed to his suit last night. I'd barely even spoken with him before that.

Last night. Had it truly only been last night? Dancing with Ashe at the Midsummer's Ball already felt like a lifetime ago.

A breeze played with my hair as we walked along the path in front of the cottages, thankfully away from the palace rather than toward it. I tipped my head upward so the cool air could better reach my heated cheeks and tried to convince myself again that this was a good thing. This...courtship, or whatever it was with Lord Ashe. He was honorable, handsome, unattached, and apparently attracted to me—all good reasons to stay with him rather than run back to my house and hide like I wanted to. He might not have been having second thoughts in the, albeit dimming, light of day, but I certainly was. What had I been thinking to have agreed to this?

"Lord Ashe, I—"

"How are you—"

He grinned as we both spoke, and stopped, at the same time. "You first."

I gulped back a breath, feeling like a fish thrown on land and ordered to thrive. Where was Alina when I needed her? She, at least, could hold a conversation with a man without tripping over her own tongue. What had I been about to say anyway? *Lord Ashe, I think you should choose someone else? Lord Ashe, I'm not the girl you think I am?* Oh sure, that would work.

"I just wondered if you enjoyed the ball last night," I said instead, pulling out the first topic that came to mind.

"Certainly. Although, with the exception of dancing with you, the dinner was definitely the highlight. That food…" His sigh was one of bliss and delight. "You won't find better."

A smile tugged at my mouth before I could stop it. Ben loved the dinners best too. They were his favorite part of each of the balls, especially when the menu included Three Meats and Dumpling stew with bread rolls straight from the oven, slathered in butter. He never could get enough of that dish. Had they served it last night? Had he missed it, because of me? I'd never forgive myself if that were the case, although I hadn't been the one to ask him to leave dinner to say goodbye. I just hoped he'd gotten back before the king noticed he was missing.

"I don't remember seeing you there," Ashe said.

I smiled at a passerby and walked a few more steps before answering. "I wasn't feeling well and left early, but I'm fine now."

He stopped. "You're certain? We can go back if you're not."

Much as I wanted to take his suggestion and the out I'd so easily given myself, I couldn't lie. "No, I'm well. I spent the day sleeping, remember?"

"Ah yes, my sleeping beauty."

My cheeks heated again as his eyes caressed my face. I turned away, redirecting the subject before he could say more. "Tell me about dinner. What did I miss?"

"Well, you know they always start with soup."

I sighed in relief when he started walking again, matching his stride to mine as we ambled our way along the cobblestone street. I could feel the edges of the stones through the thin soles of my shoes. Not sharp, but there. Like the ache in my chest.

"This was a vegetable soup, but they'd added herbs or spices or something to the broth because it was..."

He kept talking as we crossed a road and walked toward the crowded marketplace, regaling me with enough culinary details to fill a chef's memoir. It was when I saw the first royal guard that I stopped listening. Like someone had slid a switch, the pounding in my head turned up in volume until I couldn't have heard Ashe even if I tried.

Kenna, how could you have forgotten?

It was the day after a ball. Evening, the day after a ball.

Ben would be here.

My gaze darted around the marketplace, searching for Ben, silently begging him to have forgotten, even though I knew he never would. His heart was too big for that.

He'd started the tradition three years ago, after a particularly warm King's Ball, when twelve courses of food had been prepared but no one felt like eating. The food would have been disposed of the next day, but Ben heard of it and claimed every last bit of it for the people. It wasn't right, he'd said, that food was being wasted when there were those in town who were hungry.

Alina had been busy entertaining one of the visiting princesses, but Mother and I had gone with Ben to help distribute it. I hadn't expected to enjoy it so much—seeing those who had so little, knowing then for certain that poverty truly did exist in Peverell. I thought I would feel guilt, or at the very least, discomfort. Instead, I felt humbled. I ate well every day but had never been as thankful as these people for a mere plate of food.

One man had come back four times to thank us. Another, wife and three children in tow, had cried as he handed bowls of soup to his family and accepted a loaf of bread. When I asked him if he was well, he'd smiled through the tears, nodding before taking my hand and kissing it, too overcome to even attempt words.

It had been one of the most incredible nights of my life, and the first time I'd truly been thankful for the privileged life I'd been granted which allowed me to be a help to those who needed it. It must have impacted Ben also, though we'd never spoken of it, for every Tuesday, from that day on, Ben visited the village to deliver bread and soup to those who needed it.

The evening after each of the kingdom's four balls, he delivered a feast.

Should anyone have asked, it was all leftovers, but no chef worth their position in the palace was that bad at estimation.

I was a fool to have forgotten he'd be here tonight. My steps slowed as we wound our way through the marketplace directly to where I knew the food table would be. King's edict aside, I didn't want to see Ben tonight. Whether due to cowardice or prudence, I wasn't ready to face him. I laid a hand on Ashe's shoulder.

"Lord Ashe, I'm more tired than I thought. Perhaps we might—"

"Ah, there they are." Ashe waved a hand above his head, trying to capture Ben's attention over the crowd. I ducked my head, hoping the same crowd would hide me. They didn't, unwitting traitors that they were.

"It's Lady Mackenna," I heard whispered from one person to the next as the mass slowly parted. I tried to smile as I nodded and shook hands with those closest to me, but it was difficult with the panic clawing its way up my windpipe, squeezing as it went. I'd never had a panic attack before, but I imagined this was what it felt like. The fight for each breath, the burning flush of my cheeks, the spots dancing across my vision.

"Lord Ashe, please take me home," I tried again. Was it my imagination or were people looking back and forth between Ashe, Ben, and me? No doubt they were wondering what I was doing standing there, looking like the complete fool I felt. At least I was still standing. For now.

Smile, Kenna. Wave. They're your friends. They care.

The last few people parted, and I saw Wenderley standing beside Ben, piling food onto the plates as quickly as he handed them out.

That had been my role in the past, mine and Alina's. It seemed Wenderley had wasted no time in making it hers. I should have been proud. My two friends together, serving the people they would one day call theirs. Instead I felt like crying. *Stupid tears.*

Of course, Ben chose that exact moment to look our way, smiling as he waved Ashe and me over. Ashe walked three steps before realizing I hadn't followed. I blinked away the tears I couldn't let escape as he turned to me.

"Something in my eye," I told him, rubbing at it as if to re-move a speck of dust. "You go. I'll wait here."

"There will be water at the table. We can wash it out. Come on. Thoraben's waiting for us. I told him we'd be here."

"No." My outburst raised some eyebrows, reminding me how many people were listening in on our conversation. I had to calm down. I took a deep breath. "That is, it's almost gone now and it would be a shame to get this outfit wet for no reason." I almost rolled my eyes at the shallowness of such an answer, the first one to come to my mind. Like I truly cared about a little water on my dress. Still, the answer had made a few people laugh, which could only be called a good thing at this point in time. Perhaps they'd stop paying so much attention to me now. I could only hope.

Ashe wasn't laughing. He was looking at me as if I'd lost my mind, or something else. My frivolous comment hadn't fooled him. And here I'd thought he didn't know me well.

"Please don't..." My plea barely even had enough breath be-hind it to be called a whisper, but Ashe heard. He stared at me for a moment longer before nodding once and turning. I watched his feet on the dusty ground as he walked toward the serving table. Ben must have said something to the guards, for they let Ashe pass without a word.

"Lady Kenna!"

Ella. My salvation in the form of the three-foot-high girl with a tumble of curls barreling toward me. I leaned down and braced for impact, Ella's tight hug squeezing out most, if not all, of my uncertainty.

She pulled back as quickly as she'd come, frowning at me. "You're late. I thought you weren't coming at all."

"I'm sorry, sweetie. I—" What? Am not a princess anymore? When I was never one to start with? She wouldn't understand. None of the people smiling at me like I was all their dreams come true did.

Except Esme, maybe, standing behind her rambunctious daughter like she wasn't quite sure whether to reprimand Ella or offer me an embrace of her own. There was something about the expression on her face as she looked at me. Part sympathy, part question, part acceptance—all asking me if I was okay.

"Lady Kenna?" Ella asked, tugging on my sleeve. "It's okay that you're late. You're here now and my mommy always says better late than never. I have to tell you about my teddy. I took him on a picnic last week and..."

Wenderley bumped Ben with her shoulder, trilling with laughter at something he said before handing him another plate. He smiled as he took it, still chatting with Ashe. Then all three of them were looking directly at me. I ducked my head quickly, berating myself for caring.

"...and strawberries, and apples, and..."

Ashe was coming back. Finally. It had only been a few minutes, but it felt far longer. People staring at you had a way of making it feel like that.

"I'm sorry, sweetie. I have to go," I told Ella. "I'll see you next time?"

Her grin was far more forgiving than I deserved, given my complete lack of attention. "Sure. See ya."

She skipped back to her mom. I barely remembered to wave to the crowd before taking Ashe's arm and heading back the way we came.

"Wait. Lady Mackenna," came a voice almost out of breath behind me.

Where the strength came from, I didn't know, but somehow I found a smile for Mrs. Olive, running toward me, a bouquet of miniature pink, orange, and yellow roses in her hand. When she gave them to me, I couldn't help but lift the fragrant bunch to my nose and breathe in their scent. Sunset laced with all the sweet goodness of spring. "They're beautiful. Thank you."

Mrs. Olive beamed. "Beautiful flowers for a beautiful woman."

My breath hitched, my smile tremulous as Mother's words haunted me. *They want you to be their queen. Surely you've seen the respect they have for you?*

My hands shook under the flowers. I had to get away from here. In a move as rude as it was offensive, I spun and walked away.

"I couldn't agree more," I heard Ashe say behind me. "I'm afraid Lady Mackenna isn't feeling well. Excuse us."

His arm was under mine before I'd even realized he was beside me, lending a strength I didn't deserve but greatly appreciated. It wasn't until we turned a corner and I knew we were well out of the town's sight that my breath calmed to a normal pace.

"Want to tell me what that was about?"

I sighed into the dimming sky. No, I didn't, but that wasn't fair. Ashe had done what I'd asked and not made a scene when he so easily could have. It was only right that he should know why. At least, as much of the reason as I could tell him.

"I'm not Lady Mackenna anymore. All those people were expecting me to take my usual place beside the prince and Wenderley, only I don't belong there anymore. I left that life at the palace this morning." Was it enough? I wasn't sure. "I have to figure out who I am outside of the royal family."

Ashe was nodding, though I didn't know whether that was simply to show me he was listening or because he actually understood that rambling explanation. I barely did.

"He asked about you."

"Oh?"

"He wanted to know if you were okay."

So, Ben was thinking about the way we'd parted last night. Was he wondering whether I wanted an apology? If I would tell? Or if I would expect something of him now, despite the fact that he'd claimed nothing of the sort? Or was the guilt which still tormented me making me look too deep into the question? Maybe Ben was simply wondering, like the rest of his people, why I hadn't gone over to greet him. "What did you tell him?"

"That you were with me, so of course you were. How could you be anything but happy with me by your side?"

"Ashe." His playful hubris brought a genuine smile to my face.

"Hey, he had his chance to make you happy. His loss is my gain." Ashe squeezed my hand. I hadn't even remembered until that moment he was holding it, proving how flustered the events of the past few minutes had made me. I thought about pulling my hand away but found I didn't mind holding his. It was nice to think he liked me enough to want to. Unexpected, but definitely nice.

"He asked where your guards were. I'd like to know too."

Frustrated with another question I couldn't properly answer, I kicked at a pebble on the path, scuffing dirt across the toe of my shoe. Great. Just what I needed. I'd have to remember to wipe it off when I got home. Would a damp cloth ruin the suede? Perhaps a dry one would be better. My maids would have known. Only they weren't here.

"I'm a commoner. Commoners don't need guards."

Ashe's snort sent two birds flying from a nearby tree, their trilling cries evidence to their displeasure. I felt their pain but envied their freedom. They could fly away to heights where people and politics were reduced to the size of ants. I had no choice but to stand and face my problems.

"Truly? You're not exactly a common, uh, commoner. You know more about the palace and Peverell's royal family than anyone else in the kingdom. You're closer to them too."

"Not anymore."

Ashe stopped, pulling me around to face him. He dropped my hand, crossing his arms across his chest, and stood there, shaking his head.

"What is it?" I asked, wondering if I actually wanted to know.

"King Everson really hates you, doesn't he?"

Ashe was proving himself far too perceptive. I could have denied his accusations against the king but there was little point. No one else but Ben had the authority to order my guards away, and Ben's asking Ashe where they were proved he hadn't done so. "It doesn't matter."

"Well, he's a fool."

"Ashe." First my mother, now Ashe. Was I the only one who had any respect for the king these days? Even if I'd been the sole person in a radius of one hundred miles, I wouldn't have been brave enough to say such a thing out loud.

"No, really. Even if you weren't worth protecting simply for yourself—which you definitely are, I might add, the beautiful, talented woman you are—the knowledge you hold alone is enough to warrant guards. Were the king's enemies to kidnap and question you, that knowledge could bring down the kingdom."

"I would never betray Peverell."

"You might not have a choice."

Fear dropped like a cloak around me. A heavy one, five sizes too big. I tried to push it off, but the more I struggled, the more it tangled until it all but suffocated me. The Rebels. Their sole purpose was to take down the royal family and strip them of their power. Caught up in everything else which had happened, I hadn't even considered the threat they'd be to me now, unprotected as I was. They could take me and torture me for the information I knew about the palace. Ashe was right. Even as the princess's companion, not having attended any governance or military meetings, I knew enough.

My gaze skittered from tree to shrub to path around us as if the Rebels he spoke of were hiding there even though I knew they weren't. I liked to think I was strong, but would I be strong enough to resist if the Rebels ever did get hold of me?

I'd have to lock the doors at home, not venture out alone. The cottages were close to the palace and my neighbors all loyal servants to the king. If I were to yell, someone would help. I hoped.

"Thank you for your concern, but I will be fine."

The unease still clearly etched across his face did little to instill confidence in me. "Maybe I should talk to someone," he said. "I have friends in the royal guard..."

I shook my head quickly, it being all too easy to imagine what the king would think of guards leaving his side to protect me. "Please don't. I'll be careful, I promise. Just take me home."

"Very well."

The sky darkened quickly as we walked the rest of the way to my new home, the sun having fallen beyond the horizon some time ago. Ashe took my hand again, and this time I was the one to grip it tightly, thoughts of Rebels and kidnappers making me far more nervous than I should have been. My heart skidded and started at every noise and almost stopped when a frog jumped onto the path.

Mother and Father had arrived home while Ashe and I had been talking, the lights in the cottage giving it a glow which beckoned me with welcoming comfort. It might not have felt like home yet, but for the second time today, I felt incredible relief at seeing the little cottage.

"Do you want to come in?" I asked Ashe at the door, not certain of the right protocol for such a situation but feeling safe enough to offer given my parents were home. I didn't mind when he shook his head.

"I should be going home, but I'll see you. Soon. It's been a pleasure, Lady Mackenna."

I smiled at his determination to still call me that. It was sweet. Like our walk had been, or would have been had I not ruined it with my fears and insecurities. From the moment I'd opened the door to see Ashe there, I'd been nervous, only becoming more so the longer we'd been gone. It was a wonder he ever wanted to see me again.

With a final smile, he turned and walked the long path back in the direction of the palace. I watched until he disappeared from view, the blossoming contentment inside me hesitant as it worked to push its way through the fear but definitely there. And alongside the contentment, anticipation. Much to my surprise, I was looking forward to seeing Lord Ashe again, whenever that might be. I had thought my life over when I walked away from the palace this morning, but I'd been wrong.

My life was only just beginning.

TWELVE

Three weeks later, I decided that had been far too hasty a conclusion. My life was well and truly over.

I was bored, and I missed my maids. Alina and Ben, too. And the guards. And Mr. Stanley. Even the laundry staff who I'd barely said a word to in my life. At least I'd known they were there if I ever wanted to chat. Of all the things I thought I'd miss most about the palace, its perpetual noise wasn't one of them. The cottage was so quiet and only made even more so by the fact that Mother and Father still spent much of their time at the palace. They weren't a threat to the king.

I kicked the wall in frustration before dropping down onto the lounge's one sofa. A pen dug into my side. I tugged it out along with the notepad it was attached to, grimacing at the flower sketched on the front page. There was nothing wrong with the flower, per se, except that it wasn't the list of next steps I was supposed to have been making. Had been trying to make since the day after I'd left the palace.

What was an ex-royal supposed to do with her time?

Three weeks ago, my life had been full of social engagements. Charity work, mostly. Meeting people, shaking hands, watching Alina charm a room with her effervescent smile, assuring her that her makeup was still perfection itself. Mondays visiting kids at the hospital, Thursdays too, whenever I could make it. Tuesdays handing out soup with Ben in the marketplace. Wednesday and Friday were usually reserved for our work with various charities, as were the weekends.

I'd gone to the hospital my first Thursday away from the palace, only to be told by the very apologetic Nurse Beth that I needed proper authorization to continue volunteering there, now that I didn't have the title of a royal behind my name. A month of training, she'd said, possibly less because of the three years' experience I already had. I couldn't even visit Roni as her parents weren't there to approve the visit and wouldn't be back until later. The most Beth had been able to tell me was that she was recovering well.

Though I'd smiled and thanked Beth, taking the thick pile of paperwork, questionnaires and modules required of their volunteers, my heart had been as heavy as the dejected cloud above me as I'd walked away. First my home, then my name, now my ability to contribute to society. How many other things would be taken from me before my demotion was complete?

It was a short-term setback, I knew. As soon as I completed the paperwork, training, and background checks, I could be back at the hospital, same as always, but was that where I should be focusing my time? Sooner or later, I'd need more than volunteer work to sustain me. The king wouldn't be providing for my needs anymore, and I couldn't live with my parents forever.

I hadn't realized how much I would miss it all. Not the glitz and glamor, the handshaking, speeches, or photo opportunities but the knowledge that we were making a difference. That *I* was. Just by sitting listening to someone's story while Alina shook all the right hands. Or drawing silly pictures and making faces with a child who'd seen far too few smiles in their short life. Or handing out food at the marketplace.

I hadn't been back there since my walk with Ashe that night. It wasn't my fear of the Rebels or even the way my heart dropped into my stomach at the thought of seeing Ben which kept me away, though they were good enough reasons in themselves. It was the fact that I'd see anyone at all.

I couldn't face people. Not yet. Not until I had some answers for the questions they were certain to ask. *What are you doing now? Why did you leave the palace so suddenly? Will you still be in Princess Alina's wedding?* And, the one I feared the most, *What happened between you and Prince Thoraben? Are you still friends?* Because they would ask. And I had no answers. Not for them or myself.

Staying home had been easy enough for the first two weeks. I'd slept a lot, organized my room, realized how much my three maids had spoiled me, spied on my neighbors, cried a little, written in my journal, wondered what Alina was doing and if Lord Ashe was ever going to call like he'd promised, pulled a few weeds from the garden, quickly replanted the ones that turned out not to be weeds, and slept some more. A life of liberty.

A life of utter boredom. I stopped myself short of throwing the notepad on the floor.

"Give it a month or two," Mother had said when I told her about the hospital. "Take some time to adjust and figure out what you want for yourself before you start committing to everyone else."

It had sounded like good advice at the time, overwhelmed as I'd been, but now I wondered if it had only been a cover for what she really thought. That any day Ben was going to come and whisk me back to the palace and propose, like some fairy-tale prince come to save his poor, impoverished love. Ha. I might not have known what to do with my life now it was mine to direct, but I did know that that was as ludicrous as an elephant learning to ski.

Mother hadn't seen the cold hatred in King Everson's eyes when he'd washed his hands of me in the throne room that day. The white marble columns either side of his throne had been warmer, and likely had more heart. No, I wouldn't be returning to the palace. This was my life now. Overwhelming as it currently seemed.

Come on, Kenna. Stop moping. There's a whole world out there for you to discover. No more rules, regulations, schedules, or people telling you what to do. You can do whatever you want. Be whoever you want.

But that was the thing. I didn't know what I wanted. Foolish as it now seemed, I'd never thought beyond this moment. What did normal people my age do? Those who hadn't been coddled their whole life by the delusion that they were special? What *could* I do? There had to be something. I refused to believe that the last seventeen—almost eighteen—years of my life had been a waste.

No more moping.

I tore the top page off the notebook I held and scrunched it up before drawing five dots down the left-hand side of the next clean page. Five things. Surely, I could come up with five things I enjoyed doing. I'd narrow it down from there.

Five things...

I rubbed the end of the pen against my lips as I considered the blank page. Keeping Alina in line didn't seem worth writing down. Nor skiing.

Ten minutes later, my page was still blank. At least this time I'd refrained from filling it with pointless scribbles.

If only I had someone to talk to. Everyone else seemed to—a friend, a sibling or parent. My parents were out, I'd already established that. Mother was biased in Ben's direction and Father a man of few words, unless you were a horse. Alina was my usual sounding board, when I got a word in edgewise, but neither she nor Ben could help me in this instance. I considered Wenderley for a whole half second before scratching her from my mental list too. All her sentences started, or ended, with the word Thoraben, usually with a few terms of affection in the middle. Even if I could get her to stop talking about him, I couldn't see how she would be of any help. My goal was to find a life outside of the palace and its royal family. Wenderley's was to get in.

Another face came to mind. I banished it almost as quickly as it appeared. I couldn't ask her. I'd never spoken a word to her in my life, let alone formed a close friendship. But still, the woman's face lingered.

Esme Smoak.

Ella's mother. The shy woman who stood a few steps back from her young daughter, smiling as Ella and I chatted about teddy bears and favorite dresses each time Ben and I delivered food to the marketplace. The woman I'd felt an instant connection with, though I couldn't explain why. Perhaps it was a shared love for her daughter, the girl who never failed to make me laugh. Or the sincerity of her smile. Perhaps it was simply the way she, too, knew what it was like to stand one step behind a princess—albeit one three-foot-high in a well-worn dress.

But, kind as I knew she'd be, could I really show up at Esme's door, invite myself in, and blurt out all my doubts and insecurities? I'd never even shared them with Alina, and I'd known her my whole life.

Give it a break. You'll get there. You'll think of something. Really, you will.

Even the cheerleader in my head sounded tired today.

I had two options—find something within the cottage to occupy my time while I secluded myself away like a hermit, or find the courage to walk outside.

Bravery had never been my strong suit. Tossing the incriminatingly empty notepad aside—again—I found a recipe book and got to work making a disaster zone of the kitchen.

An hour later, I knew without a shadow of a doubt that I'd definitely made the wrong choice. I should have gone into the village. Nothing anyone there might have asked or said could have come close to demoralizing me as much as the pile of soggy, black and white mush currently burning a hole in the kitchen bin.

How could the humble potato be so hard to cook? It had sounded so straightforward in the recipe book. Peel potato—wash spots of blood from where I'd nicked my finger—chop, place in water, and boil. Simple.

Apparently not.

Either the simple spud was more complex than it looked, or I was a fool. I hoped, more than believed, the former to be true.

The entire cottage now smelled of acrid burnt potato, even with all the windows and the door wide open. At least the smell would eventually dissipate. I hoped. The black on the bottom of the pot certainly had no intentions of doing so.

I scraped a fingernail across the char. Not even a scratch. I might as well throw it out—only I didn't know where to get another one, or if we could afford it.

I think I opened my mouth to sigh, but a frustrated howl found its way out instead. Was there nothing I could do? I felt utterly useless. Why hadn't I thought to ask for everyday skill lessons alongside how to look pretty and rule a country? I shook my head. At least I had the diplomacy to talk my way out of the mess. I'd excelled at diplomacy.

"Lady Mackenna. I came by to... What is th—? Forgive me. How are you today?"

I placed the pan carefully in the sink, covering it with water before wiping my hands dry and turning to greet my visitor. Stench or not, I should have shut the door. At least then I would have had the chance to take off my apron and check my appearance before seeing Lord Ashe now he'd finally come to call. I'd been fighting a losing battle with a vegetable for the past half hour. He probably wouldn't even recognize me as the woman he'd once called beautiful.

"I'm fine, it's potato, or at least, it was. And it really is Miss, not Lady. I left that title at the palace." Trying to hide my failure would be pointless with the house smelling so pungent. There was nothing for it but to own up to it and count on his honor as a gentleman not to laugh. He smiled, but I didn't get the impression he was laughing at me.

"Ah. Burnt potato, a particular specialty of mine. You'd think I would have recognized the smell. And whether you live at the palace or not, you'll always be a lady to me."

I wondered when Ashe would cease to amaze me. "You've burned potato?"

"Much to my brother's annoyance. Though, fortunately, not for a while. The trick's in the amount of water."

"Water. Got it."

"You did put water in there, didn't you?"

"Of course." Wait, did I? As Ashe stood there, staring at me, I wasn't so sure. Could I have forgotten the water altogether? My finger had been bleeding quite profusely at that point, not helped in the least by the water I ran over it to try to clean it. "Well, actually..."

To Ashe's credit, he did try to hold back his laughter, but I saw it lurking there in the crinkles of his eyes.

"Any idea where to buy new pans?" Pathetic. Absolutely pathetic. I might as well tell him here and now to leave. There was no way he'd want to court me now.

"Actually, I do."

"You do." Definitely underestimated him. Why had I thought Lord Ashe another handsome fop spending time with the prince? In the space of a few minutes, I'd learned not only that he had a brother and cooked but that he wasn't too proud to admit his failures and was respectful to the degree of flattery. And knew where to shop. Courting him, assuming he still wanted to, was proving to be far more interesting than I'd thought it would be.

He winked at me before grinning. "I wasn't merely being nice when I told you it was a specialty of mine. Would you care for a walk? It would be my pleasure to escort you. Unless you'd like to protect your innocence."

"My innocence?" I swallowed, self-consciously taking a step backwards. He couldn't mean what it sounded like. Ashe was the one who'd protected me in the crowded marketplace and brought me safely home the first night, warning me to be wary of the Rebels. He wouldn't now turn around and take advantage of me. Would he? "Where exactly do you plan to take me?"

"Merely to buy a new pan. It's, well, there's no kind way to say this but..."

"Tell me."

"The house isn't the only thing that absorbs smells..."

It took me a moment to realize what he meant, and when I did, I wasn't sure I wanted to. It wasn't my virtue he was worried about. "Are you saying I smell?" He was right. There was no nice way to say that.

"No. Not you. I'm certain you smell lovely but uh, your clothes and well, maybe your hair."

"I smell."

"Maybe a little." His apologetic grin more than made up for the reproach. "But between that and you coming in to buy a new pan... Well, they'll know you've been, uh, cooking. I could purchase one for you, if you like. They know me well. I lost any reputation I might have had as a successful cook a long time ago, but your innocence could remain intact."

He was sweet to offer, but my reputation as a cook wasn't exactly high on my list of things to hold on to. I wasn't that pampered princess anymore. This was my life—burnt potatoes and all. And I had to get out of this house. With him beside me, people weren't likely to ask the questions I feared.

"Let's take that walk." Swapping my apron for a light coat, I walked past him and out the door. I didn't blame Ashe for the laughter I heard behind me. The situation was seeming more and more amusing by the minute, and if he still wanted to spend time with me after smelling proof of my dismal cooking skills, then there was definitely more to him than good looks.

"Someone has some admirers," Ashe whispered as we walked along the same path we had last time. I looked up, surprised to see an older couple watching us. Not with furtive glances either. They were outright staring. "They're probably wondering how I got so lucky, having you on my arm."

I blushed at his flattery. Smooth, Ashe. Sweet and smooth. Like chocolate. And like chocolate, probably taken best in small amounts if one didn't want to get a headache.

I waved to two little girls a few houses down, sitting in their garden. The younger of the two waved back but the older one, who I guessed to be around four or five, ducked her head shyly before grabbing her little sister's arm and dragging her inside. Perhaps their mother had taught them not to talk to strangers.

I smiled as I saw their two heads pop up to watch me through a window. Don't talk to strangers, but feel free to gawk at them. They weren't the only ones.

I could almost see the gossip spreading, laying a carpet of intrigue before us as we got closer to the center of town. Some people were subtle, glancing our way before turning their attention back to whatever they were doing. Most blatantly stared, walking right outside their houses or shops to stand on the footpath and watch us pass.

It was a good thing, I told myself, moving closer to Ashe's side. He smiled down at me. I tried not to look guilty. I wasn't using him. Not at all. We were courting, and that was what people who were courting did. If it also helped to dispel the rumors of a relationship between Ben and me, then so much the better.

"Here we are." Ashe stopped, gesturing with his hand toward the shop we now stood in front of. "Mrs. McCloud's General Store. Best place to buy pots and pans. Word of the not-so-wise, speak loudly, but don't make it obvious. She's almost deaf but refuses to admit it."

"Oh?"

"She's a little touchy about it."

"I see."

"Threw me out of her shop once because I happened to mention it."

"Really?" He was certainly full of secrets—and not ashamed to share them. "Yet you came back?"

"Of course. She thinks I'm wonderful."

I shook my head, grinning at his pretentiousness. I was more amused than surprised by it. Handsome, kind, sweet, and fun with a healthy dose of high-class arrogance thrown in. He opened the door to Mrs. McCloud's store, standing aside to allow me to precede him.

"The pans are right over—" Ashe stopped.

I turned around. "Right over where?" Ashe didn't hear me, staring instead at something over my shoulder. The door softly closed behind him. It probably could have slammed and he wouldn't have noticed.

"Lord Ashe?"

"Hmmm?"

"The pans?"

"Oh. Uh. There." He thrust an arm out to his left, barely missing my nose in the process. His line of sight didn't follow his arm. I looked over my shoulder, trying to see what had him so captivated.

It wasn't something.

It was someone.

I couldn't remember ever having met Mrs. McCloud before but was almost certain the young woman who'd claimed Ashe's undivided attention wasn't her. Tall and slim, with dark brown hair, she was attractive enough but not so much that a man would stop in his tracks. Although there was something familiar about her.

She walked toward Ashe, head down as she rifled through her handbag. Stunned as he was, the collision was inevitable.

"Oh, excuse m—" Courtesy gave way to silence unhindered as the woman raised a hand to her mouth. The feeling that I was intruding on something important pushed me behind a shelf. Far enough to hide, close enough to hear. "Ashe."

"Jade."

It *was* her then. I'd thought as much but hadn't been certain.

Jade Davis. Wenderley's older sister. I hadn't realized she and Ashe knew each other so well. Or at all. The wall of pots and pans lost its pull as I unashamedly eavesdropped.

THIRTEEN

A she was the first to break the silence, shock still evident in his tone even from where I hid. "What are you doing here?"

"We're back."

"All of you? I mean, I saw Wenderley at the ball last month but thought she—"

"All of us."

Silence. And then, "To stay?"

I could almost hear the smile in Jade's voice. "Yes."

"Then Emmett and Eder—?"

"All will be well with them."

"And—?"

A gap between some hats provided enough vision for me to see as Ashe tilted his head, apparently asking with his eyes what he wouldn't say aloud. Whether his silence was because he knew I was listening or simply because extra words were superfluous, he was understood. I hadn't thought it possible that Jade could have gotten any more beautiful but, in that moment, she shone.

"With her too."

"Thank G—" Ashe shot a wary look around the store. I ducked quickly, though I knew he couldn't see me. "—goodness. Thank goodness for that. I am so pleased to hear it. And that you're back."

Silence stretched. I ventured another peek through the hats. They were staring at each other again. Ashe might have called me the most beautiful woman at the Midsummer's Ball but he hadn't once stared at me like that. I should have been jealous. I wasn't. One had to know someone to be jealous, and two dances and a walk shared didn't count as knowing someone.

The door to the shop opened, letting in a couple I recognized as two of my new neighbors. I hoped they hadn't tracked me down to complain about the smell emanating from my house. They didn't even look at me, instead walking over to a rack of sunglasses, debating which ones to try on. I turned my attention back to the far more intriguing conversation happening between the man I was courting and the woman he loved. I hadn't missed anything. They were still staring. It was Jade this time who broke the silence.

"Forgive me. You must have come in for a reason."

"Oh. Yes. Pots."

"Pots?"

"One, actually, and it's for Lady Mackenna, not me. She burned a pot and needs a new one."

I covered the roll of my eyes with the hat I was pretending to find fascinating. I knew I'd said my innocence wasn't all that important, but Ashe could have been a little subtler about it.

"You're with Lady Mackenna?"

"Yes, we came together. She's right over..." He looked around again.

I took pity on him, stepping into view, though I could have quite happily clobbered him for his complete insensitivity. The two of them were clearly in love and he'd admitted to being with me. The only reason he'd be with me was if we were courting, a truth he could have hidden. I added another adjective to the list I was compiling regarding Ashe.

Clueless.

"Jade. How nice to see you again."

"Mackenna? Wow. I thought Wenderley foolish when she said she didn't recognize you, but you've really changed. And you're...?" She gestured toward Ashe. I decided for her sake to play dumb.

"Looking for a new pot? Yes, certainly. Who knew potato could be so potent?"

She missed the joke. She must have never burned potato. Good for her.

"I think I saw them over here."

She walked over to the shelves full of pots and pans. I followed, Ashe toddling along behind us like a lovesick puppy. It didn't take me long to find a pot that exactly matched the one I'd ruined. I knew even less about choosing a pot than cooking in one so figured the same type would be my best option.

"Allow me," Ashe said, taking it from my hand as he walked with Jade to the counter. I went to protest, but he was already gone and where I would have followed, something stopped me. Perhaps it was the excitement that had found its way back to Jade's face as they talked quietly together. I couldn't hear them anymore, but that was probably for the best. Everyone should be allowed some secrets, though there was one in particular I wasn't content to allow to stay that way.

I waited only until Jade and Ashe had said goodbye and we were outside before asking. "What's wrong with Emmett and Eder?" Though Ashe held his arm out for me to hold, I didn't take it, instead keeping my arms behind my back. We might have been out of Jade's hearing, but I had no doubt she was still watching us as we walked away.

"What?"

I frowned. "Emmett and Eder. You asked Jade about them, and she said they were well. Had they been ill?"

Ashe didn't answer immediately, serving only to increase my worry. I hadn't known Wenderley's younger brothers well, but I knew Wenderley and Jade both doted on them. If they were important to Wenderley, they were important to me. And I was curious. Had this been the reason the family had left? It must have been quite a serious illness for the whole family to leave Peverell for so long. Though, after the way the queen had died, I didn't blame Wenderley's parents for wanting to do whatever

129

they could to seek the best medical care possible for their sons. Even if it did mean leaving behind everything they knew.

"Ashe? They weren't ill, were they?"

"In a manner of speaking."

That wasn't an answer. I stopped walking, making Ashe look at me. I wasn't unhappy with his answer, but neither was I satisfied. "Either they were, or they weren't."

"Forgive me. I'm not trying to be vague, but I can't talk about it. Not with you."

Yet he could with Jade. That was telling in itself. He kept walking. I followed at a slower pace. What was the great mystery behind the Davises? Was I wrong in thinking they'd returned to Peverell for any reason other than Thoraben?

I caught up with Ashe where he'd stopped under a tree. He might have been looking in my direction, but he wasn't looking at me. Though not a mind reader, I was pretty sure I could guess who he was thinking about.

"She's beautiful."

Ashe sighed. Actually sighed. "The most gorgeous woman I've ever known."

I looked away before he caught me smiling. It took him only a few seconds to realize his mistake.

"I mean, of course, you're beautiful also, Lady Mackenna."

Oh? So he did remember he was technically courting me and not the most gorgeous Jade? If we could even call it that anymore. I certainly wasn't thinking of our relationship in that light. How could I after what I'd seen? I didn't know how it had happened, nor when, but they were definitely in love.

"Thank you. How long have you known Jade?" I sat down on a rock, content to waste a little time here. The day wasn't too hot to enjoy the sun on my back, and I was in no rush to return to my foul-smelling house. "Or is that a grand secret also?"

I was pleased when he smiled and took a seat himself, wrapping his hands around one bent leg while stretching the other. I'd never seen him so relaxed.

"It's no secret. I spent a year traveling after finishing my schooling, thinking it would be good to see more of the world before settling down. Or, at least, that was my plan when I set out. I had an unfortunate accident two months in and, by complete chance, it was Jade's father who came to my rescue. Hearing I was from Peverell, he insisted I stay with their family until it was all sorted out. I offered to work for him in exchange for their hospitality and ended up staying for the next eight months, far longer than it took to sort out the problem. Needless to say, I got to know the whole family well during that time. They're wonderful people. I kept in contact with them for a while after I left but, as you probably heard, had no idea they'd returned."

I didn't know Ashe had traveled for so long, but then, I'd never known him well, seeing him only on occasion at the palace when he came to visit Ben and attend balls. It wasn't too much of a stretch to believe he'd been away for a year without me noticing.

"Traveling must have been exciting, though I suppose you didn't travel as much as you thought you would."

"It was, and while I didn't travel as much as I'd planned, I found far more than I ever expected."

"Like Jade Davis?" I raised my eyebrows. "The future Lady Ashe Marsh?"

His head flung in my direction so fast I was certain he'd have whiplash tomorrow. "What? I never said—"

"Really? You're going to deny you love her? After what I witnessed in Mrs. McCloud's shop?" I tried to keep my voice teasing but he was so serious it was difficult. "Do you truly think I was that interested in the pots and pans? Believe me, they're not all that interesting. I was trying to give you space. You looked like you needed it. Was Jade the reason you stayed so long with the Davis family? Because you loved her?"

"Actually, it wasn't, though she was the one it was most difficult to leave when I did." He shook his head, sighing again before looking back at me. "I'm sorry, Lady Mackenna. You must think me an absolute cad, but I truly had no idea I'd ever see Jade again when I asked to court you, especially not today."

"Their returning was a surprise to us all. I don't hold that against you, nor your affection for Jade."

"You're not mad?"

"Not to be rude, but I barely know you." It was actually more of a relief than anything else. I'd never felt worthy of Lord Ashe's affections. He was wonderful, but even in the short time we'd been courting, I hadn't felt anything more than appreciation for him. Certainly not the affection Jade carried on her sleeve.

"I'm a nice guy."

I grinned. "Jade certainly seems to think so."

"Truly?"

Clueless. Totally clueless.

The couple who'd been looking at sunglasses walked along the path, strolling as if they had all day to get home. Though they looked at us and nodded a greeting, they didn't say anything. I waited until they'd passed and were well out of listening range before continuing.

"I think you should go back to Mrs. McCloud's shop, tell Jade in no uncertain terms that you're not in a relationship with me as she's probably torturing herself thinking right now, and ask her to dinner—or to marry you. I'm certain she'd be thrilled with either. Although, if you wouldn't mind walking me home first, I'd appreciate it. I'm guessing you two will have a lot to talk about, and I have a meal to salvage."

Ashe didn't move. If anything, he seemed to fall further into his melancholy, his shoulders drooping along with his smile.

"I wish I could. I haven't even told her I love her."

"What? Why on earth not?" It was so obvious that he did, even to someone hiding behind a row of shelves and merely eavesdropping.

"It's not that simple. There are...complications, I suppose you could call them. I can't make any promises to her at the moment, and until I can, neither can I give her hope."

He stood then, wiping grass off his hands before holding them out to me. I took them, letting him pull me to my feet.

Complications. He sounded like Ben. Was every relationship

so complicated? Perhaps I was better off alone. Not that I had much choice in the matter. It wasn't as if there were lines of men waiting at my door.

Ashe walked beside me on the way home, but I might as well have left him behind. His mind was a long way from the cobblestone paths we trod. I could have been taken by Rebels and he wouldn't have even noticed. The moment we got within view of the cottages, I took the pot and sent him on his way. He had Jade to think about, and I had problems of my own.

Visitors.

And if the number of guards outside my cottage were any indication, one of them was the king.

ℱOURTEEN

It wasn't the king, it was the princess. I could have collapsed with relief. I'd never seen Alina with so many guards—but then, she'd never been engaged before either. Peverell wasn't the only country she was beholden to anymore. It would make sense that Hodenia would want to keep her safe as well.

"Alina. This is a surprise."

Though I smiled at Alina, my gaze skittered around the cottage, cringing at its less than perfect state. I hadn't been expecting visitors when I'd decided to try my hand at cooking this morning. My apron had slipped off the coatrack and fallen to the floor, a pile of recipe books sat scattered across the bench alongside a shelf full of cups and pans in various states of cleanliness I'd pulled out while looking for a particular sized pot. And my half-eaten lunch still sat at the table where I'd left it upon realizing the potato was burning. Ashe had stood in the doorway for several minutes as we'd conversed earlier, and I'd barely even noticed the mess. Alina stood there, and I was aware of every single crumb.

"What's that smell?"

Oh. And the house still smelled like the aftereffects of a fire. Wonderful. At least the doors to the bedrooms were closed. I couldn't remember what state they were in.

"Can I get you a drink? Any of you?" I wasn't sure the cottage had enough glasses to serve Alina and her entire entourage of maids and guards, but it would be rude not to offer. I congratulated myself on my brilliance as I walked into the kitchen. I could swipe aside some of the mess with one hand while pulling glasses out of a cupboard with the other. Of course, the effort would be moot if Alina had already seen the mess, but it would make me feel better.

"No, no. That's fine."

I told myself not to be offended at the way Alina scrunched up her nose as she answered, or the way she perched on the edge of the chair as if it might contaminate her. What she thought of the cottage I lived in didn't matter. I was happy here. Relatively anyway, but my discontent had nothing to do with the cottage itself or any of its furnishings. I poured myself a drink of water before joining Alina at the round dining table.

"It's nice to see you, Alina. I hadn't expected to see you so soon."

"Oh, well, in the rush in which you left the palace, I forgot to give you your schedule. I could have sent it with someone else, but I missed you so thought I'd bring it myself."

"My...schedule?" I still had one of those? The two of us had lived by our schedules at the palace, having almost every minute of our lives dictated by those copious pieces of paper, but I'd thought I was free of them now. "What schedule?"

"For my wedding, of course," Alina said with a laugh, gesturing one of her maids over. I watched almost in horror as the maid placed an oversized planner on the table, almost surprised the table didn't buckle under the book's weight. It was thicker than any schedule I'd had before. And it had my name written in bold black script on the front. This was not a good sign. I'd been certain my invitation to her wedding would have been revoked after what the king had said.

Alina pulled it toward her, opening the cover. "In the front, here, are a list of the dignitaries who'll be at the wedding for you to learn their titles. You know most of them already so you can probably skip that page. And the next few," she flicked through another twenty pages or so, "which are what we can and can't say to each of them. Boring..." She rolled her eyes. "Oh, here. Our gown fitting times."

"Gowns? I need a gown?" Then I truly was invited?

Alina stared at me. "Of course, you need a gown. What did you think you were going to stand beside me in? Jeans?"

"Stand beside you?" The dread which birthed in my stomach at the sight of the planner expanded with each word Alina spoke. I reached for my water glass and took another sip.

"Mackenna. You're my maid of honor. We decided this years ago. Did you think I would change my mind just because you didn't live in the same house as me anymore?"

The palace could hardly be called a mere house but...*maid of honor? Truly?* That would mean going back to the palace—albeit only for one day—and gown fittings and rules and regulations and facing B—No, I couldn't do it. But neither could I find the strength to tell her no. I chose my next words carefully.

"Does your father know you've chosen me?"

"Of course."

"And he approved?"

"Sure. Why wouldn't he? He knows you're my best friend. Who else would I choose? You're being very strange today. Has three weeks really made such a difference?"

Not so much three weeks as one man. Her father. Alina had no idea the disgrace I'd left in. "Sorry. The agreement my parents had with your father ended upon your betrothal, hence me moving out of the palace. I assumed that meant not coming to your wedding."

"You're kidding."

I wished I was. Alina grabbed my hands, pulling me toward her until the table bit into my ribs, and I had no choice but to stare into her eyes. "Mackenna Sparrow, you are my best friend and you will be at my wedding, standing beside me as my maid of honor, dressed in a beautiful gown. You have your first fitting for in three days. Understand?"

"Yes," I mumbled. "But—"

"No. There is no 'but,' Kenna. You have to be there." Her voice gentled to the point of tears, and for a moment I saw in her the child I'd once known, who begged me to curl up beside her when she was missing having a mother so much she couldn't sleep. "I want you there. Your parents too. Please? I can't do this without you. Say you'll be there."

How could I? I'd have to stand there smiling and pretending everything was as it had always been with the king, and the prince, while knowing nothing could have been further from the truth.

Ben I could handle, given enough time to prepare. I was merely confused and embarrassed where he was concerned. But the king? To look at him with the same adoration I'd always had despite the knowledge that he hated me? And I'd have to. There would be photographers capturing every moment from twenty different angles at least. There would be no hiding. If I showed even the tiniest glimpse of fear or animosity toward him, all of Peverell would see it. Papers would pick up the story—or make up their own—and we'd all be ruined. The Rebels would have no need to take down the royal family, I'd hand them the pieces on a platter.

Yet, how could I not agree to do this? I'd promised Alina years ago that I'd be there for her and, childish promise or not, I couldn't break it. This was to be the biggest day of her life so far, the joining of not only two people but two kingdoms. I had to be there for my friend. It was only one day. I could do it. I'd have to.

"I'll be there."

"Oh, thank you. You have no idea how much that means to me." The lost child I'd seen in her was gone as suddenly as it had come as Alina flicked through a few more pages.

"I asked Wenderley and Jade to be bridesmaids too. It was such fortunate timing that they came back when they did. Don't you think?"

"Certainly." I'd guessed Wenderley would be part of Alina's party but— "Jade?"

"Oh, I know. Jade and I haven't been the best of friends, but she's as close as anyone else I might have chosen. I thought perhaps Father might have allowed Nicola back, on occasion of it being my wedding and all, but he is adamant he will not. He refused to even consider it."

Knowing what I now knew of the king, that didn't surprise me. What did surprise me was that Alina had even asked in the first place.

"Nicola is a Rebel," I reminded her. "She deserved the punishment she received."

"Oh, come on. She was only thirteen when Father sent her away. Barely even old enough to know her own mind let alone take down a kingdom. Do you truly think she deserved to be exiled from Peverell for life?"

"It was not as if she went alone. Her family went too. Rebels, the whole lot of them."

"Thirteen, Kenna."

"I know!" I shouted in frustration. One of the guards outside looked through a window to see what was going on. I waved a hand in apology. I shouldn't have shouted at Alina, but did she really think I had forgotten Nicola? Though neither Alina nor I had been allowed to attend Nicola's trial, no one in the kingdom could forget Peverell's youngest ever convicted Rebel, least of all me. Before she'd been branded a Rebel, she'd been our friend.

I might not have been allowed into Nicola's trial, but I remembered vividly the sight of her coming out of it. She'd been smiling. It radiated from within her as if she held the sun itself inside. I'd rushed to embrace her, thrilled she'd been exonerated, only to have the guards hold me back. It was only as she passed that I saw her hands, cuffed behind her back as they led her away. Exiled that very day, we'd never seen her again. Not even to say goodbye.

Alina had begged and begged her father to change his ruling, but he'd been adamant. Nicola, even at thirteen, had been certain of her beliefs. Before a hall full of witnesses, she had declared herself a Rebel and refused to recant or even consider being persuaded otherwise.

It was the worst thing she could have done.

With any other criminal, the king was fair. Unflinchingly just, but fair. With the Rebels, he was brutal. With no consideration to age or gender, he threw them out. Exiled, never to return. And that was merely the fate of the followers. Rebel leaders were imprisoned for life.

I had never understood the king's hatred toward the Rebels but couldn't deny the effectiveness of his purging. Since the day Alina and I had been born, there hadn't been a single attack on the palace.

I often wondered if, had Nicola not been friends with Alina, the king might have been more lenient. After all, she was only thirteen. But Alina was too easily trusting, and as surely as the people inside the palace knew it, the Rebels must have too. What better way to take down the kingdom of Peverell than through its own princess?

And what better time to act than in the middle of Alina's wedding?

"I'm sorry, Alina. Nicola was my friend too, and I know you miss her, but I hardly think having a known, convicted Rebel in your bridal party a prudent choice. It would put not only you but the whole kingdom in danger. No, not one but two kingdoms. The entire royal lines of both Peverell and Hodenia will be in attendance. It is far too dangerous."

Alina sighed, shrugging in defeat. "It does not matter anyway for Father forbade it." I placed my hand on her shoulder, hoping to be of some comfort even though I knew there was nothing about her sadness that I could change. "Still, at least I have you."

"I'll be there. I promise." No matter how exhausting the day turned out to be. It might kill me, but I'd be there. For Alina.

"Good." Her smile was back, if a little less bright than before. "I told Wenderley and Jade that you'd be able to help them with all of this, they having only recently come back to Peverell. I know this isn't a real wedding but—"

"Wait. What?"

"What?"

"You said it wasn't a real wedding. What do you mean?"

"Oh. That. Since Marcos is the Crown Prince of Hodenia, we have to get married there, but I wanted to get married here, with my people, so he agreed that I could have two weddings. Our official one will be in Hodenia, but we're having another celebration here in Peverell, the week before. Isn't he kind? That's why the planner is so big. It has the details for both weddings."

I didn't even want to ask, but I had no choice. "I'm going to be at both?" I sounded like I was going to be sick. Probably because I was.

"Of course." Alina frowned. "I thought you'd be excited. We've been planning this since we were girls. It's finally here. I'm getting married. Aren't you even a little bit excited?"

"Sure, I am."

My flat words had neither of us convinced. I needed air. And time. In the course of a few minutes, I'd gone from thinking I'd never see the royal family again to being Alina's maid of honor at not one but two royal weddings.

"It's a big planner."

Alina laughed, my completely nonplussed words setting her mind at ease. Though I was glad to be of service, my mind was far from the same.

"It's tiny compared to the one the palace gave me."

I looked at the bulging planner sitting so innocently on the table. I didn't want to even contemplate how large Alina's was.

"I suppose I'd better start reading then."

"Yes. And I should get back to the palace. Perhaps I'll see you at your gown fitting on Thursday. Mine is the one before, so we might overlap."

"I'll come early so we do."

"Oh do. Please do."

Standing, I walked forward to embrace Alina. She was being strong, and I knew she was excited, but I knew her too well to know she wasn't also a tiny bit terrified—and missing the fact that she didn't have her mother here at such a momentous time. Pulling back, she gave me a tremulous smile.

"Thanks, Kenna."

I smiled, giving her one more hug before letting her go.

"Oh." Alina started rummaging around in her purse, pushing aside papers, makeup, and various other bits and pieces before pulling forth a sealed envelope. Straightening a bent edge, she held it out to me. "Ben sent this for you. Thank goodness I remembered. He wouldn't have been happy if I'd come home still holding it. He said to make sure you read it. I don't know why he didn't come with me. I would have waited. Who knows what my brother is thinking... Anyway, read it, so I can tell him you did."

The instant thudding of my heart did nothing to help the queasiness of my stomach. The letter shook as I took it. I tucked it in my pocket and locked my hands behind me. "Thanks. I'll read it later." Maybe. Or maybe I'd burn it. I was doing my best to forget Thoraben. Admittedly, I was doing a terrible job, but I was trying.

"No, he said I had to make sure. He was pretty adamant."

I didn't know what the letter said, but I could guess, and there was no way I was reading it in front of Alina. I might have fooled her with my indifference toward the missive so far, but I wasn't that good an actor. I pasted on a smile. "I don't want to keep you waiting. I'm sure your schedule didn't account for standing watching me read. I'll read it. I promise I will. You can tell Thoraben that."

"Promise?"

Much as I feared what I might find in there, I owed him that much. "Yes."

"That's good, because I think he misses you. Of course, it's hard to tell with Wenderley around so much these days, but he does ask about you. It's so strange not having you at the palace. I keep running to your room to tell you things only to remember you're not there."

"Your room will be just as empty soon."

"I know. Can you believe I'll be a married woman in less than three months? Goodness, I can't. And then I'll be moving to Hodenia with Prince Marcos and—Kenna, you'll come visit me, won't you? I mean, I'll be back to visit Peverell every few months—Marcos has promised I can do that—but please say you'll come and visit me in Hodenia? It's not very far. I could send a car for you, or our plane. I'm sure we'll have one."

"I will try." It wasn't a promise, but it was enough to satisfy her. I wished I could have told her I'd come, but I didn't know if I could. For all I knew, King Everson wanted to cut me off from his children altogether, despite his allowing me to stand beside Alina at her wedding. No—I swallowed—*weddings*. I wouldn't go against his wishes but neither could I deny my friend the happiness of knowing there was a chance I might come. I could only hope.

"Thank you, thank you, thank you. Oh, I should go. I have another three meetings this afternoon alone. My maids are probably pacing your grass to mud as they wait for me. I'll see you Thursday then?"

"Yes."

"Good. Well, bye."

I lifted my hand to wave, but Alina was already out the door and off to her next appointment. There were lots of things I missed about that life. Rushing from one appointment to the next was not one of them.

Pulling Ben's letter out of my pocket, I walked into my room and shut the door, locking it behind me. My parents weren't home, nor did I expect them anytime soon, but somehow that extra bit of security gave me courage. I already felt like crying and I hadn't even opened the envelope.

I sat on the floor, back against the wall, my legs tucked up against me as I stared at the paper in my hands. My heart beat so strong I was certain any moment it would burst out of my throat. Dirty dishes, burnt meals, schedules, and all thoughts of weddings flew from my head as I fingered my name across the front.

I could put the letter away. I'd promised I'd read it but hadn't said when. I could put it away until I was ready. Until I didn't care quite so much what it said. But I wouldn't. Because the truth of it was that as much as I dreaded whatever explanation it held—and I knew Ben well enough to know it would—I wanted to hear it. I had to know why he'd kissed me. Maybe then I could truly let it go.

With shaking hands, I opened the envelope, unfolding the two pieces of paper it held. Blinking away unwelcome tears, I began to read.

Kenna,

Before I say anything else, let me tell you that I spoke with Father about your leaving. I thought it strange that you should leave so suddenly. I would have been content to abide by your decision had you not also forbidden me to visit and avoided me altogether in the marketplace. That was so out of character for you that I knew there had to be more to the story. Now I know. Father threatened you. He claims it was justified, that you are distracting me, but he is wrong. Like I told you that day on the tower, I have already chosen my bride.

Unfortunately, despite me reminding Father of that fact, he is unmoving and determined to follow through with his threats. He wants me to marry a woman of his choosing, but I am determined to wait for the one I love. (Yes, Kenna. There is the answer to the question you stubbornly refused to ask that day. I do love her.) Until the day I can convince Father of my sincerity, or find a way around his edict, I think it best we both obey.

I will not come to the cottage nor seek you out in town but, no matter what Father says, I value our friendship too much to let it go. I hope you still do also, though I wonder if you will ever want to see my family again after the way Father treated you. And I, myself.

Kenna, can you ever forgive me? I won't write it in case this letter falls into the wrong hands, but you know what I am talking about. Every time I think of it, I feel sick with regret. I hurt you, both in what I did and how I handled it. I can see you now, shaking your head at me, telling me it was nothing to worry about, but I'm not a fool. I saw the hurt on your face as you stared at me. You were already upset, and I only made it worse. And when I could have stayed to explain, I walked away. I cannot change what happened, all I can ask is that you forgive me and hope you can find it in yourself to do so.

The palace is different without you here. Alina is, as you predicted, busy preparing for her marriage to Prince Marcos. You'll be happy to know, she hasn't lost that monstrosity of an engagement ring yet. Why someone would want to wear something so ridiculously big is beyond me. Perhaps it is a female thing, though I can't imagine you thinking the same. Perhaps it is simply Alina.

I talked with your father last week and he said you are all adjusting well to your new lives. I hope for all your sakes that is true. Please know that, should you ever need anything at all, you need only ask. Not everyone at the palace feels the same way Father does.

Until,

Ben

My finger traced over the last word. Ben. He'd signed the letter Ben. I don't know why that meant so much to me, but it did. He still considered me a friend. He'd said as much in the letter, but the simple, informal signature proved it more than words ever could. Without meaning to, I found myself looking at the photo he'd given me that night. It had been the first thing I'd found a place for in my new room. The three of us were so happy there. This letter gave me hope that we might one day be again.

I read through the letter one more time, searching for the answers I had hoped it contained. They weren't there. He hadn't explained the kiss. Perhaps there was no explanation. He loved another woman and regretted kissing me. That was all there was to it. At least he knew it had meant something. Mistake or not, it had been my first kiss, and that wasn't something easily forgotten. Regret and pain would dull with time but not the memory. I'd tried to let our friendship go but hadn't yet succeeded. A lifelong relationship took more than a few weeks to die. And that was assuming I wanted it to, which I knew in my heart I didn't. Forgiving Ben that moment would be easy. I'd already done it. Forgetting was quite another story.

FIFTEEN

Queen Elsie's youngest sister, Lady Stephany (husband—Herbert Lance, children—Jashlyn (13), Fletcher (10) and Merari (8)), enjoys conversing about fashion, chamber music, and her family. Do not approach any topic pertaining to crime or criminals in Hodenia.

Other topics of interest are books, baking, and the color green.

I sat back in my chair and rubbed a hand across my eyes. The color green? Really? How many things could one possibly have to say about the color green? I could see it now...

"Lady Stephany?"

"Why, yes."

"How delightful to meet you. I hear you like the color green..."

Perhaps not. Still, it was strange enough that it would probably stick in my head, unlike the seventeen pages of information I'd already read. The guest list for Alina's wedding was predictably extensive. I knew all the details for the Peverell guests, having had to study them before, but was starting to wonder if the royal family of Hodenia had invited every person in their kingdom to attend. I'd already forgotten more than I could ever remember regarding the dos and don'ts of conversation with them. Was it King Dorien's second or third brother who had a crippling fear of bears? And one of the aunts was completely deaf in her left ear. Or was it her right?

I started flipping through pages, searching for her name. Timina, Dimity, Eshton, *Mrs.* Daughty—don't ever address her by her first name—Carin, Calissa, Marie. My eyes slid shut. Too many names. Too many details. I slammed the planner closed. The nameless aunt could wait until tomorrow. I had to get out of this house before my head burst from the pain.

Mother looked up from the book she'd been reading on the other side of the table. "Done already?"

If only that were the case. "I hate schedules."

I tuned out her laughter as I put all my attention into choosing an apple from the bowl in the kitchen. It was petty, especially as I didn't have the luxury of being choosy anymore, but I hated biting into an apple only to find it bruised or mushy. My morning had been depressing enough already without adding a disappointing apple to it. On a whim, I grabbed a bread roll also. Might as well make a picnic of it. I certainly had no desire to pick up that tome of a schedule any time soon. My frequent sighing was probably ruining Mother's day off anyway, despite her assurances of the opposite.

"I'm going for a walk."

"Good idea. That always clears your head. Don't be gone too long though. I heard there's a big storm coming, and you have your next dress fitting for Alina's wedding later."

Frowning, I leaned back far enough to peer out the window at the brilliantly blue sky. It certainly didn't look like there was a storm coming, but then, what did I know? No doubt Mother had heard from someone far more in tune with the weather than me.

"I'll be back in time for lunch," I assured her.

"Maybe you should wait for—" She cut off.

Though I waited for her to finish the thought, she didn't. "For...?" I prompted.

"Never mind. Which way are you going?"

"The marketplace, I think."

"Sounds good. Enjoy yourself."

Sunlight hit me in the face the moment I stepped out the door, the perfect antidote to a dull morning of study. *Definitely a good idea.*

The path to the marketplace was a familiar one, having walked it twice with Ashe already but, though I started in that direction, it wasn't long before I looped back around and followed the river instead as it wound its way toward the hills. I'd had my fill of people today. Nature's symphony was what I craved.

The song of the birds, so clear and unafraid.

The river's constancy as it rushed past.

The wind dancing through the trees, sending leaves into outbursts of applause.

The walk was long, taking almost an hour to reach the bottom of the hills, but the weather was perfect and the break welcome. The breeze tugged at my hair, invigorating me as it whisked my worries away.

I'd never been this close to the hills before. I'd admired them from a distance and been driven past and through them but had never stood on them and felt the grass whisper against my bare legs. I probably should have worn jeans rather than shorts, but I hadn't planned on such a long walk when I'd set out. Had it been a need to escape which had driven me? Or that perpetual aching feeling inside that there was more to this life than I saw? That there was something more for me than this. If only I knew what it was I was looking for.

The path I followed forked, stopping me for a moment as I considered where to go next. The walking track or the road? It didn't take more than a few seconds to decide. The walking track circled the bottom of the hills, the road climbed upward and through them to the sky. I chose the road.

The first fifty yards were fine. The next stole my breath away, leaving me gasping for air. I hadn't realized how steep the road was. It had never felt particularly steep from inside a car. My calves burned with the strain, begging me to turn back. I allowed myself to stop only for a minute before continuing on at a slower pace. Hard as the terrain was—and right now, it felt far more like a mountain than a mere hill—I relished the challenge. Lists of names, preferences, and unfulfilled desires were pushed from my mind as all my attention was claimed by merely remembering how to breathe. *Left foot. Right foot. Breathe in. Left foot. Right foot. Breathe out.*

The higher I climbed, the easier the rhythm came. Or perhaps it was only that I slowed down enough to find a rhythm. I climbed until I came to a clearing, deciding this would be as good a place as any to stop.

Turning around, I gasped. Had there ever been so breathtaking a view? It was Peverell, yet as I'd never seen it before. It was...backwards. The same town, the same houses and streets I'd found comfort in a hundred times as I stared at them from the tower but almost completely unrecognizable.

And the palace. Was it truly so imposing a structure? Tall and stately, I couldn't decide whether it looked impressive or downright foreboding. It was difficult to believe those high stone walls bracketed the warm, comfortable home I'd grown up in.

I looked for my tower, yearning for that piece of familiarity, but couldn't see it. The copse of trees to my right hid it from view. It shouldn't have mattered, but for some reason, it did. I needed to see it. If only I could get higher.

A thought tickled me, so scandalous that I almost brushed it aside without even a consideration. The trees around me were tall and had enough branches to draw me near. I could almost hear them whispering encouragement as they beckoned me to climb them. I rested my hand lightly on the trunk of the closest one.

I shouldn't. Hadn't I been scolded for that enough over the years growing up? *"Princesses don't climb trees, Lady Mackenna. It's far too dangerous and highly improper. Why, imagine what a man were to think should he come across you perched high above his head, skirts around your waist."*

I looped my bag over my shoulder and grasped the lowest branch. I wasn't a princess, there were no men present, and I was wearing shorts.

The bark bit into my skin as I pulled myself up but wasn't rough enough to break it. I would have kept climbing anyway. The urge to see my tower felt like a hunger inside me, clawing at my chest, charging up my throat until it was all I could think about. I had to see that tower.

The leaves grew denser and the branches flimsier the higher I climbed, forcing me to test each hold before trusting my weight on it but finally, hugging my body to the trunk of the tree as it swayed, I saw it. My tower. It still stood. I knew it would, I would have heard about it had part of the palace fallen or been attacked, but there was something so comforting about seeing it with my own eyes.

My life was complete.

I rolled my eyes at my own foolishness. *It's a tower, Kenna. Not that big a deal.* And it technically wasn't even mine. I'd never held claim to it, and even if I had, I'd "given" it to Ben that day he'd found me there. Perhaps he was even there right now, looking out over the same village I did. My hand jerked upward before I realized what I was doing and pulled it back. I'd already climbed a tree, to see a tower no less. Waving at a prince who couldn't see me, and likely wasn't even there, was beyond ridiculous.

I tried to pick out my cottage instead. I'd just found the right street when a flicker of red seized my attention. I wasn't alone. Someone was coming up the path I'd climbed. A man. A very tall, blond—Oh no. My heart skidded out of time as the man walked close enough to recognize.

Lord Ashe Marsh. Of course, it was him.

And I was up a tree.

I didn't even have the luxury of groaning. He'd hear me and then all hope of remaining invisible would be lost. If I could keep still enough, and quiet enough, he'd continue on his way and never know the difference. Easy.

Not so easy.

He stopped right under the tree beside mine, sitting down and making himself comfortable. Was he planning on staying—I swallowed—long? *Come on, Ashe. Get up. Move. It's really not that comfortable. You don't want to stay here. You really want to keep going and go home. Right away. Now, Ashe. Go away.*

He didn't respond to my silent encouragements. Worse, he closed his eyes. Was he sleeping? Here? Up in the hills leaned up against a tree? Truly? But then, perhaps that was good. I'd give him five minutes, maybe ten, to fall well and truly asleep and then I'd quietly climb down and sneak away. I could do it. How hard could it be?

Very. Apparently.

Climbing up had been easy. Reach, pull, stand, reach, test weight, pull. Climbing down—I wiggled my foot, trying to bring feeling into it—a bit more of a challenge. Pins and needles pricked at my foot as feeling crept back in. Make that a lot more of a challenge.

My hand slipped on the branch I held. I sucked a quick breath through my teeth as the bark sliced through the skin on my palm and fingers, leaving a long, thin cut right down the middle. Perfect. Just perfect. I still had four more branches to climb down, both hands required. I'd have to be more careful. I placed my bleeding palm against the branch, forcing my fingers to wrap around it despite the pain.

"Lady Mackenna?"

I yelped, my hand slipping again. Tears pricked at my eyes as the pain registered. I didn't even want to see how much damage the bark had caused this time. I should never have climbed the tree.

"Lord Ashe."

"What are you doing in a tree?"

Ouch. Ouch. Ouch. "Hurting myself?" My joke fell flat. It probably didn't help me any that a couple of tears had fallen free and were now meandering their way unhindered down my right cheek. I held up my hand, showing Ashe the mess the bark had made of it. "Not purposely. It was an accident. I slipped."

His eyes widened. I hoped that was sympathy I saw there, alongside the pity. "What were you doing? Using the bark as a grater?" He shook his head. "Where are your guards?"

"What guards?"

"Greyson? Lach? Leisha? Kallie? You know, they live next door to you. Follow you everywhere you go."

Greyson, Lach...? Was he talking about the two couples who'd moved into the cottages the day after I had? The pair who'd been looking at sunglasses in Mrs. McCloud's shop? "They're guards?" I'd assumed they were Hodenians sent to assist Alina with her wedding preparations, given the timing of their arrival.

"Thoraben didn't tell you?"

I shook my head, still trying to comprehend the fact that I'd had guards with me, all this time. Was that who Mother had been about to tell me to wait for?

"He was furious when I told him you had none. He sent them the very next day. You haven't noticed them?"

"I thought they were Alina's."

Pain was making my hand shake, the drops of blood pooling in my palm not helping. I had to get out of this tree before I fell. Only now I was stuck. I couldn't climb down with only one hand, and I couldn't bear the thought of putting my injured hand anywhere near that bark again. I wished the guards I apparently had were here. Then I wouldn't have had to ask Ashe for help.

Again.

"Ashe, I can't—"

"Wait there, I'll help you down."

Believe me, I wasn't going anywhere.

If it weren't for the pain, and Jade, I might have relished the next few moments—a strong man climbing up beside me, wrapping my arms around his neck and cradling me against him as he gently carried me down the tree. Saved by my knight in not-so-shiny armor. I probably would have fallen in love with him there and then. Throbbing hand aside, the only thing that would have made it more romantic would have been if it had happened in the late afternoon. So he could carry me off into the sunset professing his undying love.

Unfortunately for me, it was still hours till sunset and his undying love was for another girl. This was no hero, coming to save his princess. He was a gallant man saving a poor, embarrassed girl from her own foolishness. And I was dripping blood on him. The romance quickly dissipated. I stepped away as soon as we reached the ground, brushing pieces of bark and a few lone leaves off my shirt. My deportment teacher had been right, climbing trees was dangerous.

At least I wasn't wearing a skirt.

"Since you've no guards here—something they'll no doubt be answering to—let's see about bandaging that hand."

My gaze skittered around the clearing, looking everywhere but at the man in front of me. Bandages? Made of what exactly? The only fabric here was what we were both wearing, and I certainly wasn't ripping anything off mine. What was he going to do, tear his shirt? *Oh, please don't. Please, please don't.* I didn't want to see Ashe without his shirt on. I'd distracted myself from his nearness while he carried me down the tree, counting my heartbeats as they throbbed in my throat, but my strength had limits. Jade or no Jade, Ashe's height and warrior's physique were attractive, and my eyes worked perfectly well. Almost as well as my imagination.

"No, thanks. I'll see to it at home."

"Don't be a fool. I can do it here."

I blushed. Couldn't he have a little bit of pity on me and my feminine weakness for tall, handsome men? "I have...uh...bandages...at home." I assumed.

"And I have a perfectly good one here."

"You do?" I looked up—and wished I could disappear then and there. He was holding a bandage in his hand. A long, white, rolled bandage. His other hand held a bottle of water ready to pour on my hand.

"What did you think I was going to use?"

"Never mind." I held out my shredded hand and looked at the ground, suddenly finding it incredibly fascinating. Was that an ant walking there? And another. Two ants and two...uh...bugs. The water splashed over my hand, creating rivulets on the ground below. Me and my overactive imagination. I knew it would get me in trouble one day.

"You okay?"

I forced myself to look up and smile at the man holding my hand so gently as he began to bandage it. The smile was pained, but it would do. At least my cheeks began to cool.

Somewhat.

"I'll be fine. You carry a first aid kit with you?"

"When I go hiking, yes. Don't you?"

No, just an overactive imagination. "I didn't plan on hiking. I was going for a short walk."

"And climbing a tree."

"I wanted to see the palace."

He stopped bandaging my hand for a moment to turn and look at the palace, standing there in all its glory, before turning back to me. That annoying blush started to creep into my cheeks. "I wanted to see a particular tower." And there went the last of my credibility.

"Right. Well." He tucked the edge of the bandage into a fold. "All done."

I took back my hand, holding it against my stomach. "Thanks. Again. You're getting good at this."

"What, bandaging?"

"Rescuing me. First at the ball, then from the wrath of a pota-to, now a tree... What you must think of me..." I shook my head, unwilling to consider it further. Wishing I hadn't even opened my mouth. But Ashe was laughing.

"I'll admit, you're not the pampered princess I took you for, but don't think that's a bad thing. You're fun."

Fun. Well, it could have been worse. He could have said I had a great personality.

"I think I'll go now." Before I did or said anything even more mortifying.

"Don't rush off because of me. I was going to sit a bit. Why don't you join me? Give your guards a chance to catch up since they've obviously lost you. I couldn't ask for better company. I might even share my cookies."

"Food, first aid kit, water. My, didn't you come prepared."

"Don't forget the change of clothing."

"Seriously?"

"It's supposed to storm later. I thought I might need it."

Ah yes, the storm Mother had warned me about. I checked the sky again. Still clear, though the wind had picked up a bit. I should probably go home soon or Mother would start to worry, but a few more minutes wouldn't matter. I owed Ashe that much after he'd so gallantly rescued me.

Taking care not to put my newly bandaged hand in the dirt, I sat down. I don't think Ashe actually expected me to do so but, if the smile on his face was anything to go by, he was pleased I had. He sat down, pulling a bag full of chocolate chip cookies from his backpack and offering them to me. I took one. He didn't, putting the bag beside him and picking up a stone instead, rolling it around his hand.

"So, what are you doing here?" It was probably rude to ask, but I had to say something.

He shrugged. "Probably the same as you."

"Hiding from reality?"

"Thinking."

Ah. About Jade, no doubt. He had that lovesick look about him. Serious, dejected, yet somehow still hopeful. "Still haven't told her?"

He threw the stone. It arced through the air before hitting a tree trunk and rolling to a stop in the grass. If he was meaning to hit that particular tree, he had incredible aim. I wasn't sure. I didn't ask, instead watching as he threw another. This one bounced once before disappearing down the hill.

"You make it sound so easy," he said.

"Why is it so hard? You love her. She loves you. Her family clearly adore you or they wouldn't have allowed you to stay with them for so long. I have no doubt they approve..."

"My father doesn't."

"Truly? Has he even met her?" How could anyone disapprove of someone as sweet as Jade? Even when she'd thought I was being courted by the man she loved, Jade had treated me kindly, even offering me a compliment. I doubt I could have been so charitable had our situations been reversed.

"He doesn't need to. Her reputation has preceded her."

"Jade has a reputation?" As what, exactly? True, I hadn't kept in contact with her or any of her family since they moved, but could she really have done anything worth shunning someone over?

"You don't know why they left, do you."

I shook my head. "No one ever said."

"Perhaps it is better that way."

"No." I closed my eyes, taking a deep breath and letting it out before opening them again. "Please. Tell me?" I felt like I was begging, and perhaps I was, but I had to know. There was too much mystery, and far too many assumptions on my part, surrounding Wenderley's family. I needed something real.

"You couldn't tell Alina, or the king."

I bit out a laugh. "The king and I aren't exactly on speaking terms, as you well know, but I promise I won't tell Alina." He didn't mention my parents in the list of people who couldn't know. Did they already know? It wouldn't have surprised me, though the fact that they hadn't told me hurt.

"Truly. You can't tell anyone."

"I promise I won't."

Ashe considered me for a few more moments. Perhaps he was testing my loyalty, perhaps he was simply searching for the right words, I wasn't certain. Whatever it was, he found it.

"Jade swears allegiance to a different ruler."

SIXTEEN

My mouth dropped open. I quickly closed it, my mind reeling. Of all the things I'd been expecting Ashe to say, that hadn't even been considered. "Jade's a Rebel?" My eyes narrowed, as if somehow that might give me better sight to test the sincerity of his words. I couldn't believe it. Not Jade. She was too good to be a Rebel. But then, Nicola had been too, and why would Ashe lie about something so serious?

"That's what the king calls them, but they have no desire to usurp the throne in any way. The ruler they serve is—"

"How do you know this?" He still might be wrong. The rumor mill often was. Anyone could have started a story like that in an effort to besmirch Jade's good name, though what anyone would have to gain by having Jade exiled was beyond me. She'd only recently returned as it was.

"I...spent time with her family."

It was the hesitance in his voice which gave me pause. There was more to the story. Ashe was hiding something, something more dangerous than that which he'd already revealed. He didn't look away as I expected of liars but— "You're one of them too."

His gaze didn't waver, even for an instant. "I am."

No wonder he'd sworn me to secrecy.

I picked at some grass, twirling it between my fingers, pondering the calm I felt at his declaration. It should have sent me running back to my house in terror, if not straight to the palace to report him. My whole life I'd lived in fear of meeting a Rebel face to face, and yet here I was sitting with one, no one else in sight, completely at his mercy, playing with grass. It didn't say much for my judgement that the one person I'd trusted outside the palace was the one person I shouldn't have.

But Jade did. And, for some strange reason, I did too.

"Your father doesn't approve of you marrying a Rebel."

"No."

"But you could marry her anyway, assuming her father approves. You're old enough. You don't require your father's permission."

"No, but I want it. No matter what my father believes, he is my father and that position demands respect."

"What if he never changes his mind?"

Ashe shrugged, smiling wryly. "Why do you think I'm pacing the hills?"

"It's complicated." He'd said that. I hadn't realized how complicated.

"Yeah."

We lapsed into silence, both lost in our thoughts. For my part, I was realizing how little I knew of these two people I thought I knew. How many times had I seen Ashe in the palace and thought him simply another pretentious friend of Ben's? But here he was, a self-proclaimed Rebel. One who'd put his own desires aside out of respect for his father. Any man who would do that was no threat to the kingdom.

And Jade. I'd known her all my life. Spent time in her house as a child. She was kind, compassionate, loved her family, and used to have a toy unicorn sitting on her bed. All that and...Rebel? I knew Ashe was telling the truth—one didn't joke about being a Rebel any more than they did holding a bomb—but I couldn't make this new information fit in my mind. It was as if I was trying to finish a puzzle, only with a piece from a different set. No matter how I turned it, it still stuck out.

"You wouldn't hurt Thoraben or Alina?"

"I'd protect them with my life."

"Then why—"

A gust of wind whipped hair into my eyes, momentarily blinding me. I pushed it back behind my ears. It didn't stay long. The sky above us was still clear, but the wind was growing stronger by the minute, its urgency wreaking havoc on the questions bubbling up in my mind.

"I should get back."

"Yeah, me too." Ashe sighed, trying a smile. It dropped the instant he looked up. Something behind me had him scrambling to his feet and pulling me roughly to mine. "Let's go. Now."

"What? What is it?" He didn't answer, instead grabbing my hand and jerking me down the road toward the village. He was going too fast. I stumbled twice, held up only by the strength of his hold on my arm. "Ashe, slow down. What is it?"

He stopped, though I could tell he didn't want to. "There. See it? Out to the west?"

I followed the direction he pointed, my heart almost stopping when I spotted what he'd already seen. The wind I'd thought strong was nothing compared to the whirlwind that was coming. Mother had been right.

"Are we going to make it back in time?"

"We'll have to."

Ashe's face was as grim as I'd ever seen it, but there was a determination there. He'd get us home or die trying. I grabbed his hand and started running.

This was no ordinary storm.

The wind was getting stronger. It had been buffeting the cottage doors and windows for the past three hours but now it was pushing its way in. A picture flew off the wall, clattering to the ground. I held my skirt down to keep it from flying too. I should have stayed in the clothes I'd been wearing rather than changing when Ashe had delivered me safely home. They might have been sweaty and covered in dust from our harried run back, but they

HEART OF A ROYAL

were far more practical than the skirt and tank top I'd replaced them with. Clothes which were quickly becoming just as dusty.

It was useless. Mother and I had boarded up the windows best we could, but the wind was far too strong for our flimsy protections.

"Quick, Kenna. Under the table."

I looked around the room one more time, cataloguing everything in my head, hoping desperately to find something I'd missed to fortify our little cottage further. There was nothing. I ran to hide with Mother under the table, loathing to admit what I already knew—even with all we'd done, it wasn't enough.

At least Father would be safe. The palace had been built to withstand Rebel army attacks. Surely it would hold out through a windstorm. Much as I wanted Mother to be safe there also, I couldn't make myself wish she'd gone there today. It was selfish, especially since the chances of making it through this unscathed were dwindling fast, but I was so glad she was here with me.

Ashe had offered to stay, but I could see how much the gesture pained him. His family needed him, and so did Jade. I'd told him to leave, that we would be fine. Hope, rather than belief, fueled such bravado.

I'd stopped feeling that bravado an hour ago. The cottage which had yesterday seemed so sturdy now felt like a pile of twigs waiting to be swept away, with us inside. It was a matter of waiting now. It must have only been around four in the afternoon, but the darkness the storm brought with it made it feel much later.

Something crashed onto the table above us. I hadn't thought anything could scare me more than I already was, but that did. My scream was swallowed up in Mother's blouse as she tugged me against her.

"Mackenna."

I looked up. The fear I was certain blazed from my eyes was absent in hers. There was an intensity there, but it wasn't fear. Fear carried a level of shaking and uncertainty, darting, tear-washed eyes. Mother's held none of those things.

"All will be well."

I wished I had her faith.

I lost track of the time as we huddled together there under the table. Seconds stretched into hours and minutes decades. My back ached with the strain of holding myself together. After a while, Mother began to sing. With all the battering and whistling going on outside, it took me a few moments to pick the tune she sang but when I did, it brought a small smile to my face.

It was an old song, one I hadn't heard since I was very young when I'd been confined to bed with an illness for several days. As I'd lapsed in and out of consciousness, Mother had sat by my bed and sung it, over and over.

The lord surrounds his people, now and forevermore. His love will chase them, his arms embrace them. There is hope when he is near.

I mouthed the words of the chorus along with her. From what I remembered, the song was about a lord caring for his people. He sounded kind. Far more so than the king who'd thrown me out of his castle and told me not to come back. I'd have to ask Mother about the rest of the story one day. No doubt it was a good one if it brought her such comfort.

A loud bang at the door made me gasp. That was the closest one yet. I peeked up long enough to see the door shudder as another thud sounded from outside, then another. They were too rhythmic to be random. Could someone be at the door? I didn't want to open it, what little shelter it still afforded us, but I couldn't leave whoever it was out there. Not in this storm and certainly not with darkness so quickly approaching.

Mother grasped my hand as I unfolded myself from the floor. I thought she would hold me back, but she only asked me to wait while she rose to stand beside me. She wasn't stopping me from facing the danger, but neither was she letting me face it alone. I nodded my gratitude, unable to do much else.

Splinters pricked my fingers as I pulled at the old wood we'd found piled outside and wedged across the door. I ignored them and kept pulling as the pounding continued. The hand I'd scraped along the tree bark burned with the effort, but at least the bandage was protecting it from further damage. If only I had gloves to protect both hands, but I didn't have the time. Someone was out there, and whoever it was, they were in even greater danger than us. My hands would heal, but a life taken would never be returned.

"Adel...ken ... are y...there?"

I broke my attention away from the door for a split second to glance at Mother before doubling my efforts to tug at the wood. I didn't recognize the voice but, distorted as it was by the wind, it could have been anyone. Even Father. We had to get the door open.

"We're here," I screamed, as loud as I could. "In here."

"Stand back."

The order was still registering in my mind when Mother tugged me aside, pulling me in against her as she wrapped her arms around me. The pounding stopped for a moment before changing. Whoever it was had found something heavier to use. They weren't trying to pound on the door anymore, they were trying to break it down.

I closed my eyes, tucking my head against my mother's chest like I had so many times as a child. She was singing again. Even through the noise of the storm and the battering, I could hear it.

My skirt flew aside, my hair blinding me as the door suddenly broke open, letting in a gust of wind so strong it toppled both of us. Strong hands reached for me, and I found myself pulled roughly into another embrace. Even before I saw his face, I knew it was Ben. I was bent back awkwardly as he reached down to pull Mother in, crushing us both against him.

"You're alive. Thank God, you're alive."

The words rumbled his chest where it lay against my ear. I wanted to be furious at him for coming and being so stupid as to put his life in danger for us. He could have been killed. He still might. Instead I clung to him like the anchor he was, grateful beyond anything I could ever put into words that he was here.

"Come on, we have to go," Ben shouted as he tugged us toward the still open door.

"What? No." We couldn't. Even the scant bit of protection the cottage offered was better than being out there. We'd never make it. And even if by some miracle we did, I'd be better off dead if the king saw us together.

"Kenna, we have to. This wind is nothing compared to what's coming. The worst of it hasn't arrived yet. We have to get back to the palace. Now." He pushed me out the door before I could protest again. The wind took away anything I might have said anyway.

"I can't—"

A strong arm clamped around my back. "Let's go."

There was so much dust in the air I could barely see, yet Ben seemed to know where to go. Huddled together like a six-legged beast, Ben in the middle, his strength urging Mother and me forward, the three of us staggered toward the palace. No one was foolish enough to still be out in this whirlwind, yet Ben had come for us. I didn't know whether I thought him brave, stupid, or plain out of his mind crazy, but I was thankful. Or, at least, I would be once we made it to the palace. Right now, I was quite happy to hate him.

A tree branch flew past us, followed quickly by a fence paling. I closed my eyes, not wanting to see what came next. The last time I'd come across this field, it had been covered with purple wildflowers. Today, they were all gone. Every single one of them. The wind had taken them prisoner the same way it was threatening to take us.

I stumbled, falling to the ground. The wind wasn't merely threatening. It was taking us. I couldn't do it. Much as I wanted to, I couldn't make my legs go anymore.

The temptation to give into it was almost stronger than the wind itself. I was already exhausted from climbing the hills before racing the storm home. Would it really be so bad to give up?

Two sets of hands pulled me to my feet again, taking the choice from me. Now I was the one in the middle as Mother and

Ben all but carried me forward. With every step, the wind tried to pry us apart. With an almost inhuman strength, we held fast. Staying together was our only hope of making it.

"There it is."

Looming above us, like an island appearing out of the mist, was the palace. That which I'd thought so foreboding this morning had suddenly become a haven. *Our* haven.

Though walking was easier once we reached the outer walls, being sheltered at least on one side from the wind, it was no less dangerous with so much debris being hurled around. I knew I wouldn't breathe easily until we were safely ensconced within them.

"In here." I heard Ben say only moments before being pushed through an opening. We weren't inside the palace yet—only an outer courtyard—but the wind was immediately quieter, almost as if it knew it wasn't allowed beyond the palace walls. It was a fanciful thought, but I welcomed it, holding its whimsy close as I felt a fear barge in which had nothing to do with the whirlwind.

I was with Ben, and if the king didn't know it already, he would soon enough. It wouldn't matter that I hadn't been the one to seek Ben out or that my mother was with us. All the king would see would be my failure to obey him.

I pulled my arm out of Ben's, creating some distance between us. All it gained me was a frown as Ben tugged me back, putting his vice of an arm around me. We were even closer than we'd been before, yet I didn't have the strength to pull away again. Not physically, and not emotionally. Perhaps the king would be lenient given the circumstances. I could only hope.

We reached the outer door, Ben refusing to let go of me even as he pounded on it. His arm would be aching tomorrow—if we made it through tonight. Suddenly, I wasn't so sure. I'd never been in a wind so strong. Would the castle walls hold? Would all this around me be rubble tomorrow?

Before the morbid thoughts could take root, the door was opened. You would have thought the man guarding it had seen a ghost the way his sword clattered to the ground.

"Prince Thoraben. You're alive."

Ben shoved Mother and me inside, straining against the wind to pull the heavy door closed behind us. The guard, too, lent his strength to the battle. It took the combined strength of both men to secure it. I clung to Mother, my legs barely holding me as Ben and the guard conversed. "Hudson. Where is my father?"

"The Great Hall, Your Highness."

"Thank you. See to it that the rest of the guards know Lady Mackenna and her mother have been found, would you?"

"Of course, Your Highness. Right away. They will be relieved to hear it."

"As am I. Then get to the hall yourself. You'll be safe there."

Hudson shook his head. "No, Your Highness. With all due respect, I'll stay at my post. There may be others."

Ben was silent for a moment before clamping a hand on the guard's shoulder.

"Your loyalty is admirable, sir. I am in your debt."

Despite the wind and the urgency of the hour, I am certain Hudson had never stood taller than he did at that moment. It was one thing to claim to be loyal but another to stare down danger in the face for it. Even so, I hoped we were the last and that he wouldn't have to open the door again. With it shut, he should be safe. If he had to open it again? I didn't know what would become of him for, as Ben had said, the worst of the storm was still to come.

"The king is waiting, Your Highness. He's been asking for you."

"No doubt."

Something passed between the two men, something grim, but before I could wonder at its meaning, it was gone, and Ben was once again urging Mother and me forward. Hall after hall passed unseen as we ran until, there before us, loomed the wooden doors of the Great Hall. My lungs ached, my eyes stung, and I wondered if my legs would ever walk again, but we'd made it.

The doors flung open the instant Ben knocked. Silence washed like a wave from the door to the dais as people turned to see who'd come. I didn't see any of them, my eyes drawn instead to the king. He sat on his throne, at the front of the Great Hall, but there was nothing regal about his stance. His eyes were downcast as he leaned forward on his elbow, not even Alina's hand on his arm enough to draw his attention.

Until a guard whispered in his ear.

I didn't need to be beside him to know what he'd been told. His eyes immediately came up, searching out the door. The incredible relief he felt when he spotted Ben was visible even from this distance. Unfortunately, so was his instant displeasure.

His son had come home.

And he'd brought me. The enemy.

SEVENTEEN

To say the king was unhappy to see me was beyond a mere understatement. I half expected him to throw me back out into the whirlwind, in front of what seemed to be three quarters of the kingdom. He didn't, but I'm certain he wanted to, the way he glowered at me.

With a wave of his hand, he gestured for Ben to join him. Ben shook his head. The king tried again, more emphatically this time. Again, Ben shook his head, before doing the worst thing he could have—turning his attention to me. I waited nervously for the shout to come sealing my fate.

"Mackenna?"

What? Oh. Ben must have said something. "Sorry. What did you say?" Over Ben's shoulder, the king was speaking to the guard again. They kept looking our way. This was it. My end. The king had ordered me not to go near his son and here I was, standing right beside him, Ben's arm around my back the only thing holding me up. With a final nod and a quick bow, the guard walked off the dais and began picking his way around people toward us.

"Mackenna."

I'd missed what Ben said again. "Sorry."

He shook his head. "Let's go."

"Where?"

"To find you a bandage. You might not care that you're dripping blood, but I do."

I looked down at my hand. Sure enough, the bandage was not only soaked with deep red blood but studded with splinters. I held my other hand up. It was almost as bad. Amidst the terror of the past half hour, I hadn't even noticed. But like Ben had turned on a switch with his words, my hands started throbbing.

"Don't worry. Mother can—"

"Go and find your father. Yes, what a wonderful idea."

What? That wasn't what I was going to suggest, and he knew it. But Mother was nodding.

"Thank you, Thoraben. You'll stay with Mackenna?"

"Of course, Mrs. Adeline."

Wait. Did I have any say in this? Had my opinion ceased to matter?

"We'll find you later. Take care."

Ben reached out to embrace Mother, whispering something in her ear, before she thanked him again and left. She didn't even say goodbye to me. I wanted to be angry at her but was too ashamed of how selfish I'd been, so caught up in my own world that I hadn't even thought to look for Father. Of course, Mother would want to know he was safe. I did too. I hoped they both came back soon. Together.

"Now. Let's go."

"I can go myself."

"And collapse somewhere on your own? Kenna, don't be a fool. You can barely walk as it is."

I gritted my teeth, both against the pain and his overactive sense of duty. I wasn't his sister to protect. I wasn't even supposed to be his friend. One only had to look at the king, still glowering at me, to know that. Thank heavens for the huddled crowd which had slowed down the guard. I still had time to get away.

"I'd hardly be alone with all these people around. Thank you for coming for Mother and me—I have no doubt we owe you our lives—but you're forgetting your responsibility is to the people and the king."

"Truly, Kenna? You think far too little of yourself. Last I

checked, you are a person and, like you said, the best way I can serve the king right now is to care for the people. What sort of ruler would it make me if I saw one of my people hurt and didn't stop to help?" He took a blanket from one of the servants handing them out and wrapped it around my shoulders. "Now, stop arguing."

"But—"

"Let's go."

I closed my mouth, swallowing back what I'd been about to suggest. Casual as his words were, there was no mistaking them for anything other than a command. I'd heard him use that voice before, the one I'd secretly dubbed his "king voice," and there was no point in arguing. As it was, I almost curtseyed my acquiescence.

"Very well. But then you'll go back to your father."

"If you still want me to."

If Ben had looked at my face, he would have seen the scowl there. Directed entirely at him and his high-handedness. He didn't look. It was probably for the best. He was the prince after all, and that position demanded respect, even if it was begrudgingly given. Still, I gave the blanket away to the first person I saw who needed it. The elderly gentleman thanked me profusely. I smiled at him and reminded myself that I would have given it away even if it hadn't been in protest. I might not have been a princess, but these were my people as much as they were Ben's.

It didn't take long to find Doctor Merler and his assembly of helpers, something I was most thankful for. Ben had been right about how weary I was. I could have sat down in the middle of a mud puddle in the pouring rain and not even cared. We joined the end of the line waiting for medical help. It was long. Too long, apparently, for Ben.

"Wait here. I'll be right back."

He was gone before I could assure him I wasn't going anywhere.

My heart ached almost as much as my hand as I looked at those around me, so many of them injured, though not seriously.

To my immense relief. Scratches, gashes, dust-induced cough-ing, a few splinted arms and legs. Painful, certainly, but not life-threatening. Of course, these were only the people who'd made it inside. There was no telling what we'd find outside the palace once the storm had passed.

Ella and Esme. Had they made it? Mrs. Olive? Mr. Slaughter? Mr. Stanley, the doorman? The farmers on the outskirts of Pe-verell. Had they found shelter in time? They had to have. Surely, or else—I pushed the morbid thought from my mind, unable to bear to finish it. There was nothing I could do about it tonight, and I'd only torture myself worrying.

"Here, let me help," I said instead to the mother in front of me, trying one-handedly to put a coat on her toddler while holding a bandage against a gash on her other child's arm. Not that I was much help, the tips of my fingers the only parts of my hands now not covered in blood. I sent a grateful smile Ben's way when he got back and took over, tickling laughter out of the child in the process.

"Now you," Ben said to me as soon as the toddler was dressed. He held up bandages and two tubes of ointment, his expression refusing to brook any disagreement. I should have argued him anyway—there were people who needed his help far more than me—but I'd be no use to anyone with my hands like this. I hoped at least one of those ointments was a painkiller.

"Let's sit..." Ben looked around the room. For a chair, I as-sumed. He was wasting his time. There weren't any. The Great Hall was so crowded with people huddled in their little groups that there was barely any room to sit at all. "Over there."

He pointed to the very back of the hall, near one of the arches which led to the kitchens. People sat there but it wasn't nearly as crowded as the rest of the hall. Of course, that would involve picking our way over and through a few hundred more people to get there.

"Let's just stay here," I suggested, not sure my legs would make it that far.

"I could carry you..."

On second thoughts, I'd make them. There was no way I was letting Ben carry me in full view of half our kingdom. Or ever.

It took far longer than it should have to reach the back of the hall, partly because my legs shook, threatening to collapse with every step I took but mostly because we stopped to talk to so many people on the way. Or rather, I did. Ben hurried me away each time I even thought about saying more than just a hello.

Finally, we made it. Ben plonked himself down on the floor beside an arch, kicking off his shoes to more comfortably sit. I let my legs collapse like they'd been begging to do for the past half hour and ungracefully followed suit, wincing as my left hand hit the floor.

Ben placed the ointment and bandages beside him before reaching out. "Give me your hands."

I kept them in my lap. "I can do it."

"And I can do it better. Give them to me."

I didn't want to but didn't really have a choice. Stubborn as I was, and full of far too much pride, I could barely move my fingers anymore, let alone unwrap, anoint, and re-wrap them. I cringed looking at them. Ashe hadn't been too far off blaming a grater for the damage. There were splinters on top of splinters and more cuts than I cared to count. And that was only what I could see. The worst of it was still bandaged from this morning's tree-climbing escapade. I closed my eyes, taking in a deep breath before letting it out again and opening them. That seemed a lifetime ago. Had it truly only been this morning? If only coming up with an excuse for being in a tree was my biggest problem right now.

"Sorry, this is going to hurt."

It already did. I gritted my teeth. "Do it."

Despite my resolve to be strong, tears dribbled down my face as he slowly extricated the bandage from the mess the bark had made of my hand. I looked away, trying to focus instead on something else. Anything else.

The guard the king had sent was standing still, his head the only thing moving as he searched. He must have lost us once we sat down. It was a reprieve, but not much of one. He'd find us soon enough.

Everywhere I looked, there were people. Old, young, rich, poor—social standings swept away as servants and highborn took shelter beside each other. The last time the Great Hall had been this full had been at the Midsummer's Ball. Only that night, everyone had been clothed in ballgowns and finery. Now, many of those same people sat in solemn groups, clothed in various styles of dress, all coated in dust. Every so often, I heard a laugh, but even they were dry, as if a parent was trying to distract their child from the misery of it all but couldn't quite distract themselves. I hated that I could do nothing to help them.

"The hospital..." Roni, Martin, Jordana—they'd never have the strength to make it to the palace. The Rebels wouldn't attack it, but weather had no code of ethics. It struck rich and poor, sick and well.

"They'll be fine. The hospital is as strong as the palace."

"Are you sure?"

"Yes, I'm—What happened to your hand?"

Ben's horror pulled my attention back to his ministrations. It didn't take more than a glance to see what had him so shocked. I'd been grateful for the bandage covering my hand as I'd been fortifying the cottage, and then pulling those fortifications down again to let Ben in. I'd thought it was protecting my injuries. Now, much of the bandage removed, I saw how wrong I'd been. It hadn't been protecting my hand at all. It had been making it worse. The bandage had become embedded inside the gashes.

"I slipped."

He let out a short laugh. "On what? A gravel road? A tiger's claw?"

"Tree bark. I was climbing a tree."

"Why?"

"It seemed like a good idea at the time." The real answer felt even more foolish now than it had when Ashe had asked earlier.

"Princesses don't climb trees," Ben teased.

I shrugged. "In case you haven't noticed, I'm not a princess."

"Believe me, I've noticed."

I didn't know what to make of that comment, so I said nothing at all, letting the conversation fall flat. It was taking all my concentration not to pull my hand away and huddle in a ball and cry anyway. I didn't have any left to consider what his cryptic words might mean. If they meant anything.

"Almost there..."

I tried to feel grateful for his help, knowing it had to be done, but it was a challenge. I almost wished he'd stop being so careful and rip the bandage off, no matter how much of my hand it took with it. At least once that was done, he could get on with the process of healing them.

"How's Ashe?" I heard him ask through a daze of pain.

"What?"

"Ashe Marsh. You've forgotten him already? He must have made quite a poor impression."

"I didn't forget him. I saw him this morning."

"Oh? And I suppose he's swept you off your feet already?"

Despite the pain, I almost laughed at that question. Ashe hadn't literally swept me off my feet, to be exact, but he had rescued me twice now and carried me down a tree in his arms.

Not that that was what Ben was asking. Still...

"No, but you know that tree I climbed? He carried me down."

I wasn't going to say it, but I couldn't resist. Ben's reaction was well worth the embarrassment of the admission. His eyebrows shot up into his hair and he almost dropped the tweezers he'd been using.

"Do I want to know how that came about?"

"Probably not."

"I could ask Ashe."

"He'd be too much of a gentleman to tell you."

"You know him well then. He must have made quite an impression after all."

He'd made an impression, certainly, but not what Ben was thinking.

I sighed. "Honestly? He's in love with someone else."

I watched Ben's face closely as I said it, intrigued by the slight smile I saw there.

"Ah. Jade. I wondered when he'd realize she was back."

So, Ben knew about Jade. Ashe must have told him, or perhaps Wenderley. From what Alina had told me, Ben and Wenderley had been spending a lot of time together. Of course, he'd enquire after Wenderley's family. I wondered how much Ben knew. Did he know Jade was one of the Rebels?

Did he know Ashe was?

I was still trying to understand what it meant myself. Did it make me an accessory to their crime if I knew but didn't report it? Maybe I should tell Ben. Unlike his father, I trusted Ben. He would do what was right. I could tell him right now, casually drop it into the conversation. We'd been talking about Jade and Ashe anyway. It wouldn't be that difficult.

"Okay. All clean. Ready for the sting?"

Or I could wait for a better time. I sighed again. Had I always been such a coward?

"No. But go ahead anyway."

I didn't know what the ointment was that Ben splashed on both my hands but it might as well have been acid. I gasped at the pain, blinking furiously to try to stop more tears falling. He dabbed the excess away with a cotton ball before lathering a far more soothing cream over top. The bandage was next. For the second time in a day, I watched while a man bandaged my hand. Only Ben went one step further than Ashe had. When he was finished, he raised my bandaged hand to his lips and kissed it.

I rolled my eyes. "A kiss, really, Thoraben?"

"A kiss makes everything better—and this hand definitely needs to get better."

"A kiss from a mother, perhaps."

"Oh, is that how it works?" He grinned. Like he didn't know.

"You're crazy."

"You're—"

"Prince Thoraben." A voice interrupted whatever Ben had been about to say. I looked up, peering into the face of a man

I vaguely recognized but didn't know by name. The guard had finally found us. I wished he'd waited a second more to speak. I wanted to know what Ben had been about to call me. "The king requests your presence immediately."

"Yes. I thought as much." Though acknowledging the message, Ben made no move to stand. Wiping his hands clean with a cloth, he stared up at the guard. "Your name, sir?"

"Gunn Maxwell, Your Highness."

Ben nodded. "Thank you, Mr. Maxwell, for delivering my father's message. If you wouldn't mind passing one to him, you may tell him that I am seeing to the needs of the people and will not be joining him tonight. I will speak with him tomorrow."

Maxwell didn't move. "The king was quite adamant that you join him."

"As am I adamant that I will not. Please see that my father gets the message. If he is unhappy with you because of it, you may tell him that I am only doing what he has told me every day of my life—that a king's greatest responsibility is to his people."

"Yes, Your Highness."

I watched as Maxwell bowed and started picking his way back through the people. I didn't blame him for taking the long way. I wouldn't have wanted to face the king either—especially being the bearer of bad news.

The door behind us opened, letting out a gust of air along with the trio of servants carrying cups, bread rolls, and jugs of water. I took a drink and snack gratefully, wishing I'd thought of it myself. The kitchens were just behind that door. Ben and I could—I groaned. Do nothing. Absolutely nothing. Not with my hands bandaged like they were. Useless. Utterly useless. Still, Ben could—

"Don't even think about it, Kenna. I'm staying with you."

He knew me far too well.

"He's going to be in trouble, you know," I said instead, trying to distract myself from the frustration of it all. "Maxwell, I mean."

Ben leaned back against the wall. "I doubt it. Father is a fair man—and he knew already what my response would be."

"He'll blame me. He already does."

"And, like I said in my letter which I would like to assume you read, he's wrong. You're not the enemy here. Father might have treated you abominably, but that doesn't mean I have to follow suit."

"Still, you should go to him."

"I told your mother I'd wait with you."

"Thorab—"

"How are your hands?"

He wasn't going to listen to my convincing. Fine. I would stop trying. "Better. Thanks."

"Any other injuries I should know about?"

"No." Fortunately. It could have been far worse. "A little cold. I wish I had my red hoodie right now." It was stupid but, now my hands had been taken care of, it was all I wanted. That familiar piece of comfort and warmth. A shiver trembled through me, prickling the skin on my bare arms.

"What happened to your blanket?"

"Gave it away."

"Of course you did." He started to stand. "Wait here, I'll find you another one."

I stopped him before he could. "No, don't. I'll be fine."

"Kenna..."

"They need them more."

He sighed and shook his head as he sat down before shrugging out of his jacket and handing it to me. "Take this then."

Though I took it, I didn't put it on. "Then you'll be cold."

"I'll be fine. I had more layers than you to start with."

I frowned. His dress shirt's sleeves might have buttoned at his wrists, but the thin cotton would do little to protect him from the evening's rapidly-dropping temperature. Still, I held the jacket to my chest, debating with myself. It was warm, yet it was his.

"I shouldn't."

"Put it on, Kenna."

With a small yet grateful smile, I wrapped the jacket around my shoulders, reveling in its instant warmth. This was the Ben I'd missed—kind, considerate, just as stubborn as me.

"Better?"

I nodded. "Thanks."

Though my hands were taken care of, Ben continued to stare at me as if I were the only person in the room. I didn't know why. My long hair was so knotted it would likely have to be cut off at the nape to ever have a chance of being straight again. With my hands bandaged, I couldn't even try to neaten it. My skirt and top were as brown as the dust around us and felt just as gritty. I didn't even want to know what the mixture of tears, blood, and dirt had painted on my face. My cheeks alternately stung and prickled as if my hair continued to whip against them, even though I knew it didn't.

Ben opened his mouth, then closed it again, shaking his head. Still he didn't take his eyes off me. A tear trickled down his cheek, forging a shiny path through the dust for two more to follow.

"Thoraben?"

He shook his head again. "I was so worried. No one knew where you were, and the storm was getting worse. I had the palace searched and watched every person entering the hall for hours but still you didn't come. I thought the worst."

"And you came out anyway?"

"I had to try."

I reached out a bandaged hand to touch his arm, the tips of my fingers brushing down it for less than a second before pulling back. I shouldn't touch him, especially not with so many people witness to it, though few—if any—looked our way. But I'd never seen Ben cry before and seeing it now tore at my heart with an almost physical pain. He was supposed to be the strong one. He always had been. He couldn't fall apart now. If he did, I knew I would.

The door opened again, letting two more servants and their refreshments through. I waited for them to pass before speaking again.

"I'm so sorry. I didn't know I had guards. I wouldn't have left the house without them if I had."

"I probably should have told you, but I didn't want you to feel threatened by their presence. They were there to watch and protect you, not make you feel as if you were still chained to the palace and this life you'd left. They had orders to keep their distance and not approach you unless absolutely necessary. If I'd told them to stick closer, this would never have happened. I'm sorry."

"No, please, it's not your fault. Nor theirs." Though I'd have to apologize to them, once we were actually introduced. They must have been frantic. "We're safe now, thanks to you. You saved us."

Ben offered a tremulous smile. "I wasn't alone."

He must have been speaking about Hudson, who'd let us into the palace, or perhaps the guards who'd helped him look for there hadn't been anyone else with Ben when he knocked down our door. Certainly not the king, who hadn't stopped glowering at me since I arrived.

Ben swiped the tears from his face, the weakness he'd shown along with them. A smear of mud across his white sleeve cuff the only proof left that he'd even cried. There he was, in control again. "You're shaking," he said. "You should try to get some sleep."

"Here?" The floor was hard wood, the wind still whistled through the turrets, and every few minutes, it seemed, the door behind us would open to let servants through from the kitchens. Dust filled the air, laughing at the strength of the bricks not able to keep it out and giving each light a halo. People talked. Babies and young children cried. Likely many of the adults did too. It would be an uncomfortable slumber at best.

"You'll be safe here."

"You'll stay?"

I didn't want to ask it of him. Didn't want to sound so needy, especially when there were so many people here worse off than me. But I also didn't want to be alone in this crowd of people. I'd never been truly alone in a crowd before—people always kept a safe distance from Alina and me and the guards watching us wherever we went. It was so different tonight. Alina sat on the dais with the king, and Mother and Father still hadn't returned, though I had to believe they were both safe. Ben was all I had.

"For as long as you need me."

I went to sleep determined to ignore the voice in my head which told me that that might just be forever.

EIGHTEEN

It was snowing. Tiny flakes of ice fell on my face, kissing my cheeks and turning instantly to water. I should have gone inside, but I'd never felt so warm. Nor so cherished.

"Can't catch me," I yelled, giggling as I took off again, knowing it would be only moments before I'd be caught. The snow was deep, trapping each step I took before reluctantly releasing it, and Ben had always been a faster runner than me. Plus, we both knew I wasn't really trying. I wanted him to catch me.

I heard his shout of glee the instant before his arms closed around my waist, pulling me to him. "Gotcha," he whispered against my ear. The shivers racing down my spine had nothing to do with the temperature outside. "Going to run again, Kenna?"

"Going to catch me?"

I didn't need to see his face to know he was grinning. "Every time."

I couldn't help the goofy smile that covered my own face. I loved it when he quit being a prince and was simply my husband. "Maybe I'll stay."

"Maybe I'll like it."

"Oh yeah?"

"Yeah."

I turned around to face him, still captured in his arms and looped my arms around his neck. I could have stared at that contented smile on his face all day. Knowing that I'd been the one to put it there felt...absolutely wonderful.

"I love you, my Kenna."

It was hard to tell with the snow falling and trees applauding in the wind, but I think I might have sighed with happiness. "And I love you, B—"

A handful of icy slush slid down my neck.

"Ben!"

My mock outrage only made him laugh more as he loped out of retaliation's reach. I chased him a whole two steps before losing my balance and falling into the snow. At least I managed to twist enough to land on my shoulder rather than my face. I lay there long enough to bring Ben back, a silhouette against the brightness of the sky above.

"Need a hand?"

"Sure."

He held one out to pull me up. I tugged at it instead, pulling him down beside me, grinning in silent victory—until he rubbed his icy face against mine. My squeal was lost in his kisses, his strong arm pulling me close...

"Do you think it's stopped?"

"I hope so. Can you imagine how much destruction it must have caused?"

Nearby voices cut sharply into my sleepy bliss. I snuggled further into the dream, hoping it would stay. I wasn't ready to let it go yet. The bright snow on the mountains, Ben's bear-eared beanie he insisted on wearing which I secretly loved despite my protests, the way he held me close as we lay there together...

"Kenna..."

"Ben..."

"Wake up, sleepyhead."

My eyes flung open. That muttering right beside my ear was no dream. Nor was his arm across my shoulder or the blanket covering me. Partly covering him. This was not—That was not—He couldn't— My thoughts skipped from revelation to revelation, never quite landing, except on one thing. Ben wasn't my husband.

"Get away from me."

I sat up quickly, throwing the blanket aside and skittering out of Ben's reach as my terrified screech filled the hall. Whispers turned into low mutterings as I and my welfare became the center of attention. My stomach roiled. What had I done? Far from frozen, my face burned with humiliation. I wished I could take the words back, especially when I saw Ben's hands raised in the air, shock and pleading on his face.

"Kenna, what—?"

His gentle whisper was more than I could bear. I closed my eyes against the confusion I saw in his. That's when I heard what people were saying.

"...touched her..."

"...Prince Thoraben and Lady Mackenna..."

"...the law..."

"...because he's the prince?"

My heart sank more and more with each phrase I caught but it almost stopped when I heard one word repeated above the rest: "marriage."

"No!" I all but shouted. The murmurs stopped. "It was all a mistake. Just a dream. He didn't—"

"Mackenna, stop. It doesn't matter."

I shrank back from the hand Ben went to put on my arm. I couldn't let him touch me. At all. I shrugged out of his jacket and handed that back too, shivering at the sudden change in temperature. People thought—I put my hands to my face, wishing for some snow right now to cool it. Cool me. Dump an avalanche on me even. Anything to rescue me from this disaster of my own making.

"What am I going to do?"

"Nothing. There's no need to do anything. Well..." Ben smiled wryly. "You could calm down. That would help. Your terror isn't really helping the situation any. It looks to everyone here like you're scared of me."

I looked down at my hands, bandaged and likely scarred forever. He was closer to the truth than he realized, though not for the reasons he was thinking. I wasn't scared of him acting inappropriately toward me, I was scared of the way he'd made me feel in the dream—and utterly terrified my heart would believe it could be real.

"Try breathing. You know. In, out, in, out. Ah, there's that smile. It almost looks like you mean it. Would you like me to tell you a yeti joke? I've been coming up with some good ones."

That made me laugh. Albeit shakily. Ben was a great prince, but he'd yet to master the art of telling jokes—not that Alina or I had managed to convince him of the fact. His timing was perfect, but his punchlines made no sense. Of course, that was amusing in itself.

"Thanks, but no thanks."

"I'm hurt."

"You'll live." I, on the other hand... I took a breath, willing the oxygen to fix my life along with my lungs. *Kenna, what have you done? Get up. Walk away. Before you ruin Ben's life as well as yours.*

My legs felt sluggish when I tried to move them. If not for their ache registering in my mind, I would have wondered if they belonged to someone else's body. I put a hand to the floor to steady myself, reminded with a gasping flash of pain what a bad idea that was. The hand shook as I cradled it against my chest, resigned to the fact that I'd be staying here on the ground until someone helped me up. Someone *not* Ben, who was still looking at me with that amused half-grin, as if this was all some grand joke.

"What did you dream?"

"What?" There was no way I was telling him about my dream. Ever. I couldn't even look him in the eye now without remembering the way his dream-self had looked at me.

"Was I in it?"

"No."

"Liar."

"Says who?"

"That blush painting your face red."

Betrayed by my own face. The enduring trials of the auburn-haired. I could have tried to convince him it was windburn, but he'd never believe it. He would have merely told me I protested too much.

"You're rude," I said instead.

"And you're still blushing. Oh dear. Did you know your ears are purple? Actually purple. Well, maybe burgundy. It must have been a really good dream..."

"Oh, be quiet." I wasn't normally this grumpy in the morning. I was definitely blaming Ben for it—both the man sitting in front of me and his dream version.

"Nope. This is good. You're breathing, laughing, and talking to me. And if you'd look up from the floor long enough to look around, you'd see that we're no longer the center of attention. You convinced them it was nothing."

"I did?" I looked around, shocked to see that he was right. With the exception of a few still staring our way, indulgent smiles on their faces, most of the people had gone back to their conversations or gone from the hall altogether.

"You did." He leaned a little closer, bestowing upon me an almost imperceptible wink. "But I'd still like to know about that dream."

Ben didn't need to tell me my ears were purple, or burgundy, or whatever color he'd now decided. I could feel them burning. It was a wonder my hair didn't catch fire.

"So, the storm has stopped?"

He laughed at my not so subtle attempt to change the topic but graciously let me have it. Even so, I doubted that would be the end of it. He'd ask again, when I least expected it. I'd blushed far too much through his questioning to pass the dream off as nothing.

"The guards will know. Here come two now. Look, it's Maxwell. You see? My father hasn't stripped him of his employment. I told you Father would be fair." Ben waited until the two men were within a yard or so before talking. "Gentlemen, Lady Mackenna wishes to know about the storm. You've been outside the hall, I take it? How does the rest of Peverell fare?"

Neither of the guards smiled. Nor did they answer Ben's question. Instead, they looked directly at me. My smile vanished, fear once again taking its place.

"Miss Mackenna Sparrow, you are hereby summoned to appear before the king. You will come with us now."

Ben stood to his feet, putting himself between me and the guards. "What? Why? What has she done?"

"We are only following the king's orders, Your Highness."

"Then I'm coming too."

"As you wish."

I didn't say a word as Ben helped me up. There was nothing to say. I brushed some of the dust off my skirt but couldn't get it all. My clothes were gritty, my hands covered in cuts and bandages, my hair a mess, and my whole body aching from sleeping on the floor. I couldn't have felt any less prepared to stand before the king.

I made the mistake of looking at Ben. He was telling me something with his eyes, begging me to understand, but I was too mortified by the situation to pay enough attention. More than anything, I wanted to go hide, only I couldn't even do that.

"Don't worry, Mackenna," I heard Ben whisper. "All will be well."

We were being taken to the throne room. The guards, normally so casual with Ben and me, were stone-faced. I half expected them to put the two of us in shackles. We might as well have been. We were being led to our judgement. At least, I was. The doors to the throne room loomed. I didn't know what we'd face once we walked through them. I had to get Ben's attention now.

"Hey," I breathed out, turning my head in his direction, wishing I had the time to say more. "Sorry."

"Not your fault."

"But it was." One of the guards turned and frowned at me. I lowered my voice to a whisper. "You didn't do anything."

"I know, and Father will too. We'll explain. All will be well, Kenna. Trust me."

The doors opened, and I gasped. Now I knew where all the people from the Great Hall had gone. They must have come directly here. I'd never seen the room so crowded with people. No, that was wrong. I'd seen it with this many people before, only they'd been lined up formally as they waited to speak with the king, or sitting in chairs listening, not packed in groups whispering loudly to each other.

Not even the king was exempt from the mess, surrounded by wildly gesturing advisors speaking over one another in an attempt to be heard. Mr. Grant-Hartley was the one exception. He stood back, silent and considering. Would he take my side if it came to it? As my parents' friend, he'd always seemed the most approachable of the king's advisors.

"Miss Mackenna Sparrow."

My name rang clear from the king's lips, silencing the disgruntled crowd. They parted, leaving a wide walkway between me and the king. I took a deep breath, desperately searching for a courage I didn't have. Surrounded by so many witnesses, there was nowhere to hide.

"Wait."

Walking around in front of me, Ben turned his back on his father and shielded me from the king's gaze. Even knowing it couldn't last, I clung to the moment's respite.

"Kenna, I know you think this is all a mistake and you're probably already planning your escape to some far-off country that's never even heard of Peverell, let alone its royal family, but it'll be okay. It really will. Trust me." He offered me his arm again. I ached to take it and accept the support it—he—offered, but I couldn't. If ever there was a time to keep my distance, it was now. I shook my head. He dropped the arm but not the invitation. "Come on. Let's go sort this out."

If I had been bolder, more awake even, I would have told Ben to stay behind. The king had called only for me. I wasn't bold.

It was a long, silent walk.

I curtsied before the king, shame as thick on me as the dust. Ben stood tall at my side. He seemed so strong. I wondered if he was. It must have been strange for him to be on this side of the throne. Usually, Ben sat beside his father as the king meted out judgements. I couldn't remember a time he'd ever been on the side of the one awaiting judgement. King Everson was none too happy about it either.

"I didn't ask for you, Thoraben."

"And yet, this matter involves us both. Mackenna would not be here, standing before you today, if not for me. She might not have even made it through the storm."

"I will deal with the matter of your disobedience later. You can be assured of that. Right now, I wish only to hear from Miss Sparrow. I would appreciate it if you would let me."

Ben ducked his head slightly. "Yes, Father."

The touch on my arm was so light it would have looked to everyone else like Ben accidentally bumped me, but I knew it was no accident. Ben could have walked away. He should have. His father had made that more than clear. Instead, he continued to stand beside me, lending me his strength. No matter what happened today, I would find a way to thank him for that.

"Miss Mackenna Sparrow, did you or did you not accuse my son of inappropriate behavior this morning in the Great Hall?"

"No, Your Majesty. I did not."

"Then you accuse these witnesses here who claim you told Prince Thoraben to get away from you of lying?"

"No. I did—"

"Either you did or you didn't, Miss Sparrow. It is not that difficult a question."

"I told Prince Thoraben to get away from me but—"

"Why?"

It was a demand more than a question, and one that came with no right answer. Anything I said would earn me the king's censure.

"I was dreaming, Your Majesty. Prince Thoraben startled me."

"Did he touch you?"

I felt as if every answer I gave dug my grave deeper. What had happened was so inconsequential—or, it would have been had it been any other man. Had I been any other girl. What should have been an honest mistake to laugh over was now a matter of the court of the king. I could only imagine what my fate would have been had they known Ben had once kissed me. At least that would have been partially worth this ridiculous circus. Ben had merely touched me on the shoulder.

"Yes, but it wasn't—"

"Ah. You see, Your Majesty? She admits to it. Your son claimed this woman as his own."

My stomach wretched at the advisor's words. "No!" I cried. "He didn't. It was my shoulder. He only touched my shoulder. He was trying to wake me."

My protests were ignored as the advisor swooped in on the king's attention.

"And what of during the night, Your Majesty? Can anyone vouch for their integrity then? The people claim Prince Thoraben slept beside this woman, giving her his coat, sharing his blanket."

I shook my head, swallowing back the fear that threatened to overcome me and the incredulity of the man's claims. They'd all been in the Great Hall last night. Hundreds of people had. Were they all to be questioned also? And to question Ben's integrity simply for giving away his coat was ridiculous. He should have been commended for his compassion, not condemned. As to the blanket, where had it even come from?

Fury gripped the king like a puppet as it pulled him from his throne, silencing me before I could offer any defense on Ben's behalf. For once, though, it wasn't me his anger was directed at. The nosy advisor held that honor.

"I have no need for anyone to vouch for such a thing and you, sir, overstep your authority to even suggest it. What you and they are insinuating occurred is ludicrous. My son would never behave so inappropriately. With her of all people. He knows the law."

My mind full of defenses and dread-filled scenarios, the barb the king's words sent my way barely even hurt, though it certainly caused the murmurs to start up again. The whole kingdom now knew exactly what their king thought of the girl who'd once been like a daughter to him. I couldn't believe this was happening. Everyone knew—at least, everyone whose opinion mattered—that we had done nothing wrong.

Mr. Grant-Hartley stepped forward then, putting a hand on his pushy colleague's shoulder, silencing him with a stare before looking at me. I wanted to shrink down, to somehow hide within myself so he couldn't see me. Instead, I stood taller, daring him to find me guilty. With a slow nod that sealed my fate, he turned to the king.

"The people are demanding a wedding."

NINETEEN

I gasped at Mr. Grant-Hartley's words. He hadn't proclaimed me guilty, but he might as well have. There would have been no need for a marriage if he'd thought us innocent, and though he'd claimed it was the people demanding it, he never would have announced it to the king unless he agreed with them. But for me to marry Ben? Peverell's crown prince? He couldn't be serious.

The dream echoed in my head. It had been wonderful, a feeling of being cherished beyond anything I could have ever wished. But there was no way it was real, or ever could be. Not only did Prince Thoraben not love me that way, but he would never marry a commoner. It would benefit no one. I didn't even know why the people were demanding it, except—

No. I did know. They wanted me to be queen, and suddenly they had a way to make it happen. For all I knew, they'd planned it. Seen an opportunity and placed a blanket over us while we slept. Whether or not Ben had done anything wrong, there was enough suspicion to force a marriage.

But would suspicion be enough to convict us? Especially regarding such an outdated law. There was no proof to be had. King Everson was staunchly against the idea, and I'd already denied anything happening. All it would take was Ben's word and this whole craziness would be over. I was surprised he'd been so silent.

"The law states that if a man touches an unmarried woman inappropriately, he is to marry her immediately," Mr. Grant-Hartley said. "Prince Thoraben is not exempt from the law. He must face the same consequences any other man would."

King Everson sat back down, calmly adjusting his coat before speaking. "The law also states that a man must be guilty. You have no proof, therefore you have no case."

"He was seen coming into the Great Hall last night with the girl in tow, he stayed with her rather than returning to your side when you summoned him, even going so far as to choose the furthest place from anyone else to be with her, tucked in that archway as they were. She wore his clothing and shared his blanket, and her scream for him to get away from her was what most of the room woke up to. You cannot deny the facts, Your Majesty."

"But I can deny he acted wrongly with this woman."

"This woman grew up in your palace, Your Majesty."

"Something I am most assuredly regretting right now. I should have sent her away long ago. My son, however, is blameless. By Miss Sparrow's own admission, Thoraben did nothing wrong. Where there is no crime, there will be no punishment and certainly no wedding."

I let my gaze drop to the floor, relief making me weak. There would be no wedding. No matter what else the men decided, that much was certain.

"But the people, they're all saying—"

"The people are under my authority, as are you."

The king hadn't given me leave to go, but I was under no illusions that he wanted me to stay. The whirlwind had passed, and my presence here was no longer needed. I had no wish to hear again, in front of so many witnesses, how much the king detested me. This debate could take hours. When King Everson and his advisors finally came to a decision, they'd know where to find me.

I turned to leave, but Ben's warm hand on my arm stilled me. "I'll do it."

What? No. Ben couldn't be saying what it sounded like. He'd take back the words any second now. We all knew this whole thing was utter foolishness. The king rose out of his throne again, face reddening as he threw aside an offending advisor.

"I'll marry her."

I gasped, protests flying out of my mouth. "No. You can't. I won't."

King Everson slowly sat back in his throne, breathing deeply. The room was so silent I could almost hear him counting in his head.

One, breathe in.

Two, breathe out.

Three, don't get angry.

Four, stay in control.

Five, keep breathing.

When he spoke, it was calm. Relieved. "For once, it appears Miss Sparrow and I are in complete agreement. I will not let you marry this girl, Thoraben. As both your father and king, I forbid it. That is my final decision and it will not be entered into."

My relief was short-lived as Ben, unmoved by the king's edict, spoke again.

"No, Father. With all due respect, you're wrong. I will marry Lady Mackenna. You know I must. It is the only way to placate the people."

I dared not look anywhere but at the ground for fear that anything I said or did be further misconstrued. What was Ben doing, challenging his father in front of so many witnesses? Had he forgotten they were here? I certainly hadn't, though they barely even breathed lest they miss a word of the heated exchange.

"You would have these people believe you did something wrong?"

"They already do."

"Marrying this woman will only make that misguided assumption fact in their minds."

Still Ben stood strong. "Nevertheless, it is the right thing to do."

"You planned this."

Ben let out a short laugh. "I planned a whirlwind? Father, not even you are that powerful."

"This is not a time for jokes, Thoraben."

"No, it isn't. It's a time for standing up and proving our honor to the people. Of proving that we, as men and as rulers, can be trusted. It is a time for putting the people ahead of our own agendas. Isn't that what you've always taught me? That the good of the kingdom lies in the good of the people?"

His speech was so impassioned, I wanted to applaud at the end of it—as someone at the edge of the hall actually did.

Instead, I was foolish enough to open my mouth. "Prince Thoraben. This is not about the people. This is a matter of honor."

He looked directly at me. "Yes, Lady Mackenna. It is."

I don't think we were talking about the same thing.

Ignoring the withering glare King Everson was leveling my way, I tugged Ben aside, far enough from the king and his advisors to let loose on him my own questions.

"What are you doing?" I hissed, barely keeping my temper in check.

"Marrying you." His casual answer only infuriated me more. If this was some foolish plan to save my honor at his own expense, I wouldn't do it. I was one person. One insignificant person. He was the future king. The people would forget this moment eventually. It would fade in their minds as more interesting occurrences took its place. But if he went through with this and actually married me? It would be written in the history books forever, the question of his integrity recorded for all eternity. I couldn't let him do it.

"You can't—"

"Do you hate me, Kenna?"

I sighed, shaking my head. Whatever I felt toward this man, it certainly wasn't hate. "No."

"Then trust me."

Giving me a look I couldn't decipher, he shrugged off the hand I'd placed on his arm and stalked over to the fray.

That was the third time this morning Ben had asked me to

simply trust him. Three times. Did he actually have a plan in all
this mess? I wished I could trust him like I had once, but I didn't
know if I could trust anyone right now. Not even myself. Yet it
didn't matter, for the decision had been taken out of my hands.
My marriage had potentially become as much a political stunt as
Alina's.

"A word, Father, in private, if you will."

"Clear the room."

I walked out of the room with everyone else, feeling as if my
life, not just my future, hung in the balance. All because of that
stupid dream. I should have let it go.

I spotted my parents talking quietly in a little alcove. I ran to
them, throwing myself into Mother's arms. Father wrapped his
arms around us both. They were safe. And they were here. Surely, they would be on my side.

"Mother, please, go talk some sense into Thoraben. He's telling the king he'll marry me."

"I know."

"Then you'll talk to him?"

"I can't, Mackenna. You know that."

Under normal circumstances, I would have agreed. No one interrupted the king. But nothing about this morning was normal.
Ben wouldn't listen to me, but I knew how much he respected
my parents. "Of course you can. You're my mother and you're
practically his too. He'll listen to you."

She barely even considered my plea before answering. "Perhaps. But would marrying him truly be so terrible?"

"What?" I moved out of their arms and tried to ignore the
muttering of people around us. At least if they were muttering,
they probably weren't eavesdropping. I hoped. "I'm not marrying
him, Mother." She'd missed the point entirely if she was thinking
that. Of all the times to start enforcing a law which should have
been thrown out decades ago. It had made sense once, certainly,
back when women had no rights and were more pawns than
people. But times changed. We didn't live in that world anymore.

There had to be some grace. Waitrose certainly claimed enough of it. "Shouldn't it be my choice too?"

"If you're scared of his affections, you needn't be. Thoraben has always cared for you. He would treat you well."

"I'm not scared of him." I couldn't believe she even thought that. I wasn't scared. Not of Ben. Confused by him, irritated no end, but not scared. At least, that's what I was telling myself.

"That's good to hear."

"Then you'll talk to him? Or Mr. Grant-Hartley? He'd listen."

Mother and Father looked at each other, leaving me out of their silent conversation. Their eyes were tired as they turned to me, but there was a resolve there that went beyond exhaustion. "No."

"Why not? You think we're guilty?"

Mother shook her head immediately. "Mackenna, you know that's not the case. We know you and Thoraben would never behave like that." I guiltily pushed aside the memory of Ben's kiss. "Your virtue, and Thoraben's, has nothing to do with our silence."

I could feel what little strength I still clung to draining away as time stretched on. I didn't know what was being said inside that throne room, but I doubted either the king or his son were on my side. My parents were my last hope. "Then why?"

"I told you. I agree with the people. I think you would make a good and wise queen."

"You would force me to marry Thoraben?"

"No one is forcing anything."

"The king is. Or will." Whether he decreed Ben and I marry or sent me away from Peverell—one of which I knew would be the case—my life as I'd known it would be over. For the second time in less than a month.

Father placed a hand on my arm. I shook it off. He tried again anyway. "Mackenna, you trust Thoraben, don't you?"

I took a step backwards, out of Father's reach. There was that word again. Trust. First Ben, now my father. But I couldn't. One after the other, they'd let me down. Ben by claiming he'd marry me against my will and Father for doing nothing to stop it. I desperately wanted to trust someone, but I had no one left.

"Thoraben is a good man. I cannot think of anyone more suited to be his bride than you, Mackenna."

I walked away. Staying, listening to their betrayal, only fueled my anger more. I would get no help from my parents. My fate lay in the hands of the two men debating in that room—the king, who despised me, and his son, who'd kissed me once and regretted it.

Wonderful.

I paced the hall, not knowing what else to do. People stared my way as they waited to hear the king's pronouncement. I tried not to make eye contact. They'd betrayed me too. Every single one of them. Mother claimed they knew the truth of my character but not one of them had stood up for it.

It felt like hours before we were allowed back in. King Everson sat on his throne. Ben stood tall, once again at his father's right hand where I was so accustomed to him standing. I tried to tell from their expressions what decision they had come to, but they each looked as grim as the other. An entire kingdom had likely been blown apart by a whirlwind, their people's homes and livelihoods destroyed, and they were discussing marriage. Had the wind blown the sense from their heads?

"Miss Mackenna Sparrow, please join us."

I felt like a criminal as I walked the lonely path to the dais. Were there more people here than before? Perhaps it was simply the tension in the room making it feel like it. My heart thudded as heavily as a bass drum. Two beats to every step I took. I tucked a piece of hair behind my ear and concentrated on keeping my hands from shaking. Ten more steps...five...two...

When Ben pointed to a spot a few steps away from him on the platform and gestured me to it, I went, almost stumbling on the tiny step. My jaw clenched.

Hold it together, Kenna. Not long now until this will be over. You can do this. Just a few more minutes...

With no small amount of trepidation, I faced the gathered

crowd. My head pounded in time with my heart, but I boldly kept it raised. This was not a moment to show weakness. I'd already done that once today. It was what had gotten me here.

"Regarding the matter of the commoner, Miss Mackenna Sparrow, and my son, Crown Prince Thoraben of Peverell, I have come to the decision that—"

King Everson stopped, or perhaps it was simply my heart that stopped. I'd been wrong. I couldn't do this. I squeezed my eyes shut, willing away the stares of the crowd. A hand grasped mine. I flinched, then tried to pull away. Ben didn't let go. In that instant, I knew what was coming.

A dizzying orange haze started poking holes behind my eyes. I opened them, trying to blink it away. It continued to come.

"—they will marry. Tomorrow evening, the thirty-first day of July, at five o'clock, Crown Prince Thoraben of Peverell will marry Miss Mackenna Sparrow."

He might have said more but the blood rushing past my ears was too loud for me to hear. Whether my eyes were open or shut anymore, I didn't know for there, on the raised dais in front of half the kingdom, I let the darkness take me.

TWENTY

I woke to the worried eyes of my mother. Ben, the king, and the crowd were fortunately nowhere to be seen. I didn't recognize the room I was in, though the dripping opulence of the furnishings was enough to assure me I was still in the palace. Gold-gilt molded cornices, crystal chandeliers, the elaborate flower and vine motif carved into the dark wood of the four-poster bed I lay in. It was beautiful—and too much—all at once. I focused on Mother's green eyes before the dizziness took me again.

"Where am I?"

"Promise me you won't faint?"

Dread made my stomach roil even more than it already was. There were few rooms in the palace Alina and I hadn't explored over the years. The servants' rooms, though the lavishness of my current room's décor told me it wasn't one of them, the suites belonging to the king and queen and—

"I'm in the Princess Suite, aren't I."

I didn't really need Mother's nod to confirm it, nor her sympathy. Any doubts I might have had about what happened those few moments before I fainted fled. The Princess Suite, the one reserved for Ben's bride. There was only one reason I would have been put in this room. For better or worse, that bride was now me. Poor Wenderley. How would I ever face her again? And Alina? This month was supposed to be all about her—and now I'd be married first, to her brother of all people.

But neither of them was the person I most dreaded confronting. Not even the king held that place, even knowing how adamantly he opposed this marriage.

Ben. I dreaded seeing Ben again. It didn't matter that he'd been the one to offer marriage. I knew he'd only done it to save me. His reputation for mine, the honorable thing to do, as he'd so neatly put it. I wished he hadn't. My life wasn't worth ruining his.

How could I look into his eyes, knowing my foolish mistake had cost him his future? His virtue, even. He'd been my best friend once but now he was...what? My fiancé? I couldn't avoid him if I tried. Tomorrow, five o'clock, I'd be more than facing him. I'd be marrying him. Unless he had a plan to get us out of this. Could he have a plan? Was that it? He had asked me to trust him.

"If you're feeling better, we have a lot to do," Mother said, taking a lined notebook from the table beside my bed and opening it. I swallowed back fear.

"Do?"

"Fitting your gown, choosing menus, getting settled back into the palace, rehearsals..."

"Rehearsals?"

Mother looked at me as if I were daft before placing a hand on my forehead, checking for fever. I shook it away. I wasn't ill. Even if I was, it wouldn't have made a difference. The only thing that would at this point was if all of this were another dream. But even I didn't have that much hope.

"For the ceremony. You're marrying Peverell's future king, Mackenna. There are protocols, dignitaries, things you have to say. The whole kingdom and beyond will be watching."

And here I'd thought my day couldn't get any worse. "It'll be a real wedding?"

"Of course. What did you think?"

"We'd sign a few forms," I muttered. "It's—" I shook my head. What it was, was a charade. A farce. A political stunt. The people of Peverell had been watching their prince, documenting each milestone since the day he was born. First birthday, first day of school, first official speech, first ball, first charity match. Since his eighteenth birthday, they'd been waiting in eager anticipation for one thing—his wedding. It should have been a day of pomp and prestige, happiness and love. Streets lined with flags, commemorative dinner sets in every store, visiting royalty in their finest gowns.

This would be rushed, forced at best, with people assuming the worst of us both. The only thing the streets would be lined with was the aftermath of the whirlwind.

The king didn't approve, that much was obvious, but I had yet to figure out what Ben's motive was. Honor, he'd said. But whose honor? And why did it feel so...so... I didn't even know.

"Mackenna, no matter how it came about, nor the speed at which is it happening, it is still the wedding of the Crown Prince of Peverell and will be treated as such. By everyone."

I swallowed again. "A real wedding."

"And a real marriage. You will be Thoraben's wife and Peverell's future queen." Mother placed a hand on my arm. "Are you going to faint again?"

If only I could. "Would it change anything?"

"No."

"Then there's no point. What's first?"

Instead of answering, Mother looked at me in that way that made me feel like she could see right to my heart. And I had no way of hiding. "I'm proud of you, you know. Doing all this. Handling it so willingly."

"Don't be. I haven't done anything yet."

"But you will."

I sighed as I sat up. Yes, I would. But did it still count as willingness when I had no choice? "Let's get this over with."

Five hours later, I knew without a doubt that I should have refused Ben's rescue and taken my chance with the whirlwind. It had been terrifying at the time, but this was so much worse.

"Arms out. And down. Oh no, no, no. That won't do."

I could have set a table for tea on Mrs. Rosina's frown, it protruded so far. Peverell's premier dressmaker muttered to herself as she walked around me again, pushing her assistants out of the way as she stared at me from every direction. Or rather, stared at the profusion of white satin and lace I was currently draped in. I didn't know what had her in such a fuss, but I very much hoped it was able to be fixed. Soon. The stress of this fitting was getting to us all.

Well, almost all. It didn't seem to affect Meri and Avrel, sitting on chairs out of Mrs. Rosina's way, grinning none too repentantly at my misfortune. They were thrilled to be back serving me and, I had to admit, I was as thrilled to see them.

Their return, and that of Elayna, clustered in another corner of the suite with two new maids, was the one good thing which had come from this mess of a wedding. If anyone could get me through these next few days, it would be them. I'd be well cared for with five personal maids at my disposal, that was for certain.

"Arms up."

Mrs. Rosina tucked a few more pins into the bodice of the gown under my arm before motioning to an assistant to make note of her changes. I'd have to remember to put my arms down slowly. I had enough holes in my body already thanks to all the splinters. At least they'd almost healed. The hand the bark had ravaged was still bandaged and almost completely unusable.

"Arms down. Yes. Yes. Better."

Was that a smile on Mrs. Rosina's face? I'd started to wonder if she was physically capable of smiling.

"Stop slouching."

And there it went. I reined in my weariness and forced myself upright again. I'd been standing on this block for an hour already and I hadn't slept well last night, neither making good posture easy.

Mrs. Rosina was turning her attention to the gown's waist when Alina burst through my door.

"Out," Alina told the dressmaker and her assistants flitting around me. Dropping their tape measures and pins where they stood, they obeyed, leaving me quickly clutching for enough fabric to keep me decent.

"Alina. That was rude."

"Wow. Coming from you, that's rich. Tell me it isn't true."

It would have been easy, and completely pointless, to feign confusion. I knew exactly what she was talking about. And I was clearly being fitted for a wedding gown.

"It's true."

"You're marrying my brother."

"Yes."

"Well, that would explain why the whole palace has gone crazy. They're saying you seduced Thoraben. Was that why he ignored Father's summons last night during the whirlwind? Because you had him in your devious clutches? Of all the low..."

I flinched as she hurled my water glass at the floor, shattering it into a mess of tiny, wet shards. Mrs. Rosina's scissors were next, followed by a table lamp. I didn't envy the maid tasked with cleaning that up.

"Alina. Calm down."

"Why should I? You ruined my life. I trusted you and this is how you repay me? Forcing yourself onto my brother, taking the wedding which was supposed to be mine. How could you do this to me?"

"I didn't *do* anything, least of all seduce Thoraben." Couldn't she hear how ludicrous that sounded? I'd never even had a man interested in me before Ashe Marsh, who had been in love with someone else all along. Me. Seduce someone. It was laughable.

"That's what they're saying."

"And you believe them?" How could she think that? It didn't surprise me that she'd heard such rumors. Alina had always cared far too much about what people said about her family, as had I, but it shocked me that she'd believe such a thing about me. She knew me. She'd known me her whole life. I didn't know what angered me more—her lack of faith in me or the belief that Ben could have done such a thing. I might have been her friend, but Ben was her brother. Surely that relationship demanded a level of faith.

"Why else would Thoraben be marrying you? It's not like he loves you. You're nothing. Less than nothing. You two-faced, conniving, malicious—"

With a swipe of her hand through the air, Alina stomped to the door, stopping just inside it to turn back. I braced myself for a final attack only to have her voice turn quiet. Lethally so.

"I can't believe I thought you were my friend. All along, you were biding your time, waiting for the right moment to ruin all of our lives. Well, there you go. Congratulations, you succeeded. Who needs Rebels?"

"Alina." I'd never seen her so angry. She was determined to blame me for this. I didn't know if I could convince her of the truth, but I had to try. If she went out that door like this, I might never have another chance. "You have to know I didn't do anything. None of whatever they're saying is true."

"You didn't seduce Thoraben?"

"Of course not."

"You haven't been carrying on a secret love affair with him for the past ten years?"

I scoffed. *That* was what they were saying? "Hardly. That would make me, what, seven, when it started? Believe me. There is nothing between your brother and me but the same friendship I have with you."

"Then why are you getting married?"

I wish I knew. "Ask Thoraben."

"I can't. He's not here. Apparently he went to meet some photographer friend of his. Like there aren't enough of those around already."

The photographer. It must be the one who had taken the photos of us that day we were skiing. Even in the craziness of this forced, rushed wedding, Ben was keeping his promise. It was a comfort, if only a small one. I was still too confused by Ben's motives to let him off altogether. Was he truly going to go through with this? I couldn't believe it, yet I'd seen nothing to convince me otherwise.

"Your father then."

"Also out. Why can't you tell me?"

"Because I don't know."

She crossed her arms, leveling me with a glare. "It's your wedding."

"You think this is my choice? You think *any* of this is my choice? It's not, Alina. I had no choice!"

"This was supposed to be my wedding. *My wedding!* What am I supposed to do now? Be your bridesmaid?"

She might as well have thrown the glass shards at me, the way she bit out each word. I should have been wounded. Instead, all I could think was how much I wanted exactly that. With her by my side tomorrow, her smile assuring me not everything was changing, maybe I could get through this. I couldn't imagine anyone else I'd want more.

"I'd like that," I said softly. I might as well have asked the king to go dress shopping with me, the way she scoffed.

"Not a chance. You took what was mine and you're not even sorry."

"I am."

"No. If you were sorry, you would never have agreed to it."

This again? Had she heard nothing I'd said in the past few minutes? "I told you. I didn't have a choice."

"You always have a choice."

She left in a huff and a wave of perfume. I tried to brush off her words, knowing they were wrong, but the hatred still seeped in, burning me inside. I'd thought, with time, Alina might forgive me. I'd thought, given her own arranged marriage, she might understand. Now, I knew. She never would.

She might have had a choice, being the princess and all, but I was…a pawn. A pawn in a much bigger plan. One that Ben had clearly forgotten to tell his sister about. And me. Was he truly going to go through with this?

Ben, what are you doing?

"For dessert, we'll have a selection of pastries, tarts, and miniature cakes to augment the wedding cake itself. Is that right, my lady?"

I tried not to laugh at the chef's solemnity. It would be a miracle if anyone could still fit in dessert, even miniaturized, after eating the rest of the nine courses I'd already approved. I reminded myself once again that this was the wedding of Peverell's future king. Mother had been right. Even rushed, it was never going to be simple.

"Yes, sir. They all look wonderful. Your work is exquisite." I patted my uncomfortably full stomach, hoping he would get the message that I'd eaten enough without me having to decline his latest offering. Every plate he presented me might as well have been a child of his given the love and affection he poured into it. And how personally he took my comments regarding them.

"Very well then, that is all. Thank you for your time." He gestured his sous-chef to start packing up the samples strewn across the otherwise empty stainless-steel kitchen while he made more notations in his planner. It took a moment for his words to take hold in my far too detail-saturated mind.

"That's all?" I could go? Really?

"Unless you have any further questions or concerns about the menu? Samples you'd like to taste?"

The assistant paused, raspberry tart in hand, the hope on his face matching Chef's.

"No." I cringed at my overly eager voice. They wouldn't be offended if I left so soon, would they? "Every dish you've given me has been delicious and I'm certain the rest will look and taste just as remarkable."

"Of course." Chef nodded and went back to taking notes.

I smiled at his hubris. *Of course.* Silly me for intimating his food would be anything but wonderful. I thanked him again and ran out of the room before I could insult him further.

I was free. At least, that was what my new schedule said—the one which was even thicker than the one Alina had brought me regarding her wedding. I couldn't believe it when it was delivered to the door of the Princess Suite this morning minutes after Alina stormed out. How could they, whoever they were, have gotten it together so quickly? I'd been back in the palace less than a day and already my life was color-coded and planned to the minute.

Except for the next hour. My indecisive nature had won me a whole hour of freedom. After almost hyperventilating when I saw the thirty options I had to choose from for the entrée alone, I'd decided upon a plan. I'd chosen the eleventh option. Every course. My hour and a half scheduled for menu choosing was finished in a third of the time.

My presence wasn't required anywhere else until dinner, which I planned to eat in my room. Tomorrow, I'd give up my freedom forever. Tonight, I was going to savor the last of it. Not even my tower was far enough away. I was getting out of the palace.

I made it all the way to the front door.

"I'm sorry, my lady, but I can't allow you to go out there."

I groaned at the unfamiliar guard's words. Why couldn't Mr. Stanley have been at his post? He would have let me past. This guard had no intention of doing so.

"I have to."

"I'm sorry. King's orders."

"I wasn't aware I was a prisoner."

"You're not."

"Then I'm leaving."

"I can't allow that. Not without guards."

I counted the buttons on the man's vest as I told myself to calm down. He hadn't said no. He'd said I had to go with protection. I could work with that. For now.

"Then find me some guards, because I'm going out."

"If you'll wait..."

I didn't want to wait. I wanted to leave. Now. I only had an hour and precious minutes of freedom ticked away while I stood waiting. The moment two guards came into sight, I walked out the door. They were well trained. They'd find me fast enough.

My plan to walk to the hills again was thwarted by the amount of destruction I saw the closer I got to the marketplace. I didn't need the dire warnings of my guards to tell me I couldn't go far. It was almost enough to make me pivot on my heel and run straight back to the safety of the palace. I knew the whirlwind had been fierce, but this was more than I could have imagined.

Broken windows, scattered and missing roof tiles, gardens torn apart, fenceposts standing at odd angles—those not up-rooted entirely. Though someone had come through and cleared the road, the trees and branches piled up either side of it and still strewn everywhere else were proof enough of the wind's strength. Did any still stand? I couldn't see a single house that looked untouched. Mere wind had done this?

It was almost impossible to believe, and yet I knew it had. I'd felt its force as I ran through it, and that hadn't even been its angriest. I turned to my guards, addressing the kinder-looking of the two.

"You, sir. Are there..." I stopped, not wanting to ask but desperate to know. "How many are dead?"

He shook his head. "None yet, but—"

He broke off, gesturing with a hand to the mess around us. I nodded, turning away before he saw the tears on my face. He didn't need to finish the sentence for me to know what this life-hardened guard refused to say. It had only been twelve hours. Not nearly long enough to account for everyone. It was too much to hope that no one had died. Not amidst such fury.

Mr. Slaughter. He lived alone. Had someone, a neighbor or friend, taken him to the safety of the palace before the wind grew too strong? Ella and Esme? Which house was theirs? Why hadn't I taken the time to visit them when I could have? What if it was too late?

I swiped the tears off my face and kept walking. Down the cobblestone road, through the marketplace, to the center of town, almost unrecognizable from the last time I'd been here. Yet, already, it was being repaired. All around me, people worked together, making piles of debris, boarding up broken windows, sweeping paths.

Even children helped, buckets and sponges in their hands as they washed dust from the walls. They had something I didn't—hope—and like they'd taken their sponges to me, I felt my despair start to ebb away. Before one of the guards could tell me otherwise, I walked over to join a group of them, happily accepting a wet cloth, wiping the higher parts they couldn't reach. Even amidst disaster, somehow, life would go on.

"Lady Mackenna."

I spun at the sound of my name, searching for Ashe. That was his voice, I was certain of it. I turned a full circle before one of the guards pointed upward. No wonder I hadn't seen him, perched high on a roof three houses down. I waved, watching as he gingerly edged his way across the eaves before climbing down the waiting ladder.

"I can't believe you're here," he said, wiping grubby hands on his equally grubby pants before walking over to me.

"Me? What are you doing up on that roof?"

"Trying to fix it, though I'll admit, I'm none too good with a hammer." He held up a finger already beginning to bruise. I tried not to laugh but it was difficult, especially with him grinning like that.

"I'm sure you'll do a fine job all the same."

"I hope so. I aim to take my wife there tonight."

My jaw dropped open, letting out a sound that might have been a gasp but sounded more like a strangled frog. "What? You're married? When? To who?"

"Jade."

"But I thought... Yesterday, you said..."

"I know, but then the whirlwind came and I realized what a gift every moment was, and how I didn't want to waste another one without Jade. I wasn't the only one whose perspective was changed by the whirlwind either. Father was so happy to see me alive that he gave me his approval. We married this morning."

"You didn't waste any time."

"I'd been waiting two years already."

Sweat dripped down Ashe's face, mingling with the dust still clinging to everything. His hair was a shade darker than his usual blond, no doubt due to running muddy hands through it as he worked, and his shirt had a large tear in the sleeve—but I'd never seen him happier.

"Congratulations."

"Thank you. I hear you are also to be married. Tomorrow, isn't it?"

My stomach dropped to somewhere around my toes. For a few minutes, surrounded by such a confronting combination of destruction and hope, I'd almost been able to forget. But, unlike the rest of the whirlwind's damage, my future couldn't be fixed with sponges, hammers, or brooms. "Word travels fast."

"Thoraben's a good man. He'll make you a good husband."

The words sounded eerily familiar. Ben had said them when he'd been reassuring me about Prince Marcos. I nodded, knowing Ashe was right even if his assurances didn't help. Ashe always seemed to turn up when I was in trouble, but not even he could help me this time. No one could.

The more serious of my guards started toward me. I knew before he opened his mouth that my time here was up. An hour might not have passed, but my freedom was at an end. I thought it would have bothered me more than it did. I nodded to the guard, acknowledging his unspoken message before turning to Ashe.

"Congratulations again. It's been nice to see you, but I need to be getting back to the palace."

This walk hadn't been the relaxing stroll I'd hoped. The destruction had seen to that. But it had put my problems into perspective. In the past forty-eight hours, I'd ripped my hand to shreds on tree bark, run through a whirlwind twice, slept on a hard wood floor, had my character besmirched in front of half the kingdom, stood in judgement before the king, and been forced into a marriage I'd never asked for—but I was alive. No matter what else I felt, I had to remember that.

"All will be well, Mackenna."

I nodded, half smiling, wishing more than believing what he said to be true. I was thrilled to hear about Ashe and Jade's marriage. The thought of mine, on the other hand, still filled me with dread.

TWENTY-ONE

My gown was far too beautiful for the sham of a wedding I was about to undertake. Made of pure white satin in a princess cut design, it was strapless except for the lacy cap sleeves skimming my upper arms. Tiny crystals studded the bodice and skirt—not enough to be gaudy, but enough to make it sparkle when I moved and throw rainbows across the walls each time I walked through a patch of sunlight.

My favorite part, though, was the belted ribbon tied at my waist from which the skirt flowed out. It had been painstakingly stitched with silver threaded vines, diamonds and sapphires in the shape of flowers perfectly complementing my silver tiara.

I'd wondered if I would be made to wear a crown, given I was marrying the prince. Instead, to my delight, the dressers performing miracles on my wind-tangled hair had used my tiara. It was the one part of me that felt real.

No matter what Mother said, nor Ben or anyone else, I knew the wedding was all a show. A pretense. Another façade.

I refused to cry any more. I'd done enough of that already. People wouldn't mind, they'd think it was the emotion of the day. They'd be right, only for the wrong reason. These weren't happy tears. They were furious ones. Alina hadn't been the only one to fantasize about her wedding growing up. I had too and, dream of a gown aside, this political stunt wasn't it.

"Ready?"

I blinked back tears as Father took my arm and reminded myself that this was yet another thing I had no choice in. Had it been up to me, I would have walked the long aisle alone, forced as I was to walk it at all. I was angry at him. Mother too. Either of them could have talked sense into the king, or at least tried. They'd both stayed silent.

The music started and, on cue, the doors opened. The gasps of those fortunate enough to earn themselves a seat within the grand cathedral followed close behind. I tried to smile, knowing how many cameras were watching me, but it was shaky at best. The thick, floor-length veil I wore had been another part of the façade when it was put on me. Now, it was my savior. If Ben had a plan to stop this wedding, he'd better do it soon. Time was definitely running out.

"All will be well, Mackenna," I heard Father whisper. I tried my best to ignore him—and everyone else. *Left foot, right foot, left foot, right foot. Focus on the music. The strings, the melody. Left foot, right foot.* "All will be well."

I gritted my teeth behind my smile, my jaw aching with the strain. Everyone needed to stop saying that. All had stopped being well a long time ago, and I doubted it would rectify itself any time soon. I took another deep breath and kept walking. *Focus on the music, Kenna. Left foot, right foot, smile.*

I couldn't look at Ben. I felt him looking at me, even from the other end of the cathedral, even with five hundred other eyes on me, but I couldn't look at him. If he were happy, I'd be angry. If he looked at me with pity, I knew I'd cry. If he were angry, I'd know it was my fault. And if his face showed anything else? I didn't want to know.

I'd been avoiding him all day, a task made far easier by the lines of people demanding my attention. Mrs. Rosina and her ladies sewing me into my gown as I stood again on that block, maids flitting about, officials with papers to sign and read me, hairdressers, makeup artists—the list went on and on.

Nor had I seen him at either of the two rehearsals, our schedules too full to allow for both of us to be there at one time. I'd been walked through the ceremony alone, told when to stand,

when to walk, when to sit. *Prince Thoraben will be waiting here...*
Prince Thoraben will take your hand...Prince Thoraben will say...

At least no one expected me to memorize my vows or any of
the other statements in such a short time. It was one of very few
reprieves. For better or worse, it seemed I was marrying Prince
Thoraben.

Long before I was ready, Father was kissing my hand and
walking to his seat. The five hundred people staring at my back
didn't bother me. The man beside me did. I wanted to scream at
him. Beg him to make me understand what his purpose was for
all this. But I couldn't. It was too late for that.

"Come."

Ben's hand brushed mine as we knelt before the officiate in
the age-old cathedral. It took everything in me not to flinch and
pull away. I looked instead beyond the officiate to the tall, brick
arches making up the front wall. Elaborate and stately, they'd
been grayed with time, the plaster between them missing in
some sections. I imagined my heart looked similar. Were they as
cold and weary of holding the weight of expectations as my heart
too?

I'd never been in here before, the building being used solely
for royal weddings and coronations. There had been none of
those in my lifetime. Alina's wedding would have been the first.
I'd taken that honor from her. I knew she sat in the front row—
the seating chart in my planner had told me that—but I refused
to look at her either. I was nervous enough without seeing her
scorn.

Though I tried to listen to the man speaking, I knew I'd remember none of what he said. It was as if his words, so solemnly
spoken, washed over me without ever penetrating my mind. I
heard his voice, but it might as well have been another language
for all the comprehension I had. My mind was far from on him.

"Are you okay?"

Somehow, amidst the officiate's drone, loud enough to reach
every ear here, I heard Ben's low whisper. I nodded in answer,
though I wondered if it was a lie. Could I truly tell him I was

okay when my entire life felt as if it had been pulled up in the whirlwind and thrown around the kingdom for people to claim?

"And your hand?"

I looked briefly down at my injured hand. Mrs. Rosina hadn't been the only one to argue that the thick bandage surrounding it wasn't appropriate for a royal wedding. She and Doctor Merler had debated back and forth about how to hide the injury for a full half hour before I told them to leave it be. In the face of the destruction I'd witnessed yesterday, a simple bandage on my hand seemed insignificant. No one would begrudge me it. It might not have complimented my gown, but I wore the bandage with the pride of a survivor. Albeit a weary one.

"It's fine."

I let Ben help me to my feet again when the officiate directed. Cameras clicked around us, catching the moment. They thought it was romantic. My own reasoning was much more practical. My gown, with its layers of heavy satin, shaped petticoats, and three-yard-long train was not the easiest piece of clothing to move about in, stunning as it might be.

I looked down at the floor, unwilling to look into Ben's eyes even though we stood facing each other now, my hands held gently in his. I should look up, the cameras would love it, but I was afraid they might capture more than I was willing to show.

The truth.

I was in love with Prince Thoraben of Peverell, the man who would soon be my husband. I'd denied it for so long, even to myself. Especially to myself. The dream the night of the whirlwind had only confirmed it. I'd been in love with him for years.

"Shiny enough?"

Ben's whisper interrupted my moment of unwanted discovery. I had no idea what the officiate was talking about, yet I heard every breath Ben took. If this was love, I wanted no part of it. It hurt too much.

"Excuse me?"

"My shoes. You've been staring at them for a while now. Do they pass?"

Shoes. He was asking about his shoes. We were in the middle of our wedding ceremony and he was asking me about his shoes. "Um. Yes."

"Good."

Apparently satisfied, he went back to listening, even going so far as to nod occasionally. I felt his movement, though my eyes stayed downcast.

"In as much as these two have consented to matrimony..."

"How about my buttons?"

"Your buttons." First his shoes, now his buttons. He was losing his mind. Had he not looked in the mirror before turning up to his own wedding? Surely he had a valet or manservant to answer these questions.

"Yes. Are they shiny enough? I had them polished also."

I let my gaze drift upward to his buttons, so black against the crimson of his jacket. I didn't notice any vast difference, but then, they were always well polished. They wouldn't dare sport a mote of dust or fingerprint on such an auspicious occasion. With the exception of his coronation, this day would be the most important—and certainly most watched—day of Ben's life. And I was by his side. A wave of nausea swept over me at the thought. How could this have happened?

"Your buttons are fine."

"How about my tiara?"

"Wha—" My eyes flew up in time to catch his wink.

"Gotcha."

"Thora—"

"Ben, please. Can't you call me Ben? We are almost married."

Did he have any idea how ridiculous he was being? "We shouldn't be talking," I whispered back, hoping he'd take the hint. He didn't.

"They can't hear."

"What if we miss something?"

"I'll blame you."

"Ben!"

"Ah. There you go. That wasn't so difficult now, was it?" He squeezed my good hand. "All will be well, Kenna. You needn't be afraid."

"Who said I was afraid?"

"You're gripping my hands like I'm the only thing holding you up."

I immediately loosened my hold. He grinned. I decided to ignore him. At least as much as I could, given I was about to commit my life to him. Right after he pledged his to me.

"Thoraben Philippe Kendrick Everson, wilt thou have this woman to be thy wedded wife, to live together according to the law of Peverell in the revered estate of matrimony? Wilt thou love her, comfort her, honor and keep her, and forsaking all others, keep only unto her so long as you both shall live?"

"I will."

"Mackenna Faith, wilt thou..."

I stared at Ben. His words were so sure, so certain—and so surprising. He'd agreed to all that. In front of all these witnesses. I hadn't realized until that moment how much I'd been expecting him to say no. I'd been holding on to the hope that he would find a way out of this, having a plan in place to do so. Did he truly then mean to marry me? Even knowing nothing short of our deaths could break the vows he made today?

"Mackenna?"

The officiate was staring at me, waiting. I was so confused by Ben's response that I'd missed my own.

Uh...what was I supposed to say again? "I wilt."

A low laugh from Ben was quickly turned into a cough. Heat crept up my neck, burning my ears as I realized what I'd said, but I refused to correct it. It was close enough, and probably closer to the truth than anyone knew. The long, lacy veil might have been covering up my fears and foibles, but it also let very little air through to my face. The hot lights blazing down on us weren't helping either.

The officiate continued as if he hadn't noticed my mistake. Perhaps he hadn't. I determined to pay better attention lest I be caught out again.

"I, Thoraben Philippe Kendrick Everson, take thee, Mackenna Faith, to be my wife. To have and to hold from this day forward, for better, for worse; for richer, for poorer; in sickness and in health; to love and to cherish, till death do us part, according to the law of Peverell; and thereto I give thee my troth."

"Mackenna?"

The words were right in front of me, there on a piece of paper. All I had to do was read them. Easy.

If only they were simply words instead of vows that would change my life forever.

"I, Mackenna Faith..." My voice shook. I stopped, taking in as deep a breath as I could manage, holding it there in my lungs before slowly releasing it back into the world. Ben rubbed his thumbs over the back of my hands, reminding me I wasn't alone. He'd committed himself to me already. If Ben could do it, I could. I refused to be bested by him, even in this. I started again.

"I, Mackenna Faith, take thee, Thoraben Philippe Kendrick Everson, to be my husband. To have and to hold from this day forward, for better, for worse; for richer, for poorer; in sickness and in health; to love and to cherish, till death do us part, according to the law of Peverell; and thereto I give thee my troth."

There. I'd done it. There was no turning back now.

The ring Ben produced for me sparkled as he slid it on my finger. In the rare moments I'd been allowed to think in the last two days, I'd wondered briefly what my ring would look like. If it would be as ostentatious as Alina's. This simple band, with its row of diamonds and single blue sapphire, was more perfect than I cared to admit. I wondered where Ben had found it on such short notice. Then again, my elaborate gown had materialized from nothing to perfection in twenty-four hours. No doubt a ring could do the same.

His was plain. A simple gold band with no decoration whatsoever, not even any etchings. It caught on his knuckle as I tried to slip it on but eventually found its place.

"Forasmuch as Thoraben and Mackenna have consented together in wedlock, and have witnessed the same before the king and this company, and thereto have given and pledged their troth to each other, and have declared the same by giving and receiving of a ring and by joining of hands...I now pronounce that they be man and wife together.

"Thoraben, you may kiss your bride."

My gaze flew to the officiate, questioning whether I'd heard him right. This hadn't been in the rehearsals. I'd even checked, relieved beyond reason to be assured that due to the nature of our wedding, the devastation much of Peverell was still dealing with, and the tradition of *not* kissing at royal weddings, the kiss would be left out entirely. The man was supposed to finish his address, usher us toward the table in the annex where I would sign my life away, say a closing speech, and send the two of us down the aisle in the grand recessional. No kissing required.

Apparently, that was no longer the case.

My heart thudded so loud I was certain even the people at the back of the cathedral could hear it. Kiss Ben? In front of all these people? I couldn't do it. What if...? What if...?

I'd held myself together for what felt like hours already, smiling through this lengthy ceremony. I was reaching the edge of my control. If Ben touched me—no, *kissed* me—I'd be lost. He'd kissed me once and it had shattered me, even before I'd known I was in love with him.

I closed my eyes, desperate to hide the truth written there. A few more minutes. I only had to keep up the masquerade for a few more minutes. I felt him lift my veil and drop it back over my head. I held my breath, feeling as if the entire cathedral full of people did the same. One single traitorous tear dribbled its way down my face. Ben's thumb, at my cheek, caught it an instant before he kissed me.

Then it was over. Almost as suddenly as his lips had been on mine, they were gone. I wasn't sure whether to laugh with relief or let loose the rest of that single tear's friends. I did far worse.

I opened my eyes.

And stared right into Ben's. Captured by his gaze, I couldn't look away. There was something in his eyes as he looked at me that I'd seen only once before. In my dream as we played in the snow.

Pure, unmistakable love.

TWENTY-TWO

The reception had been going on for hours—and no one seemed in any rush to end it. For a marriage the king had been so adamantly against, he'd certainly supported it all day—proof of how much he adored his son, if not me. Or perhaps how much image meant to him. After all, the people were watching and he was the king. It wouldn't do for him to be seen as anything less than in complete control of the situation.

I perused the room again, wondering if I'd talked to everyone I was supposed to yet. Hoping I had. The empty corner of the Banquet Hall I'd claimed would gain me a moment's respite, but I knew it wouldn't last long. Sooner or later, someone would notice the bride missing and find me. I selfishly hoped it was later. There was only so much subterfuge a person could take in one day.

Stubborn pride, rather than strength, had gotten me this far. There were too many cameras watching to let myself shatter—including Ben's photographer friend, whichever one he was, who I knew could capture far more in a single picture than most. When the cameras turned off, I'd have nothing left to hold me.

Not even my husband.

The love I thought I'd seen in his eyes after our kiss had vanished by the time the ceremony finished. There had been nothing but studied respect there ever since—through reception lines, all ten dinner courses, even our bridal waltz. I knew. I'd checked. Right after I'd stepped on his toes. For the third time. He'd laughed, looked at me with pity, attempted a joke, and gone back to silence.

I tried to tell myself over and over that this was the same Ben I'd always known, but nothing about this, nor him, felt the same. We were married now. Married. Ben and I. It was as impossible as it was true.

"Hiding, Mackenna? Or, should I say, *Princess* Mackenna?"

I took my time turning to face Lord Waitrose. I'd seen him skulking around at a distance not long ago but, to my relief, his name hadn't been on the list of people I'd been ordered to speak with. I'd walked in the opposite direction, having no desire whatsoever to talk with him. Unfortunately, I now had no choice. I pasted the smile back on my face.

"Good evening, Lord Waitrose. And no, not hiding. Resting after a wonderful meal and even more exceptional day."

I should have offered him my hand along with the greeting. I kept it beside me. He smirked but didn't mention it.

"May I offer my congratulations on your marriage."

"Thank you."

"I must say, I didn't think you had it in you. It seems we have more in common than I thought." He walked two steps forward. Uncomfortable, I took one step back.

"I don't know what you mean."

He laughed, but there was no amusement in it. Only derision. The dim corner I'd moments ago considered my refuge suddenly became the worst place I could have chosen. Waitrose couldn't physically hurt me, not in a room full of people, but I feared him all the same.

"Oh, come on, Mackenna. There's no need to be coy with me. It seems you've already done enough of that with Thoraben. Yes, it appears I grossly misjudged you. And here I thought you were an innocent."

My hands fisted at my sides, jerking forward before I tucked them securely behind my back. I'd been told to project calm in situations like this, where one's character was wrongly maligned.

The lessons had never mentioned how difficult such a thing would actually be.

"I beg your pardon, Lord Waitrose. I don't know what you're suggesting, nor do I want to know, but neither I nor Prince Thoraben did anything wrong."

"Then why the rushed wedding? It's not as if the king approved of you. He made that much clear at the Midsummer's Ball. Banished from his presence without so much as a hello. And yet, here you are, not even two months later, married to his son. We all know there's only one way that could have happened. So, Princess Mackenna, how far along are you?" His gaze lowered to my stomach, leaving no doubt this time what he was insinuating. "Should I buy gifts in pink or blue?"

I held my head as high as I could in an attempt to stay in control, a fruitless exercise given I'm certain Waitrose could see me shaking. It was a wonder the wall I braced myself against hadn't fallen over already. "I suggest you leave. Now."

He didn't even take one step.

"I notice you didn't deny it."

"I shouldn't have to. I would have thought you'd have had more faith in your friend than that, even if you don't in me."

"He's a man, Mackenna. Don't think he's any better than the rest of us simply because he's a prince. Speaking of which, where is that husband of yours? Tired of his conniving bride already?"

"How dare you."

"Come see me when you tire of Thoraben. I always have time for women like you..."

Fury had me gasping as Waitrose left laughing. He hadn't touched me, not even once, and yet I felt filthier than when I'd run through the whirlwind. Only no amount of water could wash me clean this time—not of Waitrose's leering nor his insinuations. This was exactly what I'd feared people would think about this wedding—that it was required. As far as they were concerned, the wedding merely proved our guilt. Few would say it as bluntly as Waitrose but it didn't mean they weren't convinced of it.

The whole room thought the two of us guilty—my parents being the sole exception. They didn't think we were guilty. They just didn't think our innocence worth fighting for. I didn't know what hurt more.

"Kenna. Here you are." Reaching for the hand I'd refused to give to Waitrose, Ben lifted it to his mouth and kissed it. Bright flashes from two different directions gave evidence to the fact that he'd been followed by the ever-present photographers, capturing the moment. I tried to smile and look like the blushing bride I was supposed to be, but even without a mirror I could tell I failed. I didn't even have the strength left to blush let alone act. With a frown and a wave of his hand, Ben sent the photographers away, angling his body to shield me from the rest of the room.

"What is it?"

I shook my head. I couldn't tell him. Not when he was looking at me like that, as if he would take on the world for me. For all I knew, he'd challenge Waitrose to a duel there and then. He'd already married me for honor. I couldn't bear to watch him fight for me as well.

"Nothing Prince Th—uh, Ben." I closed my eyes, fighting back frustration at the fact that I didn't even know what to call him anymore. Probably whatever I wanted. We were married, after all. Opening them, I took a breath and tried again. "Did you want something?"

"Simply to see my wife. Are you as tired as I am of this?"

Was he serious? "Yes."

"Then come on. Let's leave."

"We can do that?" I didn't want to let myself hope in case he was teasing.

He grinned. "Probably not, but despite what our schedules say, and the day being scripted down to our toilet breaks, they're still our names on the invites and I say that means we're in charge."

"And that means we can leave?"

"Definitely."

"Then let's go."

Ben snuck the two of us past three amused guards and an abundance of distracted dignitaries before finding the side door which would be our escape. I breathed easily for the first time in hours. I'd been following the rules all day. It felt wonderful to break them.

"Wait." I stopped suddenly. "You got toilet breaks?"

Ben laughed, shaking his head at the joke. I giggled as he grabbed my good hand and dragged me down another passage. The freedom was going to my head already. Or perhaps that was the abundance of bubbly drinks.

"Come on, Kenna. Quick. Before they catch us."

He must have been talking about his father or the kingdom's officials because the guards certainly didn't seem to mind, watching as we ran past, grinning their approval. They must have thought we had more in mind than sneaking out. I wasn't so sure Ben didn't.

Still, we were out, and it felt so deliciously like the old days of following along with Ben's mischief that I couldn't help but enjoy myself.

Ben led me up to the East Tower, helping me onto a bench before sitting in the chair beside me. I thought we'd talk. I kept expecting him to, but he didn't. I didn't either, content to relax in my thoughts for the first time since Meri had woken me at four this morning to begin preparing.

I'd barely finished the breakfast they'd given me before being whisked off to the old cathedral in the pre-morning dark for a final rehearsal. Then the maids had descended with force.

I'd thought my three maids taking seven hours to prepare me for the Midsummer's Ball was excessive. That had been mere child's play. After all, as my cavalcade of maids and dressers reminded me every two minutes, I was Peverell's future queen. I felt like I should say it with pomp, perhaps borrow the palace crier to announce it to the world. *Here she is. Peverell's Future Queen.*

Albeit one they clearly didn't plan on feeding. It had been

close to two-thirty in the afternoon before my loudly grumbling stomach had forced them to set aside their ministrations to allow me a whole ten minutes to eat. Even then, I'd had two maids behind me pulling my hair through and into various confections before raking it back behind my head in some type of updo. I didn't ask for a mirror. I didn't want to know.

"You've been decorating," I said, breaking the silence. I assumed it was Ben who'd had the wrought iron garden table setting brought up. I'd never seen anyone else up here. It was nice. Fitting. I liked the way the wrought iron looked against the centuries old stone of the tower wall. If they stayed, I'd be more tempted than ever to spend all my time up here, especially given the iciness the rest of Ben's family felt toward me.

"Do you mind?"

"Why would I? I told you the tower was yours." Even if it still felt like mine.

"Ours."

I smiled into the darkness, pleased with the compromise. I could share. As long as it was only with Ben.

He leaned forward, reaching for my unbandaged hand, covering it with his own as it rested on my lap. "I thought about you every time I came up here, you know. It made you feel closer somehow. I was up here the morning of the whirlwind."

The morning of the whirlwind, I'd climbed a tree to see this tower, thinking of him as I'd done so. I'd almost waved, before telling myself it was foolish. Yet he had been up here then, thinking of me.

"Kenna, I know you probably hate me, but—"

I sighed, breaking in on Ben's apology. This wasn't his fault. None of it was. If anyone was to blame, it was me, letting him spend so much time in my thoughts that he wandered into my dreams. "I don't hate you." I was confused by him, intimidated by him, disappointed for the loss of our easygoing friendship and fighting to keep my feelings hidden, but I certainly didn't hate him.

"Really?" He seemed relieved. "That's so much more than I hoped for."

I wondered what he would say if I admitted I loved him. I shivered at the thought.

"Cold?"

"A little."

I heard him moving an instant before he settled in beside me on the bench. His arm came around my shoulders as he pulled me in against his side. I was instantly warmer, which was probably as much because of his closeness as it was the warmth he shared. I thought he'd say something, do something. I held myself tense, waiting for it. But he didn't do or say anything more. He simply held me until finally I relaxed against him.

The night was so still and clear, music from the Banquet Hall dancing easily across the distance to my ears. I didn't regret that we'd left before the reception officially ended. I did wonder if we'd get in trouble for it.

"Warmer?" Ben asked. I nodded.

More than simply warm, I felt protected.

Up here in the tower, Ben's arm around my shoulder, the darkness tucking us in, Waitrose's insults seemed to fade. It would be all too easy to imagine Ben and I truly were in love, a newly-married couple sitting under a benediction of starlight. For a selfish moment, I allowed myself to enjoy it.

"Hey...Kenna..."

I opened my eyes as something brushed against my hair. A kiss? Probably not. I hoped it wasn't a bug. Wait, had I fallen asleep? Here? In the tower?

"Come on, sleeping beauty. Let's get you to bed."

Ben stood to his feet before helping me to mine. I wobbled a little, still finding my way out of the sleepy maze I'd been lulled into. I hadn't meant to fall asleep. Certainly not as deeply as I must have to be so disorientated. It took me twice as long as usual to capture the length of my gown and train over my arm.

"Ready?"

I took a deep breath, wondering what exactly he was asking,

deciding it didn't really matter. Not anymore. I was married to the Crown Prince of Peverell, nothing was my decision anymore.

"Yes."

TWENTY-THREE

The instant Ben touched me I knew I'd lied. I wasn't ready. Not for the way he bent down and picked me up, not for the way he cradled me like a child against his chest, not for the way my heart thudded almost to a stop behind my ribs. We'd danced together a thousand times and not once had I come even close to comprehending the strength he hid in those arms. Wrapped around me as they were now, they were all I could think of. Almost.

"Put me down."

"And have you trip on this ridiculously long train of yours and fall down the stairs?" He huffed. "Not likely."

"You'll drop me." He wouldn't. I knew that. He'd break his own back protecting me before he dropped me. But I had to get out of his arms before I did something stupid like sighing with pleasure or kissing the side of his neck which smelled so distinctly of Ben. He couldn't know what I felt. I couldn't let him. I flailed about, trying to get free.

"Kenna, stop it or I will drop you."

"I can walk."

"And I can carry you. You're tired, you were literally shaking in the Banquet Hall when I came to you—whatever the reason was—and not two minutes ago you were so soundly asleep it took me saying your name four times for you to wake. Call me an old-fashioned fool, but I care about my wife too much to risk her falling down the stairs on our wedding night. I'll put you down as soon as we reach the bottom, but please, allow me this?"

I stopped, realizing how childish I was being, resigned to the fact that he truly would carry me, and enjoying it far too much to protest further. I could feel his heartbeat against my arm. It was fast. Almost as fast as mine had become. I focused on it, rather than my emotions, as he carried me down the stairs.

True to his word, Ben put me down as soon as we reached the bottom, though he kept his arm against my back as we wove our way down hallways and stairs to our new rooms. I almost tripped at one particular corner, my body walking toward my old suite before my brain could remind it I'd moved. Ben didn't say anything, instead putting an arm on mine until I was steady. It all felt like a dream. Perhaps it was, and I was still asleep, up in the tower, my head resting on Ben's shoulder.

The line of maids and servants standing at attention outside our adjoining suites brought me back down to earth. The time on the tower had been stolen—this was reality.

Ben swished his hand. "You may go, all of you."

Nine out of ten obeyed instantly. Elayna, of course, stood her ground.

"Forgive me, Your Highness, but Lady Mackenna will need assistance with her gown."

"I'll do it."

Elayna's eyes turned wide before a blush bloomed across her cheeks, turning her ears red. "Of course, Your Highness."

She ran away, scuttling down the stairs before I could call her back. I turned to Ben instead.

"You sent them away."

Confusion had him frowning. "I thought you wanted to sleep."

I did, but not everyone got what they wanted. "But I need them to prepare me for...uh, it's our...that is, don't you want... shouldn't we..." My blush rivaled Elayna's for color and, I'm positive, would have won. With ease. I wouldn't have been surprised if even my toes were red.

I hadn't expected to see a matching blush creep up Ben's

neck. Even in the dimly lit hallway, it was clear. Despite my bumbling mess of an explanation, he'd understood me—and I'd embarrassed us both. Rather than coming closer, he dropped his hands and took a half step back. His smile was as forced as I'm sure mine had been all day.

"No. That's, uh... Thanks but, well...Not tonight." He shrugged, a rueful smile playing at the corners of his mouth. "It would be a little strange, don't you think? I mean, two days ago, we were forbidden to even see each other. Now we're married. Let's get used to that before we rush into anything else. I'll see you tomorrow, though. Perhaps we could have breakfast together?"

Truth struck so hard it was a wonder it didn't force the gathering tears from my eyes. He didn't want me. I should have felt relieved. I was exhausted and completely overwhelmed already by everything that had happened these past two days. My body craved sleep more than I'd ever known. Yet all I felt was rejected. My husband of less than a day didn't want me.

"Kenna? Is that...okay?"

Understanding came in a rush, and a single name. Wenderley. Of course. I'd been so caught up in my dream coming true that I'd forgotten I'd crushed hers. No, *theirs*. Both Wenderley's and Ben's. Until two days ago, Ben had planned on marrying Wenderley. Mine wasn't the only future which had changed the night of the whirlwind.

"Yes. Of course." I wouldn't cry. Not here. Not now. Certainly not in front of my new husband.

"Good. Well, goodnight." Offering one final smile, he leaned over and kissed my cheek before walking toward his door.

I didn't move. I didn't speak either, uncertain of what to say. Elayna hadn't been merely causing trouble when she'd said I needed assistance with my gown. I really did. There were buttons I couldn't reach, all the way down the back. I could call my maids back, but Ben had already sent them away. They were no doubt preparing for bed, having had as long a day as I. The temptation to fall into bed fully dressed was strong but I knew I'd regret it in the morning. And probably ruin the gown in the process. Though I'd never wear it again, something about that seemed wrong.

"Thoraben?" He stopped, turning back, his hand on the door. "I actually do need help with my gown. Do you think you could...?" He frowned. I immediately regretted asking. I should have called for Mother. She would be here somewhere. The servants had moved Mother and Father back to their old suite this morning. I hadn't even thought of her until this moment. "Forget it. I'll call Mother."

"No, I can do it. I did offer, after all."

But... My heart raced faster as I felt panic swell my throat. What had I been thinking to ask Ben to help me undress? He couldn't. He just couldn't. It would be too...too... "Really, I can call Mother."

"It's fine." It would have been easier to believe him if he hadn't still been frowning. "Come on."

It was a few buttons, I told myself. Just a few buttons. "Okay."

Bending down, he gathered the long train of my gown under his arm, instantly halving its weight. I was certain the gown weighed almost as much as I did. It wasn't completely to blame for my fatigue, but it certainly hadn't helped.

Together we walked into my room. I gasped, unprepared for the sight. My maids had been busy while they'd been waiting for me. There were candles lit all around the room, softening even further the already beautiful suite. Twin goblets sat on a table clothed with white lace that hadn't been there earlier, a bottle of some sort of beverage lazing in a bowl of ice beside them. My bed was turned down, a filmy nightgown laid across it which had me blushing again and hoping Ben hadn't seen it. I would have rushed over to hide it except he still held my gown.

"I had no idea—" I gestured to the glasses and candles. "I didn't mean for this, this..." This romance. I shook my head in wonder as I looked again around the room. It was beautiful. Or, at least, it would have been, had I walked through the door with a man who loved me. Instead, it looked like I was trying to seduce him. He who'd already rejected me.

"It's fine. I know you didn't. My suite probably looks the same. They must have thought—Well, let's get this over with, shall we?"

The gown's train fell to the floor as his hands reached for me. I stiffened at his touch on my shoulder, wondering what his cryptic words meant. Had he changed his mind about—I blinked, trying to steady my breathing—tonight? I crossed my arms over my chest, staring at his face as I tried to read his intentions. It was impossible, especially in this light. I could turn on a light switch but then he'd be able to see my face better, and I had far too much to hide.

"I could reach the buttons on your gown better if you turned around," Ben said in a voice so low it was almost a whisper.

Buttons, buttons... Oh. My gown. He'd come in to help me with my gown. That's what I'd asked him to do. I turned my back to him before he saw the relief on my face—and the terror. I hadn't expected my room to feel so intimate when I'd invited him in.

I held my arms in tight across my chest as he unbuttoned my gown, silently begging the heavy creation not to fall, willing myself not to either. I felt his fingers on every one of those buttons. He was twenty-three buttons down when I spun around.

"I can do the rest." My voice was as mortifyingly raspy as his had been. The tiredness. It was the tiredness. Not his closeness. Definitely not his closeness. "Thanks."

I thought he'd look at me. He looked everywhere but. The floor, the table, the bed. He must have counted every single one of those candles as he avoided my eyes. I had to get him out of here before one of us did or said something we'd regret. There had been far too much of that already in the past two days.

"Thoraben?"

"Mmmm?"

"Go to bed."

With a rueful laugh, he finally looked at me. This close, I could see the flicker of candlelight reflected in his eyes. They were sad, just as they had been that night in the tower, when he'd begged me not to leave the palace. It was that sadness which almost made me ask him to stay. Whatever else he'd become, Ben had always been my friend, and I couldn't bear to see him sad when I could do something about it.

But then I remembered. I couldn't. It was his wedding night and he'd married the wrong girl. Nothing I could do could fix that.

Leaning forward, I placed the tiniest of kisses on the side of his jaw. That, at least, I could give him. "Goodnight, Thoraben."

He continued to stare, those sad eyes taking in my hair, my cheeks, my eyes, my lips. I wanted to cry, yell, berate, apologize, and kiss him—all in the same breath. I did none of them, simply standing, waiting. For what, I didn't know.

He swallowed four times before finally finding his voice. "You looked truly beautiful today, Kenna. Thank you for marrying me."

The tears began then, one falling after the other. Arms clutched around my gown, I couldn't even wipe them away. I'd held them at bay all day, except that one during the ceremony. In the end, it hadn't been people's opinions, Waitrose's accusations, or Ben's rejection that had set them free. It had been one word of gratitude.

Ben wiped the tears away with his hands, holding his palms against my face as he opened his mouth to speak again. I closed my eyes against the onslaught of more tears. He waited one exhaustion-charged moment longer before touching his lips to mine. My surprise was swallowed up in his kiss, my eyes flying open in time to see him step away.

And then he was gone.

I think I heard him say all would be well as he walked through the door to his suite. I wondered which of us he was trying to reassure.

TWENTY-FOUR

I was too exhausted not to sleep well, though I woke in a haze of dreams. They were impressions, more than anything I could describe. Wedding gowns drowning me, Alina accusing me, and Ben, his mouth moving over and over in an attempt to tell me something but having no sound to carry the message.

Silly dreams. It was them which had gotten me into this mess in the first place. I sat up, determined to rise before my subconscious once again accosted me. No amount of guards could protect me from my dreams.

"Good morning, Your Highness." I turned my head to see Avrel sitting by the window, a book in her hand, looking as if she'd been there for some time. "Or, should I say, good afternoon."

I started at that, dreams banished in an instant at Avrel's words. Was it truly that late? A clock on the wall verified the truth of her statement. It was almost one o'clock. Without meaning to, I'd slept half the day away. No wonder Avrel looked so comfortable. She'd probably been sitting there for hours. I hoped the kitchens hadn't gone to any great effort on my breakfast.

Breakfast. Ben had invited me to breakfast with him. And I'd slept through it. *Well done, Kenna. Your first day as a wife and already you've let your husband down.*

Husband. I had a husband. Ben was my husband. I was Peverell's future queen.

And I was still sitting in bed.

I swung my legs around, sliding off the tall bed to the floor. I might have missed the morning, but that didn't allow me the liberty of wasting the rest of the day. Of course, I had no idea what my responsibilities entailed now I was actually a princess, but no doubt there was a schedule around somewhere to tell me. If there was one thing I'd learned growing up in the palace, it was that there was always a schedule.

"I'll ring for some lunch then, shall I? Or would you prefer a breakfast tray?"

"Lunch, please. And if I might send word to, or speak with, uh..." I broke off. I didn't even know how to speak with Ben anymore. Was there a protocol? His suite adjoined mine, but the thought of opening that door had me blushing. Yet again. Was there no end to the humiliation? There was no guarantee he'd be there anyway. "I was supposed to meet Prince Thoraben for breakfast. I should apologize."

"There's no need, my lady. He knows you were sleeping."

"Oh."

"He's come by a few times to check on you, insisting I and the other maids let you sleep each time. He said to tell you when you woke that he'll see you later."

Oh. I didn't quite know what to make of that. Nor did I know what to do with the longing inside me to see him. Strange as our parting last night had been, the disappointment at the thought I'd missed our breakfast was overwhelming. I wanted to see him and to prove nothing had changed between us—even though everything had.

"Now, what gown would you like to wear, Your Highness?"

"I don't—" *Have any gowns* was how I planned on finishing that sentence, until Avrel opened a door I had yet to explore and I saw inside. It wasn't an exit, as I'd thought. It was a closet, if one could even call it that. I'd thought the dressing room in my old suite large. This was the size of half my previous suite, and already lined with clothing. Some pieces I recognized as those I'd left here, most I didn't. I walked inside, lightly running my hand over satin ballgowns, floaty dresses, heavy coats, and plain-colored ensembles.

"These are all mine?"

"Yes. There will be more, of course. These were the only ones Mrs. Rosina and her assistants had finished."

"But...so many?" I'd only been married a day. There were easily twenty gowns there—if not more—alongside the other outfits. And that was only one wall. Matching shoes in more colors than I could name lined another wall while hats and fascinators of various sizes and shapes sat like tropical birds on more shelves. Surely even Mrs. Rosina with her vast convoy of assistants hadn't had time to make all these so quickly, especially given they'd also created my spectacle of a wedding gown.

Apparently they had.

Avrel shrugged, though I could see a grin peeking through around her eyes. She was loving every bit of this new prestige. "You're the princess. Peverell's future queen. You could hardly go about dressed in rags. No, you must look the part. They'll need adjustments, of course, but nothing major. Mrs. Rosina set her assistants to work the minute she heard you were to be married. She already had all your measurements." Of course, from my bridesmaid gown fitting. There the finished gown was, easy to pick out with its pink frills pushing aside more demure satins as it fought to be noticed. Would I even have the chance to wear it now?

Alina had come to the wedding—I doubt she had a choice otherwise—but she hadn't spoken with me. The day might have been easier if she had.

Avrel pulled out a silky pant suit in turquoise green and a sleek, ivory-colored hat, topped with a matching flower. "May I suggest this ensemble for the parade later? Beautiful and practical, it's perfect for your first outing as our princess."

"My first...outing?" What outing? Did she say parade? I'd never liked my schedule, but I desperately wanted to see it right now. Wherever it was.

"Of course, I realize you would have liked a long honeymoon, somewhere romantic with your new husband—and well you deserve it—but with the wedding catching us all by surprise and Peverell having been torn apart by the whirlwind, it's not a feasible option right now.

"The king explained this to you already, did he not?"

I shook my head.

"Oh. Well, I'm sure with his excitement about the wedding and all, it merely slipped his mind."

No doubt. Though I wondered if "excitement" was quite the right word to describe the king's state of mind. He hadn't spoken with me any more than required either.

"I'm going out in public? Today?"

"With the prince, of course. You'll take the royal carriage, make a tour through Main Street, wave to the people, and then serve food at the marketplace the same way you would after a ball. From what I hear, Prince Thoraben went to the kitchens himself yesterday to ensure enough would be made for everyone."

Of course he did. It was so like Ben to see to the needs of his people, even while he was sacrificing his life, heart, and future happiness for them. They didn't know that. They probably thought he'd married me for love, a romantic story. I alone knew the truth. The only romance in the story was the incredible love he'd shown for them, his people. He'd given up his chosen one for them.

A knock at the door admitted my lunch. Though I ate everything the tray held, I couldn't have told anyone what it was I'd eaten, my mind too full of what today—and the future—might hold to even notice. I'd thought I had a pretty good idea of what it meant to be a princess of Peverell. If the wall of gowns now gracing my suite was any indication, my lessons had only just begun.

Four hours later, I tried to tell myself this was like all the other times we'd taken food to the marketplace. Same people, same food, same route, same guards.

I failed. Drastically. Nothing about this felt the same.

To start with, we were in a horse-drawn carriage. A very elaborately decorated one. Velvet seats in a red so dark it was almost purple. Four guards—two at the front and two at the back—dressed in regalia so decorative it was a wonder they could move at all. And gold. So much gold. It swirled along the sides of the carriage, dancing gracefully along the tops of the seats before twirling down to the center of each of the four wheels. Elegant. Effortless. Opulent.

Definitely not the plain, black car we normally took.

And definitely not the positions we normally sat.

Rather than being across from me, Ben sat beside me. Close beside me. I knew he did it on purpose. It was the same reason I took his hand where it lay between us and held it. The same reason I was here today, rather than hiding in my new chamber pretending the past forty-eight hours hadn't occurred.

For the people. Everything was for the people.

Smile and wave, Mackenna. Smile, wave, and look like all your dreams have come true. And don't look guilty. Don't you dare look guilty.

"I'm sorry I missed breakfast," I told Ben quietly as the carriage continued its journey.

Wave, smile.

"Don't worry about it. I'm glad you got some sleep. I know it's rude of me to say it, but you looked exhausted last night." *Smile, wave.* "Are you feeling better now?"

"I am. Thank you."

I barely stopped myself from groaning aloud at how ridiculous our conversation sounded. Almost as staged as our smiles and waves. I hated it. This was Ben, the closest friend I'd had growing up. And here we were, talking like strangers. Would it always be like this now? Or could we somehow find a way to move past it and forge a new relationship, even if we never regained the closeness of the past?

"Then you'll join me for dinner?"

I tried my hand at a real smile, turning my head to bestow it upon Ben. His face was closer to mine than I'd expected, making it easy to see the pleasure there when I nodded. "I'd like that."

Perhaps there was hope for us after all.

"I'm sorry Wenderley wasn't at the wedding."

And perhaps not. I turned my attention to the people lined up along the street cheering as we passed. How many of them had been in the throne room two days ago proclaiming our guilt? They'd gotten what they wanted. We were married. I would be their next queen. Were they happy now their hopes had come to fruition? *Smile and wave, Mackenna. Smile and wave.*

"I know you would have liked to have her there," Ben continued. "She was invited, you know. I made sure Father put her on the invite list, but with Jade's wedding and the cleanup from the whirlwind, she was unable to come. She sent her regrets though. I don't know if you knew that."

See Wenderley front and center as I married the man she was in love with? I was glad she hadn't come. Alina and the king glaring holes through my back had been enough. Fortunately, I was saved from making any sort of comment by the fact that we'd arrived at the marketplace. The food was there, already set up, stacks of plates and cutlery on a table beside it. All it was waiting for was someone to serve it.

"Come on, future king," I said, pushing aside the bitterness becoming all too normal inside me. I couldn't change what had happened, and there were hundreds of people far worse off than me standing waiting for us. "Let's go feed these people."

I was glad I'd slept the morning away for I never would have been able to hold back the tears otherwise. Though I'd fought against her words, Mother had been right. The people were thrilled I would be their queen. Whether they knew the truth or believed the rumors about how the marriage had come about, they were happy it had. It was humbling.

Ben and I stood there, side by side, for an hour as we handed out plates of food. I caught him looking at me a few times and knew I must have looked as happy as I felt. Compared to the silence of the palace, the marketplace with all its people was pure chaos—and yet I loved every bit of it. There was a freedom outside the palace which I'd never felt inside it where protocols and etiquettes reigned. Every decision within the palace was political—what to wear, who to talk to, what could be said. Though it was necessary, it was also stifling. Out here, none of that mattered. Parents made decisions not with foreign countries in mind, but for the good of their children.

And, for an hour at least, I had the privilege of being a part of it. I couldn't have stopped smiling had I tried.

"Are you really a princess now?"

"Ella!" The plate I'd been holding clattered to the table as I ran to embrace the girl I wondered if I'd ever see again. Her brown ringlets tickled my nose, the dust in them making me sneeze and probably turning my tears to mud, but I didn't care. She was here. She was alive.

She wriggled out of my arms, pulling back to hold out a child's plastic tiara. "I brought this for you. Mama said you were a princess but you're not wearing a tiara, so I thought maybe yours got lost in the big storm like my teddy. You can borrow mine, if you want, until they find yours."

Kneeling in front of her, I took off my hat, likely costing more than I wanted to consider, and ducked my head so Ella could position the tiara atop my hair. The way the too-small costume piece dug into my scalp was well worth the smile on her face. I could have told her my tiara was fine but, in the face of her selfless gift, couldn't find the words. When I returned it in a few days' time along with the assurance mine was safe, I'd send with it the cuddliest teddy bear I could find. It might not ever replace the one she'd lost, but hopefully, it would at least let her know how much I'd appreciated her kindness.

"Thank you, Ella." I handed her my hat, loving the way she fingered the flower. "Why don't you give this to your mother? She'd look beautiful in it, don't you think?"

Ella's eyes widened. "Wow. Really?" At my nod, she skipped off, clutching the hat to her chest. I waved to Esme, watching, as always, from a distance. Close enough to watch her daughter, far enough not to impose. One day, when life settled down a bit, I'd properly introduce myself to her. Not as Princess Mackenna or Peverell's future queen but as Kenna. The girl looking for a friend.

Mrs. Olive was waiting when I stood. Her head was down, hands clutched together at her stomach. It was a few seconds before I noticed the flower held between them. Far from the usual elegant bouquets she gave me, this flower was small, unadorned, missing a few petals.

"Mrs. Olive?"

When the woman didn't move, I walked forward, placing a hesitant hand on her arm. It was when she lifted her head that I saw the despair written across her face. The wetness of her eyes.

"The whirlwind took them all. This was the only one left," she said sadly.

I reached for the tiny flower, cradling it in my hand. "It's beautiful."

"You deserve so much more."

I shook my head again. "I'm a woman, just like you. We made it through the whirlwind, all of us. Battered and shaken, a little worse for wear, but we'll grow again, as will your flowers. They'll be filling this place, and my life, with beauty again before you know it."

Though her mouth didn't smile, her eyes brightened. "I'll water them every day, bring you a whole bunch next time you come."

My voice cracked, overwhelmed with emotion as I answered. "I'd be honored to accept it."

A guard cleared his throat beside me, pulling my attention to the food table, now empty. "Forgive me, Your Highness, but it's time to leave."

I thanked the guard, turning back to Mrs. Olive to say good-bye. It would have been nice to stay and eat with the people, but even I knew that the time of peace we'd had while serving wouldn't last forever. It was foolish to think that everyone was as happy with the way the royal family ran Peverell as those who'd come today. Sooner or later, the Rebels would descend. The forty guards patrolling the marketplace weren't here for show.

And Ben had invited me to dinner.

I looked around me. Where was Ben? He was supposed to be beside me. How long had he been gone? Charmed by the people, I hadn't even noticed him walk away.

"Prince Thoraben?" I asked the guard, turning my gaze to the direction he nodded. There Ben was, to the left of the crowd, speaking with a small group of people. I didn't think I recognized any of them, but it was difficult to tell the way the sun cast them in silhouette. I was trying to decide whether I would be welcome to join them or not when Ben saw me looking and waved me over, making the decision for me. The other option would have been to wait in the carriage for him to finish his conversation, and I found that far less appealing. To sit in that golden carriage was to once again separate myself from the people. I was more than happy to put that off for as long as possible.

I'd walked only two steps before one of the guards stopped me.

"Princess Mackenna, we really must go."

"I know, but Prince Thoraben has requested my presence, and who am I to disobey Peverell's future king?" It was low of me, playing on the guard's sense of duty, but I really didn't want to sit in that carriage alone. "I'm sure we'll only be a moment. I'll tell him it is time to leave."

The guard looked at his watch before once again surveying the still peaceful crowd. I could tell he didn't want to let me. Unfortunately for him, unless there was a direct attack happening or imminent, both Ben and I outranked him.

"Very well, Your Highness. You have two minutes."

I had no doubt he would count every one of those hundred and twenty seconds. I left before he could start.

Ben reached for my hand as I approached, smiling as he welcomed me into the little circle. He dropped my hand as soon as I stopped, but the arm he put around my waist as we stood side by side more than made up for it.

"Princess Mackenna, may I present Morley Clarkson, Mike Taylor, Terrance Nathan, Joha Samson and Leon Starc—good friends of mine."

I nodded to each of the men in turn, doing my best to commit their names to memory. I'd never met any of them before, nor did they seem familiar, despite Ben calling them good friends, further proof that while I'd grow up alongside the man I now called my husband, I didn't know everything about him.

I did wonder how he'd met them. Clarkson had to be in his seventies at least, and Starc wasn't far behind. The man he'd called Joe, or something like that, seemed to be around Ben's age, but the others must be at least a decade older, if not two or three. They certainly weren't the friends I usually saw Ben with.

Still, they seemed amiable enough.

"It's a pleasure to meet you, gentlemen."

"And you also, Your Highness," Clarkson said. "May we offer our congratulations on your recent marriage."

"Thank you. Were you able to attend the ceremony?" Though I didn't recall seeing any of them there, that didn't mean they hadn't been. If they were such good friends of Ben, surely he'd invited them.

"No, Your Highness," Clarkson spoke again. "I'm not sure they let beggars like us through the doors, especially on such an auspicious occasion." He said it with a smile. One echoed around the circle on each man's face. Even Ben let out a quiet laugh. I missed the joke.

"Still, it would have been wonderful to have had you there. Allow me to add my invitation to the one I'm certain the prince has already given you. Any friend of Thoraben's is always welcome at the palace."

Clarkson ducked his head again. "Your kindness does you credit, Princess."

"She believes then?" Nathan asked. Ben shook his head, leaving me once again feeling like the outsider. Believes what?

"But I thought—"

"All will be well, my friend."

That wasn't an answer. It wasn't even half an answer. But it satisfied Nathan and must have laid to rest the doubts any of the others might have carried, given their nods. They could have at least waited until I'd left to start talking about me. I'd be going soon enough.

I groaned. Going. I was supposed to tell Ben we had to leave. I glanced behind me at the guard, still waiting some twenty yards away. He hadn't come, though two minutes must have passed, but he didn't look happy.

"It's been a pleasure, gentlemen, but it is time for Prince Thoraben and me to depart. Our carriage awaits. Perhaps we'll see you at the palace sometime?"

"Perhaps," was the only answer I received.

Ben said goodbye, and we walked to the carriage together, his hand in mine. He let go only long enough to wave to the assembled crowd before assisting me into the carriage. The instant he sat down beside me, he took my hand in his again. Though my heart still thudded at what should have been a casual touch, I was all too quickly becoming accustomed to the feel of it. And wanting far more.

The carriage pulled out as soon as we were settled, the guards far more eager than I was to depart. We were almost back at the palace before I found the courage to ask. "Do I believe what?"

To his credit, Ben didn't pretend not to understand, but the instant he grinned, I knew I wasn't going to hear the real answer. I might not have known his friends, but I knew that teasing smile far too well.

"That I'm wonderful."

Very funny. I might have let him get away with it too, except he'd told them I didn't.

"You shook your head."

"Maybe I wasn't sure you still did." His smile drooped a little and, whether or not he meant me to, I heard the yearning in his voice to know the truth. Though he'd said it to tease me—likely the first thing that had come into his mind—he desperately wanted to know now what my answer was. What did I think of him?

"I think you're a wonderful prince and friend."

"And...husband?"

The smile was completely gone now as he looked into my eyes. Even if I'd wanted to look away, I couldn't have. He'd captured me there. I took a deep breath and forced away the four words that raced far too quickly from my heart to my mouth.

I love you, Ben.

I hid them instead behind teasing of my own. "It's a little too early to make a decision on that, don't you think? We've only been married a day."

"Perhaps dinner will help you decide."

He looked away then, back at the road ahead of us. Had he continued to look into my eyes, he would have seen the fear I wasn't strong enough to hide. The fear his words put there. All of a sudden, dinner seemed like far more than a simple meal.

TWENTY-FIVE

No one but a few guards and some grooms were around when we arrived at the palace. After being surrounded by so many people for the past two hours, it felt strange, but not unwelcome. I began walking toward the dining room, but Ben's hand on my shoulder stopped me.

"Come this way."

I frowned. There was nothing in the direction he pointed except more rooms, unless he planned on taking a scenic route and doubling back at some point. "I thought we were going to dinner."

"We are."

The unease I already felt grew as I wondered what exactly he had planned. "Thoraben..."

"Come on. I promise. You'll like it."

And I'd promised to trust him—for better or worse. "Fine."

I let him take my hand as we all but ran down the hall. Wherever dinner was, Ben wanted to get there quickly. The few maids we passed moved to the side, allowing us through. I was so busy trying to keep up that I didn't realize until we started climbing that we were at my—our—tower. Even then, Ben didn't slow, though fortunately, he let go of my hand. I envied his flat shoes. The tall heels I wore were beautiful, no doubt, but they'd not been designed for climbing stone staircases. I took them off halfway up.

"Come on, Kenna. Can't you go any faster? You'll miss it."

"Miss what?"

I saw it the moment I looked up. The sunset.

It had been dropping while we talked to Ben's friends at the marketplace and at a headache-inducing height on the way home but now—

Now it was magnificent.

In the time it had taken for us to exit the carriage and run to the top of the tower, the sun had cast a pink spell over every cloud in the sky, gilding their edges with gold. The rays bursting up from one particular cloud, the one the sun hid behind, crowned the sky with a magnificence not even a king could lay claim to.

I dropped my shoes and ran to the edge of the wall, desperate to take in every bit of it I could. Forget dinner. This sight alone was a prize worth moving back to the palace for. I hoped Ben wasn't too hungry because I planned on standing here, breathing in the sky's beauty, until that last ray faded.

I jumped when Ben's hands cupped my shoulders, his body behind mine instantly setting every nerve on fire. I hadn't heard him approach. I'd thought nothing could distract me from the incredible scene before me. I was wrong. Ben's hands, slowly moving down my arms until they captured mine around my waist had me struggling to breathe. Not because they were tight. Simply because they were there. I told myself they were just hands with no power whatsoever over me, but neither my head nor my heart believed it.

The pounding began in my chest, quickly spreading to my stomach and within moments, my whole body was throbbing with the beat, right down to the tips of my fingers. Could Ben feel it? Did he have any idea the effect him merely standing behind me, his arms around me, was having? He had to have, surely. But he took no advantage of it. Though I could feel his breath against my hair, he didn't move nor speak, not until the sun's final ray faded into the horizon.

And then, he stepped back, walking, I assumed, to the seat he'd sat in last night. I stood there at the wall, staring out at the darkening sky for another full minute before finding the courage to turn around.

The tower was covered in white fairy lights. Whether Ben had only just turned them on or I'd simply missed them in the brightness of the sunset, I hadn't seen them before. They criss-crossed above me, making a roof of starlight, and rippled around the stone walls.

Bright. White. Achingly beautiful.

And there stood Ben beside the table, not sitting as I'd thought, but patiently waiting. For me.

"Will you join me for dinner, my lady?"

"Certainly, kind sir." He waited until I'd sat then helped push my chair in, deftly laying a napkin across my lap. I couldn't help but tease him.

"Trying to convince me you're wonderful?"

He grinned as he sat down across from me. "Is it working?"

Well and truly. "Maybe."

"Well then, let me present...your dinner."

With an overabundance of flair, Ben pulled the silver dome off the large plate in the middle of the table. Stunned laughter bubbled out of me before I could stop it. That wasn't dinner. And yet—

"You remembered."

"Of course."

If I hadn't already loved him, I would have fallen hard there and then. It was a wonder I wasn't glowing with it as brightly as the fairy lights above my head. Surely any moment my heart would explode.

Dinner was pancakes—three huge stacks of them, a bowl of fresh blueberries on the side ready to pile on top. Steam was still rising from a silver jug filled with thick chocolate sauce. I checked, though I knew already what it would be. There was only one thing missing from my fantasy dinner.

"Where's the—?"

From somewhere near his legs, Ben produced a tub of vanilla ice cream, holding it just out of my reach.

"Admit it first. I'm a wonderful husband."

I had no reason not to. "You're a wonderful husband." He beamed. I held out my hand. "Now hand over the ice cream."

I couldn't believe he'd ordered pancakes for dinner.

I had been fourteen, maybe fifteen—and having a rebellious day—when I'd claimed this would be the perfect dinner. King Everson had been out of the country for two weeks, leaving Ben, Alina, and me to dine alone. Without the king overseeing our etiquette, we'd been far freer than usual. Alina had sent back to the kitchens three meals one particular night before settling on one she was content with. Talk had turned to "the perfect meal" after that.

Ben had claimed his to be a spit roast with four different meats at the very least, hot bread rolls, an abundance of roast vegetables—especially potatoes—and chocolate pudding drowned in hot fudge sauce for dessert. And the permission to eat as much as he liked without being considered a glutton.

Alina had listed off eight courses of supposed delights, all of which made me sick at the thought. It was as if she'd combed the world, searching out the most expensive dishes and claiming them her favorites. I doubted she'd ever eaten snails—garlic, gold-flaked, or otherwise—as she frequently told me how disgusting a creature they were. Still, if snails were on her list of the perfect meal, who were we to take them from her?

By the time Alina had finally settled on her eight courses, being as particular as she was, dinner was long finished. She and I were about to walk out of the dining room when Ben, still sitting at the table, had asked what my perfect meal would be.

"Pancakes. Just pancakes," I'd said defiantly. It was the simplest, tastiest thing I could think of.

They'd both laughed, of course. "Pancakes? That's it? Not even sauce on them?"

"Fine. Pancakes with blueberries, vanilla ice cream, and chocolate sauce." I'd walked out alone, leaving Alina still laughing at what a simpleton I was. I thought Ben had been laughing too. I never dreamed he'd remember all these years later.

I took a bite, relishing the taste. There was no way the two of us would be able to eat all of this, but I'd certainly enjoy every mouthful I did manage.

"Did the maids do all this?" I asked Ben, gesturing to the fairy lights.

"No, I did."

"Oh." I took another bite, then another, making my way through half the pancake as I considered his answer. When had he had time to do all this? And—the even greater question in my mind—why? "You put up fairy lights."

"I know you like them. And I had to find something to do while you were snoring the day away."

"I don't snore."

"Do."

"Do not."

Ben shrugged, teasing grin still firmly in place. "It's okay. I don't mind."

"How very chivalrous of you. But I don't snore."

"Sorry, Kenna, but you actually do."

"How would you know anyway?" I grumbled. Ben had never been in my room while I was sleeping, despite what Waitrose and however many others seemed to believe. He hadn't even been in it while I was awake until that night he kissed me.

"You forget, I stayed beside you the night of the whirlwind."

The whirlwind. The night everything fell apart. I could have argued that there were hundreds of people in the hall that night so he had no way of knowing it was me, but Ben was more certain than I was at this point. The air had been so thick with dust, I might have.

"And you still married me?"

"You needed a hero."

He was teasing me—I knew that—but I couldn't find any laughter in me to play along. I still didn't understand why he'd married me, and having him joke that it was because I needed a hero made me feel like a pathetic weakling who couldn't even stand up by herself. What woman wanted the man she loved to think that of her?

"I was going to propose up here, you know. I had it all planned."

My fork clattered out of my hand onto the plate. I left it there, staring down at it as if it was a foreign object I'd never seen before. It gave me something to focus my eyes on while my mind tried to process Ben's words. I wanted him to take them back, or at least convince myself I'd heard him wrongly, but neither happened.

"Pr— Propose?" I stuttered on the word.

"I was going to. That was my plan. Your little dream, which you still haven't told me about I might add, negated the need for a proposal, but I couldn't bear to waste those plans altogether so..." He waved his hand, palm upward over the table, like a stall owner showcasing his wares. "Our dinner."

The fairy lights, the setting sun painting the sky stunning shades of orange and pink, each cloud gilt with gold, a private dinner with not even a guard in sight. And I'd been foolish enough to think he'd planned it for me.

My stomach roiled. Here before me was my fantasy dinner, and I couldn't eat another bite of it. Not after hearing that. This dream of a place was where he'd planned to propose to Wenderley. The fairy lights lost their beauty, even the sunset seemed overly gaudy. I'd told Ben when I left the first time that he could have my tower. I hadn't considered how much it would hurt to see him share it with someone else.

"Kenna? I thought you'd like it."

"I do." Or, at least, I did. "Thoraben, it's beautiful, all of it, truly. But you don't have to do this. It's like you're courting me or something."

"I am."

He was? "Why?"

"With the rush of the wedding, I never got the chance to court you."

There it was again. The fear. Rushing up my throat, pounding in my ears, squeezing the air from my lungs. It shouldn't have scared me, the thought of Ben trying to come closer, but it did. I'd fallen in love with him without him ever doing anything to make me. What hope did I have of hiding my true feelings if he purposely tried to court me? It might have been different, had I not known about Wenderley, but that was the point. I did.

"It's what normal people do before they get married, you know."

Nothing about our relationship could be considered normal. "We're already married."

"I know. I was at the wedding."

I rolled my eyes. He was being ridiculous. There was no need for this chivalry. It felt as fake to me as the smiles at the wedding had. I knew he didn't love me. It was almost insulting of him to pretend otherwise.

"You don't have to."

"Did it ever occur to you that I might want to?"

"I get it, you're the prince. You always do what's right."

"Kenna—"

"No. Dinner up here, in my favorite place, the sunset, the lights coming on and everything—it's beautiful, truly. I couldn't imagine a more perfect setting." Or a more perfect person to share it with. "But I can't do this now. You said it yourself last night, we need time. *I* need time. I've spent my whole life pretending, but I can't do it anymore. I can't pretend everything is fine when it's not."

"You don't have to."

"Yes, I do."

"Not with me."

I sighed. Especially with him.

He reached for my hand across the table. I drew it back before he could touch it. Though he frowned, he didn't try again, instead simply looking at me, more compassion in his eyes than I could bear. "What are you so afraid of?"

I shook my head, angered as much by his patience as I was disgusted by my own emotions. I had to get away from him. The napkin he'd placed with such care on my lap joined the mess of pancakes on the table as I scrambled to my feet.

"Bye, Thoraben. Thanks for dinner."

"Don't go, please. Stay. We don't have to eat. We can talk."

Leaving my discarded shoes behind, I fled down the stairs before my anger got the better of me.

That was the problem—there was nothing left to say.

TWENTY-SIX

The days passed, and my room became my sanctuary—or perhaps it was my prison. I wasn't sure anymore. My maids came and went, not staying any longer than required to perform their duties—not even Meri. I wouldn't have wanted to be around me either. I was back in the palace, the place I knew so well—and yet, nothing was the same. All because of this little ring sitting on my finger. It might as well have been a ball and chain for all the freedom it gave me.

I twisted it on my finger, wondering how long it would take to become accustomed to the rigidity of it. I'd never really worn rings before, not for more than a few hours at a time, and they'd all been dress rings. Ostentatious, meant to be seen and admired. This was far simpler. A small sapphire on a white gold band studded with square-cut diamonds.

Compared to Alina's, it was downright dowdy, and yet, I liked it. Like the wildflowers my mother loved so much, its beauty lay in its simplicity. And, whether it had been made to or not, it matched my silver forget-me-not tiara.

I liked the ring. I didn't like what it represented.

Marriage.

It reminded me every moment of every day that I was married. To Ben.

The man I was in love with.

The man my heart ached to be with.

The man I avoided every chance I got.

I didn't know how to act around him anymore. It was easier to stay in my room than it was to figure it out. With Alina and the king detesting my very presence and Ben respecting my request for time, no one complained that I took the vast majority of my meals alone.

My head warred with my heart back and forth on the issue until I felt ill. My dream the night of the whirlwind had proven how much I wanted to be Ben's wife, yet it hadn't been my choice, nor his. And now, it never could be. I felt as if my worth as a person had been taken along with my freedom.

I missed my little room in the cottage with its normal sized bed and simple furniture. And my picture. The one Ben had given me of us in the snow. I'd sent a maid there to look for it. She'd returned empty-handed. It had been foolish to think it would have survived the storm anyway. I'd seen plenty of photos from our wedding already but, despite their glamour, not one of them had come close to being as precious as that photo had been. Ben would have another copy of it. I'd ask him one day—if I ever found the courage to face him again.

My list of friends shrank smaller each day. The king hated me, Alina was mad at me, my parents had betrayed me, I doubted Wenderley would ever forgive me for taking the man she loved, and Ben? I didn't know where I stood with him, but I couldn't go to him. He was in love with Wenderley, and he was married to me.

I had no one.

But, as if to prove not everything had changed, I once again had a schedule. Every minute of every day mapped out for me with where I should be, what I should wear, and who I should talk to—along with hundreds more rules and etiquettes to learn now I was the future queen. The day in the tower when Ben had first told me about his bride, I'd pitied her and all the adjustments her new life would entail. I'd been right to. I just hadn't thought it would be me.

Alongside Beth and Michala, my two new maids, I had a personal advisor, an event planner, and a stylist—all of whom I met with weekly—and various other staff I was both responsible for and accountable to. I also had an etiquette coach who came daily to teach me how to be a queen. As far as I could tell, it was the same as "how to be a princess" only with more power and fewer frills.

It was almost surprising I had any time to mope at all.

I sketched a heart on the top of my page, swirling flounces and edging around it, belatedly hoping the folder of pages I'd been given was a proof copy of Peverell's trade agreement with Hodenia and not the original itself. No number of flounces could ever make the reading more interesting, but I was pretty sure I'd be in trouble for it all the same if it were the original.

A knock came at my door. I put down the paper with relief. Lunch had arrived. Finally. I'd have to go back to reading it again later—I was the future queen now with matching responsibilities—but even queens had to eat.

"Come in." I packed the papers inside the folder, closing it far more forcefully than the task required. If only I never had to open it again. "Thanks for bringing—"

I stopped. That wasn't my lunch. And it wasn't my maids.

"Waitrose..."

"Princess Mackenna. What a charming suite you have here."

I picked up my oversized planner, hugging it against my chest as if it could protect me from his leering eyes.

"Get out."

"What? No welcome? And here I thought princesses were supposed to be charming. Or is that only the prince?"

"I'll call the guards."

"Oh, didn't you know? There was a little...hmm, what shall we call it?" He raised an eyebrow, walking a few steps closer. "*Disturbance*...in the throne room. All the guards were called to assist." He closed the door behind him, taking with it what felt like all the oxygen in the room.

"What have you done?" Ben was in the throne room this morning. It was written on my schedule. If Waitrose had hurt him...

"Oh, don't look so worried, princess. Goodness. Anyone would think you actually cared for your new husband. It was nothing more than a scuffle with an overly inebriated man. Well, inebriated is probably stretching the truth a little. Perhaps I should call him a good actor. He'd better be, with what I'm paying him."

"Get out, Waitrose. I mean it."

"You do? How sweet. Worried your husband might catch me here or that you might actually care for my...affections." His wink rolled my stomach. The edges of the planner bit into my fingers where I gripped it. If he wasn't going to leave then I had to. Only I had no idea how. There were three doors out of here—to the hall, the balcony, and Ben's suite—and Waitrose stood closer than I to all three. The bathroom and dressing room were options, but neither of them would offer me much protection or means of escape.

"If you so much as lay a hand on me, I'll scream. There are servants everywhere in the palace. Someone will hear me."

"Touch you? Oh no. I came to talk. Though now you mention it, you are looking quite fetching today in that sundress. I always did have a partiality for women in pink."

And blue, and green, and purple, and... He should have stopped at "women." The whole palace knew how much he liked women. If only any of the women had ever liked him back.

"I'll have you thrown out of the palace."

"On what grounds, exactly?"

"You're not welcome here."

"On the contrary. Should you mention this visit to anyone, I'll tell them you invited me."

"You wouldn't."

"Ah, but I would. And we both know who the king would believe."

"You don't think my word holds any weight?" Much as it goaded me to admit it, he was right. The king would believe Waitrose over me any day.

His sneer was obvious, and as terrifying as his leer had been.

"Come now, Mackenna. It's not as if the king's distrust of you is a secret. Not that I blame him. He could hardly be expected to care for someone who's only a threat to him. You might have smiled through the wedding, but we all heard in the throne room how much you protested it ever occurring. It wouldn't be a stretch at all to convince the king that I was already your lover. I'll bet you haven't even been in Thoraben's chamber yet."

That was no business of his, although there was clearly no doubt in his mind that it was true, especially with the betraying blush spreading across my face. "At the reception, you claimed I was pregnant."

"I changed my mind."

"Get out."

"No, I do believe I'll stay. It's not like anyone can force a wedding on us even if we were caught in a—shall we say—compromising position. Not with you already married and all. Princess Mackenna, our *future queen...*"

I swallowed back the revulsion threatening to choke me, clutching at the folder so tight it bit into my fingers. "I'll tell Ben. He'll believe me."

"Aha. So, it's *Ben* now, is it? How sweet. You trust him, then? Tell me, does he trust you?"

"Why wouldn't he?"

"Has he told you his dirty little secret yet?"

My stomach clenched, fear pulling the strength from my body. I lined my hip up with the edge of my desk and focused on its rigidity. Waitrose wanted me to be afraid. He was trying to plant doubts. He was thoroughly succeeding at both, but I refused to give him the satisfaction of showing it.

"Oh yes, perfect Prince Thoraben isn't as perfect as he's led you to believe."

Waitrose took a step closer to me. There was nothing for it. If I waited any longer, he'd be close enough to grab me. Words I could block out. If he got hold of me... I didn't even want to think what would happen next. I had to run. Catch him off guard.

One.

"You're not going to ask me what it is?" he goaded.

Two.

"It's only fair that you know, being his wife and all."

Three.

I ran as fast as I could, ignoring his shout behind me. The bathroom door crashed against the wall behind as I flung it open, knocking my knee when it bounced instantly back. Spinning so fast I slipped, I slammed the door shut.

On Waitrose's arm.

I tried to push the door closed but my strength was nothing compared to his. With very little effort Waitrose opened it and walked inside, blocking my only escape. I'd never had a pet, but I knew enough about wild animals to know that pain only made them angrier, and even more dangerous.

A gasp of terror rose in my throat. I hadn't been fast enough.

"Nice try, Mackenna," he sneered. "My, isn't this cozy."

There was nowhere else to run. Not even anything to defend myself with.

"I've always wanted to know what it would be like to be with a princess. I never got my chance with Alina, but you..."

He took a step closer, trailing a hand up my arm. My gaze skittered down, spotting the planner, still clutched against my chest. I'd never before been so thankful for its bulky size. Using every bit of strength I could muster, I smacked it against the side of Waitrose's head. He stumbled backward.

"You will never be even half the man Ben is."

"Ben? *Ben?*" Waitrose roared, putting a hand to his head. "Do you even know him? He's not the man you think he is."

"You have no right to speak of him that way. He is your future king."

Waitrose laughed bitterly. "However mistakenly highly you think of him today, Thoraben will never be king. His father will exile him long before he ever ascends the throne, and you with him, princess." He spat out the word like one would a vile taste. My fear grew more intense by the second. "I'm surprised the king hasn't done so already. He must think there is still hope. If he does, he is as much a fool as his son. The future of Peverell lies in ruin, Mackenna—and all because of your dear Ben."

"I'll have you tried for treason."

"Me?" He laughed again, his voice a sneer. "Thoraben is the one who should be tried, not me. Oh, but you don't know. Do you."

"Get out."

"You can't ignore the truth forever."

"Like I'd believe anything you told me as truth."

"Thoraben's a Rebel."

"How dare you."

Fury made me strong where fear had crippled me. Waitrose had crossed the line the instant he walked through my door. He'd defamed me and now he'd defamed my husband. I couldn't push him out—he'd already proved himself far stronger than me—but I still had my planner. I raised it to hit him again, but this time he was ready. He caught it in one hand, using my lack of balance to draw me closer. He stopped a breath short of touching my face.

"Ask him yourself. *I* dare *you*."

"Leave. Now."

"You know what? I will. I did what I came for." He stepped back suddenly, throwing me off balance again. The planner dropped to the floor with a thump. "Come running to me when your perfect marriage falls apart, Mackenna. I'll be waiting."

With a final smirk, he walked out of the bathroom and out of my suite, leaving me shaking with fear. I was still standing in front of the sink, arms braced against it, trying to find control when the door opened again. I tensed for a moment, fearing he'd come back, before Avrel called my name. She must have brought my lunch.

"I'll just be a minute." I called, quickly turning on the tap. The face staring back at me in the mirror was strange in its normality. After all I'd been through in the last five minutes, I somehow expected it to look different. My insides were shaking, my heart still pounding, but my face looked the same as always. I felt as if it, too, had somehow betrayed me. Though, once again, it was probably for the best. I knew enough of Waitrose's reputation to know he had the power to destroy mine. It was why he knew he could get away with it.

I ate lunch slowly, forcing down each bite, refusing to let my tremulous emotions steal another meal, though they certainly came close.

It wasn't only that Waitrose had come and threatened me, although that would have been enough to nauseate me alone. He'd called Ben a Rebel. Ben, my husband, the future king. A Rebel. It was a lie. Nothing more than pure defamation. It had to be.

Yet, the more I tried to push Waitrose's claims from my head, the harder they stuck. *Thoraben's a Rebel. Thoraben's a Rebel.*

No, Waitrose was wrong. Ben couldn't be a Rebel. He was the prince. How could he pledge allegiance to another ruler when he would be king himself one day? To do so would be to doom Peverell as a kingdom to... But then, that's what Waitrose had claimed. The future of Peverell lay in ruins.

But Ben wasn't a Rebel. So none of this mattered.

Unless he was.

Ashe had been, and I hadn't known. Jade also. Could Ben be? That day with Roni in the hospital, he'd tried to tell me something about them before brushing it aside. *Did* he know more about them than he let on? Surely not.

I'd been witness to the king convicting Rebels in the past and exiling them. Nicola and her family aside, they'd mostly been older couples who, while accepting their sentences with dignity, had been determined to tell the king how wrong he was in thinking he could govern the kingdom alone. One had even been sentenced to prison for life after suggesting Queen Ciera would have wanted the king to know the truth. Alina and I had been rushed out of the throne room before I'd heard what that truth might be.

I'd never held any sympathy for the Rebels, believing that they chose their fate when they pledged their allegiance elsewhere. Exile seemed kind. But they'd all been older, set in their ways. Ashe, Jade—they were young, their whole lives ahead of them. They'd spoken with a respect for Peverell and its royal family that couldn't be feigned.

But then, if Ben were a Rebel himself, it wouldn't need to be.

And there were those odd friends he'd introduced me to—Clarkson and the others—who'd laughed at the notion that they'd be allowed in the palace. Nathan had asked if I believed. Ben never had explained what he meant. Were they asking if I, too, was a Rebel?

This was ridiculous. Ben wasn't a Rebel, and I was torturing myself thinking about it. Waitrose had dared me to ask Ben. I would.

Someday.

TWENTY-SEVEN

I was sitting at the same desk again three days later when the wooden door to my suite thumped open, with not even a knock to warn me. The startled screech that shot out of my mouth was tiny compared to the noise my heart was still making as it tried to escape my ribcage. I put a hand against my chest to hold it in. The man who swept through the door into my room this time wasn't Waitrose, but I feared him almost as much.

"Thoraben. You gave me a fright. What are you doing here?"

He didn't apologize, nor say hello. Instead, he turned around and closed the door before walking over toward me, stopping a yard short of where I sat. I didn't know whether to stand and greet him or prostrate myself on the floor before him. I'd never seen him so angry.

"Thoraben?"

"I've had it, Mackenna. This has gone on long enough. It's been two weeks. Tell me, what did I do? And before you get any ideas, I'm staying until you answer me. As are you. Your maids and everyone else has been told to leave us alone until I tell them otherwise.

"I've given you time to get used to me and your new position but we can't go on like this. *I* can't go on like this. So, tell me, what did I do?"

I dropped my gaze to the floor. "Nothing."

"Then why are you avoiding me?"

"I'm not."

"Don't lie to me, Kenna!"

He wanted the truth? "Fine. I am avoiding you."

"Why?"

Stupid tears. There they were, again, clawing their way up the back of my throat, threatening to break free the second I opened my mouth. Why did I have to be so emotional? There were a hundred ways I could answer Ben's question. Ninety-five of them were lies. I'd been lying to myself my whole life, it seemed. And I hadn't even known it.

I'd been so angry at Ben and the king for putting me in this position but now the full brunt of my anger rested solely on myself. I shook my head, pursing my lips and clenching my teeth together as I tried to keep my face from scrunching into an unattractive ball of sobs.

"Kenna..."

"Go away." I bit out the words, even though I knew he'd never do it.

"No."

"Then I will."

"I locked the doors."

"You locked me in?"

He crossed his arms, staring down at me. The angrier I got, the calmer he seemed. It was infuriating. "Until we work this out."

"How could you?"

"I have to know what I did wrong."

"You married me!"

I spat the words out, covering my face as I ran to the window and stared at the glass. My eyes were too full of tears to see anything but shades of color beyond it. There was silence behind me, but I wasn't foolish enough to think Ben had left. His patience was undeserved. And annoying.

"Kenna..."

He was behind me now, close enough to touch me yet he hadn't. I closed my eyes against the pain that tiny distance caused. I ached to lean back into his arms and let him love me.

Even if he didn't love me, hold me, like he had in the tower that night as we watched the sunset. I wanted someone to hold me.

No. Not someone. I wanted Ben.

"You're angry I married you?" He was completely calm now, all the anger gone from his voice. There was surprise in his tone. Or perhaps it was sympathy. Maybe even a yearning to understand me.

Yet how could I make him understand my roiling emotions when I didn't understand myself? Was I angry he'd married me? Yes, absolutely. And no. Was there any right answer to that question? "I wish I understood."

"Understood what?"

"Why you did it. And don't tell me it was because of the people. You could have told them nothing happened between us in the throne room that day. Your father was opposed to our marriage. He would have found a way around it. You turned your back on Wenderley, you—"

"Wenderley? What does she have to do with this? She wasn't even there."

I glared at the window, wishing I was brave enough to face him. I was already in pain. Did he have to make it worse?

"I know she was the one you'd chosen to marry."

"You do, do you?" I could hear the smile in his voice. He was laughing at me. Here I was, aching with the pain of all that had happened, and he was laughing at me. Anger overthrew my fear as I spun around, almost bumping into him, he was so close. I walked back a step, the window behind me holding me up as I stared him down.

"I'm not blind."

He crossed his arms, that half grin on his face only infuriating me further, if that was even possible. Any second now I'd throw him out. He might have locked the doors but there were plenty of windows.

"No, but you are wrong."

And he was a fool. "You're denying Wenderley loves you?" Everyone knew it. It was as common knowledge as the king's name, Wenderley having made no secret of where her affections lay.

"I'm denying she was ever the woman I chose as my bride. I don't love her. I never have. At least, not in the way a husband should love his wife."

Oh. "Fine, so it wasn't Wenderley. So I've taken someone else's place. Even better. Somewhere in the world, there's a girl moping over the fact that I've taken the husband who should have been hers. Oh, but wait, she didn't know yet, did she? And now she never will. She'll die not knowing she might have been queen one day. And you're stuck with me, the girl you never would have married if not for a stupid mistake of a dream."

He looked at the floor, still grinning, like he was the sole guardian of some grand secret. Well, I wasn't waiting around to hear what it was. The doors locked from the inside, not the outside—something that, foolishly, had only now occurred to me. Enough was enough. I was leaving. There, he'd succeeded. He'd gotten me out of my room. All it had taken was for him to walk into it.

"Forget it, I'm going." I stalked toward the door.

"Wait."

Wrong thing to say. Spinning around, I unleashed every bit of frustration I'd built up in the past month. I didn't care what he thought of me anymore. He wanted the truth? I'd give him it. I just hoped the room was soundproof.

"No, Thoraben. I won't wait. This conversation is ridiculous and I'm tired of your games. If you're not going to explain what I want to know or answer any of my questions, then—"

"You didn't take anyone's place."

"What?" I flung the word out, barely even caring what he said. Didn't he get it? I'd had enough. I couldn't deal with any more speeches about honor or the good of the people or—

"You were the one I chose. The only one I chose."

My head started to spin, and I grabbed at the bedpost beside me for support, relieved when I made contact with it. He couldn't be saying what it sounded like. That would mean...

"Me?"

"Yeah."

"Why?"

"Because I loved you."

Silence pulsed in my ears. I'd stood beside a gong as it was being hit once. The initial noise had been loud but the ringing in my ears, even after the sound had ceased, had remained for almost an hour after. His words were just as shattering. "You what?"

"I love you, Mackenna. And this is not how I meant to tell you."

The strength left my body along with the fight. "You said it was because of honor."

"It was the only reasoning Father would listen to. I'd already told him I loved you and it hadn't been enough. He was never going to let me marry you. But then the people were demanding we marry, and I knew it might be my only chance. Father might be opinionated and stubborn, but he'll do anything for his people."

Though I heard Ben's words, I couldn't make them real. It was as if I was witnessing the conversation from a distance rather than having it myself. Any second now, he'd laugh and tell me he'd fooled me. Only he wasn't joking. He couldn't be.

"You told your father you loved me?"

"The day I turned eighteen. He told me it was time to choose a wife. I told him I already had."

"Eighteen? But I was only fifteen. Barely even a woman."

"Old enough for me to know that there was no one else I'd want for my wife. It's always been you, Kenna. Your parents knew too. I'd spoken with them, gained their permission. I was only waiting for you."

"You're kidding." He shook his head, daring me to believe him, never once taking his eyes off mine. "You never said anything. Never even hinted that you...well...that you..." I couldn't even say it. It wasn't real. It couldn't be.

"That I loved you? I couldn't. Not back then. You were too young to marry and Father didn't approve. He wanted me to marry a princess or, at the very least, a high-class woman like Wenderley who he could mold into the queen he desired her to be. He thought I'd change my mind about you if he paraded enough other women in front of me. He failed, by the way."

"But...that day in the tower, when you told me you'd chosen a bride and all but begged me to ask who it was. It was me? Even then?"

"Yes."

"What would you have done had I given into your pushing me?"

"I knew you wouldn't. You're too stubborn. And I was right."

"But if you hadn't been?"

He shrugged. "I would have told you. I wanted to. I almost did—twice—the night of the Midsummer's Ball. I'd been waiting for so long, knowing it was only a matter of months left until you would be eighteen and I could declare myself. That was the agreement I'd had with my father, you see, that I'd not say anything to you about my intentions until you were of age.

"And then I saw you standing outside the ballroom looking far too beautiful for any man's sanity, let alone mine when I'd loved you for years. Had Waitrose and Ashe's presence not given me pause, I know I would have ignored Father's edict altogether and knelt down there and then to declare myself.

"But then Wenderley showed up and Ashe pulled me aside to tell me of his plans to court you and you shocked me with the news that you were leaving. I know I shouldn't have come to your room that night, but I couldn't let you leave without at least knowing I cared. Only I scared you even further away with that kiss."

"I knew it was a mistake." I'd been telling myself that ever since it happened.

But Ben was shaking his head. "Believe me, it wasn't a mistake. I'd been wanting to kiss you for so long. I should have told you how I felt then, even despite Father's edict. I tried but—"

"I sent you away."

"You were right to, much as I hated to admit it at the time.

I lay awake most of the rest of the night trying to think how I could have handled that better."

I'd lain awake too, only for an entirely different reason. "I thought you regretted it. I convinced myself you were in love with Wenderley and that it was merely goodbye."

He shook his head slowly, eyes still on mine. He wasn't smiling, exactly, but there was something warm in his gaze. "Kenna, you're the only one I've ever kissed."

It was too much to take in at once. I sat on the edge of my bed, opening and closing my eyes as I stared at air, willing my mind to make sense of all Ben had said. I kept coming back to one thing.

Ben loved me. Except—

"But our wedding night. You didn't want me."

He let out a short laugh, crossing his arms as he stared down at me, an expression I couldn't interpret on his face. "Oh, I wanted you all right."

"You sent me away. Told me it would be too strange to...be with me."

"It was late, and you were exhausted. You'd already been forced into the marriage. What sort of husband—friend even— would that make me if I demanded more?"

"I thought you were thinking of Wenderley."

Ben came over and sat on the bed beside me, still not touching me, but close enough that if I moved my hand even the smallest bit, we would be. It was like he was still giving me that choice. To accept him or to send him away. Again. Ever since the wedding, I'd thought the power lay in his hands. I'd never realized he'd relinquished it to me.

"Kenna, you were the only one I was thinking of as I stood in your room that night reminding myself of all the reasons I should leave. You'd done everything I'd asked of you all day, trusting me even though I knew you hated it, playing the part of a bride, smiling for the cameras. I couldn't have been more proud of you, nor more desperate to stay. But you hated Father and what he'd done to you and for all I knew, you hated me too. I couldn't stay.

But I wanted to. So, so wanted to. I'd waited years already to be able to tell you I loved you and there we were, actually married.

"You've always been beautiful but you, in that gown, my tiara, the candles... It took all the strength I had to kiss you once and walk away. Even then, I don't think I slept all night, knowing you were on the other side of that door."

I was the one he'd chosen. Not the replacement or the mistake but the one he'd always wanted. I hadn't taken Wenderley's or some other woman's place. I'd only taken mine. All that time— when we'd played with Alina in the snow, talked in the tower, when he'd tried to convince me to stay, when he'd asked me to trust him and married me. All that time, he'd loved me.

"When you said you were going to propose in the tower, you meant to me."

"Of course. The fairy lights, the food, the sunset, your tower... How could it have been for anyone—" He stopped. "You thought I meant Wenderley." It hurt too much to agree so I merely shrugged. "No wonder you ran away. I'm so sorry, Kenna. I thought you understood. It's only ever been you."

I'd made such a mess of this. All this time, I'd thought it was Wenderley he loved, when it had been me. Every time he'd kissed me, teased me, held my hand—he hadn't been doing it because people were watching. He'd actually wanted to. As much as I had.

"What's going on in that head of yours now, Kenna?"

"You love me."

I felt him sigh, turning my head in time to catch his smile. "Yeah, I do. I think I always have."

Lifting a hand, he touched the side of my face. I leaned into it, relishing the connection. I didn't have the courage to reciprocate, it was all still too new, but I considered it.

"Wait." I drew my head back, breaking the contact. "Your tiara?"

"I designed it and had it made for your sixteenth birthday."

"But...your father..." The king had been the one to give me that gift, not Ben.

"He found out I'd commissioned it and refused to allow me to give it to you, saying it would be an inappropriate gift from me, given we weren't engaged. I would have been happy to rectify that shortcoming but Father reminded me of our agreement. It was too late to return the tiara, as the jeweler already knew it was for you and Father didn't want to lose face, so he had another made for Alina, giving them to both of you as your gifts that year. I comforted myself with the fact that one day you'd know the truth."

"That it had been from you?"

"And that I loved you, even then." He smiled, then just as quickly frowned, his eyebrows pulling together as he scrutinized my face. "Are you going to cry again?"

I laughed, shaking my head. Two months ago, I would have thought it an absurd question coming from Ben. I'd stubbornly refused to ever cry in front of him, thinking I'd never live it down. I'd cried every time I'd seen him of late. It felt good to laugh instead.

"Well, that's a relief."

"I'm sorry. I know I've been a mess lately. It's been…crazy."

"I know. For me too, though I've had longer to prepare. Kenna, I want you to know that I'm not going to force you to feel anything for me. I know you never asked for any of this, but I hope in time, we can at least regain the friendship we once had. I'm still the same person you've known all your life."

"Except now I know you love me."

"Well…" He shrugged, grinning and unrepentant. "There is that."

I stared down at my hand, the one he'd so tenderly bandaged and kissed that night. He'd loved me even then.

Without letting myself think, I reached out that hand and took his, marveling at the way it felt in mine. Strong. Sure. Certain as the man himself. He made me want to be strong while giving me the space to be weak. He'd given me so much today, breaking his way into my self-imposed prison and turning it into a place of joy. I ached to tell him I loved him too, yet there was one thing holding me back. One thing stopping me from giving him my love and everything I had.

"Ben?"

"Yes?"

"Are you a Rebel?"

TWENTY-EIGHT

My question echoed in the silence, filling the air before dissipating into time and space. The silence stretched so long I started to wonder whether I'd even spoken. Perhaps I'd dreamed it. I knew it was stupid. Waitrose wasn't a man to be trusted. He never had been. This was Ben—future king. My best friend. I knew him. I'd known him all my life. I loved him, and he loved me. I would have known if he was—

"Yes."

"What?"

"I am."

My mind went blank. My heart begging him to take the admission back.

"No." The whisper tore out of my mouth. He couldn't be. Only moments ago, I'd wondered if I could have possibly been happier. With a single word, he'd dashed it all.

"It's not what you—"

"How long?" I didn't want to hear his excuses or explanations. I wanted to know if it was real. Perhaps it was a recent decision and I could convince him to change his mind. He'd said he loved me. He'd waited years and publicly defied his father to marry me. Surely my opinion held some weight. There were other ways to prove himself different to his father. He didn't have to take down the kingdom to do it.

"All my life."

I'd said I wouldn't cry. Any second now I'd prove myself wrong.

"When Nicola—?" He'd watched her be exiled, all the while knowing his crime matched hers, if not overshadowed it entirely. She was just a girl. He was the prince, with far more power, access, and influence than she'd ever have. Had he not felt even the slightest bit of guilt?

"She didn't go alone, neither has she been since. We've kept up with every one of the Rebels who've been exiled or condemned, speaking with them regularly, as they can with us. The contact goes both ways."

With every word Ben said, the depth of his betrayal stretched further. He wasn't just a Rebel. "You're their leader."

"No, not a leader, but I do have access to information and people many of the others don't."

Ben was a traitor. I tore my hand out of his, shoving it between my knees, steeling myself against the hurt on his face. Had he expected anything less? Surely he hadn't thought I would merely tell him I loved him and ignore the fact that he was a traitor to crown and country. Or, worse yet, become one myself. I might have loved him, but I wasn't a fool.

"It's not what you think, Kenna. We're not trying to override Father or take down the kingdom. We simply believe something different. There's a better way to live than what you know."

We. He, Ashe, Jade, and who knew how many others. Prince Thoraben, Crown Prince of Peverell—the man I was joined to for the rest of my life, the man I loved with everything I had—was a Rebel. He could try to justify it all he liked but it still came down to that one truth.

"Rebels killed your mother."

"Complications in childbirth killed Mother after a group of insurrectionists, long since caught and punished, attacked the palace. It wasn't the Rebels you fear."

The flowers on my skirt swirled into a mass of color as I fought the anger his calm answer stirred. He was deluded. There was no other explanation. Brainwashed by the Rebel group he claimed to be a part of. Had Ashe, whom I'd trusted, been feeding him lies all these years? I should have reported Ashe and Jade when I had the chance. I'd do it now, except... But that was the thing. I couldn't. Not now Ben and I were married.

"You're not going to ask what we believe?"

"Will it make a difference?" What was I supposed to do? They certainly didn't cover this in Princess school, nor any of the Future Queen lessons I'd had. *What to do when your husband turns out to be a traitor to the throne...*

"It will to me."

"Fine." What did it matter at this point? He'd already shattered every misconception I had. It wasn't as if he could fall any lower. "What do you believe?"

"That there is a God."

Actually, he could. "God? That's what this is all about?"

"Yes."

"Then you're even greater fools than I thought. No wonder your father wants the kingdom rid of you all."

"He's real, Kenna."

"There is no god, Ben. For once, I agree with your father."

"Ask your father."

I blinked into the lengthening silence, trying to gain control of my quivering emotions. Ben couldn't be saying what I thought he was. I didn't want to ask, but I couldn't keep the question in. "Mine?"

"He believes too. As does your mother."

He was making it up. He had to be. Perhaps it was a test, to see what I would do with this information. First, he tells me he loves me, then he tests my loyalty by telling me this? It was the only level of sense I could find in this madness.

Yet, in that moment of turning to face him, I knew it was no test. He wasn't making it up. Any of it. The truth was there, in the eyes I desperately wanted to look away from but couldn't. Ben wanted me to believe him. More than that, he needed me to.

But I couldn't.

"My parents..." The two people who'd loved me and given up

their whole lives for me, moving to the palace so I could stay. Lying. All this time. Rebels. Both of them.

I closed my eyes, blocking out Ben's desperation. His sympathy. Or was it empathy? I didn't know anymore. I didn't know him. All my life, I'd thought I did. Now, I knew for sure, I didn't know him at all. Him or my parents.

"All will be well, Kenna."

My hands clenched so hard I felt the nails bite into my palms. I welcomed the pain. Anything to distract me from the fact that my world was not just crashing but disintegrating faster than I could grab at the fractured pieces. I hated that phrase.

"All will be well! All will be well! Why does everyone keep saying that? You can't know it."

My fury didn't faze him. He barely even paused in the face of it. "Yes, I can."

"How?"

"Because God is good, and no matter what happens to me, all will be well, because he still will be."

"God? This is about God?"

"Yes. It's a statement of faith."

A statement of faith. It all made sense now. I was so foolish for not having seen it before. "It marks the Rebels."

My parents, Ben, Ashe, Jade, Clarkson and the men in the village—I'd heard them all say it. Its brilliance lay in its simplicity. Not an obvious mark like a tattoo someone might notice or a medallion worn. A statement, not commonly thrown about but neither strange enough to be questioned. *All will be well.*

"It's also something we believe."

"Because of your god."

"Because of God."

"Does your father know his son is a criminal?"

"No."

"And you've never thought of what he might do if he found out?"

"Of course I have. But he's just one man, Kenna."

Just one man. Perhaps to Ben, but certainly not to me. "He's the king. He could take away everything you have."

"He could never take what's most important to me."

"Your god."

"Yes."

I wanted to cry at the sincerity of his delusions but the hot anger burning inside me wouldn't let the sadness through. He truly believed this. All of it. Even at the risk of his life.

"What am I supposed to say if the king asks me about you?"

"The truth. I would never ask you to lie."

"He could have you killed."

"Perhaps. But it's the choice I have made."

But I hadn't. Unknown to me, I'd married a man with a death sentence.

"I think I want you to leave now." To be honest, I didn't know what I wanted. But I also knew I wouldn't be very good company until I figured it out.

"Are you okay?"

Of course, I wasn't okay. I'd found out not only that my husband loved me and had for years, but that he was a Rebel. One of the most hated people in the kingdom. And might one day be stripped of everything he had because of it.

My parents too. Was I to lose everyone I loved?

"It's a lot to think about," I said cryptically. I doubted he fell for it. He knew me too well for that. I flinched as he reached his arms toward me, as desperate for him to hold me as I was to keep my distance. And I had to keep my distance. If I let him touch me now, all the fears and doubts his declaration had put in my mind would disappear, swallowed up by the overwhelming love I felt for him. It sounded wonderful now, but it wouldn't last. The moment he walked out, the doubts would return.

"Go. Please." Before I gave in to his love like the fool I wanted to be.

Standing, Ben placed a hand on my shoulder. I tried not to notice that it was shaking. I didn't want to consider how difficult this was for him, not until I muddled my way out of my own pain.

"Talk to your father. He's a wise man."

All will be well.

Ben might not have said it out loud, but I heard the words anyway as I watched him walk away. He stopped when his hand clasped the doorknob, turning back and opening his mouth as if to say one more thing. But then he closed it, walking out the door without another word. The instant I heard the door click shut, I fell back on the bed, tears dripping down my cheeks and running into my ears as I tried to make sense of the mess I'd found myself in. All wouldn't be well. Not today. Maybe not ever again.

The urge to run away and never return pressed on me like a vice. Ben was a Rebel. My husband, Crown Prince of Peverell, was a Rebel. And the king thought marrying me was his son's greatest felony.

What would the king do when he found out? I didn't even want to think about it. And now, willing or not, I was part of that felony too. Where Ben went, I would go.

Unless I left. No one need know where I'd gone. I could sneak away in the night, disappear into obscurity in a poor province, as so many did. Move to Hodenia, perhaps. Or Allegria. I knew enough people who would protect me—especially if I told them none of this had ever been my choice.

But even as the thought passed through my mind, I knew I couldn't do it.

Because Ben loved me.

The knowledge of that still felt like a dream I couldn't quite capture and wasn't sure I could claim, and yet it was enough to make me stay.

I went to dinner that night, and the next, pretending once again that all was fine as I'd done the day of my wedding. As I walked back to my prison of a suite, I wondered if I'd ever stop.

It was a full week before I took Ben's advice and went to see my father. Ben came each morning to check on me, and each morning I sent him away, telling him I needed more time. It was the days after the wedding all over again, only now I knew he loved me. I knew how much I was hurting him to keep sending him away. If he hadn't come each day, I might have been able to pretend it didn't matter, but I couldn't keep sending him away, and I couldn't see him knowing what I knew.

I found my father in the stables, curry brush in his hand, right where I knew he'd be. He was always happiest when he was grooming his horses.

"Mackenna. This is a nice surprise. How is Peverell's future queen?"

I was too uptight to appreciate his teasing.

"Why didn't you tell me?"

"Tell you what?"

That you're a Rebel. That you believe this foolishness. That all along you'd planned my downfall. "About your god."

He brushed three more circles in the horse's dark hair before putting down the brush and wiping his hands together. That done, he turned his entire attention to me. I knew in that moment how serious he was.

"Who told you?"

He might as well have reached inside me and torn out my heart, the way it stung. And with it, my last sliver of hope that this was all a misunderstanding. He hadn't denied it. Not even flinched.

"It doesn't matter who did. You should have."

"There were...other things...to consider."

That wasn't good enough. There were always other things to consider. I was his daughter. I deserved to know.

"Would you die for this faith?"

"Yes." I noticed he didn't need to think about that answer.

"Yet it wasn't important enough to tell your only daughter? You or Mother?"

"Of course it was. We wanted to tell you, your mother especially. You have no idea how many tears she's shed over this. But we couldn't."

"Couldn't or wouldn't?" There was a big difference between the two.

"You don't know the whole story, Mackenna."

"You're right. I didn't know that my parents were Rebels, nor the man I am now married to. I've lived my whole life jumping at shadows, terrified of what the Rebels might do to me only to find out I've been surrounded by them all this time. If you're the pacifists Ben claims you to be, why all the secrecy? Why is King Everson so eager to wipe you from the kingdom? Do you have any idea what position this now puts me in? What am I supposed to do? Tell the king? Suddenly believe? Simply because everyone I've ever respected does?"

"No. If you choose to believe, it has to be for you."

"*If* I choose to believe? Father, I don't know what to believe. How could I? I don't even know what *you* believe." My hands flew about in frustration. Any second I'd hit a post or rail or something and break a nail, if not a bone. Good. I'd welcome it. At least then the agonizing pain of betrayal in my heart would have somewhere physical to go.

"I believe that there is a God, one God, high above all else— even the king. I believe that he cares about each person he's created on this earth—right down to the pattern and number of stripes on their littlest fingerprint. I believe the only reason I have life and worth is because he gave it to me. I believe I am nothing on my own. I believe, because of his son's sacrifice, I can stand blameless before him. I believe, one day, God will rule supreme over everyone and that all evil, pain, and injustice will be gone.

"And because of all that—I believe all will be well."

My hands stopped swinging, my restless feet stilled, stunned to silence by my father's words. I'd never once known him to say so much, let alone with such passionate certainty.

But he still hadn't told me, not until I'd asked. How could I trust the word of someone who'd kept something so important from me?

"We never meant to hurt you, Mackenna."

"You could have told me."

"We couldn't."

"Why? Tell me, Father. Why was something you were willing to die for not important enough to tell your daughter about?"

"It was important enough. You were important enough. But... we couldn't."

"Why?"

"Because of Thoraben."

Like his name was the link I'd been missing, a thousand unrelated moments fell into place, bringing with them a wave of comprehension almost blinding in its clarity. My parents' choice to still work at the palace, even after the king sent me away. Their silence the morning after the whirlwind, and faith in Ben during it. The amount of time Ben spent in the stables. It wasn't for the horses, or even to avoid women who weren't at the palace anywhere near as often as he escaped there. It was an excuse to spend time with my father.

"You love him more than me."

Father's protest was immediate. "No! How could you think that? You're my daughter."

It didn't matter what he said. It was all too clear to me now to be anything but convinced.

"No, that's what it is. I should have seen it. He's the son you never had, taking after you in far more ways than he does his own father. The morning after the whirlwind, you could have defended my honor. You knew I didn't do what the people were claiming but instead you stayed silent, choosing Ben over me. I told you I didn't want to marry him, and you still made me, because you knew he'd chosen me. You sacrificed my love for his. I can't believe how blind I've been, all this time."

"You're wrong, Mackenna. Very wrong." I watched as Father put a hand on the side of the horse, whether to calm it or himself,

I didn't know, but when he turned around, there was something different in his expression. "Wait here."

"Fine." I didn't know what I was waiting for but I couldn't have moved if I'd tried. My mind whirred with too many thoughts to even consider something as mundane as making my feet move.

Father walked to his office, returning moments later with an envelope. Even from a distance I could see it had my name on it. He held it, considering it in his hand before finally handing it to me. I recognized Mother's writing right away.

"Take this. Read it. Your mother wrote it years ago and had me hide it here. We couldn't risk anyone else finding it but hoped—prayed—that one day you might be ready to know what it contained. I hope it helps you understand. And Mackenna, know that your mother and I love you. We all do."

He meant Ben. Somehow, I knew.

I took the letter and walked outside, spinning the envelope between my fingers as I wandered the garden paths searching for the courage to open it. I was far more fearful of what it might contain than I had been of Ben's letter, that day so long past. Yet, like Ben's letter, my heart ached to know the answers it contained. I passed a deserted garden bench three times before I finally sat, opened the envelope, and began to read.

TWENTY-NINE

My precious Mackenna Faith,

I've always wondered if I mothered you wrongly, following the law rather than what I knew to be true. Since the day you could speak, you've been asking questions—and I've been trying to find ways to tell you the truth while still obeying the king. I never lied to you, but neither did I tell you the truth. You weren't old enough to understand how dangerous it could be. One word of any of it repeated to the wrong person and we would all have been thrown out, and not only out of the palace but of Peverell altogether. But then, by the time you were old enough, you'd stopped asking.

There is a God, Mackenna, and yes, he cares about you. He knows your name, your heart, your hopes, and fears. I think you already know that. I think you always have.

King Everson believed that once. The years before you were born were very different than what you now know. Chapels abounded and people worshiped freely, without fear. But all that ended when Queen Ciera died. It was as if the king's faith died with her. Within a year, speaking of a deity higher than the king himself had been outlawed. Chapels were burned, their teachers either exiled or killed. Rebel uprisings, it said in your history books. Every one of those Rebels was a believer who refused to be silent about their faith in the one true God and was punished because of it.

By the time you and Alina were two, faith in God had been all but driven from Peverell. Believers were allowed to talk about God amongst themselves but could not speak of him or their faith to anyone else—not even their children. Many of my friends left Peverell during this time because of it, but your Father and I stayed.

We could have left. Alina was weaned and no longer needed my care and, as much as I've appreciated the king's kindness in providing for our family—you especially—neither did we stay because of that. The truth was, we had actually decided to leave, believing, like our friends, that it was more important to teach you the truth about God than to stay for our comfort.

And then, late one night, little Thoraben came to your father and me. He climbed up on our bed and sat there, considering me in that serious way I'm certain you know. I asked him what was wrong. I'll never forget his words. "Mrs. Adeline, did God die too? Mama said he's always with me, but I can't find him anymore."

Thoraben had been three when his mother died and for the past two years he'd been wondering where God went. As we sat there in the dark, assuring the five-year-old Thoraben that God was still with him, like his mother had said, I knew we had to stay. Unlike us, Thoraben couldn't leave, and someone had to teach him about his mother's God.

I could tell Thoraben about God because, young as he was, he already believed. He could ask questions, and your father and I could answer them without breaking the law. Even as a five-year-old, he understood the need for discretion.

It was never as simple with you and Alina. I couldn't tell you the truth—the only truth—without breaking the law. So, I prayed. Every day of your lives, I've prayed that you'd come to know God despite the law. That somehow, you'd start asking the right questions for yourself and find your way to his arms. That one day you'd know the sacrifice his son made for you.

Should I have been bolder? Should I have told you the truth even despite the king's edict and what it might have meant had he found out? You will never know how much this question has troubled me over the years. Yet, your father and I both felt as if God told us to stay, even knowing that meant our silence. He asked of us a faith greater than we'd ever had before—the faith that God could teach you his ways and find you despite our silence.

If you're reading this, you've finally started asking the questions I've always hoped you'd ask, yet no doubt fighting against accepting the answers. But you must, my precious Mackenna. You'll never be at peace until you accept them.

There is a God, and he loves you more than you'll ever know.

Know that, and everything else will fall into place.

I love you, Mackenna. Every day I thank God that you are my daughter. You make me so proud.

Mother

I was still sitting there, staring at the paper in my hand, trying to reconcile what I knew with what it said an hour later when Ben found me. I think I told him hello but my mind was in such a state of confusion that I wasn't sure. He came to me anyway, kissing my forehead before sitting beside me on the bench. I didn't know what to say so I handed him Mother's letter, watching his knees as he read it. I was silent only until he put the letter down and turned to face me.

"Did you know?" I asked him quietly.

"That your parents stayed because of me?"

I nodded.

"I suspected. I knew as well as you my father's hate for the Rebels, yet your parents always took the time to teach me and encourage me in my faith despite it. Your father has been as much a mentor to me as my own, if not more so, meeting with me each week to discuss life and faith. So many others left, especially those with young children, yet your parents stayed. I always wondered if it was because of me, though it felt like such a selfish thought that I never asked."

He handed the letter back to me, watching as I folded it along its lines and tucked it inside the envelope. When I looked up, he was still staring at me.

"Do you...hate me for it? Your whole life could have been so different had I not—"

"Been you?" I smiled wryly, though I doubted it reached my eyes. My thoughts still tumbled about, not knowing where to land, or if they even should.

"Gone to your parents that night."

I shook my head. "You were a child missing your mother. I could never hate you for that."

There was no way Ben could have known the decision my parents would make because of it. I didn't even know if I was angry at them anymore. I wanted to be. I wanted to be utterly furious at them for choosing him over me. I could have been too, were it not for the little voice in my head reminding me that had they not stayed, I wouldn't have known Ben the way I did. I certainly wouldn't have married him.

"Thanks," he said.

I didn't know how to reply to that.

Most people's lives seemed to follow a fairly straight path. An expected one. They lived the life they were born into, grew up, chose professions and partners, had families, and watched those families grow up much the same way they had.

My life seemed to be made up of single moments, each one drastically altering its course forever. Queen Ciera's death had brought me to the palace, five-year-old Ben's question had kept me there, the whirlwind had forced my marriage. Would this moment, this decision I had to make, be the next?

I let my gaze wander over the manicured shrubs surrounding us. They were cut back shorter than usual, most likely due to the whirlwind's destruction, but not one leaf was out of line.

"And God?" I asked. "This king you've all pledged your allegiance to?"

"You don't know what to think, do you?"

I sighed. Not at all. "Honestly? I feel like I'm back in the middle of that whirlwind. Everything I thought I knew was apparently wrong, and the place I thought was safe is crashing in around me. Only this time, you're not pounding on the door to come and save me."

"But God is."

"I wish I could believe that." I said it without thinking, only to realize it was the truth. I really did want to believe as they did. Ben, Ashe, Jade, my parents—they all had a confidence I craved. It had to come from their faith.

"What's stopping you?"

"I don't know. Fear? Maybe the fact that all my life, an allegiance pledged to anyone but the king has been akin to treason? You were there, Ben. You saw how many people were sent away. And now you're telling me not only that it wasn't treason at all but that you've believed it too, your entire life? And you want me to. Is it any wonder I don't know what to think?"

My eyes sank closed for an instant as another thought fell into place. "Wenderley believes too, doesn't she? That's why her family left, and the reason they came back." I knew even before I saw Ben's nod that I was right. It all made sense now. Wenderley's parents had done what my parents hadn't. They'd left Peverell for the sake of their children. When Jade had told Ashe that all would be well with Emmett and Eder, she'd meant that they now believed. King Everson mustn't have known that Wenderley was a Rebel or he would never have chosen her for his son.

And Ashe, he must have made his decision while he stayed with the Davises. He'd said the lengthy stay hadn't been because of Jade. He must have been learning, being mentored by Wenderley's father the same way my father had mentored Ben.

How many others hid the same secret?

"Does Alina believe like you?"

"No."

I felt guilty at the wave of relief that came with Ben's answer. He wanted Alina to believe as desperately as he wanted me to, but I was glad she didn't. It meant I wasn't the only one. I was starting to wonder if I knew any of my friends or family at all. Alina might currently be furious with me, but I had far more in common with her than anyone else I knew. I wasn't a Rebel.

Yet.

A frustrated sigh escaped me. What did I believe? Ben made it sound so simple—just believe—but then, he'd followed this god his whole life. His whole identity was caught up in it. Me, I'd found out that the truth I'd staked my whole life on might be wrong. The whirlwind had nothing on the force or number of thoughts rushing around my head right now.

Ben leaned over and kissed my cheek, smiling as he sat back. "It's okay, Kenna. None of us expected you'd change your mind overnight. Take your time. But...don't stop asking questions, okay?"

I gave him a half-hearted smile, the best I could manage. He was so patient with me. I wanted to turn to him there and then and declare my faith. It would have made him so happy. But I couldn't do it. Not right now. Not even for this man I loved so much. If this god of my husband and parents was who they said he was, he was even more powerful than the king, and one didn't swear allegiance to a being that powerful unless they were absolutely certain.

My life had changed completely the day of the whirlwind.

And like the aftermath of that whirlwind, I had no doubt I would be changed every bit as drastically if I chose to surrender to the one inside me.

"I'll try."

"Your parents weren't the only ones praying for you, you know. I've prayed for you too. Both you and Alina, for years. God hasn't given up on either of you and neither will your parents or I. You might feel like you're in a whirlwind, Kenna, but you're not alone in it."

Perhaps not, but none of them could make this decision for me.

"And don't forget, every whirlwind comes to an end eventually."

I smiled, though it was as uncertain as my emotions. Yes, every whirlwind ended. But would I still be in one piece when it did?

ℭHIRTY

My dreams that night were as muddled and terrifying as they had been the night of my wedding. I was surprised I slept at all given the proof of my parents'—and Ben's—treason resting beneath a pile of memories in the drawer beside my bed. Dangerous as the letter was, I couldn't bear to throw it away.

Ben had left for a meeting not long after speaking with me in the garden. He'd offered to miss it, but I'd told him to go. I'd needed to think, and I couldn't do that with him beside me. Ben and his steady love were far too distracting.

But even without him there, I hadn't come to any conclusion. There was too much at stake. In the end, I'd given up and gone back to my room.

I'd tried to read, write in my journal, study policies, even re-organize the gowns in my oversized wardrobe—much to Elayna's disgust—but I hadn't been able to focus on any of them. Elayna ended up pushing me out of the wardrobe after I'd pulled all but three gowns off the long rail they hung on and flung them to the floor in frustration. I might as well have been a three-year-old throwing a tantrum.

Patient beyond what I deserved, Elayna had drawn me a warm bath, poured in half a bottle of lavender-scented soap—no doubt an attempt to calm me down—and told me not to come out for an hour at least. All the lavender had done was give me a headache. I'd gone to bed not long after and woken just as conflicted.

My schedule was empty for the morning, but I would have

canceled whatever was on there even if it hadn't been. I'd be no good to anyone until I figured this out. Talking to Mother might help. Father would have told her I'd read the letter by now. I was surprised she hadn't sought me out herself. And yet, alongside the surprise, I was thankful. She would have answers, but I needed more.

I needed a reason.

Not what to believe but why.

Perhaps a walk would help. If nothing else, it would give my scattered mind something to focus on.

The halls were deserted, to my relief. I had no strength left in me to fight, whether against my attraction to Ben, my distrust of my parents, or King Everson and Alina's hate. I stopped only to assure the guard at the door that I wasn't going further than the Queen's Garden before slipping out into the welcome sunshine.

I hadn't decided until the moment I spoke with the guard where I would go, but even as I said it, I knew it was perfect.

The Queen's Garden, planted in memory of Queen Ciera, the woman whose death had brought me to the palace, and whose son had kept me here. Though I'd never known her, her life had influenced mine more than I cared to admit. And all of Peverell. According to Mother's letter, it had been Ciera's death which had created the Rebels.

I fingered a rose petal before plucking it off and holding it in my hand, marveling at its velvety delicacy. Had the god the Rebels believed in been the one to create this petal and tell it when to bloom? Was that why Mother had always loved wildflowers? Because they reminded her of her god?

I threw the petal to the ground. This was ridiculous. I couldn't believe I was even considering the existence of this god, let alone him taking such an interest in the world—and having the power—to order about a single rose.

"Mackenna?"

I spun around, shocked to see Wenderley sitting on a bench not two yards from where I stood. The guards hadn't said anyone was here, so I hadn't even thought to look. Sunlight caught the wet trails on her cheeks that I might have missed otherwise. She'd been crying. And I was interrupting.

"Sorry. I didn't see you there. I'll go."

"No. Don't."

Her quiet plea stopped my exit.

"Please, stay. I...was hoping to speak with you."

Wenderley patted the seat beside her, inviting me to sit. Still, I hesitated. She loved Ben. Ben loved me. In a competition I'd never entered, I'd won. Were they angry tears? Despairing ones? The wrenching sobs of a broken heart? I knew she wouldn't hurt me, but she had every right to be mad.

"You must despise me," I finally said.

"Despise is a strong word."

"Hate me, then."

She sighed, shaking her head. "No. I thought I did, when I first heard you were marrying Thoraben. I was so angry at you. It didn't help that Alina was the one to tell me."

Wenderley didn't elaborate on that, but she didn't need to. I knew exactly what Alina thought of me. She hadn't talked to me once since the wedding. The first of her two weddings was just over three weeks away, and I still hadn't found the courage to ask her if I was part of it. I'd be there—I was part of the royal family now—but would she still want me standing beside her?

"But then I saw the way Ashe looked at Jade when he came to tell her he loved her, and I realized Thoraben's never once looked at me that way. I've loved him all my life but, if I'm honest with myself, which I'm doing my best to be, he never gave any indication that he loved me back. Maybe he considered me once—my battered heart would like to think he did—but when it came down to it, it's you he chose."

"He loves me." I saw her flinch when I admitted it, though she tried to hide it behind a smile. I hadn't meant to say that and hurt her further when she was already being so gracious. It was all so new it kind of slipped out. "Sorry." I sat down, wondering how much more of a mess I could make of my life. Ben should have married Wenderley. At least she wanted to be queen. And she already believed as he did.

"It's okay. I already knew."

I didn't ask her how. "And you're okay with that?"

She swiped at one tear then another as they began to fall again, wiping the wetness from her hand to her skirt. I berated myself for the stupidity of my question. Of course she wasn't okay with it. She was sitting alone in a garden crying, and probably had been for some time given how long it had taken me to notice her.

"Honestly? No. But I pray one day I will be. And I don't hate you. Jade told me Thoraben loved you, Ashe and my parents too. I just didn't want to hear it. I thought I could make him love me. Now I know that was never an option."

Wenderley turned her sad smile to me, grasping my hand for a moment before letting it go. "You'll make a wonderful queen, Mackenna."

I shook my head, feeling as if the weight of all that had happened—all I now knew—grew heavier with each day. "Queen, perhaps. I'm already failing at being a wife."

"I doubt that."

Whether she doubted it or not, it was the truth. Though I was Ben's wife, Wenderley had far more in common with him than I did.

"Thoraben's whole life revolves around a belief I don't share."

Wenderley opened her mouth to say something before apparently thinking better of it and closing it again. I didn't blame her. She didn't know where my loyalties stood any more than I did. One wrong word and I could have her sent away forever. I sighed. "I know Ben is a Rebel, as are my parents, Ashe, and your entire family. You have nothing to fear from me."

"But it terrifies you."

I turned away before she saw the tears which instantly sprang to my eyes. They weren't tears of frustration but of relief. Someone understood.

Of all the people to understand what I was feeling, I hadn't expected it to be Wenderley. I'd thought she hated me, and by her account, she had. Could it be the person I thought would hate me the most might be the one person I could actually talk to?

"I don't know what to do."

"And you have to do something."

I nodded, my face still turned away. Neither Ben nor my parents were pressuring me to decide, yet by telling me, they were. I could choose to accept their god or I could choose to deny him, but I couldn't pretend he had nothing to do with me anymore. Not when everyone I loved had pledged their lives to him.

"I know a bit of what you're feeling," Wenderley said. "I mean, not completely. I'm not making a decision as Peverell's future queen. But I know what it's like to have everyone you love believe one thing while you don't."

"You do?"

She looked away again, following the path of an indecisive butterfly as it wandered into the garden, almost landing on three different flowers before floating out of sight. I kept silent, waiting for her to continue, anxious to hear what she might say.

I never would have come to the Queen's Garden today if I'd known Wenderley would be here, and yet, I was so thankful she had been. Her acceptance of the situation we'd both found ourselves in, of me still as a friend, had already laid to rest some of the fears I hadn't known I held. I desperately wanted to hear what else she had to say, especially if, by some chance, she really did know what I felt.

"I was the last of my family to believe. Even Eder, young as he is, believed. But I couldn't. It all seemed too far-fetched, the idea of an invisible God holding life and everything in his control. Holding me. I didn't want to accept that anyone held my future except me. I refused to believe any of it.

"My parents didn't force me, but I knew my decision, or lack of, hurt them. Jade reminded me almost every day of the privilege it was to even be able to talk about this God, let alone believe in him without retribution. 'Do you know how much our parents sacrificed so that you might know the truth?' she'd ask me.

"I knew, but I also knew that I hadn't asked them to do it. As far as I was concerned, they'd taken me away from the man I loved, and that was enough to turn me away from their faith forever."

"But you believed anyway. I mean, you do now, don't you?"

"Yes. Absolutely. But it took me a long time. Longer than everyone else in my family."

"What changed your mind?"

She was silent for a moment as she considered the answer. I hoped it wasn't too personal to share. I didn't want to sound desperate, but I had to know. Ben had believed all his life, my parents also. They didn't know what it was like to have to choose. Wenderley did. And had.

Why? That's what I had to know. What made someone choose to believe in something they couldn't see, especially when doing so could have them punished and thrown out of the kingdom? Wenderley couldn't make my decision for me, no one could, but maybe, she might help.

"Actually, it was the realization one day that the only way I'd ever see Thoraben again and convince him to marry me was if I believed. My family were never going to move back to Peverell otherwise. So, I told God that I'd believe in him and pledge my allegiance to him if he brought us home. Only what started out as a bargain turned out to be the best decision of my life."

Except for one thing. "But you didn't marry Thoraben."

"No."

"So your god can't be trusted after all."

Again, she didn't answer right away, instead considering her words. I appreciated that. I already had enough people in my life who were certain. It was refreshing to be with someone who didn't have all the answers.

"No, I don't think that's it. I think that's the true test of faith— when we don't get what we ask for. I'd like to think I've passed it, but I think it's going to be a long battle."

"But you still believe. You'd still stake your life on this god's love for you, even though you weren't the one to marry Thoraben."

"Yes." She didn't need to think about that one. The certainty was in her peace-filled smile as much as it was her eyes. I envied her it.

"What if I can't do that?"

She shrugged, not bothered by the same doubts I was. "I think you will."

"Why?"

"Because I think you already do."

THIRTY-ONE

With an embrace from Wenderley and a promise to catch up again soon, I left the Queen's Garden and went back to wandering, my thoughts plodding in time with my steps.

To believe in the Rebel's god, or not to.

Accept what I'd been told all my life, or reject it.

A life of safety, or a life of uncertainty.

Yet was it truly a life of uncertainty? None of the Rebels I'd talked to had seemed uncertain, despite the law and what it would mean for them were King Everson to ever discover their true loyalties.

And could it truly be any more uncertain than I felt right now?

Without meaning to, I ended up at the tower. It had always been a good place to think, and I definitely needed to think. And more than think, I needed to make a decision. I'd never be at peace again until I did.

Nothing in my life had ever been my choice—not where I lived, not the clothes I wore, not even who I married. But this—this was my choice alone.

For the first time ever.

The words from Mother's letter seemed etched in my heart. *There is a God, Mackenna, and yes, he cares about you. He knows your name, your heart, your hopes and fears. Know that and everything else will fall into place.*

It would be nice to give up control to a God who cared that

much, and to know all truly would be well. I gave my allegiance to King Everson, and I didn't even like him. He certainly didn't care about me.

Yet this God apparently did.

What would it be like to give my allegiance to a power like that? Was he watching me now as I walked back and forth from one side of the tower to the other? Had he been the one to send Wenderley to the garden, for me? Did he know how difficult a decision this was for me?

And was it really so difficult a decision?

It didn't feel strange to consider the existence of God, a power higher and more worthy of praise than King Everson. Both Mother and Wenderley were right. Somewhere, so deep within me I hadn't even realized it was there, I'd always had a yearning for someone greater. My decision lay not in whether he existed or not but whether I could trust him. Whether I could give him my allegiance.

And whether I was willing to accept the consequences.

Would I risk imprisonment for this faith? Be exiled for it? King Everson already hated me. If I chose the Rebels' God, and King Everson ever found out, it would be reason enough to rid the kingdom of me forever, even despite being married to his son and heir. Ben and my parents would never let me go alone. They'd be forced to proclaim their own faiths and then—

I stopped. Waitrose had been right. The whole kingdom would fall. One decision was powerful enough to crumble it. Ben had decided it worth the risk, but could I?

It would have been an easier decision to make if I hadn't married Peverell's future king. I wasn't making this decision for myself. I was making it for an entire kingdom. Sooner or later, Ben would become king, and I had no doubt his first decree would be to abolish the law forbidding the people from worshipping and teaching about God. When that happened, Peverell would look to Ben first as king, but then they would look to me, wondering what I believed. Whether I believed as their new king did.

Queen Ciera had.

Not for the first time, I wished I'd known her. She alone knew what it was like to stand overlooking the people who would one day be mine and have them look to me. The pressure felt insurmountable. I wondered what she would say to me. What advice she might give.

And yet, I would never have been standing here in this tower, facing this decision, if she had lived. I wouldn't have been raised in the palace, nor known the friendship of Ben or Alina. I was here because Queen Ciera had died. In a way, she'd given up her life for mine.

It was a sobering thought, and I knew it could not be for nothing.

The kingdom and its pressures fell out of sight as I dropped to my knees. The stone floor was rough against my skin, but if this God was king, he deserved that much respect and more.

I'd put my faith in Ben to get me out of the whirlwind because I trusted him. He'd said God would save me from the whirlwind inside me. I didn't know Ben's God well, but somehow, I knew I could trust him. Because Ben did. Because my parents did. Because, somewhere deep within me, in that same place where I knew God existed, I believed he cared.

"God of the Rebels, I don't know what you want from me, I don't know if I can claim to believe everything my father does yet, but I want to try. I want to believe as they do."

I closed my eyes, blocking out everything but my breathing and the thudding of my heart. This was crazy, what I was about to do, and yet, nothing had ever felt so sane.

Words from my wedding ceremony came back to me as I knelt there, pledging my allegiance to this God I'd only now come to acknowledge. They felt as foreign now as they had that day, but I meant them every bit as surely. Even more, because I said them of my own free will.

"God of the Rebels, I commit my life to you from this day forward—for better, for worse; for richer, for poorer; in sickness and in health; to love and to cherish, till death do us part, and thereto I give thee my troth."

It was likely the wrong thing to say to pledge my allegiance to the God of the Rebels. I knew so little about him, certainly not the right pledge but, in that moment, I knew there was no truer commitment I could give him.

For better or worse, I was now a traitor to the king. Come what may, I, like my husband and parents, was a Rebel.

And it felt wonderful.

My eyes stayed shut as my mind luxuriated in a stillness I hadn't felt in days, if ever. I'd found peace in the middle of the whirlwind. Or perhaps it was peace that had found me. It didn't make sense that I would instantly feel so different, and yet I couldn't deny that I did.

The king still hated me, Alina might never forgive me, and the future of Peverell rested precariously on the shoulders of a man who might never be king—but for the first time ever, I had hope. I understood now how someone could truly claim that all would be well. I believed it myself.

The smile on my face as I slowly stood to my feet couldn't have been bigger had I painted it on. I wasn't even sure what I'd committed to, but I knew, without a doubt, that I'd made the right choice. There would be plenty of time to learn, and plenty of people to teach me.

My parents. What would they think? All this time, they'd trusted in silence that one day I'd choose their God. And now I had, for better or worse. I couldn't wait to tell them. All those moments, those forks in the journey of my life which I'd thought too much to handle had brought me to this place. Queen Ciera's death, King Everson's hate, the whirlwind's destruction, my forced marriage. Even Waitrose and his attempts to ruin my marriage.

My marriage.

Ben. I had to tell Ben.

I ran all the way to our suite, not even bothering to knock before bursting through his door.

"Ben! Ben! Where are you?" He had to be here. I had to tell

him. My whole body might explode with the joy of it all if I tried to keep the thrill of my decision to myself much longer.

I checked every corner of the suite. He wasn't here. I refused to let disappointment slow me. I'd find him. I had to. Perhaps he was at a meeting, or in the dining hall. Was it lunchtime? Dinner? I didn't even know. Time seemed a mere irrelevance on such a day.

A schedule. Surely Ben's schedule would be here somewhere. I only had to find it and it would tell me where he was. And if not his schedule, then mine. I knew where mine was. Thinking it would be faster to find mine, I turned to open the door connecting our suites.

My hand stopped without touching the doorknob, my attention caught and held captive by the wall beside Ben's door. I hadn't seen it when I'd first burst through, running straight past it in my haste. Slowly, disbelieving, I walked toward it.

The wall was covered in framed photos, all blown up to magazine size, and all of the two of us. Ben had said the photographer took a series of photos that day in the snow when he gave me my picture. I hadn't even thought to consider what had happened to the rest of them.

No wonder Ben had promised the photographer his wedding and followed through with that promise, even with only a day to prepare. The photographer had caught more than our friendship that day—he'd caught our love. Even before I'd known I was in love with Ben, it had been witnessed and captured forever in these pictures by a man who didn't even know us.

There, in the way Ben looked at me over the top of Alina's shoulder.

There, in the way I grinned at him.

There, when he helped me to my feet while Alina stood spluttering and covered in snow.

There, as we clapped hands together, thrilled at our successful attack.

And there, for all the world to see, in the expression on Ben's face as he watched Alina and me walk away.

It was in every photo. I recognized it now. No wonder he hadn't shown me the rest of the photos. It would have given his love away in an instant.

And mine.

I wished now that I'd taken the time on our wedding day to meet and thank the photographer. I hadn't even asked which one he was, let alone his name. I'd been so caught up in my own bitterness that I hadn't cared. Next time, I promised myself. There would be a next time. I would make sure of it even if Ben didn't. Holidays, portraits, the births of our children... I blushed at the thought but couldn't hold back the smile of delight that accompanied it.

Yes, definitely children. Our future was uncertain at best, but if my parents could entrust the life and future of their only daughter to the God they believed in, then so could Ben and I.

"Kenna?"

"Ben!" He'd returned.

I ran to him, sure of myself now as I flung myself into his arms, thrilled when he caught me up, swinging me around. He loved me. I loved him. God loved us both.

"You're in my room."

I laughed at his bemused expression, as if he wasn't quite sure whether I was actually there or if he'd dreamed me. I planned on putting all those doubts to rest as soon as I could, beginning with one thing.

"I love you, Ben," I told him, relishing the feeling of his arms still around me.

Bemusement turned to wonder as he looked down at me. "Truly? You mean it?"

Reaching up, I looped my arms around his neck like I had in the dream. And a thousand times in my thoughts since. His smile was even better in real life than it had been in my mind.

"Truly. I think I have my entire life, though I didn't realize it until the morning after the whirlwind."

His smile only grew bigger, reaching up his face to crinkle

the corners of his eyes. "Ah. The infamous dream. It seems I have more than one reason to be thankful for it. So I was in it?"

I nodded, curling my fingers into the dark hair at his nape. "We were married. You were chasing me. We were..." I blushed, my thoughts suddenly swooping far further forward than our dream selves had gone.

Ben raised an eyebrow, grin still firmly in place, as if he knew exactly what I was thinking. "Kissing?" he supplied.

I smiled. Close enough. "In love. And I couldn't think of any place I'd rather be. I know I should have told you I loved you before now, but I was scared, of so many things. I'm sorry, Ben."

He traced a thumb across my cheek, much as he'd done at our wedding. Only this time, there were no tears to wipe away. "Then you're not afraid anymore?"

I laughed aloud. "Are you kidding? I'm terrified."

"But you want this? You want to be my wife?"

"Yes. So much."

"Because?"

I smiled, the joy of my new faith still so shiny and bright, if a little shy. "Because I love you...and because now I believe too."

I thought I'd seen delight in his face when I told him I loved him. This was a thousand times better. "Kenna. Do you truly mean it?"

"Yeah." I breathed the word out, still in awe of all that had happened to bring me—us—to this point. Only a power far higher than the king could have done it. "No matter what happens from this moment on, I choose to believe, like you and my parents and all the others, that all will be well."

His sigh was that of a full and content heart—that which had had all its long-held hopes realized. I knew it well. It was the same as mine. Twice now I'd been saved from the middle of the whirlwind. What I'd once considered the end of my life had now become the beginning.

"That it will, my Kenna. That it will."

This time, when Ben kissed me, there was nothing fast about it.

ACKNOWLEDGMENTS

I've always loved reading the acknowledgements pages of books and seeing all the different people involved—each one a beautiful reminder that none of us walk this journey alone. We need each other. And believe me, you wouldn't be holding this book in your hands if even a single one of the following people (and far too many others to name) hadn't stood up and been a part of it.

So, without further ado, a HUGE thanks goes to...

My mum, who read my first ever manuscript almost a decade ago and loved it, despite it needing five years of work to make it even close to good. Thanks for sharing your love of books, believing in me no matter what, reminding me to keep looking to God for my strength, caring for my littlest a day a week so I could spend more than an hour at a time writing, and knowing that a block of Whittaker's New Zealand chocolate (just like Kara Isaac shared once in a Facebook post) would make me smile. You are truly amazing, and I am so incredibly proud to be your daughter. (Side note... We did it!!!)

And my dad, for not only believing I could be a published author but doing whatever you could practically to make it happen. Your faith in me is humbling, but your faith in God is what inspires me most. I am so blessed to have you both in my life.

My husband, Brett. I wouldn't be me without you. Nor would this book have been published, or even written, if you hadn't given me the time, space, support, and technology to do it. You make me a better person, and I'd like to think that makes me a better author too. Even if I refuse to ever let you read this book. Believe me. I'm doing you a favor. You'd hate it. There aren't any explosions or gunfights or anything.

My two girls. Thanks for being too amazing to ever let me get lost in fictional lands for long and tempting me out with hugs when you think I have been. And my son, who always knows how to make me smile. Thanks for being the most adorable three-year-old around. I love spending every day with you. No fictitious character could ever come close to being as precious to me as you three are—not even Superman.

David and Roseanna White and the WhiteFire Publishing team. Thanks for taking a chance on an unknown author half a world away. I hope one day soon I get the chance to meet you in person and thank you for all you've done. Right from that first email, you were so encouraging and all the way along, have been amazing to work with. It's an honor to be part of the WhiteFire family.

And, Roseanna, wow! That cover!! It's absolutely gorgeous. Still can't believe I get to put my name on it. Thank you!

Karryn and Georgia. Thank you for not just believing in me and loving my writing but being over-the-top, I-can-hear-you-from-the-other-side-of-the-city, excited. Every author should be so lucky to have cheerleaders like you in their corner.

My siblings. Thanks for so many laughs growing up (some of which may have inspired scenes in this book...Joel...) but more for the privilege of still being so close today. Writing about close siblings is easy when I have you as my best friends. I love you all so much!

Jessica Kate and the Class of 2019 Debut Authors Facebook group, who have been my voice of first-time-publishing sanity this year. I've loved being on this journey with you, sharing the milestones, the frustrations, and the many, many questions. There's something so incredibly encouraging about knowing I'm not alone in it all. I keep forgetting I haven't actually met any of you in person because you sure feel like good friends!

My mum's KYB Bible Study ladies, who, though I don't know

most of their names, prayed this book into being and I will forever be thankful for. Don't ever doubt the power of prayer and that God can, and still does, do miracles. You're holding one in your hands. Thank you, faith-filled warriors!

And God. My rock in the middle of this whirlwind called life. I used to kind of roll my eyes when Christian authors thanked God in their acknowledgements, figuring they only did it because they had to. How wrong I was. I couldn't have done any of this without him. Looking back over the writing and publication of this book, all I can see is God's hand in it—from the dream that started it all to the people he sent my way at the exact moment I needed them to make it happen. This might be Kenna's story, but it's also my story of a God who has proved himself good over and over again. He is the reason I can say without a doubt, "All will be well."

To God be the glory.